ILLUMIN∆TI:

A NEW WORLD ORDER

POWDERDRY BOOKS

First published in Great Britain in 2019 by PowderDry Books Ltd

All characters and events in this publication, other than those clearly in the public domain, are fictitious and any resemblance to real persons, living or dead, is purely coincidental.

A CIP catalogue record for this book is available from the British Library.

ISBN 978-1-9160191-0-2

Typeset in Baskerville Old Face

Printed and bound in the Great Britain by

www.beamreachuk.co.uk

Papers used by www.beamreachuk.co.uk

are from well managed forests and other responsible sources

To my guideposts -

It is said, the highest hanging fruit will always prove to be the sweetest, most delicious and satisfying of all...

The Author

Δ

Have you ever wondered why financial markets rise and fall without warning? Why twenty-six of the wealthiest known individuals, own as many assets as the poorest half of the planet? Or why the world has been so dependent on oil, when the first electric car was built in 1888? The answers to all these questions, and more, will be revealed in the Illuminati series of books.

Eight novels spanning the most turbulent decades of the past two centuries, the series chronicles the rise of the 'Financial-Illuminati' as their grip extended around the globe. Also referred to as the **New World Order**, this small group of family lines has built the world we live in today. Everything you touch, everything you see, everything you consume – all because of the system they have created around you. And it is perfect. Unlike rulers of previous Empires, this faceless group cannot be toppled for it is likely you do not even know of their existence...until now, that is.

Δ

History

Δ

Before global debt stood at a figure so long, it was only intelligible on a spreadsheet. Before two towers shone resplendently in the sun and represented another time and place altogether. Before man planted a stake into the surface and marked the end of the space race. Before shots were fired across an open top car driving down Dealey Plaza. Before the Bilderberg Group held its inaugural meeting in the remote village of Oosterbeek. Before the S-1 Executive Committee met at Bohemian Grove and the Manhattan Project was conceived. And before an area was set aside on the shores of Groom Lake to build Homey Airport in Nevada...Abraham Lincoln was president of the United States...

Δ

Chapter 1: Fords Theatre

Δ

Good Friday, 14th April 1865

In the dimly lit Vermeil Room of the White House, only the flickering from the fireplace offered much light to chase away the cold and darkness penetrating from outside.

Above the marble mantelpiece, a gold-edged, convex mirror reflected a face furrowed and pinched: President Abraham Lincoln, contemplating the past, the present and the future. The Civil War that had raged across the US was on the brink of culminating in success for the Union, but it would leave the country deeply divided and unsure of its place in the world.

Across the room was his second in command, General Richard D Brown. Quietly debriefing United States military officer Harry Smithson; a young and slender man, he did his best to stand tall despite Brown towering over him.

"Every second that passes we continue to be surrounded by danger. Defeat creates martyrs who are willing to sacrifice themselves and make grand statements," Brown intoned, staring his fellow officer right in the eyes. "This is not a time to celebrate, but rather a time to be vigilant and remain on your guard."

Brown was in the grip of grave concerns about a latent attack on the president; he knew how important Lincoln was to the future of the country. Turning his focus, he pressed his good friend once more to change his mind. "Abraham" he alerted "Mr Smithson here is more than capable of accompanying you to Ford's Theatre, but I would be very happy to attend in his place if you prefer...?"

Lincoln smirked in esteem of his friend's persistence. He appreciated the concern.

But turning slowly to begin his rebuttal, he was interjected by his wife, Mary, entering the room. Marching straight towards him and reaching up, she straightened his dickie-bow, folded down his collar and patted him on the chest.

"Come on, Abe," she said, wagging a finger at him as if he were a recalcitrant child. "We'll be late again. You know how you hate to miss the start!"

Mary's comment raised a genial smile from her husband; she knew him all too well. But the smile soon faded when Lincoln returned his gaze to Brown.

"War at its best is terrible, and this war of ours, in its magnitude and in its duration, is one of the most terrible of all. It has ruined businesses in many localities and partially in all. It has destroyed property and produced unprecedented national debt. It has impelled mourning in almost every home, until one could almost say that the heavens are hung in black."

At this Mary sniffed sombrely and Brown bowed his head, while Smithson looked on thoughtfully as his president approached.

“But in the coming weeks,” Lincoln went on, dropping a hand on Brown’s shoulder, “this war of ours will be over! And in no small part that is down to you and your hard work on the frontlines.”

Brown opened his mouth to interject, but the president ignored him and continued. “I do not need you to accompany me to the theatre, Richard. I need you to set off in good time and meet our esteemed friends in the morning.”

Brown was silent, caught in two minds.

While he saw the wisdom in Lincoln’s words, he was still desperate to protect the president at all costs. His hesitancy only allowed Lincoln to press his point further.

“These men are some of the most important business owners in America and they are expecting you. Warm them up - a daft old politician like me can’t do it all on his own, can he...?”

Lincoln smiled warmly at his friend, who was once again disarmed by the president’s eternal charm.

“I need you on this one, Richard,” were Lincoln’s parting words, delivered with absolute authority, as he placed his tall hat on his head.

End of discussion.

Precious little opportunity for Brown to protest, and though they were old friends, it seemed poor form to question Lincoln's judgement after such an oration.

Brown, instead, returned his attention to Smithson and with a firm pat on the back, hurried him along the hardwood floor, to closely follow Lincoln out the room.

Standing there rigidly, resting his heavy set against the doorframe, Brown fixed his stare upon the group. Watching along the corridor as the front door creaked shut, his gut told him to rush after them: *but he did not.*

For a few more moments, which seemed like an eternity, Brown continued to stare at the entrance, willing the president to return and order his friend to accompany him that instant. Yet as the pendulum on the grandfather clock swung back and forth, ticking restlessly in time with his heartbeat, Brown remained alone. There was nothing for it but to turn his attention to the impending journey ahead.

"My bags, if you will!" he yelled out to no one in particular, knowing that someone would be about and hastily oblige.

He frowned as the seconds passed and no one sprang into sight. *Hastily oblige -well where was the haste?*

Brown may have accepted playing second fiddle to Lincoln but for the rest of the White House employees, he expected his instructions adhered. He was just opening his mouth to shout when someone came lumbering down the corridor, a large bag slung over each shoulder. The boy looked barely old enough to walk these halls, but he wore the Union Crest on his white uniform with pride.

"Okay, son, let's go," Brown said.

Within seconds of leaving the Vermeil Room, however, he saw how the boy was struggling under the weight of his bags - which, admittedly, contained several heavy books - and he felt compelled to assist.

Shaking his head, he took one of the bags. The young man looked alarmed, but Brown gave him a wry smile. After all, the lad was only trying to do his best, something the war general demanded of all his troops and appreciated in staff and colleagues alike.

"Show your respect." he instructed, gesturing to the presidential portraits lining the corridor down which they were walking. He nodded to Thomas Jefferson, immortalised in oils, and the boy quickly followed suit.

Outside, Brown pulled his thick, woollen army coat around him as he strode to the awaiting stagecoach. A battalion of men with riffles marched along the damp, cobbled street in formation and maybe he thought, just maybe; *Washington is safe enough to leave the presidents side.*

Passing his bags to the burly coachman, he stepped aboard and without a second look back at the White House, he departed on his mission. A half hour later, with his wife alongside him, he boarded a train at New Jersey Avenue Station. As the engine pulled away from the platform in a flurry of white steam, Brown settled into his private compartment. It was equipped with beds and his wife had laid out his nightclothes, but somehow he doubted he would get any sleep on their long journey ahead.

Δ

Lincoln's party - which included his wife, Smithson and the Major's young fiancée Caroline Bevan - had indeed arrived late to the theatre. At least their tardiness could go unnoticed by the many ladies and gentlemen filling the seats of the auditorium, as they were quietly ushered up the private staircase leading directly to the presidential box.

They slipped silently into the darkness of the upper balcony, which stood over three metres high and was flanked by a set of lavish gold-and-white curtains, and were about to take their seats when suddenly all action on stage was arrested. The orchestra began playing "Hail to the Chief", and the two-thousand strong audience stood to give Lincoln a rousing ovation.

With all eyes staring up in their direction, Mrs Lincoln gripped her husband's hand and whispered softly in his ear, "What will they think of me hanging on to you so?"

The president raised his top hat high into the air in recognition of the crowd's generous acknowledgment. Smiling down at all the people below, he leaned in and reassured his wife quietly, "I'm sure they won't think a thing of it, my dear." Then he took his seat, and everyone else followed suit, allowing the play to continue in earnest.

With the second act of *Our American Cousin* about to begin, Lincoln's stagecoach driver, Maurice Parker, made his way up the winding staircase and arrived outside the presidential box. Out of breath and panting lightly, he approached his friend and police officer, John Starks, who was standing guard for the night.

"John, how about a quick drink in *The Star*?" he proposed enthusiastically.

Yet as tempting as the offer was, Starks had reservations. "I really shouldn't..." he said, looking glumly from the entrance to the box to his friend.

"Come on, John, it's only next door," Parker reasoned. "The war's as good as over – what is there to worry about?"

Mulling the proposition over in his head, Starks fidgeted uneasily. He knew he shouldn't, but a beer would really hit the spot. And there was no one about here anyway; he was merely standing in the dark, staring at a blank wall.

"Okay," he said. "But on one condition: we just have the one drink and then I'm back before the intermission."

Parker agreed eagerly, and with that Starks left his post and scrambled down the stairs, before hurrying out the revolving door and into the rain.

Unaware of the desertion outside their box, Abe and his wife were deep in concentration, enjoying the farcical nature of the play and the performance of the lead actor, portraying a brainless English nobleman with aplomb.

Sat alongside them in contrast however, Major Smithson had no interest in the play whatsoever, and instead gazed longingly at his new fiancée in an almost trancelike state. Persistently holding her hand and seeking assurance she was OK, Caroline, who was quite happily watching the play, lost patience and slapped away his hand.

"Stop fussing!" she whispered sharply and he gladly sat back in his chair. Yet it wasn't long before he was once again staring in adulation, at her long blonde, flowing locks.

As the second act came to a close, the audience members began filing out for the intermission, their eyes drawn upwards towards the presidential box.

Inside, Lincoln stood to address his party. "Does anyone require refreshments?"

His kind enquiry was met with a unanimous, "No, thank you."

Lowering slowly back into his seat, the president remained unmoved by the snub, but sought himself a moment of amusement anyway "Suit yourselves then!" he gruffly replied and not one of them noticed as he turned away, hiding his mirth from his companions.

As the audience took their seats and the oil lamps were turned down ready for the final act to begin, a man walked into the foyer of the theatre. He was Oliver Carmicle, a local actor and Southern sympathiser, and he stood out at once in the refined setting. Not only did he walk in an agitated manner, but he was wearing a dark, full-length trench coat that dripped rainwater onto the carpet and a fisherman's cap pulled down low over his damp and curly hair.

"Excuse me, sir!" an usher exclaimed as he rapidly stepped towards the intruder. "Do you have a ticket for tonight's performance?"

"I'm here to check my mailbox, Marty," Carmicle replied, raising his head slightly to reveal his face. "It's me, Oliver."

"Ah, Oliver, good to see you. Yes, go right in," Marty said.

In fact, Carmicle had no intention of checking his mail.

He waited until his colleague had walked away, out of sight, and then took his opportunity to hurry across the foyer, scurry up the flight of steps - and soon arrived outside the unguarded presidential box.

On stage, the lead actor turned to his co-actress to utter his favourite line: "Don't know the manners of good society, eh? Well, I guess I know enough to turn you inside out, old gal!"

The comment caused a wave of unanimous laughter, the considerable commotion filling the gills of the theatre and creating the perfect cover for Carmicle to open the door to the presidential box. He stood there for no more than a second before raising his Derringer handgun, aiming directly at the back of Lincoln's head and pulling the trigger at close range.

As the president started to collapse, and Smithson began to rise from his seat, Carmicle was already in motion. Pushing past Mrs Lincoln, reaching for her slumping husband, he leapt up onto the balcony ledge and jumped, somehow landing on his feet on the stage, he sprinted for the rear exit.

For a moment, the audience hung suspended in silence; they were unsure whether the loud bang and the leaping man were merely part of the play or something more sinister. Their uncertainty however, was soon answered, when Mary let out an almighty, piercing scream and Smithson's young fiancée frantically rushed to close the curtains around them.

Smithson was still in a daze.

He didn't know what to do.

Seeing Lincoln lying on the floor, seeping blood, while his wife held his head aloft in a hopeless attempt to somehow aid her husband, he decided to storm out of the box - just as John Starks and Maurice Parker came dashing up the stairs.

"Where have you been?!" Smithson demanded as they peered past him and stared, aghast, at the sight of the fallen president and Mary sobbing over him uncontrollably.

"We...we went..." Starks stuttered, sick to his stomach with what he was witnessing.

"You went *where...*? You weren't supposed to leave, even if you were offered eternal fortune, you stupid, stupid man!" Smithson yelled, awash with fear for himself - the reprisal from Brown - and his repugnance for this man who had left his post when he was most needed.

Enraged, he slammed a palm into each man's chest, sending them to land roughly on the floor. Accepting the blows without any thought of retaliation, they sat there, motionless and silent and absolutely appalled by their failure to prevent this horrific act.

Then came a call from behind.

"Harry!" shrieked Caroline. "Harry, *quickly*!"

Smithson rushed back into the presidential box.

Caroline and Mary were kneeling at either side of Lincoln, who, Smithson suddenly realised, was gasping to speak.

"Harry..." Lincoln implored as Smithson quickly knelt down and leaned in close to hear his spluttered murmur. "Please... tell Brown... stick to the plan... I urge you, tell Brown... tell him to carry out the plan..."

Δ

Chapter 2: Brown's Nightmare

Δ

BANG. BANG.

The noise rippled through the cold night air like gunfire.

BANG. BANG.

A scuffle. Men shouting. The pounding of a train as it rattled along the tracks getting louder and louder and then –

Brown awoke, sitting bolt upright in the narrow bed, awash with sweat and panting. What was that? A dream. But it had felt so real...

His bleary eyes caught sight of movement.

Several figures in silhouette standing directly outside the door to his compartment. At once he was out of bed and marching towards the doorknob with his hand.

"What's going on?" he boomed at the sight of his bodyguards atop two men wriggling on the floor.

"They entered the carriage and wouldn't stop when we demanded," the night guard commandingly informed him.

"Well, what do they want?" Brown angrily enquired while watching the four of them struggle. A small part of him wondered, whether he was still dreaming.

"We don't know, sir, but we didn't want to take any chances - our orders are that no-one should be in this carriage other than you and your wife," the second guard explained. Then he pushed down hard on the man he had in an armlock, crunching his elbow and eliciting a scream of pain.

"Take them to the hold. We can deal with this in the morning," Brown ordered as he rubbed his head, hoping tomorrow would bring some clarity. "And make sure you come straight back. I'm...I'd prefer it if you kept a watchful eye," he added with more than a hint of trepidation.

Re-entering his compartment, Richard found that his wife had awoken and was staring up at him from their bed.

"What's happened?" Julia mumbled, yawning at the interruption.

"Nothing, darling," he said, wiping the worried look from his face. "Probably just a couple of drunks," he suggested to calm her nerves. And she settled back over to sleep, leaving Brown to ponder the actual reason for the kerfuffle outside their room.

Hunkering down in a chair beside the washbasin, he poured himself a large glass of whisky and stared out the window in contemplation. A thousand stars sprinkled across the pitch-black sky and stared back down at him seeking some peace, yet their sight did nothing to calm the thoughts, running relentlessly around his head.

Δ

When morning came, Julia slowly opened her eyes and was startled to see her husband exactly where she had left him the night before. "Have you been sitting there all night?"

"No, no," he said – a lie; he had been unable to rest. "I woke early and needed to think."

Julia suspected this was untrue but she did not challenge him. "Shall we head for the dining carriage then?"

Brown shook his head. "I've ordered breakfast to be brought to our compartment. But first I have business to take care of."

Then he was off, out the door. And with a nod to the night guard, still standing at attendance outside, Brown made his way down the swaying train, determined to get to the bottom of the intrusion earlier that morning.

The men who'd caused the ruckus were in the carriage designated for luggage, which was stuffed full of only the most important guests' paraphernalia. This included a large golden cage containing a set of parakeets whose squawking had induced headaches in the men waiting here for Brown all night.

Pacing back and forth with his hands behind his back, the war general glared at the captives before turning to the guard.

"Any news from these two?"

"Not a thing," replied the guard, somewhat annoyed that he was unable to offer more, having doggedly persisted in questioning the men throughout the night.

Brown walked to the captives and eyeballed them at close range. Clearly, the guard's hard stance hadn't won him answers, so Richard decided to try a different tack. "What's the game then, fellas?" He chuckled. "Here to assassinate me, were you?"

It was meant to be a joke, but his jovial manner was abruptly shattered when the two men exchanged sober looks and then hung their heads in what could easily be construed as a demonstration of guilt.

Shaken by their response but not wishing to reveal his shock, Brown slowly moved across to his colleague and told him in a low voice, "When we arrive in Philadelphia, take these men straight to the local cells."

The instruction was for the guard's ears only but the prisoners must have got the idea, yet when Brown glanced back at them as he left the carriage, he saw no reaction; their gaze remained fixed firmly on the floor.

Δ

He walked back to his carriage slowly, even more concerned than before. Caught up in second guessing himself, it was something of a shock to open the door to his compartment and be greeted by the cheeriness of his wife.

"Fantastic, you're back!" Julia beamed with happiness from across the little table that had been set up in their room. "I saved you some coffee."

"I'm not thirsty," he retorted sharply and slumped into the armchair.

Undeterred by her husband's abruptness, Julia set down the coffee pot and came over to kneel down at his side. "Now, Richard," she coaxed, "you know it helps to discuss these things... A problem shared, remember, is a problem halved."

Sitting there with his stomach in knots, Brown stared longingly at his wife. He was desperate to disclose his thoughts, but his machismo – *a war general ought to have no need to share like this* – held him back.

"Richard," Julia tried again, looking at him with loving eyes and smiling gently. "It's me. You can tell me."

Brown sighed.

He never could resist that warm and loving smile.

"Two men were caught outside our door last night after a scuffle with the guards. I went to question them just now, and asked whether they'd come to assassinate me." He shook his head in condemnation. "And the look on their faces...!"

"What!" Julia breathed and she quickly grasped her husband's hand.

Seeing the panic in her eyes, he drew her in close to comfort her. "I also had the strangest dream about Lincoln being assassinated," Brown confessed, gazing at his wife awash with uncertainty.

"Oh, Richard," she said, knowing what a nightmare that had been for him. "It's just a dream. You'll see him in a day or two," she reassured him.

"You're right... yes, I'm sure you're right..." he said, for her benefit as much as his own. "I've simply become fanciful, and need to jolly well pull myself together!" and his wife patted his hand with pride.

Brown was a complex character. As chief of the Union Army, he possessed formidable leadership qualities and could be a cold-hearted military man when required. However, he was not a warmonger, and away from the battlefield he was rather softer. Behind closed doors, he often questioned his own actions, and was not as confident as he was careful to appear. Truth be told, he preferred to be second in command, leaving the big, important decisions to someone else; which was why he and Lincoln made such a formidable team.

Feeling reassured after his wife's kind words, Brown reverted to his strong and commanding persona. He stood, puffed out his chest and instructed Julia to begin packing for their imminent arrival at Kensington Station, where the local sheriff would be waiting to take Brown to his appointment.

Chapter 3: The Union League

Δ

As the carriage pulled up outside the Union League, Brown told the driver to take his wife on to their hotel and he kissed her goodbye. Then he straightened his uniform, stepped out onto the street and took a moment to admire the building before him. Surely the most splendid in all of Philadelphia. It was a shining example of European Renaissance-style architecture, with its brick and brown-stone frontage and spectacular marble columns, and its *pièce de résistance*, the striking entrance, which was accessed via twin spiral staircases twisting from street level to the first floor.

Richard marched confidently up the stairs, and was greeted at the entrance by Martin McMichael; Mayor of Philadelphia and president of the Union League. And as Brown smiled back at the friendly face before him, both men as customary, saluted each other, before quoting in unison the founding motto: *"Love of country leads."*

"How are you?" Brown enquired warmly as the men firmly shook hands.

"I'm well, thank you," McMichael replied with a wide grin. "And you? Good journey, I hope?"

"Not great to be honest, but nothing to worry about," said Brown, hoping to forget about his troubles. "Am I the first to arrive?"

"You are indeed," McMichael confirmed. "Please, come on in."

They moved into the main entrance foyer, passing the pristine marble busts of Washington and Franklin, before making their way up to the second-floor library. And just as was requested, the bulletin board bore no reference to the meeting that was about to take place

"Good choice," commended Brown, as he scanned the space before him. Shelves and shelves of books encased the room's perimeter and in the centre, a large table, in the shape of an ellipse. Brown continued to nod in approval and his mood finally began to lift. Reassured, he wandered across to the window and perched, the perfect vantage point to look down at the street and watch the guests as they arrived.

First came fifty-two year old James Robert Harris, dressed, as usual, in black from head to toe; his bright-white ruffled hair and bushy eyebrows the only contrast to his dark attire. Looking up from the street, he spotted Brown and subtly tipped his hat in acknowledgement before entering the building in the hope of gaining a private audience, prior to the others arriving.

"Brown, old sport!" Harris declared jovially as he entered the library. "How's that bastard Lee doing? Don't hear him shouting now!"

Harris proceeded to somewhat coarsely congratulate the war general on defeating his Confederate nemesis. And while Richard was taken aback by Harris's exuberance, he could not help but be flattered by his words and recognition.

"It may be a couple of weeks yet, as they're still almost two hundred thousand strong, but without General Lee the Confederate effort is severely depleted," Brown revealed, then paused solemnly in contemplation. "Lee was their best man – a good man. But there can only be one victor on the battlefield, and history will now remember him as the loser."

JR offered a smile of solidarity in response, his eyes gleaming with the thought of victory.

"And how's your boy?" Brown asked out of nowhere.

Now JR's face turned to embarrassment.

And he searched for a plausible explanation for his son's absence today. The truth was, having walked into his father's business, Andrew John Harris was enjoying the good life on easy street, and he had decided not to take up on the invitation to this meeting, deeming it unimportant in his busy social schedule.

"Apologies, Richard," Harris said, red-faced and uncomfortable. "Andrew has been waylaid and unfortunately will be unable to attend..."

He was saved from any further interrogation by Levi Sykes entering the room to join them.

At forty-five years of age, Sykes had amassed a similar level of wealth to JR, but his manner and outlook on life were completely different. Priding himself on being a "gentlemen banker", Sykes worked at a more methodical pace, and rather than concentrating solely on work, he liked to be with his family, relaxing at home. Softly spoken, with a warm and welcoming manner, he was well regarded by all.

"Gentlemen, how are we?" Sykes enquired pleasantly.

"Great to see you!" Brown enthused while purposefully making his way across the room to shake Sykes's hand. "Glad you could make it."

Before they could continue their conversation, McMichael, who had been standing at the entranceway all this time, intervened, "Can I offer you chaps some refreshments?"

"Just some water for now, thanks," Brown responded. He grinned knowingly. "We'll save the heavy stuff for later!"

As McMichael strode out of the room to find a subordinate to bring the water, he crossed paths with another man just about to enter. Brown recognised him as the distinctly fresh-faced Alex Macdonald: the others did not. At twenty-nine, Macdonald was nowhere near as rich or powerful as the other attendees and was only just beginning his journey. However, what the Scot lacked in experience he made up for in charm and, more importantly, an insatiable appetite for study, not to mention a photographic memory.

As Alex walked hesitantly into the room with a look of trepidation on his face, Stephen Roberts appeared alongside his son Alfred, and brushed past the young Scot, simply assuming him to be a member of the club's staff. Roberts Junior - balding with a comb-over and oversized muttonchops - looked every inch a younger version of his father, albeit much rounder than the ever slimline Stephen.

"Could we not have held this meeting on the ground floor?" the elder Roberts grumbled. The seventy year old was evidently struggling to catch his breath.

Stephen, or "The Commander" as he liked to be known, had a furious temper which had earned him the epitaph "The angriest man in New York". He was by far the wealthiest individual in the room; a self-made multimillionaire from his exploits in shipping and railroads, having dragged himself up from the humblest of beginnings through his relentless obsession to work harder than his competition and undercut them until he ran them out of business.

Wishing to assert his dominance early on and drive a marker into the ground, Stephen pressed his close friend once again for an answer. "Well, Brown, could you not have arranged this on the ground floor?"

"I can only apologise, Commander." Brown grinned, well aware his associate was merely posturing. He turned his attention to bringing Macdonald into the group. "And Alex, I can only hope this is to your satisfaction?"

Now the spotlight switched focus.

"Well, I would never wish to disagree with Mr Roberts, however, I feel on this occasion, the room should suffice," Macdonald replied, having instinctively grasped the nuance of the situation and decided, smartly, to appease both men. And with his shrewd response having been warmly received, the group of men swarmed around the Scot, to offer their hand to the stranger.

With Brown, Macdonald and Sykes engaged in conversation, The Commander took the opportunity to drag his old friend, JR, away from the group. "Good to see you, James," Stephen stated before scanning the room. "Your boy not here today?" he wondered.

Not again!

"He's... a little under the weather," JR squirmed.

He need not have been so ashamed, for The Commander knew all too well his friend's situation.

"Well, keep at him, JR. Just look at my boy..." Stephen said, and they focused their attention on Alfred across the room, happily chatting amongst the group. "He used to be such a blockhead, and your lad isn't even that bad!" Stephen told his ally, who appreciated the thoughtful gesture.

Their moment, however, was rudely interrupted as Harris felt a sharp slap across his back and Jack Brunson waltzed confidently into the room, smoking a large cigar between his teeth.

"Well, well, well, what do we have here?" he boomed derisively as he walked past JR and Stephen, barely acknowledging them. "The victory gang!"

Brunson marched directly up to Brown and thrust out his hand with a confident swagger.

"How are you, Jack?" Brown asked politely, while looking fondly upon their latest arrival, but bracing himself for further eccentricities.

"I'm great, as always!" Brunson declared. "But aren't we all?" He gazed around the room, grinning wildly at those gathered, his cigar hanging loosely from the corner of his mouth.

Forty year old Jack Brunson had built his vast fortune through manipulation, determination and a sheer disregard for the consequence of anyone else. With a naturally aggressive temperament, he ramped up his exuberant personality at every opportunity in an effort to dominate people into submission. The fortune he had amassed almost put him on a level with Stephen Roberts; the two men stood as titans of industry, and were immensely proud of the fact.

"It certainly is a great day to be alive," Sykes agreed, strolling across the room to greet his good friend Brunson, just as the last of the guests made his appearance.

Christopher Worthington was a protector. His heart overflowed for those in society who, he so deemed, required assistance for a better chance in life. Not a tall man but stocky, and with a piercing gaze, it was said that he could peer deep into a man's soul, and so those with a guilty conscience did not seek to be around him. He was the only attendee at the meeting born into old money; his family wealth stretching back several generations.

"Worthington!" Brown called out heartily as the newcomer made his way across the room. "Good to see you."

"I'm... not late, am I?" Worthington gingerly enquired, looking worriedly around the library, now alive with people.

“Not at all.” Brown merrily exclaimed as he ushered him towards the table. “In fact, you’re just in time. Now we’re all here, we can commence.”

Looking around at the other men, most of whom were engaged in noisy conversation, he yelled out in a commanding voice, “Shall we begin?”

Δ

Chapter 4: The Pyramid

Δ

As the group settled down in their seats, Brown closed the double entrance doors then made his way across to the fireplace, before pausing to compose himself. Then he turned to face the expectant onlookers, sat watering at the mouth.

"I want to thank you all personally, because without your contributions, we may never have arrived on the cusp of victory where we stand today."

Hearty applause rippled around the room.

And though it was appreciated, it left Brown waiting patiently for the clapping to die down, smiling graciously at the praise. When he spoke next, he addressed Macdonald.

"Alex, as superintendent of the military railways, running the Union telegraph lines, you unlocked the railroads and supervised the transportation of troops. Without your efficient work, our eventual victory may never have come about."

Flattered by Brown's compliment but somewhat embarrassed at the same time, Macdonald joked, "First casualty of the war." He pointed to a scar on his cheek. "Got this freeing a trapped telegraph wire while out on duty..."

The group chuckled at the Scot's quip, and once the laughter quietened, Brown continued with his next acknowledgment.

"Without JR Harris & Son's offices in New York and London being the Union's financial representative in Europe, our funds would have been severely depleted and we would have been unable to pay our troops. Who knows how this would have ended otherwise?" Brown said. He received a nod of approval from JR, before moving systematically on to Sykes.

"Similarly, Levi, your firm L & W Sykes disposing of over *two hundred million dollars* in bonds, as well as supplying uniforms for the troops - both these acts scarcely less important than the Battle of Gettysburg."

The men around the table bowed their heads in a mutual show of respect for Sykes. Then the spotlight turned to Worthington.

"Christopher," the war general said, "as one of the founding members of the Union League, you have always been our staunchest supporter. Your lobbying in Washington alongside Lincoln to create the allotment system has drastically aided the livelihood of all our troops."

This elicited nods from every single member. All of whom held the army, in the highest of regards.

"Now the Roberts family..." Brown grinned playfully, wondering whether he was going to receive another tongue-lashing from The Commander. "Donating your steamers to the war effort has allowed the Union Army to maintain the upper hand at sea. Your continued commitment to releasing your ships at my request is something I shall never forget, and I thank you profoundly for your support."

Applause broke out, echoing through the library, and the usually unemotional Stephen looked deeply moved.

"And last but not least –" Brown began, but he was interrupted by the group, who began to snigger and lightly pat the table, making a drumroll with their hands.

"Don't praise him too much, Richard – his head won't fit out the door!" Stephen Roberts jested, smiling insincerely across at Brunson. Something passed between the two men, a quiet undercurrent.

"Your work alongside our good friend Mr Roach in successfully distributing Treasury Notes has been invaluable," said Richard, "as well as the access you have provided to your railroads."

More applause, but this time it died down quickly.

Then Brown, looking solemn, made his way towards the table, eyeing each of the men in turn.

"Now that we have recognised your individual contributions, we must also consider the whole. Your co-operation has laid the foundations underneath President Lincoln, at the top of our pyramid." Brown brought his index fingers and thumbs together to make a triangular-shape (Δ) and illustrate his point. "And it is his *express* wish for this group to continue that alliance to create a prosperous new America."

The men sat bolt upright with pride at being the select few chosen for this honour, and it was all they could do not to clamour for details of this great new nation they were to build together.

"What are the plans, Richard?" Harris enquired with a sense of wonderment in his voice.

"Rebuild cities, and create new ones. Expand the railroads; link every place in this country. Roll out free public schooling across the states. Improve the labour system, and massively expand commerce and finance," he announced boldly and with no small amount of gravitas.

The members of the group sat astonished by the enormity of his suggestion and quickly the mental cogs started whirring as they considered how they could best be involved. Yet as the endless possibilities rushed around his colleagues' minds, Stephen Roberts had already identified where he'd likely prosper. And wishing to make it a memorable moment, he placed his hands atop the armrests of his chair and slowly rose to his feet. Standing dominantly over the men seated around him, he paused for a moment and scanned the group intensely, until he had the full attention of each and every man.

"Gentlemen, this shall be the start of a new America. And under the guidance of Lincoln and Brown we shall hereby commit to creating a New World Order."

Inspired by the elder Roberts' proclamation, the men rose from their seats, clapping and chattering excitedly. Caught up in dreams of a glorious future for their nation, they paid no heed to McMichael who slipped back into the room, even though he was white-faced and trembling, and hurried straight to Brown and began whispering in his ear.

"Are you sure we can't do this here?" he hissed back.

McMichael shook his head gravely and in the blink of an eye the war general sensed something was amiss.

Heads were starting to turn around the table, the interruption drawing attention. Brown did not wish to quell the revelry, and so he said quickly, "Please, talk amongst yourselves, I shall return in just a moment."

An instruction, not a request: he was already walking towards the door, awash with confusion and a mounting sense of concern.

Δ

Chapter 5: A New Deal

Δ

Pacing out of the library and into the adjacent room, McMichael appeared somewhat on the verge of breakdown. His eyes roamed wildly around the small administrative office while he desperately attempted to compose himself, taking deep breaths and trying, but failing, to form the words a tip his tongue.

Brown soon lost patience.

Grabbing hold of McMichael's suit lapels, he shook him lightly and commanded authoritatively, "Pull yourself together Martin and tell me what has happened?"

And so, not wishing to irritate his friend any further and unable to figure out how to deliver the terrible news correctly, McMichael blurted out, "President Lincoln was shot last night!"

Brown didn't think; his reaction was purely instinctual. He shoved McMichael across the room in a burst of rage, causing him to hit the wall, hard. Stumbling backwards with the ferocity of his own action, Brown steadied himself on a dark oak desk. Heedless of the other men gathered just a wall away, he yelled at the top of his lungs.

"Tell me it isn't true! How could this be?"

McMichael picked himself up warily, concerned that he would face another physical assault. When Brown did not advance on him, he managed to compose himself sufficiently to carry on.

"All I know is that a local man by the name of Carmicle managed to gain access to the presidential box and he fired a shot directly at Lincoln's head," he informed.

"And did he survive?" Brown asked desperately. His collar suddenly felt tight and his beard itched with perspiration.

"I'm not sure," replied McMichael. "The message... I'm sorry, that's all I know."

The answer at least provided Richard with a modicum of optimism and he stood motionless, allowing the information to run through his brain. Unable to comprehend the full extent of the situation in such a short space of time, he could only conclude that he needed to depart immediately.

"Prepare the stagecoach. Prepare the train. I must return to Washington at once!" Brown instructed to McMichael, as if he were back on the battlefield and taking a firm hold of the situation, as would any good general. He must reassess, manoeuvre and transform this situation, no matter how grave the position in which he may find himself.

Back in the library, the group were continuing to enthusiastically plot the future of America. Brown did not wish to burden his colleagues with the news of the shooting until he knew the full story – specifically, whether Lincoln lived. So as he marched back into the room, he avoided making eye contact and hurriedly gathered up his belongings.

"Gentlemen, unfortunately I must return to Washington," he stated. "I can't explain right now, but I shall contact you again soon."

His announcement caused a ripple of surprise among the men. "Do you wish for us to do anything?" Sykes offered.

"We do nothing until our next meeting," Brown advised. "We have a plan, and that must be completed, whoever leads this group."

And with those cryptic closing words, Brown swept out of the room and pounded down the stairs to the waiting stagecoach.

Δ

The chatter in the library was far less exuberant now. Of course, the members of the group understood that as Lincoln's right-hand man had a great deal of responsibility and could be called away at a moment's notice, but he had looked rather flushed, and it seemed to them that his words had been clipped and charged with some meaning they could not quite grasp.

"I guess we just await an update from Brown then," Sykes said to Brunson as they stood together, a little apart from the rest of the group.

"I, guess so," Jack replied tersely, not particularly engaged in the conversation, nor all that concerned with Brown's departure. His concentration was fixed firmly on Stephen Roberts, towards whom he suddenly began advancing in a direct line across the room.

With the Roberts family and Brunson both holding large interests in the railroads, there was a clear conflict of interest, and in his typical style, Jack wasted no time in putting his cards firmly on the table.

"You and I both have common interests in the railroads," he said, interrupting The Commander's private discussion with his son and JR. "So we need to decide: do we slug it out or come to some form of agreement?"

Turning around to look down his nose at his adversary, Stephen was riled by Jack's discernible lack of respect, but years of practice enabled him to remain composed.

"My interests are in the east," he said simply, to avoid being dragged into any discussion over the matter, before turning his back on Jack.

Issue: dealt with.

Brunson, however, still had ideas of his own. "But if we're to be assisted by Brown then I may wish to move into those markets too," he said.

The comment caused the room to freeze, all at once. And the blood pressure of the elder Roberts rose at the challenge, heading dangerously close to boiling point. With everyone awaiting Robert's retort, not daring to take their eyes off the action nor speak, Alex Macdonald spied a large map hanging on a picture rail and grabbed it off the wall, before ambling over and laying the gold-edged frame on a table between the warring factions. Too shocked to even consider dismissing his interjection, he was allowed to launch into his mediation strategy before they could open their mouths.

"Stephen, so far as I understand it, your network extends mainly between these three cities." Macdonald tapped a finger on the cities of New York, Washington and Cleveland, leaning upon his extensive knowledge of the railroad network.

"That's correct," Stephen cautiously confirmed, feeling somewhat confused, not only by Macdonald's familiarity with his operations but also by where the young Scot was leading with his approach.

"And according to my understanding, Mr Brunson," Alex continued, turning to face Jack, "your concerns lay mainly here, here and here..." He tapped the map again, this time on the cities of Cincinnati, Washington and Cleveland.

Brunson nodded, impressed by Macdonald's accuracy but equally as perturbed.

"So, if I may suggest..." Macdonald said, with somewhat of a large lump within his throat.

Here goes nothing!

Slowly and carefully, he marked a line in the dust across the glass of the frame. And all the men gathered around, leaned in to examine the marking, which extended from Cleveland to Washington.

"If you would both allow," said Macdonald, "you could operate on either side of this line. Mr Roberts, that would give you everything to the northeast and Mr Brunson, you could work with everything else. Then neither of you need run into conflict over territory?"

To Macdonald's mind, this represented the most equitable deal, but whether the two titans would see the merits of his plan was entirely another matter.

Standing in silence, each man thoroughly considered the Scot's proposal; not only in terms of how it may benefit him but also his opponent. And each quietly concluded that the deal benefited *him* more than his rival. For Stephen, it allowed him to concentrate his efforts in the area he knew best and build upon his already tremendous success. He was happy in the knowledge that he would have the most densely populated part of America to himself, leaving Brunson with what he deemed to be desert land. For Jack, meanwhile, the plan represented an opportunity to claim a whopping ninety-five per cent of the country, allowing him to develop the western frontier. And of course, it also played well to his ego, that he would be granted the vast majority of the land.

But before either could offer their recommendation, Christopher Worthington began a slow-clap from across the other side of the room. "Bravo," he called loudly, making his way over to the men. "Bravo indeed. This is exactly the kind of considered approach we need in order to make this coalition work." He turned to Macdonald. "And well done to you, Alex," he said sincerely, offering him the warmest of smiles.

The Scots game of risk had paid off well.

"So what do you say?" Brunson propositioned The Commander, as both men desperately sought to hide their excitement at the *"better deal"* they perceived they had been granted.

"I'm happy to go with that," Stephen agreed. "For... for the sake of harmony, of course," he added in a flagrant attempt to demonstrate his most generous nature.

"Well then, it's agreed," Worthington happily announced before Jack could actually confirm his agreement, and he patted them both on the back.

With Brunson having achieved his goal for the day, he was desperate to depart in order to get straight to work, away from the prying eyes of the group.

"Good doing business with you, gentlemen," he stated. As he left the room, and he threw a quick, furtive wink Sykes's way; an invitation to leave alongside him.

Discerning the subtle gesture, Levi duly followed. "See you again soon, chaps," he called out, before catching up with his friend, who at once launched into a description of his latest extravagance.

"Did I tell you about my new island?" he boomed, knowing full well he was within earshot of the others. "I'm building the grandest house in all America..." he declared smugly, as they disappeared down the stairs.

Δ

In the library, while Macdonald was carefully returning the framed map to its rightful place, Christopher Worthington said farewell to his associates and departed as well, leaving only the four of the group remaining. But with JR hoping to speak with the Roberts men alone, he decided to take control of the situation.

"Alex," he called warmly across the room, "you should visit my boy in New York. I'm sure he'd be delighted to assist you with any business you may have."

Delighted, Macdonald began walking over, but then James abruptly added, "All the best then!" nodding towards the exit with a commanding smile.

Macdonald's euphoria instantly subsided.

But with a respectful nod to JR, he obediently directed himself out of the library. As he made his way down the stairway alone, Alex was undeterred by the dismissal. He felt content with his day's work, knowing that his ascent to the top would involve thousands of small steps, just like the one he'd taken today. "One step further ahead," he murmured to himself "One step further ahead..."

Back in the library, Harris finally had the privacy he craved, to debrief with the Roberts men. "So what do you think of all that?" he said, his voice edged with disbelief.

"I think it's a handy little deal, James, don't you?" Stephen replied, fully expecting his friend to have come to the same conclusion.

"You've given a lot of the country away!" Harris shot back, but Stephen only smiled benignly.

"I've 'given away', as you put it, JR, a barren and ungodly part of the land that is ferociously difficult to lay track on and full of Indians. Brunson will do well to conquer that part of America in his lifetime!" he contended somewhat haughtily. "I'm more than happy with Macdonald's suggestion and in fact, shall have to thank him personally the next time I see him."

Accepting that Stephen was quite content with the deal and seeing no reason to question him further on that score, JR moved the conversation on to their new acquaintance. "And what of this Macdonald chap?" He shrugged his shoulders. "Who is he? I've never even heard of him before!"

"I'm not sure," Stephen said, shaking his head from side to side. "But..." He raised his eyebrows and fixed his eyes on his friend. "But he could certainly be of use to us, James," he finished.

Harris considered for a moment, and then nodded slowly in agreement. "Indeed he could, Stephen... indeed he could." Both of them sensing, their next business opportunity may have just presented itself to them.

Δ

Chapter 6: Return to Washington

Δ

Arriving back in Washington both tired and emotional, Brown made no excuse for his mood to the coachman who obeyed his barked order to take him immediately to the presidential mansion. Time seemed to pass by in slow motion as he sat impatiently in the coach, staring out at the tree-lined streets upon a city, full of contrasts. Dominated by fields with a scattering of four storey townhouses set amongst plentiful wooden shacks; it was a humble and mainly rural landscape, yet its small residential dwellings were overshadowed by the gigantic, white-stone government buildings clustered atop the hill. And soon he would arrive amongst them.

During his return journey, Richard had tried to remain hopeful that the news delivered to him in Philadelphia might somehow be incorrect. However, upon recognising the heightened security presence around the North Lawn, he closed his eyes and swallowed the lump in his throat, in the knowledge that today was not likely to be his lucky day.

"Richard," Officer Marsh quietly acknowledged Brown as he alighted from the coach.

"Where is he?" Brown gravely enquired, filled with trepidation as he looked up at the Presidential Mansion.

"He's in the State Room, sir," solemnly said Marsh, at which Brown's chin dropped to his chest, as if it had been held up by a string atop his head that had just been cut.

"At ease," Brown allowed, signalling the end of the conversation, before making his way up to the house.

When he arrived at the State Room, he paused before the threshold, consumed by a reluctance to enter. Finally, steeling himself, he peered around the corner to see with his own eyes: President Lincoln laid atop the dining table, his body motionless and covered by a white sheet with an American flag folded neatly across his chest.

Standing frozen in the doorway, Brown felt his stomach lurch as if he were about to be violently sick. He brought his hand up to cover his whole mouth, gripping his cheeks in such an abrasive fashion that it would have caused him severe discomfort; if only he could have felt anything beyond the unrelenting grief.

A million thoughts rushed through his head.

Where do we go from here?

How did this happen?

Who is responsible?

Have we caught him?

"Because if we have," he muttered, rapidly spiralling into a chasm of anger, "if we have, then I can be a horrible man – I can tear flesh from bones – I can..."

"Richard!" someone shouted.

He turned to see Mary Lincoln dashing towards him and before he knew it, she flung herself into his arms.

"I'm... I'm so sorry, Mary. I should have been here."

"This is not your fault, Richard. Don't ever think that. *Don't ever think that!*" she shrieked.

Then she lost her composure completely.

Banging her fists on his chest and yelling, Brown allowed Mary to take her anger out on him, before pulling her into a tight embrace and leaving her sobbing uncontrollably against his chest.

They stood like that, together, until Brown noticed a man hovering outside the room, seeking his private counsel but not wishing to interrupt the tender moment. Brown nodded to acknowledge the presence of William Roach, Chief Justice of the United States, before giving Mrs Lincoln one final hug and then releasing her from his grasp.

"It will be all right, Mary," he reassured her, even if he did not fully believe that himself. "I'll make sure you're well taken care of," he promised.

Lincoln's wife did her best to force a smile, but it trembled on her tired face. Then she turned and walked out of the room, back to her bed, which was so desolate and empty, and seemed to swallow her back into the mire.

"William." Brown beckoned Roach into the room. "What can I do for you, good sir?"

"I understand you were in Philadelphia?" Roach said. The implication was clear: *Where have you been for the past twenty-four hours?*

"Yes. On a mission for the president, which I shall explain to you later on. For now, we need to get to the bottom of what the *hell* happened here." Brown pointed angrily at Lincoln's body.

"We have some initial information on Carmicle. We just need to locate his whereabouts before –"

"Before we see him *hang*!" Brown vehemently cut in.

"Before, we do whatever is deemed fit," Roach countered calmly.

Incensed by the realisation that Lincoln's assassin would likely be afforded even a modicum of legal process, Brown walked over to the window and peered out longingly into the distance. He knew the assailant could only be a day's journey at most from where he stood; the war general could almost smell his freshly laid tracks.

Returning his gaze to Lincoln's body, Brown slowly regained his composure once again. Then his thoughts suddenly turned to succession.

"And what of the presidential position?" he asked.

Roach cleared his throat. "Mr Rushbourne was sworn in this morning, sir, once word was received from the doctor."

Brown blanched at this. Lincoln was barely cold, and Vice-President Benjamin Rushbourne was already sworn in?

"We wanted to demonstrate a strong and swift resolve," Roach went on as Brown exhaled a large sigh. "We didn't want to give an advantage of any sort to the Confederates, nor diminish the spirit of our troops."

Richard swilled the notion around his gums, but he could not argue with any of that. And reluctantly, he had to acknowledge that it was the correct thing to do. It grated on him though, that he was not consulted, and deep down inside a little flame of hope had been extinguished: that *he* may have been considered for the role.

Turning once again and staring across the lawns to mask his frustration and disappointment, Richard wondered to himself whether this grandiose plan of his and Lincoln's would ever actually see the light of day. *Maybe the opportunity has already passed us by?*

A raging doubt began to creep into every fibre of his being. "That's...understandable," Richard replied belatedly as he slumped against the window casement, feeling every sense, a failure.

Waiting for Brown to continue, Roach stood patiently by his side. However, when the general uttered not a single word more and merely continued to stare out into the distance, William decided that his colleague must need some further consoling. "You'll be pleased to know that Benjamin's first piece of business was to confirm that Lincoln's Cabinet will remain in position. He wants to continue Abe's good work!" he said brightly.

But that only raised a wry smile from Richard, who looked like a man carrying the weight of the world on his shoulders. Realising he could do no more, Roach left him to his contemplations.

After standing there alone for what may have been ten minutes or could have been ten hours, Richard finally moved away from the window and slowly approached the table. As he stared intently at the president, it suddenly seemed to him that Abe was lying there with a grin upon his face! Gasping at the sight, Brown attempted to recall whether Lincoln's expression was as such when he first entered the room, but with his mind in such a haze, he simply could not remember even a minute before. Abruptly, the moment caused him to blurt out a grief-stricken chuckle, and a solitary tear trailed slowly from his eye and down onto his cheek.

Awash with emotion as he looked upon his dear friend, Brown vividly recollected how Lincoln always made the best of every situation, no matter how dire it seemed. It was this characteristic that elevated him above other men, and Brown knew that he must try to replicate that now that his leader was no longer there to guide him.

Δ

Later that afternoon, Brown arranged for Lincoln's body to be moved into the East Room of the presidential mansion and made presentable so the president could lie in state. Standing with his arms folded as he supervised the mansion staff, out of the corner of his eye Richard spotted Harry Smithson walking towards him, exuding guilt from every pore.

The moment Smithson saw he had Brown's attention, he began scrambling to defend himself.

"Richard..." his pleading began.

Brown sprang into action, stalking down the corridor towards him.

"I was..." Harry squirmed as the war general pounded ever closer.

"It wasn't my..." came Harry's final attempt.

However Richard was now directly in front of him, and he grasped the young Major by the collar with both hands and lifted him clean into the air. Smithson hung there, suspended for a moment, his feet kicking back and forth. Then Brown threw him backwards, and the two of them crashed into the hardwood floor with an almighty, forceful bang.

"You were supposed to protect him!" the war general exploded, covering Smithson in a cascade of spit.

Feeling physically bruised by the fall, but far more injured mentally by the ferocity of the attack from this man he so respected, Harry lay on the floor, fanatically shaking his head back and forth, lost in the grip of fear.

"Well...?" Richard persisted, pure anger running through his veins.

When no response was forthcoming, Brown raised his right hand and slowly made a fist in the air. Smithson creased his face up, cringing in anticipation of the imminent attack. With his full force, Brown threw a thunderous strike downwards. It landed millimetres to the side of Smithson's head, splitting timbers and cracking bones.

Heedless of his knuckles dripping blood and ballooning, Brown continued with his interrogation. "What. Happened?" he demanded.

Harry began to ramble incoherently in a desperate attempt to defend himself. "He came from nowhere... he knew the theatre... he knew the staff... the guard left his post... *there was nothing I could do!*"

Upon hearing his colleague's numerous justifications, Brown slowly began to release his fist, and panting, he slumped to the floor to sit beside Smithson.

With the tumult seemingly at an end, the cluster of staff who had been hiding in the doorways along the corridor to watch the commotion, quickly jumped back to their positions, keen to avoid being the next focal point on Brown's warpath.

Carefully, wincing with pain, Smithson sat up, and the two men sat side by side, staring at the floor and lost in their own thoughts - until that was, Smithson suddenly recalled Lincoln's message to pass to Brown.

"Sir, I must tell you..." he bravely began, his voice aquiver. "After the attack, Mr Lincoln spoke to me. He had a message for you..."

Brown gritted his teeth and breathed heavily through his nose while craning his neck to face Smithson.

"Yes?" boomed the demanding reply.

"He said for you to carry on, sir – not to stray from the plan... I don't know what he meant, but that's exactly what he told me to tell you," the young major said, oblivious to the magnitude of the message he had just delivered.

With Lincoln's final words ringing in Richard's head, and fusing with the emotional turmoil of all he had already suffered, he abruptly began hitting the top of his head in frustration, while a bemused Smithson looked on, unsure whether to run, call for help or intercede.

Coming to a rest, after several hefty blows, Brown suddenly stopped - then slowly rose to his feet. Towering over his colleague, who looked like a man facing the gallows, he extended a hand out to Smithson and pulled the astonished officer up with a firm jolt. And after patting him down and straightening his uniform, Brown quietly instructed: "Be on your way."

There could be no more internal fighting with so much at stake and so many enemies at their door.

Still sorely confused about the situation but not about to wait around and be told twice, Smithson dashed off, leaving Brown standing there alone as a great realisation dawned upon him. *Whatever has passed, must be left in the past; now is the time to move forward. From this day on I shall make it my life's work to complete Lincoln's vision, in accordance with his dying request.*

Chapter 7: Rushbourne and Roach

Δ

The sun rising over Capitol Hill on Easter Sunday brought a mellow glow to the faces of the people queuing around the block, hoping to catch a glimpse of their fallen hero and former president. Set against this quiet and sombre backdrop, Brown's attention was firmly fixed on apprehending the man responsible for the atrocity at Ford's Theatre, and he had woken early in a bullish mood, determined to turn this situation around. Dressed in his full army attire, he made his way to the Oval Room, where Rushbourne and Roach were holding their customary morning meeting. Brown's aim: to agree his arrangements with them before setting out for the day.

As he entered the Oval Room, Brown spared a second to eye Roach and Rushbourne and take their measure. Chief Justice Roach stood there in his usual judicial-type attire; a particularly tall and blockish man, he dwarfed Rushbourne, who was of much more average stature. Average in size, but not in manner – a controversial character, the newly sworn-in president despised taking advice from others and actively enjoyed going against the grain if it provided an opportunity to demonstrate his authority. A fierce drinker, but not a particularly good one, he often made a fool of himself in public spheres when left unchecked by his advisors.

"Morning, gentlemen." Brown beamed like a ray of sunshine, to Roach's considerable surprise.

"Good morning, Richard," William acknowledged, pleased that his comrade appeared to be in better spirits. "I didn't expect to see you up and about so early. Is everything okay?" he enquired, pouring himself a coffee.

"My mood is of no concern," Brown replied bluntly. "All that matters is bringing to justice Lincoln's killer." He turned his attention to Rushbourne. "Benjamin, I'd like to speak to you at some point today regarding a proposal."

The new president was immersed in a pile of papers strewn across his already messy desk. "I should be available this evening," he said, glancing up from his work briefly to acknowledge his colleague.

"Then I shall see you at dinner," Richard replied readily, before marching out of the room to pursue his business for the day, and leaving his colleagues to stare at one another in surprise at the war general's shift in temperament.

Δ

Returning to the presidential mansion late meant Brown missed out on dinner altogether, but he had little concern for his stomach. His appetite was for justice, and on that score he had had a successful day picking up several new leads in his pursuit of Lincoln's assassin and co-conspirators.

Handy little days' work, he thought to himself, striding commandingly into the dining room.

"Richard!" Roach merrily exclaimed, welcoming Brown back to the mansion "We thought you'd never return!" he joked. Evidently, Brown was a couple of drinks behind his colleagues.

"My apologies. I didn't realise the time..." the war general offered as explanation, though truthfully, had it not been for nightfall, he'd have still been out there, trying to apprehend his suspects. "However, we made good ground today," he added and a grin crept menacingly across his weathered face.

Roach congratulated him before making his way over to the drinks cabinet to pour out a well-deserved glass of bourbon. Brown knocked back the entire drink before requesting a top-up from Roach, then reached deep into his inner jacket, pulled out a thick cigar and settled himself in a seat opposite Rushbourne at the dining table. Leaving the new president to gawp at him as he struck a match and took his time lighting his smoke, until it was puffing away nicely before delivering his proposal.

"Mr Lincoln had a plan," he started, wafting the match to extinguish it by his side. "An Economic Development Plan to rebuild our country after four torrid years of war."

Looking serious now, Roach handed Brown his latest top-up and took a seat next to him.

"We have the resources to develop America into one of the leading powers of the world," Brown went on, "but we will require assistance from a group of men whom Lincoln identified."

"What men?" Benjamin interjected, somewhat tetchily.

Calm and collected, Brown used the interruption to pause for a moment and take another delightfully long draw on his cigar, before continuing.

"The members include the Roberts family, the Harris family, Jack Brunson, Alex Macdonald, Christopher Worthington and Levi Sykes," he announced.

Benjamin reacted with his usual narrow-mindedness. "That's great Richard, but I don't think we'll be requiring of any *help*," he said, gazing over at Roach and waving a hand as if physically dismissing the group.

Just as expected.

Brown, however, was not prepared to waver.

"If you want this country to flourish under *your presidency*, these are the only men who can help you achieve that," he stated with real emphasis, hoping his words would click with the personally-ambitious president.

And it worked.

With his attention now turned, Rushbourne sought to delve further into the detail. "So these men are looking to work for me, at my command, in an effort to rebuild the country?" he asked.

"Exactly," Richard allowed emphatically, before taking another long draw of thick cigar smoke.

He could just about see the new president's mouth watering at the tantalising prospect of cementing his place in the history books as 'The Man Who Carried Out Lincoln's Vision and Rebuilt America' when a flicker of disdain, twitched across his face.

Resting back in his seat and stroking his upper lip, Rushbourne considered his next move. While desperate to endorse the plan, he could not help but struggle with the fact it had not been his idea. And looking around the dimly lit room, his gaze fell on his most trusted advisor.

"William," he said, "what do you think of all this?"

Roach swilled the liquor in his glass, half-empty, and took a moment to think before answering.

"I know Jack Brunson very well," he said, "and I am aware of the others." He gave Brown a long and shrewd look, before knocking back the remaining contents of his glass. "I think they could be useful to us," he told Rushbourne, giving the president exactly what he needed: the sense it had been *their* decision to let this happen; not Brown's, and not the man lying cold and stiff in another room of the mansion.

"Well then," Benjamin said, returning his gaze to Richard. "Arrange a meeting, General Brown, so I can see for myself what these men have to offer me," he ordered conceitedly in a further effort to display his power.

Brown, however, simply nodded respectfully; he had witnessed this kind of behaviour on numerous occasions before. Let Rushbourne posture as much as he liked; all

Brown cared about was that ultimately Lincoln's word was followed. And it wasn't like the two men hadn't endured a tepid history anyway: Benjamin never really appreciating Brown's brilliance during the war, and in turn Brown never valued Rushbourne's political career. Each man viewed the other as lucky, rather than talented, yet they were both equally close to Lincoln, and it was perhaps this that had divided them more, causing jealousy over being perceived as his favourite.

No matter: with Richard's simple agreement to arrange a meeting between Rushbourne and the group, both men felt satisfied with the outcome. And the conversation soon moved on, late into the night, as Brown detailed the leads he had chased down that day, which he recounted with particular gusto as the alcohol continued to flow.

Chapter 8: Lincoln's Funeral Procession

Δ

As spring arrived, those responsible for Lincoln's assassination were duly apprehended, questioned and convicted. All apart from Carmicle that was, who had been slain in a shootout having refused to surrender or go peacefully to the law. Then, on a humid and rainy day in the capital, his three co-conspirators were led from their cells under cover of umbrella to the wooden scaffolding erected inside the yard at Washington's Arsenal Penitentiary and hanged in front of an exultant crowd; the onlookers included Rushbourne, Roach and Brown.

Meanwhile in Manhattan, outside his firm's office on Hanover Square, James Robert Harris stood on the pavement assessing the likelihood of his son, AJ, being in the building rather than still laid up in bed.

I'll give it fifty-fifty...

JR Harris & Son occupied the whole left-hand side of the upper ground floor which, whilst not the grandest or largest of banking halls, was well positioned within a whisker of Wall Street - allowing AJ to keep abreast of the latest financial updates with ease. When he bothered to turn up, that is.

With a heavy sigh, JR walked up the steps into the foyer. Purposefully bypassing the building's manager, he turned directly into the banking hall – to find his son perched on the edge of his secretary's desk, fooling around as usual. Noticing his father, AJ promptly sprang to his feet and fumbled around with whatever paperwork he could grasp hold of in a vain attempt to look like he was discussing business.

"And I'd like that written up by the end of the day," he told the bewildered secretary authoritatively, before turning to his old man. "Father!" he exclaimed loudly, approaching him with open arms.

"Keeping yourself busy, I see!" JR said sourly, knowing all too well that his son was slacking.

"Taking care of business – as usual!" AJ jokingly replied, to his father's annoyance.

He had not travelled all this way to be messed around.

And certainly not today.

But JR would not make a scene in front of the watchful eyes of their staff. "Can I speak with you in your office," he said to his son – an instruction, not a request.

Nervously, AJ led his father through the banking hall, their expensive shoes loudly annunciating each step they took across the shiny marble floor. As they entered the compact rear office, AJ was working through a mental list of possible misdemeanours for which his father may wish to reprimand him on this occasion.

JR closed the door behind them and they took a seat either side of the large green-leather-topped desk that dominated the room.

"So," the elder Harris began, "I assume you are prepared for the meeting with Brown and Rushbourne?"

At this, AJ relaxed back in his chair, relieved that this didn't appear to be another telling-off. "Oh, yes - certainly," he replied rather casually.

Far too casually for his father though.

And from the younger Harris's laidback response, JR gathered that his son had made no preparations whatsoever. Incensed by his son's immature attitude, he shot to his feet and slammed his hands down on the desk.

"Do you not understand the importance of this meeting... of this moment and what it could spell?" he barked like a disgruntled headmaster castigating a naughty pupil.

A crestfallen AJ began to sink down in his seat as it dawned on him that this was indeed, another dressing-down from his father. Peering down at his son as he slumped in silence while nodding away somewhat insecurely, JR realised he would need to employ a different tactic if he was to rouse AJ into action.

"You recently turned twenty-eight, Andrew..." he said, and AJ sat up straight, knowing it was most serious if his father was addressing him by his full name. "It's not a grand old age by any means. However, many of your peers have already made their fortunes."

It was said with such an insistent whine that it had AJ now seemingly paying full attention. And JR ran through the finer points of the meeting he had attended in Philadelphia, including the possible alliances that could be forged with the members of the group; in particular, Alex Macdonald.

"Our partners in Europe are eager to advance millions of dollars in loans, so Brown's plan could not have come at a better time. Every other opportunity will pale into insignificance if you play this one right..." he said enticingly. Leaning across the table to affectionately cup Andrew's cheek, he softened his tone. "I implore you son, prove how great you can be and make me proud."

With his father having effectively pulled on his heartstrings, AJ rose to his feet to match his father. "I'm sorry, Father. I don't want to fail you," he admitted, dropping his gaze to the floor. "I only wish I could be half the man you are," he confessed under his breath.

JR instantly grabbed hold of his son's hands and rattled them up and down. "AJ, if you get it right this time, you'll be *ten times* the man I am!"

AJ couldn't quite believe it and he raised his head in wonderment. "Really?" he whispered back.

"I can guarantee you that as a fact." And for the first time that day, James Robert Harris allowed an upturn in his frown, as he saw in his son's eyes something precious: inspiration for the future that potentially lay ahead of him.

Δ

In Washington, Lincoln's funeral train sat waiting to depart from the station, surrounded by crowds of people who had come to pay their respects. Making his way through the gaggle on the platform, Brown was caught off-guard by an unexpected sight: Alex Macdonald standing in the open-sided driver's compartment at the front of the extensive train.

"Alex!" Brown shouted enthusiastically over the hubbub, edging his way towards the Scot. "I didn't expect to see you here. Did you receive my telegram?"

"Indeed I did," Macdonald confirmed, taking off his blackened gloves. "However, driving the first few legs of the procession seemed just as important."

What a wonderful sentiment indeed.

"Well, I couldn't agree more," Brown said, full of fondness for the Scot and his show of devotion. "And who better to oversee the journey!" he commended, returning him the most heartfelt and sincerest of smiles.

Alex did not need to be present for Lincoln's funeral procession. Just like the others, he could simply have awaited Brown and Rushbourne's arrival in New York, but he had seized the opportunity to assist those in positions of power; knowing all too well it never hurt to be well thought of by those who had the ability to alter a man's destiny.

Stepping around the coal shed and onto the gangway connection, Macdonald reached down a hand to Brown and helped him up and onto the train. And the two of them soon decided to grab a swift drink before departure, so made their way through the passenger carriages towards the dining cart at the rear.

"I assume that having arranged the meeting, the president is looking to take the project forward?" Macdonald enquired informally.

Brown, walking ahead of him, could only offer a non-committed response. "I hope so," he said, but then stopped abruptly in the aisle to reconsider. "I think he sees the benefit of our collective," he added, but was clearly still undecided.

"Well, I'm sure once Rushbourne meets the members of the group, he'll be fully committed," Macdonald suggested, as optimistic and diplomatic as ever.

Continuing their journey through the carriages, chatting away like old friends, they reached the dining cart where unsurprisingly, they found Rushbourne and Roach, already standing at the bar. Latching eyes on one another simultaneously, they were unable to engage in any exchange before a sharp, loud whistling pierced the air and the train wheels began slowly grinding into a full turn. With steam cascading up from the tracks to fill the concourse around them, the men turned their attention to the exuberant crowds outside and waved out the windows until their hands and smiles ached, and the last of the bystanders had wished them well on their many stops ahead.

Chapter 9: Meeting in New York

Δ

Over the next few days, the procession passed through its scheduled destinations of Baltimore, Harrisburg and Philadelphia, before arriving on a pleasant sunny morning in Manhattan for an overnight stop. With his ceremonial duties complete, and the journey having allowed Macdonald to ingratiate himself to the new president and his right hand man, he was in a fine mood as the presidential stagecoach carried them to the headquarters of the Union League. The building, at 26 East 17th Street, was certainly not as grand or imposing as the meeting place in Philadelphia; in fact, unless you were a member, you would likely not notice it was there. A sturdy building, wedged into a row of four-storey townhouses; it was further hidden away by the hordes of people going about their daily business, around the busy, Union Square.

As they walked up to the door, it was flung wide open, and the president and his entourage were greeted warmly by Christopher Worthington, who, as one of the founding members of the League, welcomed them into the establishment as proudly as if it were his own home.

Worthington's six-year-old son, Christopher Junior, was in the reception area, sitting with his teddy bear and quietly amusing himself sketching in his Journal of Insects, the anatomy of a butterfly. He smiled up at the important men, stood dominantly all around him.

"Play quietly," his father instructed, before escorting the new arrivals down the hallway and into the Hamilton Room. It really was an outstanding space. Glorious oak panelling running vertically drew the eye up to a magnificent stucco ceiling. Each of the walls was punctuated by floor-to-ceiling windows, framed by citrine velvet curtains, which had been opened to allow just enough of the midday sun to flood in and chase away the darkness in the vast and echoey room.

And although the party from Washington had arrived in good time, all the other delegates were already in place around the large oak table in the centre of the room, sat in a state of keen anticipation. So without further ado, once the latest arrivals were seated, Brown opened with the formalities.

"My dear friends, firstly I would like to apologise for my sudden exit last week. I'm sure you'll excuse my departure, given the circumstances at the time."

Around the table his colleagues nodded in solemn and universal appreciation; no justification necessary.

"Some of you will know Mr Roach," Brown went on, "and no doubt all of you know President Rushbourne, so –" But before Richard could finish, he was interrupted by Rushbourne.

"Thank you, Richard," he said loudly, with the intention of taking a firm hold of the meeting. He had already become bored of listening to his colleague and wanted to find out exactly what this group of men had to offer him.

Rushbourne then stood. And began walking slowly around the table, closely observing the men sitting silently before him. "It's my understanding," he said, "that you have been approached by Mr Brown regarding the rebuilding of our great nation."

Slithering between them, he trailed a hand over the back of every seat, scrutinising each man for any sign of nerves. None of which were present - so he carried on his display.

"And you will be happy to know," he said finally, when he arrived back at his seat, alongside Roach, "that it's also my desire to rebuild. Therefore I would like to hear how you believe you can assist me with my plans."

The members of the group were somewhat staggered by Rushbourne's approach; unlike his predecessor, the president had little to offer in the way of pleasantries. But knowing better than to be deterred by his brusque manner, they gazed at one another, silently, deciding whom should present first.

Jack Brunson confidently stood to deliver his proposal. "My good friend Mr Roach will no doubt have vouched for my credibility already," he said, sending a grin William's way. "My plan is to open the western frontier, with the ultimate aim of creating a single railroad from east to west."

The president listened carefully, but did not respond; he merely nodded at Jack to retake his seat. Unsure as to whether his pitch had contained enough detail and desperately wishing to elaborate, Brunson dallied for a moment, staring longingly at Roach for some sign of approval. But when none was forthcoming, he sank back into his chair, silently seething, as Alex Macdonald stood to present his offer.

Further to the initial meeting in Philadelphia and with this new opportunity at his door, the Scot had been furiously deliberating over where best to position himself so that he could conquer a niche and not put himself in conflict with the others in the group.

"My iron and bridge-making company will provide the raw materials needed for the development, as well as opening up new avenues for expansion," Macdonald said simply. Truthfully, having only recently formed his company, he was flying by the seat of his pants.

Once again Rushbourne remained unmoved, and without offering a reply, he apathetically motioned for Stephen Roberts to take the floor. The Commander, however, certainly not one for being ordered around, chose not to stand as charged; a signal that he was not particularly impressed with the attitude of the new president, some fourteen years his junior.

"I hold numerous positions in both shipping and railroads, with which I'm sure you will be familiar, having travelled on one of my lines to get here today," he stated somewhat haughtily. "And that is where my interests will be of most concern to you, Mr Rushbourne."

Benjamin squinted his eyes and pursed his lips in open contempt for the fact Stephen had failed to address him by his proper title, "President Rushbourne".

An awkward standoff sprang up in the room, but Stephen showed no signs of caring and continued to enlighten the men from Washington about his plans. "Mr Brunson and I both hold interests in the railroads. However, we have agreed upon an area-split, so between us we shall effectively cover the entire country," he outlined.

As he glanced assertively across at Jack, who nodded in recognition of their deal, Roberts missed the flush creeping up the president's face.

"Is that correct?!" Rushbourne erupted, furious that he was being told how *his country* was to be divvied up.

"That it is," Stephen replied coolly and somewhat dismissively. Upsetting the new president did not remotely concern him.

Already far wealthier than he could ever have imagined, The Commander was happy to take this opportunity or leave it. But what he would never do was beg for inclusion, and especially not to someone whom he held in such poor regard. Benjamin had not even been properly elected to his position; in Stephen's opinion, he was an imposter replacing the man he so adored.

Noting the uneasy atmosphere between the two men, Sykes stepped in to move proceedings along and relieve the tension. "My firm wishes to continue our financial support for any developments under your leadership, President Rushbourne," he said politely. "And by continuing this group and rebuilding America, I wholeheartedly believe the nation will thank you eternally for your efforts."

Sykes had struck the right tone; for the first time Benjamin displayed some positive emotion, offering an appreciative smile to Levi for his good grace and warmth.

That's more what I expect.

With the meeting back on a more stable footing, Christopher Worthington stood to attention. Always one to observe the highest level of respect for authority and formality, he saluted the newly appointed president before opening up on his plans.

"I bring something different from the other men insomuch as my concerns lie in establishing social enterprises, building hospitals and providing a better place for our citizens to live. All of which will no doubt be essential if we are to build a United States for one and all," he stated.

His evident compassion tugged on the heartstrings of both the men from Washington, who nodded in consolidated agreement at Worthington's good causes.

James Harris was the last to speak.

Placing a hand on his son's shoulder, he looked down fondly at him. Then his face became resolute and stern. "Money," he said emphatically, "is the lifeblood of all economies and none shall survive without it. The only man I know who would work without pay is a slave, and thankfully, due to Lincoln, that option no longer exists."

This earned him an uncompromising nod of approval from Brown, meanwhile, Rushbourne sat chewing the comment, trying to decipher if it was aimed at him, or not.

"The bankers around this table can provide you with access to finance from around the world, but if you refuse that assistance, America shall not move forward - not even one little bit," he concluded.

As JR's powerful words rang around the room, and heads continued to nod, the message was most notably received in the ears of his son. Finally grasping the importance of this opportunity, he scanned the figures around him. Titans, ten times wealthier than him, he wondered if one day he could stand aside them? Maybe it was time to start listening somewhat closer, to his father's constant advice.

Having heard from everyone in the group and not one to waste his own time, Rushbourne immediately stood. "A fine display, men, a fine display," he declared, while tapping Roach on the shoulder and motioning that they were to depart. "I'm content with your proposals and have decided to continue with the plan of this group."

All those assembled let out a noticeable sigh of relief, and several smiles were exchanged across the table.

"However," Rushbourne continued with an edge to his tone, "you will all be required to make your submissions to my trusted colleague Mr Roach, who will deal with your requests on my behalf - good day!"

And with that, he turned and departed unceremoniously, his second in command following closely behind.

For a short while, the group remained seated in silence, somewhat shell-shocked by the whirlwind visit. Then Jack Brunson, still reeling from having made no favourable impact in the meeting, rapidly made his excuses and rushed off to chase the departing president. He caught up with Rushbourne and Roach as they boarded the waiting stagecoach.

"A wonderful meeting, President Rushbourne," he gushed, holding on to the lip of the door as the men settled themselves on the seat. "With you now on board, our plans are sure to succeed!"

Overt flattery, and yet it served its purpose: the president gave Brunson a nod of appreciation, while Roach offered him a reassuring grin.

Δ

Back in the meeting room of the Union League, a flurry of conversation had broken out concerning the president's announcement. And with a hint of worry in his voice, James Harris was the first to ask Brown, "Do you think he'll actually pass any of these plans?"

Brown replied cautiously, "He seemed happy with the proposals – but I guess only time will tell." Privately, he remained hopeful that he would be able to help push the plans along, and assist the group either way.

"Doesn't it all seem a bit arduous, though?" a disgruntled Stephen Roberts pointed out, feeling aggrieved that he would have to pander to Rushbourne now, rather than simply speak to his close friend, the war general.

"As I said before, let's see how it plays out," said Brown, trying to mask his own concerns that with matters no longer in his hands, he could not dictate how the Development Plan would unfold.

Sensing that Richard was somewhat exhausted by the conversation, Worthington moved over to him and placed a reassuring hand on his shoulder. "Gentlemen," he said firmly, "we should be celebrating the fact that Benjamin has agreed to continue Richard's plans, and not sit around second-guessing what may or may not happen." Brown shot him an appreciative look for coming to his aid.

With the meeting concluded, the men made their way down the long corridor towards the exit, filled with excitement amid a buzz of conversation. James Harris however, purposefully hung back from the ensemble, not for one bit moved by the president's approval, already hatching his next plan. And just as they were about to leave the building, he seized his opportunity to strike.

"Alex, did you say you wanted membership at the Club?"

His question caused the other members of the group to suspend their departure and instead turn their attention to Macdonald in anticipation of his response.

The Scot stood there looking sorely confused and with all eyes staring upon him - he knew a decision had to be made.

For the life in him, he could not recall mentioning membership to anyone, but a perfectionist such as Harris couldn't possibly have got it wrong; could he?

"Yes, thank you - that would be wonderful!" he simply replied. *A Membership is a Membership, after all.*

"Well, stay awhile, then, and I'll fill out your sponsorship form," said James.

The other men looked on in surprise at his unusually considerate offer, and then brushed it off as a curiosity before turning to exit through the heavy double doors.

Out on the pavement, the men exchanged their farewells, squinting against the glorious sunshine cascading over the public; completely unaware that these men, standing there in all their finery, would potentially shape their future, in so many ways unimaginable.

It was then Stephen Roberts, taking a moment to behold Union Square in all its splendour, who turned to his good friend Brown. "What a fine place to erect a statue in remembrance of our fallen comrade." he proposed.

Richard was touched by the thought.

"What a wonderful idea," he agreed, casting his gaze around the square to envisage where such a monument to Lincoln might stand.

With that consideration filling their thoughts, the men were slowly beginning to move off in different directions when The Commander suddenly yelled out, "Oh, and Richard...?"

The war general turned to face his colleague once again.

"Glad you heeded my advice about the ground floor this time!" he quipped, and they moved off towards their awaiting carriages, with amusement on both their faces.

Δ

Chapter 10: Manhattan Madness

Δ

Back in the reception area of the Union League, Alex Macdonald stood gazing around the fine establishment and relaxed aside the Harris men before him.

"So, an iron and bridge company, Alex?" JR questioned, in the hope of delving a little more into his business.

"I thought it seemed a sensible option," the Scot replied - then instantly realised he had given a little too much away.

Unfortunately for him, the slip did not go unnoticed by the ever-perceptive James. "So how many bridges have you built exactly?" enquired the elder Harris as he moved in closer to his new associate.

"We've built a few so far..." Macdonald said, silently scrambling to add more weight to his answer, "... with a full order book for the coming year!"

James was not fooled.

And his creeping grin continued to expand, as he placed a hand upon the Scot's shoulder.

"Well, then," he said genially with a smile, "sounds like you'll be a busy boy, Alex. I do hope you'll have enough time to assist with Brown's plan?"

By now Macdonald's tongue was tied in knots.

Naively, he had assumed he was merely there to sign up for a membership, and not to be interrogated was the master interrogator himself. "Erm, well, I'm sure I can expand to meet any requirements," he said, feeling his temperature rise and sweat begin to trickle down the back of his neck.

Mercifully, Alex was saved from any further questioning as the administrator returned with a form and dutifully handed it to James. And so with duties to fulfil, JR removed his gold fountain pen from his jacket pocket, leaned on the reception desk and began filling out the form.

With his father's back now turned, the younger Harris, noticing Macdonald's unease, leaned in to quietly reassure him. "Don't worry," he whispered, "he's like this with me. In fact, he's like this with everyone!"

As Macdonald smiled in gratitude, neither he nor AJ saw James grinning away too. He had heard his son's youthful derision and accepted it with absolute delight: his plan to align Macdonald with his son was transpiring just as he had hoped!

"Right then, Alex, you're in!" the elder Harris merrily announced, popping back up in between them both and handing a membership card to the Scot.

"Most generous of you," Macdonald said, smiling respectfully at his sponsor.

"Well, my business here is done," JR stated. He turned to his son with a look of intent in his eyes. "You should show our new member around the Club, you know, get him used to the facilities in preparation for his next visit," he instructed.

Slightly confused as to why he had been recruited to chaperone the completely able-bodied Macdonald around, AJ nevertheless acquiesced without question. Then James had one final request for his son. "And can you kindly assist me to my stagecoach, please, Andrew?" he said as he walked off towards the exit, not bothering to wait for an answer.

With Alex busy signing the back of his membership card, somewhat in awe of becoming a fully-fledged patron, Andrew advised him, "I'll be back in a minute," before grabbing his father's overcoat and rushing out the door.

AJ found his father already climbing into the carriage, with the coachman ready to depart. So he closed the door on his father's behalf, and just as it clicked shut James reached through the window, snatched at his son's hand, and pressed him into action.

"Right, son, this is your chance!" he whispered excitedly.

"My chance for what?" Andrew enquired, wondering why they were whispering.

"Macdonald is waiting for you, my boy. Someone like him will be a great addition to our client base. *Go and build bridges*!" he urged enthusiastically. Then he turned and boomed, "Drive on," to the coachman, who cracked his reins at once.

As the horses trotted slowly away, leaving AJ standing on the sidewalk, it was then his father's masterplan suddenly dawned upon him. *Oh the irony!*

And as he turned to walk back into the building, Andrew could not help but chuckle to himself at the sudden turn of events. After so long, disparaging him over his past misdemeanours, AJ's father now expected him to draw on his more sociable nature to serve them well in their business endeavours!

Δ

The afternoon was set to be something of an eye-opener for Alex Macdonald, who currently resided in Pittsburgh, with a mere seventy thousand inhabitants, and had never much frequented the likes of a city such as Manhattan, with its sprawling population of more than eight hundred thousand citizens.

As they progressed around all four floors of the Club, Andrew showed Macdonald the sporting facilities on offer, as well as the host of lounge and dining areas. Eventually, they settled on luxurious leather armchairs in one of the small, private enclaves and began working their way through platefuls of the club's sandwiches along with a hefty order of liquor. And as the drinks flowed and their friendship blossomed, Harris sensed his opportunity to "build bridges" as directed, and so began to delve deeper into Macdonald's business activities.

"So how are you planning on funding your iron and bridge company?" he probed, still munching on a crust. "J.R.

Harris and Sons are always seeking to establish new alliances"

The Scot was flattered by the offer and hoped to respond in kind. "I have some funds saved over from a little investment I made in Cleveland," Alex honestly revealed. He swirled the liquor in his glass and smiled wryly. "Admittedly rather speculatively, but the farm I purchased struck oil and some chap offered me four times what I paid for it."

Four times what he paid for it!

At this, AJ nearly spat his mouthful of whisky across the room. Astounded by the story, and somewhat flabbergasted that the Scot wasn't in Cleveland right now, repeating the trick, Andrew instantaneously asked, "Well, why didn't you buy another then?"

But Macdonald waved a hand dismissively at the suggestion. "I think I just got lucky," he said humbly, a look of acceptance on his face. "I suppose with a lot of funding, it may be possible to build a business like that, but not easily."

The cogs in Harris's head were now running at a thousand miles per hour - he still couldn't understand why Macdonald held such reservations? And with AJ sitting motionless, lost in his musings, Alex felt compelled to fill the silence and decided to expand on his reasoning for not pursuing the successful venture further.

"If it weren't for my interest in iron then I may have looked to develop my knowledge of oil. But so far as I understand it, this oil market is very tricky, with hundreds of small operators. It's risky, to say the least." he smartly assessed.

The simple fact of the matter was that while Macdonald possessed a brilliant mind, he liked to concentrate all his efforts on mastering one single field of expertise in order to become the greatest at that endeavour. AJ, on the other hand, was at entirely the opposite end of the spectrum, completely disinterested in scratching beneath the surface any further than was necessary in order to turn a profit from a market, before moving on to the next venture.

With both men sitting in mutual admiration and apparently seeking to outdo one another with their gestures of goodwill, AJ felt the moment right and decided to probe the Scot about his investment some more.

"Do you recall the purchaser's name at all?"

"Of course! I never forget a name," Macdonald replied, delighted to be of assistance. "The company was called Ratchet, Ratchet and Cunningham," he divulged.

AJ nodded, feigning only mild interest, as he worked to imprint the name on his brain. *Ratchet, Ratchet and Cunningham* he hummed to himself, *Ratchet, Ratchet and Cunningham.*

He was desperate to write it down, but held back to avoid appearing opportunistic. And besides, he felt sure that he had got it, so decided to move on. "Right then!" Andrew said enthusiastically, jumping to his feet in a fit of joy at the successful progression of their meeting. "How about we make our way up to Central Park? The ride will give you the opportunity to see more of the city," he said, offering his hand to help Alex up from his seat.

"Thanks," Macdonald declared, stumbling slightly on his feet. He did not realise he had consumed so much alcohol whilst sitting there for the past few hours.

"Nay bother," AJ replied in his best attempt at a Scottish accent, and both men laughed their way out of the Club and into the mid-afternoon madness of Manhattan, where Andrew hailed a stagecoach from the side of the road.

Δ

Over the hour-long journey along Fifth Avenue, Andrew acted as tour guide, pointing out places of interest to Alex. As they made their way across the low-rise metropolis of Manhattan the driver oriented himself by the church spires that stood out as markers above the buildings, with very few surpassing more than several storeys high.

Yet despite Harris's upbeat chatter, Macdonald couldn't help but notice that while the upper-class areas were clean and peaceful, the majority of the island was, in stark contrast, a much more unpleasant place. The cobbled streets were filled with manure, dead animals and rotting waste, mixed with pools of stagnant water around overflowing and blocked sewers. Little development had occurred beyond Central Park, where the landscape remained untouched - creeks and streams running through marshlands and meadows. Even the built-up areas to the south were generally hilly and difficult to traverse, yet the masses of inhabitants squeezed themselves onto this small island enclave, with more arriving each day, making for a bustling and congested place to live. And Macdonald knew from newspaper reports that the poor were faring the worst, often living on top of one another, twenty to a room and five to a bed.

Arriving at the southern tip of the park, AJ ordered the driver to join the hundreds of stagecoaches driving up and down the lanes, in the hope of impressing his guest as they meandered amongst New York's wealthiest folks. However, the Scot was more concerned with the general public standing watching at the sides: he could not quite comprehend why they would waste what precious little leisure time they had gawping at the rich?

Feeling somewhat uneasy at the situation, Macdonald instead proposed, "Shall we get out and have a walk around?"

Harris wasn't prepared for that and had several reservations about doing so, but not wishing to appear stuffy in the eyes of his new friend, he agreed to his request and stepped cautiously from the carriage.

As they wandered around the crowds, Alex's mood picked up, and he spent his time talking to young and old ladies alike; every one of them taking upon his conversation with great pleasure. All the while AJ stood shyly behind him, becoming increasingly flustered by the minute.

When they finally arrived back at their stagecoach, their driver - who had been sat waiting impatiently, still to receive any payment – snapped in their direction, "I hope you have enough money to cover all this!"

His brusqueness had them forgetting their manners and sent the two gents into a fit of laughter, which did little to reassure the driver. Seeing the man's expression, Macdonald hoped to politely reassure him, "You'll have no worries there, my good man" His respectful reply, allaying the driver's fears.

Moments later, they were back in the carriage once again.

"Where to?" called the driver.

The afternoon was drawing to an end, but Harris wanted to continue the fun, so he turned to his new acquaintance with an idea in mind. "How about we go see my girls at the office and take them out for dinner?" he proposed.

AJ's plan offered Alex the opportunity to cajole another set of ladies, while at the same time putting himself in more comfortable surroundings, amongst people he knew.

"That sounds great, Andrew!" the Scot replied gladly.

And as Macdonald straightened his hair, AJ glanced at his watch, and noticed it was past four o'clock: his office would close at five. He leaned out of the window and shouted up to the waiting driver. "If you can get us to Lower Manhattan within the hour, I'll pay you double!" And with that inducement, the driver set off on the seven-mile journey at lightning-quick pace.

Chapter 11: Delmonico's

Δ

After a frantic fifty-five minutes, the stagecoach arrived in Hanover Square, just as AJ's secretaries were closing up for the day. Spotting his staff from afar, he waved his hand high in the air and lurched out the carriage door.

"Maria!" he shouted. The unexpected call scared Maria half to death and she dropped the keys held within her hand.

Then, gripping tightly to her colleague, they spun around together and breathed a sigh of relief when they spotted Andrew, dangling - almost falling - out of the carriage and waving cheerily. When Alex popped his head out above, wearing a similarly stupid grin, the girls could not hold back their amusement and the Scot confidently introduced himself and their offer.

"Can we interest you in dinner?" he enquired.

They replied in unison without hesitation. "Of course!"

Mission accomplished!

The men stumbled out of the carriage, and AJ duly paid the driver double, as promised, whilst Alex regaled the ladies with the tale of their breakneck journey through the city. And as the stagecoach drove off, Harris joined the little group, feeling more at home, back in his own surroundings.

"Well, it's the best place in town for you then!" he declared enthusiastically, to the girls' visible excitement.

It was a short stroll down William Street to AJ's favourite restaurant in all of New York. Delmonico's, he told Alex, was Manhattan's finest dining establishment, and one of only a handful of restaurants where customers were waited on. The restaurant was spread across three floors of an iconic, wedged-shaped building, and the ladies and Alex were most impressed as they entered to see the numerous marble columns dotted around the dining space, which, AJ told them, the owner proudly informed all his patrons "were specially imported from Pompeii".

In the main dining room, they were quickly greeted by the maître d', who had seen them enter and made a beeline for the group. "Your usual table, sir?" he asked dutifully, which pleased Andrew no end, as his guests were looking on, impressed by this reception.

"Yes," said AJ. "Thank you."

The maître d' led them into a private room, off the main hall, and the gang took their seats at the large circular table, sitting boy, girl, boy, girl. A bartender arrived to take their orders, and in what seemed like the blink of an eye, the drinks were soon flowing again. With their faces gently lit by the candelabra centrepiece, the girls were merrily discussing which set of cutlery to use first when one of the waiters arrived at the door and knocked softly before entering.

"Good evening, ladies and gentlemen. Are we now ready to order?"

Macdonald, sitting closest to the man, decided to take the lead "What do you suggest?" he enquired politely, simultaneously charming the waiter and the ladies, who all but swooned at his most gracious manners.

"I would suggest the Lobster Newburg, sir. It's an 'off-menu' dish that our head chef has been working on for some time," the waiter proudly proposed.

AJ looked around the table, and when his companions nodded their assent, he agreed, "Four plates of Lobster Newburg it is then!"

"And I'll bring some more drinks for you, sirs, madams," the waiter said, nodding in turn at the gents and the ladies. "Wouldn't want you running dry," he added, smiling.

So with the orders taken care of, the girls made their excuses and slipped out to take a closer nosy at the facilities – who knows if they would ever be back here again?

And with the men left on their own, Macdonald leaned over towards AJ and poured him another glass of wine. "Do you have an interest in either of the girls?" he enquired genially, not wishing to step on anyone's toes – especially his new found friend.

"I do like Maria," AJ admitted but then sighed dolefully. "Although I doubt she feels the same." His cheeks were now becoming increasingly rosy and his nose turning a darker shade of purple the more alcohol he consumed – a condition he had become accustomed to but one that still dampened his disposition, whenever around such conversation.

"Why would you say that?" Macdonald asked, somewhat shocked by the remark.

Not wishing to discuss his shortcomings in public, AJ retreated into silently sipping his wine. There was an insecurity held deep inside that Macdonald didn't like to see, and he hated that any man would befall to such personal negativity. "Consider how she's been smiling at you!" the Scot tried to encourage him. "She's aglow when you look at her."

Harris, however, was not convinced. "She's probably just being polite – I am her boss."

"Don't be silly, Andrew!" Macdonald said, nudging him amiably in the ribs. "I tell you what, let me warm her up for you. By the end of the night, she'll be all yours!" he confidently propositioned, and raised a gentle smile from the downcast Harris, who thoroughly appreciated the gesture.

But before AJ could respond – or even decide how to respond – Maria and Audrey re-entered the room. As they took their seats, they looked a little suspiciously at their hosts, who had fallen silent upon their arrival. Exchanging glances, the ladies pulled out some pre-rolled cigarettes and lit up, and then Macdonald began his enchantment. "So, Maria, I hear from Andrew that you're his most trusted employee!"

This caused Maria to choke on her smoke in shock, before smiling bashfully at Andrew. With all eyes on Harris in anticipation of his response, Alex flashed him a cheeky wink of approval, and AJ had to stifle a chuckle at his friend's most generous approach.

Δ

The merriment continued late into the evening, with Macdonald's plan playing out like clockwork. And come midnight, Maria was sitting leaning against AJ, their arms interlinked, and at the other side of the table Macdonald and Audrey were in a similar embrace.

"I suppose we should call it a night," yawned the Scot, feeling flush with happiness for his day's hard work.

"Good idea," AJ agreed, before laboriously hauling himself to his feet. "I'll go pay the bill."

All on the company, of course! And thank god.

Because while JR Harris and Son was a wealthy bank, AJ himself was not poor, but nor was he rolling in large amounts of disposable income of his own for such splurges.

With this the group slowly stumbled out of the building and into the temperate air. Luckily, they happened upon a stagecoach, and they dashed across the street to grab it while they could. AJ helped Audrey and Maria inside before climbing in himself, but was confused when he heard the door close unmistakably behind him. He turned to see Macdonald smiling from the pavement as if to say good night.

"Are you not getting in, Alex?" Harris said, leaning out of the carriage window, as the girls sank into the comfort of the well-padded seats.

"I'm going to take a stroll," Macdonald replied. He was feeling humbled by the success of his day and knew he would not be able to sleep just yet. "Make sure you get those two home safely!" he instructed jovially.

At that the girls sprang up and leaned out of the window to wish him a drunken goodbye. Their last act of the night, blowing kisses in his direction, they slumped back into their seats before promptly beginning their descent into slumber.

Andrew extended his hand in gratitude to his new friend. "We must do this again sometime soon, Alex," he said sincerely and Alex pumped his hand and agreed heartily.

As the stagecoach began moving, Andrew called out his parting words: "Next time, I'll introduce you to the Roberts family..." Then the carriage slowly trundled off into the dark Manhattan night, leaving the Scot to soak up the enormity of his day's events in full.

Δ

Early the next morning, *very* early the next morning, AJ was rudely awoken by his father. "Wake up! Get up! I want to hear all about it...!" JR shouted as he pulled the bedcovers off his son. "Come on! No time to waste."

Head pounding from the exploits of the day before, AJ sat up and rubbed his face and peered around with bleary eyes. The early morning sun was piercing through the half-closed curtains, revealing clothes strewn across the room. Looking down, he discovered he was wearing only long-johns. "What time is it?" he asked in a haze.

His father, hovering over him, thrust a glass of water into his hand and barked, "It doesn't matter what time it is, young man – you're on my time. Now *get up*!"

Still heavily intoxicated with both love and liquor, Andrew was unable to muster the energy to argue about the intrusion, and decided he had better follow orders.

"Kitchen. Two minutes," JR instructed, and he marched straight out the room.

AJ quickly threw on some clothes and was seated at the kitchen table in the nick of time. His abode mirrored his lifestyle; a mid-sized townhouse, with two small rooms across each of the three floors, and barely a jot of food in the entire place!

Once both men were equipped with a freshly prepared cup of piping-hot coffee, Andrew began to detail the great friendship he had established with Macdonald and the gentlemen's agreement they had in place that Alex would use JR Harris & Son whenever he required finance. He left out the bit about the expensive carriage fare and didn't even touch on details about dinner at Delmonico's – not that his father would have cared too much.

"What wondrous news," JR beamed in admiration of Andrew's impeccable work. "Our associates in Europe will be most pleased to hear of this."

AJ flashed a hazy smile at his father, but it lacked the gusto of which James was expecting accompanying such news. "What's the matter?" he asked.

With the shock of the early-morning wake-up call, the younger Harris had so far been on autopilot and simply concentrating on answering the questions his father put before him. However suddenly he recalled, the conversation with Macdonald regarding his oil investment.

"I had a very intriguing conversation with Alex about an oil field he purchased last year," he began.

At this, JR put down his mug of coffee and granted his son his full attention.

"Apparently, some chap paid him quadruple his investment!" AJ exclaimed, dumbfounded.

His father scrambled to find out more. "Who was the purchaser?"

Andrew tried hard to recall the name, yet as he squeezed his eyes shut and attempted to jog his memory, the moments of the day before seemed to merge into one...

"Well?" his father persisted impatiently.

Suddenly, he regretted mentioning it at all.

Continuing to rack his brain, slowly the company name began to come back to him in bits. *Something, Something and Someone,* he thought, but he could never say that to his father! "It was three surnames," he said. Then one of the names landed on the tip of his tongue. "Cunningham, I think it was!"

"Cunningham... Cunningham," JR cogitated, rubbing his chin in mild frustration as he tried to recall whether he had ever heard of such a firm.

Then, out of nowhere, it hit his son like a train. "RATCHET...!" he blurted out gleefully, raising a fist in victory. "Ratchet, Ratchet and Cunningham," he stated, thanking his lucky stars he had remembered.

However, his exuberance was instantly deflated as his father said dismissively, "Never heard of them."

"Yes, but apparently that's the problem," AJ revealed animatedly, leaning in toward his father. "There's no single operator controlling the market, and Macdonald said it's very speculative."

JR sat in silence, staring intently at his son as he deliberated their next move. Finally, he concluded, "I think it's worth you looking into this, Junior. Maybe you can speak with these Ratchet fellas and see if they can provide you with a way in." He nodded resolutely. "In fact... yes. Go pay them a visit and let them know you can make them all very rich. I'm sure they'll be more than happy to help you out!"

Chapter 12: Oiling the Wheels

Δ

Out on the flats alongside the Cuyahoga River in Cleveland, Ohio, three young men stood in a wooden cabin, peering out of the window at their drilling tower, under the scorching heat whipped up by the midday sun. They watched in silence as the cable tool was driven to the summit of the derrick before being released at speed back down towards the earth; cracking the rock beneath the pipe with an almighty, thunderous bang. With sweat dripping down their faces and hair stuck flat to their heads, they sipped thick black coffee and tore hunks from a loaf, waiting patiently for any sign of success.

Brothers Mark and Brad Ratchet were the brawn of the operation; strong, dominant men with ferocious personalities and drinking habits to match. Mark was the default leader of the two, being somewhat more able than his brother, who could not even read or write. The real brains behind the operation, though, was Oliver Peter Cunningham, the company's methodical bookkeeper. Slight in stature and wholly unassuming - which led many people to assume he was not a man to be reckoned with, frequently at their peril.

All of a sudden a loud rattling shook up the pipe as natural gas bubbles exploded underneath the surface. Several of their workers, who had been administering the process, began to rush away from the scene, but the Ratchet brothers and Cunningham looked on at the ensuing panic with glee.

"Hold on to your hats, boys!" Mark Ratchet called out in his deep southern accent, swinging his hat in a circular motion above his head.

Then, just as they had hoped, oil gushed up the pipe and sprayed high into the sky, rapidly covering everything within a five-metre radius.

"Looks like it's our time to shine!" whooped Brad, and they stampeded out of the cabin to begin ordering their men into affirmative action.

Yet while striking oil was all well and good, the yellowy-black substance shooting out of ground was of little use unless it was refined. Anyone could set up a drilling tower and get lucky with a strike, but the distillation process required skill and expertise, making it not only the most profitable part of the industry but also the area where Cunningham concentrated all his time, along with the fourth member of their crew, the only one who did not have his name on the deeds, so to speak.

Robert Adams was a quite brilliant chemist who constantly came up with new processes in order to help the company deliver products at lower costs than their competitors. Adams was often cited as the principal founder of fractional distillation, and as such Cunningham had personally sought his employment and done his utmost to bring him into the fledgling firm – for Cunningham's vision far surpassed that of his partners, but with the business in its infancy, he was keeping his future objectives closely guarded.

As Mark and Brad instructed the men and a frantic melee of action ensued outside the hut, Cunningham quietly looked on, his head bobbing up and down while he methodically counted the seconds ticking by, and calculated the number of corresponding barrels this strike would likely produce. Coming up with their profit for the day, a satisfied smirk crept across his face, and he drained the final few drops of coffee completely, before making a note in his small, red ledger of their latest endeavour.

Δ

Meanwhile, across the other side of town, AJ Harris had just arrived at the train station with his colleague Samuel Smith. Knowing their targets were based somewhere in the vicinity, they had made the journey to Cleveland in an attempt to corner them about selling their business. The local tavern seemed a sensible first port of call for word of the Ratchet brothers and Cunningham, and they found themselves on the dusty road outside. Entering The Lonestar Saloon, AJ and Samuel were surprised by the barren nature of the establishment, which was nothing like they were used to back in Manhattan. The vast and hollow room with its basic white-washed walls contained only a single bar alongside a tatty old piano and a billiards table without balls. However, the rough wooden floorboards beneath their feet, covered in a mix of sand, dirt and oil stains, were at least a positive sign that they were heading in the right direction.

"Any idea where we might find Ratchet and Cunningham?" AJ politely enquired of the rather burly bartender, who was cleaning glasses and replacing them on the rickety, wooden shelving.

"You should find them down the flats," the man said, without looking up to acknowledge their presence.

"And where exactly may that be?" Smith jumped in curtly, trying to impress his boss with his uncompromising demeanour. However, as the bartender looked up, scowled darkly and walked around the bar towards them, Samuel's pluckiness soon disappeared, and he shrank behind the larger figure of Harris.

"You chaps see out over that there hill?" the owner growled, pointing above the swing doors of the saloon. "That's where you'll find 'em!" he directed plainly, in the hope of getting rid of these stuck-up, rich folks as soon as possible before his regulars saw them in his establishment and all hell broke loose.

Harris thanked the man courteously for what he perceived as his assistance, and then he and Smith walked swiftly back to their hired stagecoach, which was fortunately, still sat outside. As the carriage bumped over the rough road, the two of them chatted away merrily, feeling rather smug in the belief that their mission may be even easier than expected. The bartender, meanwhile, stood in his saloon and sniggered to himself at the thought of the shock that these high-flyers, dressed in all their finery, were set to encounter in the not-too-distant future.

As the stagecoach mounted the top of a hill, AJ suddenly fell silent. Spotting the gargantuan creek below, now coming into view, it was covered in hundreds of drilling towers as far as the eye could see. Leaning forward without averting his gaze, Andrew grabbed the top of the still-gabbling Smith's head and rotated it towards the window so that he would see for himself. Everything in sight was ensconced in black, sludgy oil, and even the air itself seemed thick with the crude taste of petroleum, inhaled with every breath. "Stop!" AJ called to the driver, in a tone less assured than before.

Hesitantly opening the door to begin his descent to ground level, Andrew noticed the exterior of the carriage had become covered in a mix of dust and oil, kicked up by the wheels from the dirt roads below. And as his expensive loafers squelched into the thick black paste covering the ground, he looked around and whispered to himself, "How lovely," feeling a million miles away from the comforts of home.

The next moment, out of nowhere, gunfire suddenly exploded, and acting on pure instinct Harris hunched into a ball. He waited for one heartbeat, two, and when the air was silent and he did not appear to be dead, he slowly rose from his tucked-up position.

"Andrew!" exclaimed Samuel from the stagecoach. "What happened? Are you –?"

"I'm fine," tetchily said AJ, who had just conducted a quick pat-down to confirm the fact.

He looked about and soon saw from where the shot had originated: a man stretching out a gun and pointing it towards a horse stuck deep within a pit of thick oil and mud. The horse, collapsed from exhaustion, was unable to free itself and so the choice remained, to either leave it to die or put it out of its misery. Another shot rang out and the decision had quickly been made – not that it was ever in question around here. And while AJ was not exactly put at ease by the sight, with his newfound determination and his father's words ringing in his ears, he continued to press ahead unabashed.

Remaining at the side of the road as carts passed by, laden down with barrels of oil spilling over the edges, Harris and Smith were unsure where to begin. They felt distinctly uncomfortable, knowing that they stood out like a sore thumb in their expensive suits and top hats and needed to do something quick. Their luck was in, however, as a young boy, intrigued by their presence, approached them, mouth wide open.

"Can I help ya chaps?" he asked cheerily while staring at them as if they had just landed from another planet.

"Do you know where we might find Ratchet, Ratchet and Cunningham?" Andrew enquired graciously of the oil-stained boy.

"I believe they've the tenth farm on the right," he informed them while pointing into the distance.

AJ and Smith scanned the tops of the drilling wells and counted back methodically until they reached their destination. However, not only was it some several hundred metres away, but there was no identifiable route.

"How would you like to make a quick dollar then, sonny?" Harris quickly propositioned, thinking on his feet.

The young boy's face lit up with excitement. "Yes, Mister. Please!"

"If you can tell these Ratchet fellas and Mr Cunningham to meet with me at The Lonestar by midday," said AJ, "I shall pay you a dollar for the good deed."

Beside himself at such a lucky opportunity to earn the equivalent of three days' wages, the boy jumped at the offer.

"Sure thing, Mister," he smiled, before dashing off eagerly to locate the men, leaving Harris to grin contently at his rather smart little plan.

Δ

Arriving back at The Lonestar, the men from Manhattan slowly swung open the saloon doors. It had filled up since their earlier visit, and they were met with derisory looks from several of the regulars. Approaching the bartender, who looked surprised and somewhat unhappy to see them return, Harris loudly thanked him for his earlier advice and smartly disarmed the owner, in front of his gasping patrons.

"Now we require a private space in which to discuss some business – do you have anything available?" he asked politely while sliding several dollars in his direction.

At this, the bartender nodded with something approaching begrudging courtesy, and while the locals stared on in disbelief, he led AJ and Samuel through a doorway, missing its door, at the rear of the saloon. Beyond this exposed entrance was a small room containing a long, rickety table and splintered wooden benches positioned at either side. Not exactly lavish, but they had become accustomed to what they could expect.

The city men thanked the bartender and carefully chose a suitable place to sit so as not to nick their expensive suits, and before the barman could leave, AJ had one further request. "Could you please provide us with some hot food and a bottle of your best whisky?" he asked pleasantly.

The owner trudged off to fulfil their request – the nourishment to quell their hunger while they waited, the alcohol to intoxicate their guests, and hopefully give them the edge in negotiations.

With time ticking on, however, AJ and Samuel's renewed optimism slowly drained away, and as the clock chimed one o'clock, Samuel – who had been drinking to stem his boredom – began to lose his cool.

"How dare they be late!" he moaned.

Harris tried to remain collected.

"I'm sure there's some plausible excuse. Let's give them a little while longer," he replied calmly, to convince himself as much as his colleague.

A further half hour passed, and the men from Manhattan were about to call it a day, when all of a sudden there was a commotion at the front of the saloon, and the young errand boy dashed in. With the bartender yelling at him to leave, the boy spotted his targets sitting in the back room, and skipped towards them while avoiding capture from the patrons, grasping at his oversized work clothes.

"I got them for you, Mister!" he joyfully announced between panting, his eyes alight with the prospect of receiving his payment, and feeding his family for the entire week.

"Great work, young man!" AJ commended heartily, and he reached into his jacket pocket, flicked open his wallet and pulled out two dollars holding them one atop the other. "Here's a bit extra for all your hard work." he winked.

The boy took the payment and held it up in front of his face, staring in complete amazement. Then he thanked AJ profusely before hastily departing, as the sound of heavy, stomping boots heralded the arrival of AJ's guests.

The Ratchet brothers marched across the tavern, the boards of which they had tread on so many occasions before. Still in their workwear, hands and faces blackened from handling barrels all day, with Oliver Peter Cunningham following closely behind, they took a place at the table without offering any form of acknowledgment before pouring themselves a drink, as AJ watched on contemplatively.

"So what's a fancy lot like you doing here?" Mark gruffly opened up the proceedings. His brother sniggered uncontrollably at the question as if it were the punchline of a joke.

"We've come to find some oil men, like yourselves," AJ replied genially, in the hope of building some rapport.

"Is that so..." Mark scoffed impudently. He rested his broad back against the wall and puffed out his expansive chest. "And to what do we owe the pleasure?" he asked, flashing a creepy grin across the table.

Refusing to be deterred by the strangeness of this man, Harris forged ahead regardless. "My bank has a fantastic opportunity for the right set of people. We have the means to make them the number one company in the land."

Then he rested his back as well, mirroring Mark with a little smile, and confident that those two little words "my bank" would have earned him the respect that had so far been sorely lacking.

"Well, ain't that something!" Mark replied irreverently, tapping his brother on the leg to incite him.

In response, Brad bounced his torso up and down like an excited little chimp, leaving Andrew to stare silently across the table, wide eyed at the two brothers before him. *How can these imbeciles own the biggest refinery in Cleveland?*

And while he contemplated the best way to deal with such men, Smith broke ranks beside him. "Forget this, AJ!" he said sourly. "There's a million other guys we can buy from. Let's get out of here!"

But as he went to rise, Harris put his hand on his colleague's thigh and pushed him firmly back into his seat. "No need for that," Andrew said coolly and he decided to take a more direct route in his negotiations, from which he had attempted to employ before.

"I'm here to purchase this company," he said, fixing his glare directly at Mark. "A company I can afford to buy several times over and make you *all* extremely rich. So, tell me now." He glared severely at the oil man, and finished in a deafening boom: "WHAT'S YOUR PRICE?"

At this, Mark turned to his brother, who responded with nothing more helpful, than a look of confusion. So Mark eyeballed Cunningham, who stared back at him, raised his eyebrows and nodded insistently at his partner to take the deal.

"The company's not for sale!" Mark announced joyously. He was already picturing regaling the moment, stood at the bar later on that evening. And as Mark's reply rang out across the table, it ushered in a sudden silence that permeated the room.

Aside him, Cunningham's face dropped in utter disbelief, and then he quickly stumbled into the conversation in an attempt to bring about some co-operation. "Are we, sure this is the best way forward, chaps?" he said tentatively - and a little desperately. "Surely there's some, some common ground on which we can work... maybe in a partnership with these gentlemen?"

But his colleague was not prepared to yield, and in fact was becoming increasingly hostile. “Ain’t no company in America who knows how to refine oil like us,” Mark declared arrogantly. “We don’t need you, Mister, and your money ain’t no good round here!” he concluded.

Andrew looked at his counterpart and let out a rueful sigh of acceptance. He knew that today was not to be his day, but was more than prepared to play the long game while he searched for another option.

“Look, chaps, it doesn’t appear as if we’re making much progress here,” he stated, getting to his feet and reaching into his jacket pocket. At this, the Ratchet brothers scrambled backwards, expecting a pistol to be pulled. But all that AJ produced from his pocket was a handful of plain, business cards with utilitarian inscriptions, which he tossed onto the table. “Let’s call it a day and you can contact me should you change your mind,” he said.

He turned and began making his way out of the room, with Smith following hurriedly by his side, but then stopped and looked back at Ratchet, Ratchet and Cunningham. “It’s not a hold-up, chaps,” he said with some amusement. “This is business – as we do it in New York.” And with that parting shot, he and Samuel exited the saloon and made their way to the station, leaving the three men to their own contemplations.

Cunningham did not think for long before losing his temper; he was at the end of his tether with his two burly associates. “Are you mad?!” he yelled. “Those men could have made us the biggest oil company in the country!”

The brothers looked at him in shock at his tantrum. They had never heard Cunningham raise his voice in such a tone.

“But on whose terms, Oliver?” Mark said, who had no reservations about having just turned down the opportunity.

“On a fifty-fifty basis no less!” Cunningham snarled, completely exacerbated by his partner’s lack of foresight.

The Ratchet brothers were not used to being spoken to in such a manner, by anyone, and they decided that they did not like it one bit. They got to their feet and towered over Cunningham to assert their physical dominance.

“You can’t work with men like them. They’d leave us high and dry,” Mark warned. “And what’s wrong with where we are now?” he insisted, shooting a fiery stare at his business partner.

Cunningham lowered his head in dismay.

He was sensible enough to know it was a risk to push these men any further, so he let the matter drop. And as the brothers swaggered out into the bar area to gloat, the meek and mild bookkeeper merely gathered up his belongings - and the cards lying beside him on the table.

Chapter 13: Plans to Develop

Δ

Jack Brunson was waking up to an early-morning call in his room at The Willard Hotel, Washington. The finest lodgings in the capital, it naturally hosted the most important social and political delegations from across the world and was *the* place to stay for America's wealthiest patrons. Situated at 1401 Pennsylvania Avenue NW and extending across seven glorious storeys, the hotel was perfectly positioned for his planned day of business, being located less than four hundred metres from the presidential mansion.

Jack had decided to take breakfast in his room, as part of his plan to keep his visit as clandestine as possible. He had nothing to hide, nor was there anyone around, but he hated the thought of someone stumbling upon his affairs. Giving himself until the coffee pot ran dry and his cigar was a mere stub, Jack rehearsed his speech several times over, not wanting to leave any stone unturned, when addressing the president this time round.

Down in the expansive ground-floor lobby, with its marble columns, atop its marble flooring, and presidential paintings adorning the walls, Levi Sykes stood patiently awaiting Jack's arrival. He was somewhat more relaxed than his friend, and merrily passed the time chatting with one of the hotel bellboys. Finally, Sykes saw Brunson coming down the central staircase to the foyer, and he politely excused himself from the conversation and greeted his friend warmly with open arms.

"Good morning, Jack! And what a lovely day it is," Sykes said, as happy as a man could be.

"A lovely day, we hope!" Brunson replied cautiously, remaining uneasy as to whether Rushbourne was actually interested in sanctioning any of their plans.

Sykes, however, was in possession of a constantly sunny disposition. "Nothing to worry about, Jack," he asserted confidently. "We have Roach on our side - what can possibly go wrong?!" he reminded his friend.

"No, you're right," Brunson agreed, though he remained somewhat edgy. "I just want us to be the first to get moving," he said, determined in his quest to beat the other members of the group. And so, without further ado, they left the hotel and made the short walk to the presidential mansion, arriving well in advance of time.

Δ

Having signed in at the registration desk, Sykes and Brunson were led up to the State Floor and through the entrance hall, adorned in ornate Tiffany glass screens, before being ushered into the Blue Room and told to wait there for their associates' arrival.

The oval-shaped room, painted entirely in blue, was furnished with several sofas and a few armchairs positioned to face the centre, where a circular banquette pouffe lay beneath a large and imposing chandelier. But despite the many seating options, neither men sat down. Sykes had been drawn over to one of the full length window, and gazed out over the South Lawn, taking pleasure in the view, while Brunson stood at the marble fireplace, checking in the mirror that no food was stuck in his long, unkempt beard. And just as the Denière et Matelin mantel clock chimed to mark the tenth hour of the day, the president and his number two entered at pace.

"Good morning, gentlemen," Rushbourne called loudly, and he marched across the room and seated himself on a sofa against the wall, swiftly followed by Roach.

"Good morning, Mr President," Brunson replied, scanning the room and wondering where he and Sykes ought to sit? With all other options seeming a little too distant for polite conversation, Brunson and Sykes sat on the pouffee under the chandelier and attempted to find a distinguished position as the meeting began in earnest.

"So, William tells me you have a plan to run by me?" the president enquired as his guests continued to shuffle uncomfortably.

"That's correct," Jack replied politely, feeling hesitant, for once in his life.

"Well, do go on. I don't have all day!" Rushbourne snapped in his usually crude manner.

Brunson glanced at Roach for reassurance; he wasn't quite sure how to take the remark. But his old friend gave him a swift nod of reassurance and rotated his index finger down by his side, as a signal for Jack to continue.

Taking the hint, Jack quickly pulled out a small map of America and unfolded it upon his knees. Leaning forward, he held the map out for Rushbourne and Roach to see and pointed at it to illustrate his intentions.

"I'd like to extend my railroad down to St Louis and across to Kansas City," he outlined, looking back and forth between the map and Rushbourne for any signs of approval. "This will take me halfway across America, with a view to completing a line from east to west thereafter."

Not a bad little plan.

But however impressed Benjamin was by the idea; now that he had spent several months in office, a raft of more pressing political issues had become apparent, and the Development Plan was the last thing on his list of priorities. Still, he looked around his fellow men and decided, only because Jack was a close friend of Roach, to afford Brunson a little grace. "And how do you expect all this will be paid for?" he asked.

It was then over to Sykes, who duly stepped in to clarify.

"Your role, Mr President, can be minimal," he began, seeking to reassure Rushbourne. "My bank and affiliates will provide the funding, so all you need do is grant us the land on which to build."

Well, that sounds pretty simple.

Nodding his head in quiet agreement, and once again highly impressed by Sykes's approach, the president held back for a moment while considering his next move. Then he smiled and rubbed his hands together. "Well, if that's all I need do, chaps, then I'm more than happy to back your plans," he said, and stood to indicate that the meeting was at an end.

Blunt as ever, but they had got what they had come for. And concealing their jubilance beneath polite and restrained smiles, Jack and Levi promptly rose in accordance to thank the president for the endorsement. With their words of gratitude complete, they set off as a group towards the exit; however, as they progressed across the floral rug, Roach abruptly halted. Rushbourne had come to recognise the look of contemplation in his right-hand man, and he enquired inquisitively, "What are you thinking, William?"

Wagging a solitary finger back and forth, Roach began to smile at the men awaiting his response. "To enter St Louis from Indianapolis, you'll have to bridge the Missouri River. Looks like you'll have to speak with our friend Alex Macdonald then," he proposed thoughtfully.

He wasn't wrong.

"That I shall do, William," Jack confirmed warmly, thrilled by the chance to speak with the Scot and get him on side by providing him with the first opportunity to work on a project approved by the president.

The men walked out into the Cross Hall and said their goodbyes, and Rushbourne and Roach set off to prepare for their next meeting. But when they were halfway down the corridor Jack suddenly remembered that he had neglected to extend an invitation. "Excuse me, gentlemen, just one last thing, if I may?" he called, and his associates turned back to face him. "I'm holding an 'end of summer' party at my new house and would be delighted if you would consider joining us as guests of honour?" The two men to whom he had proposed, stood glancing at one another.

"I think that would be most ideal, don't you, Benjamin?" Roach said readily, as he aimed to provide a constant stream of assistance to his good friend Brunson.

"Very good, Jack, we'll see you there," the president agreed, before turning back around and disappearing down the hallway, leaving his guests to see themselves out.

Exiting the building with Sykes at his side, Brunson struggled to keep his exuberance contained. His excitement was amplified by getting *one up* on the other members of the group, even more than the financial rewards his scheme would potentially yield. And as they walked out onto the lawn to make their way back to the hotel, Levi could only conclude, "I told you everything would be fine. We have Roach on side – nothing to worry about!"

Δ

Later that afternoon, Rushbourne attended his second formal meeting of the day, this time with his secretary of war, George Collins, as well as Brown and Roach. The fifty year old Collins came dressed for business, as usual, and wearing his trademark round, thin-wire-framed spectacles. A man of principle, educated in law, he was forthright and uncompromising, with a particular fondness for a good intellectual debate.

They held their meeting in the Treaty Room on the second floor of the mansion. Rushbourne favoured the office for all his Cabinet meetings, and as such the space was arranged to provide much more effective seating arrangements than the Blue Room, earlier that day. With his colleagues seated directly in front of his leather-topped desk and Roach at his side, as always, so Rushbourne began the meeting.

"Gentlemen, we have a number of pressing issues to discuss as I attempt to clean up the mess we have been left in!" he announced curtly.

Brown tried to assess whether he was referring to the Civil War or, indeed, to the work undertaken by Lincoln. Leaving it as a cursory thought, he decided to remain silent on the point as the president continued.

"I think we all agree that a speedy restoration of the States is a particular priority," he asserted, and the group all nodded in approval.

"They never really departed from the Union," Collins said, which elicited more nods around the room.

"Therefore, all we're left with is the bothersome issue of the Freedmen," said Rushbourne, a look of irritation washing over his face. "Which to my mind," he added bluntly, "is something that should be dealt with by the individual states."

At this, the harmony in the room abruptly evaporated.

Being a man of simplicity, Benjamin's efforts extended to only those tasks that conveyed the greatest benefit, and having already assisted Lincoln with the Emancipation Proclamation, it was Rushbourne's belief that he had done more than enough for the newly freed black man. Brown and Collins, however, were of a very differing perspective, and the former spoke now on their behalf.

"I must say, Benjamin, I'm compelled to respectfully disagree," Richard began, instantly incurring the wrath of the president, who did not suppose this to be a topic up for discussion. "The Union Army subscripted some twenty thousand Freedmen who fought on the battlefield and assisted us in winning the war," he stated compassionately, but Rushbourne was unmoved.

And he scoffed in distain at the assertion.

"I gave them freedom - what more could they desire?!"

Rubbing his chin and grimacing at the rebuttal, Collins could see this deteriorating into a heated argument. And wishing to avoid such a situation, he calmly attempted to add weight to his colleague's point in order to moderate the president's position. "A large majority of our party also feel that by granting the Freedman rights, they will be indebted to vote for us," he explained, while glancing across at Richard, who nodded firmly in agreement. "Which would surely be to all our benefit, including yours?" Collins added elegantly.

Rushbourne, however, was in no mood to listen to this reasoning, and his wrath had been severely stoked at having been verbally dismantled, so he saw it, in his own office. Still, he was astute enough to sense that he was no match for his colleagues wisdom, and that to try to outsmart them would be foolish. "We do need to organise the power struggle in the southern states," he said, feigning agreement, before pausing rather oddly. "Just give me a moment..." he asked.

His colleagues flashed an optimistic glance at one another - *Maybe Rushbourne can be reasonable after all?*

The President meanwhile leaned back in his chair, and a wicked idea flashed through his mind. Casually, he beckoned Roach to his side and whispered in his ear. His close friend, focused on the floor, listened and nodded in agreement, and then Rushbourne reverted to address his colleagues.

"Right then, Richard, I have it!" he exclaimed confidently. "As we're at loggerheads on how best to proceed, and in an attempt to gain a full understanding of these issues, I'm sending you on a fact-finding mission around the southern states." He sat back, beaming in delight - and with no small measure of glee - at his plan, which would keep the war general out of meddling with his business, while at the same time appearing to demonstrate, his faith in Brown's opinion.

Brown and Collins sat there reeling with shock, but knowing that they were powerless to change the president's mind.

"Upon your return, you can furnish me with a report of your findings, and from there we can decide the best way forward," Rushbourne said with as much sincerity as he could muster, and when Roach seconded the motion, they rose up in tandem to signal the end of the discussion.

"And what of the Economic Development Plan?" Brown enquired apprehensively as the president drifted past him.

"Don't worry about that," Rushbourne said, not even breaking stride, "William has it all in hand." Moments later, they were beyond the threshold, leaving Brown and Collins alone in a Treaty Room that had seen no negotiation whatsoever that day.

Δ

Wishing to discuss the outcome of their meeting in more private surroundings, Richard and George quietly made their way down the stairs to take a stroll around the Ellipse, outside the South Portico.

"So how do you feel about being sent on a reconnaissance mission?" George Collins instantly enquired as soon as they were out of earshot from all the White House members of staff.

"I'm not sure what he's expecting," Brown pondered with a look of confusion on his face. "Surely I'll just find evidence that confirms what *we* think already?"

"Exactly!" Collins replied emphatically. "So why send you?" he questioned suspiciously, trying to open his friend's eyes to the possibility that all was not as it seemed.

Collins and Brown had a long-standing friendship, forged during the Civil War and strengthened by their deep-held respect for one another as men. It allowed them to speak as openly and frankly as they wished to each other, while striving for what was best, for the country they so loved.

"Do you think he's sending me on a wild goose chase?" Brown asked his friend now, as he mulled over the mission and suddenly felt far from assured of its true worth.

"I'm not sure, Richard," said Collins, "but I don't trust Rushbourne one bit. Do you not remember the number of times he embarrassed Lincoln, who had to apologise for his behaviour?" he pointedly reminded his friend, who did indeed recall those drunken outbursts. "The man has no regard for anyone other than himself!" Collins finished vehemently.

Richard stopped in his tracks and stared despondently up at the second floor of the mansion, picturing the dining room where, he imagined, Rushbourne and Roach were now taking afternoon tea, seated at *Lincoln's table.*

Having taken a moment to regain his composure, and thinking tactically once again, the war general resumed strolling. It was time to set down a plan for defensive action.

"You need to be our eyes and ears while I'm away," Brown instructed Collins, while maintaining a watchful eye to ensure their conversation remained private. "Speak with

Senator Dixon and have him propose a bill in the House to extend the Freedmen's Bureau," he suggested, thinking this a cunning way to circumvent the president's indifference towards the matter.

"Are you sure we shouldn't seek to implement something a little more... combative?" Collins said brazenly, quite prepared to go straight for the president's jugular.

"If the state of our Union were not so fragile, I'd march up there and drag him out myself," Richard admitted indignantly under the mounting strain of frustration. "However, we must maintain a united front."

"That I agree," Collins affirmed, nodding pointedly at his friend. "For now..."

Δ

Chapter 14: Building Bridges

Δ

Later that week and in New York, Andrew Harris was awaiting Alex Macdonald's arrival from Pittsburgh, having invited him back to the city in order to formally introduce him to the Roberts family. AJ always liked to keep his promises, and besides, The Commander had some potential business he was itching to discuss with the Scot. Sitting in his office with his feet up on his desk, AJ had purposely left his door ajar, just enough so that he could glimpse his guest's arrival and be fully prepared to greet him. However, he was startled when a sudden knock came at the door, and he jumped to his feet, assuming he must have missed Macdonald's entrance.

Instead it was Maria who walked in, with a look of excitement about her.

"Has he not arrived yet?" AJ enquired eagerly.

"Not yet," she stated, and Andrew sank back into his seat with a thud and an impatient sigh.

AJ was so distracted that he barely noticed as Maria checked the banking hall, then surreptitiously closed the door behind her. He was just about to protest when he saw the look on her face, and then a slow grin spread across his, as she walked across the room, taking her time, and leaned over. Then his secretary - and recently acquired significant other - planted her lips onto his. He was reaching for her, to pull her in for a deeper kiss, when she pulled away, and said mock-sternly, "Now then, Mr Harris, don't go keeping Mr Macdonald all to yourself."

He blinked up at her, confused, and she broke out into giggles. "Audrey is desperate to see him again!"

Her laugh was infectious and Harris was addicted to it. "Well, I'm sure there'll be enough of him to go around," he replied and he stepped up to be at her side.

Yet before Maria could respond, or AJ could snatch that kiss again, they heard a commotion outside - which, they knew, could mean only one thing.

Alex has arrived.

Grinning together, Maria and Andrew hurried to the door and opened it at once. And staring out across the banking hall, they saw their expected arrival, chatting away to Audrey, no doubt reminiscing about the evening at Delmonico's. Passing Maria while she dutifully stood aside to hold open the door, Harris gave her a gentle and affectionate stroke on the arm, making sure it was subtle enough to go unnoticed by the other members of staff, before confidently strolling out to meet Macdonald. "Alex!" AJ beamed, raising both arms in the air. "Great to see you, my friend. Good journey down?" he enquired.

"Not bad, Andrew," the Scot confirmed cheerily as Audrey excused herself and returned to her desk.

Harris was about to continue their conversation when he suddenly became aware that he and Alex were the focal point of the room: his female members of staff and even some customers were turned their way; staring over and swooning adoringly, over Alex's boyish good-looks.

"Let's make a move," AJ suggested. "The Roberts men are expecting us." In moments, Maria had handed him his coat and he was manoeuvring his visitor, back towards the exit.

Δ

Standing on the busy street outside the office of JR Harris & Son, Macdonald could barely contain himself at the thought of their destination; *chez* Roberts, surely the grandest house in all America. Even though he was not one to be bowled over by ostentatious shows of affluence, the Scot was still tickled pink at spending an afternoon playing croquet on the lawn, or tennis on one of the many courts, no doubt.

"So, which way?" he asked enthusiastically.

"Follow me," Harris instructed with a funny little smile, and he led his visitor along Pearl Street. But when they reached the junction with Broad Street, AJ suddenly stopped.

Assuming he was simply waiting for the traffic to disperse, Macdonald stood there, blissfully unaware that Harris was doing his utmost to hold back his fit of laughter.

"Right then, here we are!" he blurted out at last, peering up at the boarding house, beside them at the crossroads.

"Are we meeting Stephen and Alfred here?" Macdonald asked, puzzled and somewhat unsettled by Andrew's irregular disposition.

"Yes, we are. Because this is where they live!" AJ revealed, thoroughly enjoying the look of confusion running across Macdonald's face.

The Scot, quite understandably baffled by the admission, attempted to puzzle this out. "They live... " He paused while scanning the somewhat decrepit-looking boarding house. "Er... here?"

"It has a bar and a laundrette, and all their meals are provided," AJ explained, forcing himself to calm down and quash his mirth. "And Stephen loves the history of the place - apparently, Burr and Hamilton attended a meeting here before their famous duel," he added, knowing that Stephen loved to tell all and sundry, about that particular little fact.

Stephen Roberts had a large extended family, and the boarding house accommodated not only his wife and their eleven grown-up children, but also Alfred with his wife and their eight children. In reality, all they were missing was a "Chateau de Roberts" sign above the door - and it was this door through which Stephen and Alfred now suddenly appeared and trotted down the few small steps to the pavement.

"Thanks for making the trip down, Alex," the younger Roberts said pleasantly, offering his hand to shake, and thus triggering a full round of pleasantries amongst the group.

With their greetings concluded, the four men did not, as Alex expected, enter the house, but instead set off along Broad Street, heading towards the East River Docks. As they manoeuvred throughout the hordes of pedestrians, a number of children popped their heads out of the top-floor windows and called "Grandfather, Grandfather!" to Stephen while waving excitedly. A gesture, he paid little attention to, now serious discussions were at hand.

Δ

They came to a stop on South Street, overlooking the East River, where the unmistakable smell of the ports hit them squarely. The streets were full of seafarers and boats continually being unpacked. Each and every one of them stood seeking The Commander's acknowledgment, but instead he began his business for the day, with his new associate, Macdonald. Pointing towards the hundreds of ships sailing back and forth, he asked, "Do you know what that is over there, Alex?"

The Scot was unsure as to what he was referring and also struggled to hear amongst the noisiness of the port. "What's that, Stephen?" Macdonald replied politely, and he moved in closer, with the hope of receiving more of a clue.

"That over there is Brooklyn, and behind it is Long Island - a land that at present, is completely unconnected to Manhattan," he informed his visitor. Then he directed him north, up the river. "In fact, if you look all around this isle, you'll find there's not a single connection to the mainland. So what do you think to that?" the elder Roberts said pointedly to the young Scot.

Responding to Stephen's tone, Alex shook his head and said, "How terrible." Silently, though, he remained confused as to where this was leading and how it affected him.

"Look," said Stephen. "See all these Periaugers?" He gestured to the hustle and bustle of the numerous tiny sailing vessels that were precariously transporting passengers across the waters. "Two simple masts and oars for rowing, and the waters are frequently rough - dangerous conditions," he said darkly, and had the stories to tell.

Wiping those disasters from his mind, he continued ahead, with Macdonald still hanging on his every word. "There are more than two hundred and fifty thousand people in Brooklyn alone. It's the third most densely populated place in America, and some days those damn folks can't even get across! And so, the point I am trying to make is: we need to build a bridge to Brooklyn."

Finally, the penny dropped for Macdonald, with a resounding *thunk*, like an anchor hitting the shore. "What a grand idea!" he exclaimed as he contemplated the huge scale of such a project and how it would propel his company into the stratosphere.

"Well, I'm glad to see you're impressed," replied Stephen, and he rubbed his hands together in glee.

Then he turned to AJ, who had been standing by silently with Alfred, waiting their turn in the conversation. "And you can provide the finance for our friend?" he asked, already knowing the answer.

"Absolutely!" was Harris's resounding reply, and the men stood together in contemplation, gazing out across the East River, envisaging the huge bridge that would extend over and above their heads.

"Well then, it's agreed!" Stephen concluded happily. "I'll have the plans drawn up and submitted to Brown this week."

As they made their way back along Broad Street towards the Roberts' house, AJ tentatively asked the group, "Did you receive your invitation to Jack's party? And... are we attending?" The latter enquiry he aimed specifically towards The Commander.

"I'm sure we can show our faces," Stephen confirmed, a wicked smile creeping across his face as he considered the plan he had in mind.

A plan that still to this point, no one else was privy to.

None the wiser, the group arrived back at the crossroads outside the boarding house, and Stephen halted and turned to Alex with one final question that he had been burning to ask his guest. "You see my place here?" he said.

Macdonald nodded, somewhat worried that he was going to be drawn into a discussion about his own personal take on a millionaire living in such humble accommodation.

"Did you know that Aaron Burr and Alexander Hamilton met in this exact building before their famous duel?" he asked, to the clear relief of the Scot.

"I... did not know that, Stephen," he replied in his most serious tone. And whilst AJ and Alfred, attempted to hold back their laughter out of sight, Stephen remained blissfully unaware and happily smug at having passed on his little-known fact to his latest associate, the ever-in-demand, Mr Alex Macdonald.

Chapter 15: Brunson's Summer Celebration

Δ

Late September, and the day of Jack Brunson's house-warming arrived, along with clear skies that promised perfectly warm and radiant weather. As the sun rose in the sky, Jack's army of staff frantically prepared every inch of the island, so that not one piece was out of place, in anticipation of receiving his most important guests.

The newly completed home was unlike any other mansion in the area. Built towards the western tip of Lake Erie and with its own dock full of small sailing boats, only the several turrets of Jack's grey-stone gothic castle could be seen, protruding above the trees surrounding the island. Internally, the hallways were narrow and the rooms dark, with dense oak-panelling and only thin window slits to draw in meagre light from outside. With statues of gargoyles and stuffed animals in attack poses mounted on the walls, the gothic mansion aimed to unnerve at every juncture, and so it did - mirroring its owner's personality, exactly as he wanted.

Come the afternoon, guests were taxied across the waters on Jack's private boat, affectionately named *The Olive*.

Worthington and Sykes, along with their respective families, as well as Macdonald who travelled alone, joined the revellers on the island, and the party began to get into full swing. Jack had placed a member of his staff atop the highest tower, the perfect observation point to alert him at certain junctures throughout the day. And upon hearing his employee call out, Jack sprang into action.

Here we go.

Jumping aboard *The Olive*, he raced across to Put-in-Bay, just in time before Rushbourne and Roach could take another boat. With his very important guests in sight, Jack struggled to hide his delight at the prospect of parading them around his party, and further confirming his status as one of the richest and most well-connected people in the land.

"Ahoy!" he shouted merrily as *The Olive* approached the shore, and ordered his deckhands to safely secure the boat.

"Good day to you," beamed Roach, approaching his friend in a jubilant mood. "Great day for it," he stated, gazing around at the calm and pleasant waters of the lake.

Soon they were on the waters and "Brunson Castle", as Jack affectionately called it, came into view. Rushbourne, like everyone else, could not fail to be impressed, and luckily for Brunson, the president now considered him an ally, otherwise he may well have taken umbrage to another man having such opulent surroundings.

"Delightful place," Benjamin conceded as they walked up the path towards the main lawns, which were crowded with people, chattering and laughing and eating food, served to them by waiters bearing silver plates.

With the most important guests now safely on the island, Jack's lookout was ready to fulfil his second duty for the day. Putting a bugle to his pursed lips, he began playing "Reveille", a song regularly performed by the Union Army during the Civil War to let the troops know they were to assemble for their morning roll call, and played now as a mark of respect for Jack's most special arrivals.

As the performance came to an end, applause broke out, exuberantly all around. Jack, forever impatient, was in too much of a rush to wait and lightly tapped a sterling-silver knife upon a flute of champagne glass, until the crowd began to settle and all eyes turned to him expectantly.

"I'd like to thank you all for attending the grand unveiling of Brunson Castle," he loudly enunciated, and the remaining guests quietened down to a complete hush. "To mark this wonderful occasion we're lucky enough to have been granted the presence of not only one but two of America's greatest patriots - President Benjamin Rushbourne and Chief Justice William Roach," he declared excitedly.

At this, the president and his number two raised their glasses high into the air, and the audience dutifully mirrored their gesture in return. Assured that his peers were now well aware of his very important guests, Jack stood there feeling satisfied to the core. There was little else for him to say. "Enjoy your day, and if you get the chance, do visit the pool!" he advised keenly.

His guests rewarded him with a rapturous round of applause, and feeling like a king amongst men, Jack offered to take his most important guests on a walking tour around the house and grounds.

Δ

Remaining on the lawn, not having been invited to partake in the excursion, Macdonald, Sykes and Worthington stood together, admiring the view across the lake and commenting on Brunson's achievements.

"What a grand job he's done with this place," Worthington said, quietly considering whether it would be worth trying to dip into the family trust fund in an effort to emulate such a splendid residence for himself.

"A most impressive job indeed," agreed Sykes, and the three men nodded in humble accord while gazing in awe at the scene of serenity around them.

"So, how's business treating you chaps?" Worthington enquired genially, seeking news of any progress under the new president, having not submitted any plans of his own as yet.

"All's, coming along, nicely," replied Sykes somewhat vaguely, and without offering any finer detail, but in a confident enough manner that informed his associates he had something to be pleased about.

"And yourself, Alex?" Worthington asked.

The question had the young Scot scrambling, unsure as to whether he could reveal his East River plan with Roberts to the group. Smartly, he decided it better not disclose any of the details until he had cleared it with Stephen. "I'm just here to assist the group where I can," he replied simply.

"Ah, yes, indeed you are," Sykes said, flashing Alex an affectionate grin. "And I believe Jack will wish to talk to you about that at some point later today," he added cryptically.

However, before they could further their discussion, a deafening honking blasted out from down the lake, causing the men to stare at one another in bemusement.

What on earth was that?!

"Must be a commercial shipping vessel that's taken a wrong turn," said Worthington.

The men tried to ignore the interjection and carry on regardless, but the noise continued unabated, and the waters around the island suddenly became choppy. Guests soon edged back towards the highest point they could find, and called for their children to stop playing and come join them at once. As the three men looked on anxiously through the gaps between the trees, Brunson's boats began crashing against his jetty, then against one another, as the waves crashed onto the lower reaches of the lawn.

Then came the source of the furore: a one-hundred-metre yacht, meandering around the corner and belching thick black smoke out of its funnel, high into the summer sky – and sat elevated at the steering column, proudly commanding *The Constellation*: Stephen Roberts.

As the yacht docked, The Commander looked down to the starboard side and gave his friend Harris a little grin. He was rewarded with a wink of satisfaction from AJ, both revelling at having spoiled Jack's tranquil proceedings. Next they disembarked the boat alongside Alfred and although their invitations had included wives and children, the men had come alone; for this was not a social visit in their book, but a business meeting and a chance for Stephen to once again try to establish his authority over the group.

While Worthington and Macdonald rushed down to meet them and welcome them to the party, with looks of disbelief across their faces, Sykes disappeared off to find the host and let him know of the situation unfolding on his front lawn.

"That was one hell of an entrance!" Macdonald shouted out to Stephen as the new arrivals proudly marched up towards the house.

"Not bad, eh, Alex?!" Stephen replied with a twinkle in his eye. He was thoroughly looking forward to seeing Brunson's reaction, and was quite hoping the owner of this faux castle would explode into a rage and reveal his true colours, out in public.

The Commander did not have to wait long for a reaction. The news spread like wildfire, and as if set alight himself, a very red-faced Brunson came speeding to the scene. "Nothing like using a hammer to crack a nut, eh, Stephen?" he said sarcastically, having just about managed to compose himself in his final few steps. "Of course, I did offer to ferry you across on a more suitable vessel..." he added, shaking his head in disgust and glaring fiercely at his adversary.

"Is that so? I must have misread the invitation," Stephen said innocently. "However, we did have a delightful journey here!" He beamed, trying to incite a reaction from Brunson.

For a long moment, the two powerhouses remained fixated on one another while the group looked on in anticipation of fireworks. Then, having enjoyed their disruption in full, Harris decided to quell the tension and move the conversation on.

"President Rushbourne and Mr Roach, lovely to see you both again," he said pleasantly, initiating the first part of his mission for the day: to develop his relationships with the men who held the keys to unlock the door.

"Well, at least we're all here now," Rushbourne responded gruffly.

However, as AJ scanned the faces around him and did a quick head count, he recognised the glaring omission in their ranks: the war general.

"Is Richard... somewhere in the party?" he enquired. It was an innocent question, and he was somewhat taken aback by the response from the president, who leered across at Roach, doing little to conceal his amusement.

"Oh, on the contrary," Rushbourne stated. "Brown's on a very important mission for me in the southern states. He left just earlier this week."

The group were surprised by the news, but saw no reason to question it, simply assuming the war general must have been compliant with the idea.

"Right then, shall we take a walk?" Brunson proposed, in the hope of lording his wealth over the three new arrivals and playing Stephen at his own game; goading them into making a wrong move in front of the men from Washington.

Following behind Jack as he led them towards the confused-looking crowd of guests, Stephen tugged lightly on the elbow of Harris's jacket so as to hold him back a little and have a private word in his ear. "Brown contacted me after he heard about our plans and said he'd been sent away. Nothing he could do about it, apparently?" The Commander revealed, while keeping a keen eye on their surroundings to ensure they were not being watched or overheard. "He said if we need assistance, we should speak with George Collins," he swiftly concluded.

AJ looked befuddled by the news and frantically tried to work out the consequences.

Jack, meanwhile, continued to walk the group around the manicured lawns while detailing the history of the island. He informed them it was once used as a lookout point for Commodore Percy during the War of 1812 against the British, from where he victoriously defeated their foreign invaders. And having deliberately aimed the tale in the direction of the elder Roberts, Brunson shouted out to him from the front, "Maybe I should go and sink your ship in honour of Commodore Percy, eh, Stephen?!"

This generated a smattering of laughter from the men, who took his half-serious comment as a friendly joke.

"Why not indeed, Jack?" The Commander responded in a similarly divisive tone to his adversary. "Let's see how your little *Olive* looks after my steamer runs straight over the top of her!" he said gleefully, smiling generously around the group - the men once again, expressing their amusement at the quip.

Touché, AJ thought, grinning mercilessly at the host.

But before things could escalate any further between Jack and Stephen, Macdonald stepped in to break the deadlock. "So what about the fishing here, Jack?" he enquired, having overheard the host boasting about his angling expeditions on the lake.

"Oh, the fishing, the fishing, my dear boy..." he eulogised as he set off once again and the others dutifully (and in some cases begrudgingly) followed. "The fishing and hunting around here are something to behold. The best in all America!" he bragged, and with that he launched into another lecture on the stunning surroundings of the lake.

Seeing that Brunson had the full attention of the group and would no doubt continue to wax lyrical for some time, Rushbourne took advantage of the moment to pull Stephen Roberts aside and quietly requested his personal audience, away from the rest of the group. Only AJ noticed as the two men discretely edged their way back through the masses and made their way towards the house, and he was careful to conceal his excitement at the sight, as he followed Jack onwards, leading the group with his continually droning brag.

Δ

Rushbourne and Roberts walked up the spiral staircase to the octagonal first-floor library, one of the few brightly lit spaces in the house thanks to the large windows on each of its eight walls, providing a three-hundred-and-sixty-degree view over the grounds and its surrounds.

The president took a seat but appeared edgy, gripping firmly onto the arms, as he began. "I wanted to bring you in for a private chat," he said, as The Commander propped himself up on the windowsill, keeping one eye on the other members of the group, visible outside near a copse of trees.

"Go on," Stephen said warily, wondering whether this was likely to be about his escalating feud with Brunson and his less-than-respectful arrival earlier.

"Firstly, I want to thank you for submitting your plans – quite a wonderful idea," Rushbourne said.

At this, Roberts was cautiously encouraged; however, an old hand at such games, he knew there was still more to be revealed. "Well, I'm glad you agree," replied The Commander, offering the president a cursory smile and gesturing for him to continue.

"However..." Rushbourne began, and no sooner was the word was out of his mouth, Stephen knew this was not going to end well for him. "However, it's such a huge project, I just don't feel it viable for me to rubber-stamp at this time," the president advised, and a deathly silence encircled the room.

His view about The Commander had been altered since their last meeting, and after speaking with Roach, he now fully appreciated the benefit of keeping the Roberts family on side. The Commander, however, still had nothing to say in reply. Standing motionless and averting his gaze from the president while he considered his next move, Stephen's attention was caught by the sound of overly-exuberant laughter: Brunson flamboyantly leading their colleagues around his splendid grounds.

You would expect this to blow his top, but suddenly, Stephen decided, that rather than fall into a torrent of abuse, he would simply make a sharp and dignified retort. "Very well then," he said loudly, finally acknowledging Rushbourne. "Shall we?" He directed, and moved off towards the exit.

Sensing that Stephen had not taken the news particularly well, but feeling no need to apologise, having granted him a private hearing over the matter; Benjamin followed silently out of the room. It was a position from which, he did not see The Commander's flared nostrils or grinding teeth, and so reflected that he was more than happy with the outcome, and looked forward to an afternoon of fun.

Chapter 16: Happy Jack

Δ

When the two men re-joined the rest of the group, Brunson was still extolling the virtues of his new home. He stopped abruptly, however, when it dawned on him that Rushbourne and Roberts were returning to the group having been absent, and had therefore held court on his island someplace without him. Filled with a mix of envy and anxiety, he felt compelled to make a point of their absence.

"Ah, welcome back, chaps," Jack said somewhat sarcastically with a tense look on his face. "Discussing plans, were we?" he asked pointedly, glaring at both the men.

"Of a sort," Rushbourne replied curtly.

Stephen, standing dejectedly by his side, was certainly not in the mood for another round of verbal jousting, so he remained silent on the matter.

If he spoke he would only likely explode.

And the chance of his humiliation becoming public knowledge caged his frustrated anger, bubbling right underneath the surface.

With an eerie atmosphere pervading the returnees, Jack also felt a jolt of insecurity and worried they were hiding a secret from him, so decided to go on the offensive.

"Well, I'm glad if you've signed off plans for Mr Roberts. Good for you, Stephen," he commended insincerely. "Looks like I won't be the only one with a project signed off then!" he added, unintentionally bringing Stephen to the end of his tether.

Without taking a split second more to mull things over, The Commander decided that he had already devoted far too much of his attention to this project and it was time, right now, to walk away. He took a deep gulp of air before graciously smiling at the men, staring upon him for a response. "I believe my ship is calling," he simply announced. "Good day to you all!" He nodded curtly before walking off towards the dock, completely content with his efforts, and reminding himself that it was always prudent to know when to cut your losses and that to outstay your welcome was embarrassing.

The remainder of the men stood there staring in amazement at one another, wondering what could have caused his sudden departure.

"Wait there, Stephen!" AJ shouted out, and he quickly said his goodbyes to the group and then hurriedly chased after his friend, hoping to change his mind.

Following in quick succession behind, Alfred caught up with his father. "What's going on?" he puffed, somewhat out of breath.

"A waste of time!" Stephen angrily muttered under his breath while marching ahead with purpose. "I'm finished with the lot of them!"

AJ and Alfred looked at each other, baffled as to the reason for Stephen's sudden change of heart. And desperate to find out more information or see whether he could offer anything to dispel his ally's concerns, a fraught AJ enquired urgently, "What happened? What did Rushbourne say?"

"He took me all the way up to that bloody library to tell me that *our* plans aren't good enough," he yelled, displaying his resentment in full. "Only to then find out that whatever Brunson has submitted, HE'S PASSED IT!"

The Commander continued to rage while AJ tried, and failed, to get a word in edgeways. "I don't need this, AJ. I know you want to saddle up with this lot, but without Brown, I can't. And nor do I need to - so I'm out!" he concluded unequivocally.

Difficult to argue with that.

They had reached *The Constellation* now, and Stephen's first mate helped him aboard. Staring back down at AJ, having left him stalled upon the jetty, Stephen waited to see whether he would come aboard. However, the younger Harris was torn: leave with his cohorts, or stay to develop his relationships with the group?

Picking up on his hesitation The Commander offered him a solution that was most generous, under the circumstances. "You stay if you wish, Andrew. I won't hold that against you," he said genuinely. "Business is business.

But *we* have no need to be here," he said, looking to his son, who quickly made his way on board to arrive alongside his disgruntled father.

Standing beside the lake and feeling thoroughly disheartened that the day had turned so sour, AJ knew he needed to make a decision, quickly, for the sake of both parties. He glanced back over his shoulder, to the group on the lawn, and saw Brunson joking with Macdonald. The sight instantly reminded him of where his loyalties lay, and Andrew suddenly felt a creeping sense of dismay with himself for even stopping to consider the fact.

"Give me a hand up then, Al," he said, before scrambling aboard the yacht for their departure. And within the blink of an eye they weighed anchor, turned the large vessel around, and then sailed off into waters sparkling in the sun.

The group on land watched their departure with varying degrees of confusion; all, that is, apart from Rushbourne, who looked on pensively as the men from Manhattan disappeared into the distance.

"Well, that was a fleeting visit!" Brunson said dryly, while privately revelling in their exit as he chalked up a win on his own personal scoreboard.

"I'm sure there's a reasonable explanation," Macdonald said sincerely, hoping to soften the perception of his business partner's departure.

However, he need not have been so worried, for his next opportunity would soon be upon him."Can we possibly steal you for a minute, Alex?"

Macdonald found Brunson and Sykes smiling at him oddly.

"Of course!" the Scot replied to Jack readily. Then they set off to find a more private and secluded area of the island, leaving Worthington standing alone with Rushbourne and Roach, and provided him with the perfect opportunity to detail them, some plans he had of his own.

Δ

Jack led Levi and Alex towards his orangery – which was, of course, impressively ornate and expansive – and settled upon it as a suitable place to begin the process of bringing the Scot under his enchantment. "I do hope you're enjoying the party, Alex?" the host enquired cordially as they slowly circled the edge of the large swimming pool, where a contingent of guests were splashing about.

"It's been most splendid," Alex replied pleasantly, watching the sun shining down through the glass roof above, shimmering against the water.

"Well, I do like my important guests to enjoy themselves," Brunson said. He glanced mischievously over at Sykes and added in a loud whisper, "Even better when the ones I don't like leave early!"

However, Levi did not react to his friend's jibe.

He was still weighing up Macdonald and saw no benefit in publicly berating the other side to a man whose loyalties remained unclear.

Moving the conversation swiftly back to the matter at hand, Sykes said to Macdonald, "Rushbourne has approved a plan of ours which requires the building of a number of bridge crossings, as well as the iron for the tracks." He laid a hand on the Scot's shoulder. "And as such we would like to bring you in on the project," he declared, as if it had been their choosing, rather than Roach's directive.

"I'd be honoured to join you!" replied an exultant Macdonald, struggling to conceal his excitement and grinning from ear to ear in acknowledgment of being so kindly considered.

"Well then, it's agreed," confirmed Jack. He offered a hand to Alex, and the two men shook hands heartily.

"And, just so that there can be no misunderstandings of expectations, Alex, both Rushbourne and I want this completing within a year, so it will require your complete and utter devotion," Jack stated firmly.

In truth, the project would not actually require all of Macdonald's energies, however, Brunson wanted to make it clear that he was to be the Scot's most important customer, and that he expected to be treated that way. Eager to be accommodating and ever the professional, the young Scot nodded his agreement.

"Well then, glad to have you on board," Sykes said, and he clapped Macdonald on the back, before leading him back out into the party.

Δ

Aboard Stephen's boat and sailing east along Lake Erie, AJ hoped that in the past half hour, since they had left Brunson's island, The Commander's anger might have abated. Now, tentatively, he approached him at the helm.

"How are you?" he asked cautiously, staring up at his friend from the deck.

"Absolutely fine, AJ," Stephen replied, doing his utmost to appear like a man without a care in the world. "I'm commanding my beloved yacht on a lovely summer's day – what more could I wish for?" he said blissfully, staring directly ahead with his head held high.

Knowing his friend had dodged the question, Harris tried again. "And what of Lincoln's Development Plan?" he asked softly, specifically naming it as such to try to press The Commander.

"Well, as I said, Andrew, it's no longer *his* plan. And as long as that remains the case, I'm happy to work alone." Stephen paused and then added pointedly, "Just as I have done for the past forty years."

AJ scrambled about for one last desperate attempt. "We could... Or perhaps if you... Then I... Oh, yes, that's it! Let me speak to Collins!" he said, suddenly recalling Brown's words. "Maybe he can help us?"

When Stephen said nothing, AJ called up to him. "Stephen, please. I'll make it work. I promise you."

His passionate proclamation raised a light chuckle of admiration from The Commander, who smiled down on his young friend in appreciation of his persistence.

"Okay then, AJ, if you think you can make it work, then be my guest." He shook his head and sighed. "But don't blame me if you find it a huge waste of your time..."

Accepting Stephen's reply as the best outcome he could possibly expect, Harris returned to his seat, set on the starboard side. And as he sat back and watched the houses dotted along the shoreline slowly passing by, his mind started to drift away. Rather than relaxing, though, in this scenic setting and quiet moment, he found himself tensing up, and a chill of worry washed through his entire body as he became racked with self-doubt.

Brooklyn Bridge plans in tatters...

Macdonald buddying up with Brunson...

Roberts out of the running...

My visit to Cleveland a disaster...

What will my father think?!

Fortunately for AJ, he wouldn't have to come face to face with his father's reaction; JR having returned back to their London offices for the foreseeable.

Sitting there all alone, with the wind combing through his hair, he held his wineglass tightly to his chest for comfort as the negativity continued to flow through him; and could do nothing but consider himself a failure.

Noticing Andrew had been sitting staring into space, Alfred whistled over to him. Immediately, AJ snapped out of his reflections and waved to reassure his friend that he was fine, just fine, and enjoying the sail in the sunshine. He raised his glass, and Alfred nodded and smiled in reply.

It was just what AJ needed.

Warmed by his friend's considerate act, he realised there was little point in feeling down and getting lost in contemplation, and he promised himself right there and then, he would do whatever it took to turn his situation around.

Δ

Chapter 17: Erie Beginnings

Δ

Brunson's island had emptied considerably, with most of the guests having made their way back to the mainland. Rushbourne and Roach were among the last to leave, and Jack made a point of personally bidding them farewell and thanking them for their attendance as they stepped aboard The Olive.

"It's been an absolute pleasure," Roach said graciously, while offering his hand in gratitude to Jack, who shook it vigorously.

"Yes, yes, ditto," he said, tripping over his tongue in his desperation to share the latest news. "And before you go, just to let you know: I spoke with Alex Macdonald, like you suggested, and he's fully on board - so full steam ahead!" he finished merrily and stood there beaming, eagerly awaiting their reply.

"Full steam ahead indeed!" Roach echoed proudly, awash with satisfaction that his friend was continuing to make all the right moves in front of the president.

The man himself, nodded in recognition of the news, then disappeared into the cabin of the boat, ready for departure. Brunson watched as they sailed the short distance back to shore, the moon providing a perfect spotlight, shining over the lake and illuminating the rippling waters below, as a thousand stars glistened in the clear dark-blue sky above and the lights of the houses dotted around the mainland reflected beautifully against the water's edge.

Feeling invincible – king of the castle and more besides – Jack pulled a large cigar out of his pocket and lit it while slowly walking back towards the house. He almost failed to notice his old friend Millard Stride sitting on the swing seat against the south-facing porch; only the squeak of the swaying chain gave him away.

Having been far too busy to speak with him earlier in the day, Jack walked over to give him an audience, now that his more important guests had departed. "How's Erie treating you, Millard?" Brunson called out boisterously as he approached his fellow railroad owner.

"Not bad, Jack," Stride replied. "You know how it is – keeping *the wolves* from the door!"

His reply was uttered in a deliberate tone. But Brunson was far too preoccupied by his own splendid thoughts, however, to pick up on the reference.

Stride, or "Uncle Millard" as he was affectionately known by his friends, was a poorly educated ex-publican who had dragged himself up from very humble beginnings. A small and slovenly sixty-eight year old, he took little care of his appearance, mainly because when he woke and arranged himself in the morning, he was often still inebriated from his exuberances the night before. "Did I see that despicable man Roberts here today?" he asked, somewhat rhetorically.

Having run a successful steamboat business that operated on the Hudson River, Millard had previous with the Roberts family and he had run into further conflict with Stephen in recent days.

"Why do you ask?" His interest suddenly piqued, Jack sat down on a bench opposite Millard. "Have you two had a run in?" he wondered.

"Roberts came to the depot yesterday and asked..." Millard shook his head. "Well, I say asked, but that's not how it was. He *told* me, Jack, that I had to sell all my shares to him," he revealed.

Brunson's eyes lit up at this: *A potential opportunity to meddle in my enemy's business!*

"I did wonder about him arriving out of the blue. But I didn't think you'd have invited him here!" Millard grumbled.

Jack paused cautiously at the question; he did not wish to reveal his connection to the group and so opted for some clever misdirection. "Roberts approached me regarding a railroad deal to split the country. We've agreed patches we'll both stick to," he explained.

Stride's look of absolute shock was not picked up by Jack, and was further lost when one of his waiters appeared and offered them a refreshing beer. His guest pounced on one like he had not drunk a drop in hours, which was, in fact, very far from the truth.

"So what's this land share you've agreed?" He chuckled. "I bet the old codger stiffed you!" he suggested cheekily, and took a gulp from his glass.

"Not at all!" Jack staunchly defended his decision. "We've split the country from Cleveland to Washington, meaning I have control of over ninety-five per cent of America!" He smiled smugly.

End of conversation – or so he thought.

"Are you serious!?" Millard spat beer all down himself. "The conditions out west are appalling for building railroads! That's why he's given that whole territory to you," he declared, before *really* upsetting Brunson's strength of conviction. "And even better for him, it keeps you away from meddling with his business in the best parts of America!"

As Millard sat there, flagrantly shaking his head in disbelief; fury and embarrassment whipped Jack into a frenzy. "Is that what you think he's done?" he roared, causing the stragglers nearby to turn their weary heads and seek out the source of the outburst, "The man is an utter disgrace!"

"I agree," Stride said righteously. "Roberts expects to walk over everyone. Just like when he came to see me yesterday," he reiterated, finally getting back to the reason he had hoped for the exchange in the first place.

Feeling fully provoked, and now desperate to exact revenge, Jack sat and thought for a moment, tapping the edge of his glass against his gritted teeth in frustration. Then he asked with a seething intent, "What are you going to do about it then?"

"What can I do?" Stride replied with a shrug, playing the helpless victim in the hope of luring Brunson into his battle. "I can't go toe-to-toe with him – he'll bankrupt me!"

"Well, I *can* go toe-to-toe with him, and you'd better believe it!" Jack snapped back, while Millard looked on, delighted at the outcome. "Whatever you need, I'm in," he said with unadulterated conviction and malice in his voice.

"But what about your areas agreement?" Stride asked, rather craftily, trying to wind his friend into a fervour.

"Forget the areas agreement," Jack barked forcefully, as the muddy patches across the flooded sections of his lawn, suddenly came acutely into view. "I'm the big man here, and it's time to show Roberts just who's boss!" And with that, he sank the remainder of his beer and stalked into the house, leaving Millard to watch his departure, muffling a chuckle of glee, like the cat that got the cream.

Δ

The following day, Brunson rose early, having been unable to sleep at all the night before. Walking around the gardens with his robe gently flowing in the light morning breeze, he sipped cautiously on a piping-hot coffee while enjoying a smoke and deliberating which of the ideas he had dreamt up last night would damage Stephen the most. With the gloves well and truly off, Jack finally decided to head straight to Union Station. Too impatient to wait for his drink to cool, he tossed the cup onto the lawn and raced back into the house. Running along the cold stone floor in bare feet, he made his way up to his bedroom, where he opened his wardrobe and flung his chosen clothes out onto the armchair.

His wife, still dozing in bed, lifted up her hazy head to see what all the commotion was about. "What's going on?" she enquired drowsily, keeping her eyes closed in the hope of a quick reply that would mean she could go back to sleep.

"Going to Erie to meet Stride. Not sure when I'll be back," Jack hurriedly told his wife - to her confusion; however, with the plan not seemingly affecting her slumber, she happily tucked herself back into bed and quizzed him no more.

Dressed in his obligatory black suit, with a long cape and grey fedora hat, Jack grabbed his wallet and watch, before leaving the bedroom. Then he made his way down to the jetty, boarded *The Olive* and sailed her along Lake Erie to arrive at Presque Isle Bay. After mooring his boat at the quayside, he walked the short distance along State Street and through Perry Square, and soon arrived outside Union Depot on Peach Street. The bleak, three-storey building looked more like a prison than a train depot, with its dark, brown-brick façade and tall, narrow windows, its only saving grace, a large dome above the concourse, which cascaded bright light into the recesses of the dingy station below.

Entering on the ground floor, Brunson scanned the U-shaped walkway above him, hoping to catch sight of Stride or his collaborator, Jim Diamond, lingering around the upper-floor offices and sleeping quarters. But unable to locate them, he turned his attention to the concourse, seeking someone in authority, anyone? But neither the tellers sitting in their gated stalls nor the staff in the hairdressing saloon fitted the bill. Becoming increasingly frustrated, Jack was about to jump the gate guarding the offices when he spotted the station controller walking between the main set of tracks, and just as he took his first tentative steps towards him, Brunson was abruptly halted by a hearty slap across his back.

"Jack!" Jim Diamond crowed, as Brunson swiftly spun around to see who had dared place his hand upon him. "Good to see you," Jim beamed, before swiftly wrapping his arms around Brunson and squeezing his large, rotund figure into his person.

"Ouch," squirmed Jack, and then, when the man finally released his hold, "Oh, it's you, Big Jim."

Jim Diamond – or Big Jim as he was known, for obvious reasons – loved to gorge on all life's little pleasures, but he had a particular penchant for food, drink and, his most favourite of all, women. Aged thirty, but looking fifty, he had trod a similar path to Stride; working in several different fields and successfully pulling himself up through each of those ventures to arrive as the railroad's main stockbroker in

New York and a controlling member of the board, alongside Millard.

"Uncle Millard said you might visit!" Jim cheerily confirmed. He looked exceedingly pleased that Jack had appeared at the depot so soon. "Let me take you up to see him and we can get the ball rolling," he said excitedly.

Jim led Brunson up the stairs to Stride's office, where they found him sitting behind his desk and scribbling away on a timetable. "Jack!" was his surprised reaction. "Great to see you!" Millard said as he leapt up to greet his esteemed guest.

Standing by the door, with both men at his side grinning in veneration at his presence, Brunson quickly assessed the severe lack of seating in the room. In the blink of an eye, he skipped between the men to sit down in Millard's seat, leaving his hosts to squeeze onto the crumpled sofa adjacent. In any usual situation Stride would never permit a single soul to take his seat; however, under the circumstances, and recognising his position in the food chain, he decided to forego his privilege and squeezed up next to Big Jim. As they attempted, unsuccessfully, to get comfortable, Jack decided to cut to the chase and reveal his masterplan.

"So, I was thinking about what you told me last night, and I've come to the conclusion... that I should just buy you out instead!" he announced.

Stunned silence instantly befell the room.

And both Millard and Big Jim stared at each other in abject disbelief, wondering whether they were going to regret, seeking Jack's involvement after all.

"Well, I'm not sure that will work," Millard said hesitantly. "I mean, Roberts already owns thirty per cent of the railroad..." Big Jim nodded in slightly panicked agreement. "... So if we sold you our shares, the problem still remains."

Jack thought about that, and paused for a very long moment, then reluctantly accepted their justification. But he wasn't finished there. "So what *is* the solution?" he demanded gruffly, leaning back in Stride's seat and lifting his feet onto the table, to rest them on the now scrunched-up timetable.

With Millard forced to bite his tongue at Jack's disrespectful display, Big Jim shuffled forward on the sofa to present their dastardly idea. "We short the share price and drive it low so we can water down his stock holdings," he announced profoundly.

What on earth does that mean?!

Seeing their visitor's confusion, Stride stepped in to try elucidate. "It's just like when I was in the droving game," he offered, in the hope of explaining their somewhat complex and elaborate scheme. "I'd make the cattle lick salt and drink water in the hours before taking them to market, so they'd bloat up. Their weight would temporarily increase, and so their value would increase, you see?" He gave a toothy smile, clearly very proud of the unscrupulous business practice. "So

Jim here will issue secondary shares in New York, which I shall purchase through the railroad, and we can sell them on to Roberts, with the best bit being - they convey no rights of ownership whatsoever."

Their ideas were coming like gunfire now.

"Even better, he won't suspect a thing – because he came to us demanding to purchase them in the first place!" Big Jim concluded excitedly, and he sat back in anticipation of Jack's response to this deceitful, little scheme.

"This sounds..."

Big Jim and Stride looked at each other, while the pause seemed endless.

"... brilliant!" said Brunson, and he leapt to his feet, grinning mercilessly at his comrades' fiendish idea.

"I thought you'd like it, Jack," Millard said haughtily, standing to shake on the deal while hiding his relief that their visitor had been convinced.

"Let's water up this stock, then chaps!" Brunson concluded coldheartedly, punching the air in celebration, and with that the room descended into a joyous frenzy at the prospect of finally getting the better of the Roberts family.

Δ

Chapter 18: Out of the Black

Δ

On a crisp and early October morning in New York, Andrew John Harris was making his way to work through the streets of Lower Manhattan, hand in hand with Maria. Determined not to be disheartened by the events at Brunson's island, AJ had since bucked up his ideas and had been working twice as hard and for twice as long as ever before. Feeling in a particularly breezy mood, not only because of the unseasonably warming sunshine beating down upon his face, but also because he had managed to arrange a secret rendezvous with George Collins for later that day, he could not help but smile at what the day may bring.

As they progressed along William Street, nearing the offices of the bank, Andrew and Maria engaged in their now daily ritual: and affectionately tipped their heads towards Delmonico's, while smiling tenderly at one another. However, their blissful moment was abruptly shattered as they turned their attention to the entrance of JR Harris & Son, and spied a man lurking on the steps, bending over and looking through the letterbox of the front door. This early in the day, there were few people about, and he stood out like a sore thumb against the morning sweepers.

Who on earth is that, and more importantly – what is he doing with my door?!

As Harris hesitantly made his final approach, and Maria followed half a pace behind, the young man suddenly turned and saw Andrew – and waved energetically in his direction.

Frowning in response, AJ scanned the face of their visitor. He thought perhaps he recognised the man from somewhere, but remained resolutely on his guard.

"Mr Harris!" the chap called excitedly, while nimbly making his way down the steps to offer his hand; he appeared even smaller than before, stood next to AJ towering over him. And as Andrew continued to rack his brain as to where he had seen this chap before, the man reached into his trouser pocket and pulled out a business card.

Andrew John Harris (Owner)
JR Harris and Son

"The oil man!" AJ exclaimed loudly, exultant at finally having remembered, but remaining vague in order to mask his ignorance – he was unable to recall the man's actual name.

"Yes, Oliver Peter Cunningham, sir. You came to see me and my associates in Cleveland," he confirmed politely.

Harris's eyes lit up with glee. "Yes, we did... we did, indeed," he replied happily, and all worry over their impromptu visitor subsided.

Now, knowing the newcomer posed no threat, Maria walked up the steps to open up the bank, and the men followed in behind her. As he led his guest into the private rear office, Harris was hopeful that if Cunningham had made such a long and arduous journey to arrive outside his door at such an ungodly hour, some positive news may be forthcoming.

"So how are you, Oliver?" he asked in an upbeat manner, bounding into his seat. However, Cunningham appeared troubled by that simplest of enquires.

Seeing the world from a different angle to most, Cunningham was often perceived as being rude: in fact, he merely had no time for incessant conversation. He had dedicated his life to work, even marrying young in order to "get it out of the way" and so that he could concentrate all his attention on building his business empire and achieving his two main goals in life (1) to live to one hundred and (2) to make one hundred thousand dollars.

Realising an awkward silence had sprung up following Harris's question regarding his wellbeing, Oliver smiled politely and replied, "Good, yes... thank you," remembering that while he found it odd to discuss one's disposition, he prided himself on being respectful and polite.

"What can I do for you then, Mr Cunningham?" Harris asked. "Here to sell me your company?" he suggested cheekily.

"Well, not exactly..." confessed Oliver, which wiped the grin off AJ's face and curbed his initial enthusiasm. "But I would like to make you a proposition," he said calmly.

"Well, do go ahead," Andrew instructed, leaning forward over his desk in anticipation of the revelation.

"Firstly, I wish to apologise for my associates' actions," Oliver stated, in an attempt to detach himself from his colleagues and to start as he meant to go on. "The Ratchet brothers have no foresight and I would have liked to have partnered up with you, had they –"

"Then why didn't you say something at the meeting?!" Harris cut in.

Oliver took the interjection calmly.

"With all due respect, Mr Harris, sometimes our colleagues take over proceedings and ruin the discussions for everyone," he stated, referring subtly to both the Ratchet brothers, as well as AJ's colleague, Samuel Smith.

Andrew stared, open mouthed at Oliver for a moment.

Then burst out laughing in amusement.

Most uncharacteristic for him; usually AJ would be riled by such a demonstration, but he was taken back by Oliver's temperament, which strangely, reminded him of his father.

He decided to get straight to the point.

"Look, Oliver, I like you. But we both agree I can't work with your colleagues. So what's the solution here?"

"We join forces and buy the Ratchet brothers out of the business," Oliver replied without a second's hesitation.

Well, I wasn't expecting that!

Andrew was a little surprised at how quickly the meeting had moved on, but nonetheless thrilled at the prospect of part-owning one of the best oil refiners around. With the deal hanging delicately in the balance, he knew the outcome would come down to cost. "So how much will you require for them to walk away?" he asked.

"Fifty thousand dollars should suffice," Oliver unerringly replied, once again, and without need for taking breath.

AJ had expected a higher figure; a much higher figure in fact, and he thrust out his hand across the desk to instantly shake on the deal.

For the remainder of the morning they settled the paperwork for their agreement, then Harris advanced the money into Cunningham's account: job done. And although it wasn't the largest loan he had signed off, it certainly was the quickest, so he leaned back in his seat to deliver a cursory warning to his new associate. "This could be the start of something very big for you and me, or it could be your short demise - don't let me down, Oliver!"

Cunningham wished to make a statement of his own. "Time shall prove to you that I am a man of the utmost integrity, and I will *never* dare disrespect you or your company. Furthermore... it is my intention to pay back every cent you have invested and to repay that within a year!" he declared.

At this, AJ beamed fit to burst, for what Oliver was promising made this even more of a win-win situation for JR Harris & Son. Even without the repayment, the deal would give them a foothold into the oil business that Andrew and his father so craved.

With the two men feeling very comfortable with their unity, AJ led his new business partner back into the banking hall. He paused in contemplation, wanting to engage some more with Cunningham, but mindful of his impending summit with George Collins. He settled on a half way house. "Have my driver take you to the St Nicholas Hotel and book yourself a room. I'll be with you at around six o'clock, okay?"

"Thank you very much, Andrew," Cunningham accepted respectfully, and they headed out onto Hannover Square, where the coachman on account with JR Harris & Son was sat waiting to take him away. With his guest being driven off into the distance, Harris surveyed the street below him from the top step of his building. Staring around at the mid-day rush he took in an almighty breath of cool, fresh air to fill his lungs, before puffing his chest out like a silverback gorilla: wholly satisfied with his first, rather unexpected, but most welcome bit of business for the day.

Δ

As AJ devoured his lunch, he took the opportunity to excitedly inform Maria of the developments from his time with Oliver Cunningham. She congratulated him, full of admiration for her trailblazer, before helping him prepare for his next meeting.

Departing his office dressed in a full-length coat with the collar turned up and a flat-cap to cover his face, Harris hoped this would be sufficient disguise to avoid his being recognised by his contemporaries. Making his way to the prearranged destination at St Paul's Chapel, he took the long way round in order to avoid Wall Street, where he would certainly be quizzed over his attire. Shooting out onto Broadway to mingle amongst the crowds, he stooped his head to avoid standing out, before dashing across the road and successfully entering the church unnoticed.

Standing in the entrance foyer, Harris took off his cap as a mark of respect and scrunched it in his hands, before making his way through the second set of doors to enter the main body of the church. At once, he was struck by the mix of elegance and simplicity inside, the fourteen cut-glass chandeliers adorning the hall contrasted with a backdrop of pale-coloured walls and well-trodden, tiled flooring - he could never fail to be impressed by the sight.

Scanning the viewing galleries above his head, Harris discerned the shape of a man sitting conspicuously alone. He could not make him out properly as he was partly obscured by one of the three large columns holding the upper balconies in place. *That'll be my man,* AJ thought instinctively, before swiftly making his way towards the side stairs and towards his second meeting for the day.

Quietly opening the stairwell doorway, Harris swiftly examined the man at close range and was pleased to find his deduction had been spot on. Those spectacles were indeed the thin wire frames of George Collins, and he turned briefly to offer AJ a nod of recognition. Andrew however, wishing to keep their meeting as covert as possible, ignored him altogether and opted to walk along the row behind, and sit down behind his associate, who flashed a cursory glance back over his shoulder.

"Thanks for making the journey," AJ whispered politely while fixing his stare upon the organist, whimsically playing the George Pike organ; the soft melody flowing throughout the chapel like the seedling florets of a dandelion floating in the wind.

"That's quite all right," George whispered in kind, offering little in the way of conversation.

"Richard said that if I needed anything while he's away, you're the man to speak with?" AJ asked, in an overt attempt to demonstrate his affiliation with Brown.

But Collins knew he had to be on his guard with what he revealed, and so decided to keep his replies to a minimum. "He mentioned that some of you may call."

It was now becoming a game of cat and mouse, which was not what these men, seeking similar outcomes, should be playing. Harris frowned behind his back. "Look, when's the damn man coming back?!" he demanded gruffly.

Down below, a couple of parishioners looked up with interest. Suddenly realising that even the slightest murmur would bring them unwanted attention, AJ calmed himself.

His outburst however, had told Collins all he needed to know, and from that he had gathered, he was firmly on the side of Brown. "It will be at least a couple more months," he revealed. "Rushbourne has planned his whole route, so he can't just up and leave, you see."

Harris mulled the information around his gums, it was annoying to say the least. "Why did Rushbourne have to get involved in the first place?" AJ moaned, and raised the cap to his mouth as if he could hide the slanderous comment. Then he dropped the cap and added mutinously, "It should be Richard sending him on the mission, not the other way round!"

At this open airing of loyalties, George responded in kind, with a grin he could not seem to shift. "I agree, Andrew, I really do, however, this is the situation we find ourselves in."

Reluctantly, AJ had to concede that there was nothing more to do at present than to accept the situation. At least the meeting had been somewhat successful; and he had secured another useful ally in Washington for the future.

"Let's get together upon Brown's return?" he suggested.

Collins nodded in confirmation, then reached a hand back and patted the only part of AJ he could reach - his knee. "Don't worry, Andrew. We'll get there."

"We will George - we will," agreed AJ, and he tried with every ounce of his being to believe it.

Meeting finished, Harris readied himself to depart. He placed his cap back on his head and dropped to a crouched position, before quickly scuttling along the bench and exiting via the stairwell. Collins held back a few minutes to make sure they were not seen leaving together, then departed the building himself, before taking the short walk across the block to his next engagement at City Hall.

Chapter 19: Into the Blue

Δ

Having returned to his office and changed back into his more standard attire, AJ jumped aboard a hired stagecoach and headed up to meet Oliver at the St Nicholas as promised. With a twenty-minute journey ahead of him and a frantic day already had, he rested back against the luxury upholstery and relaxed, with a surge of satisfaction filling his entire body. The events at Brunson's party seemed a distant memory, from which AJ felt he was learning and growing, and now he was awash with optimism and ready to do battle.

The driver pulled up outside the hotel. "Find somewhere to settle," Andrew advised him, handing the man a dollar to sustain himself while he awaited the conclusion of his evening.

As he walked up to the hotel Andrew reflected, as he always did, that its white marble frontage was "certainly something to behold". The thousand-bed St Nicholas was one of the most luxurious hotels in all Manhattan. Sprawling an entire block between Spring Street and Broome, it set a new standard of luxury when it opened, almost a decade ago. The first building in New York to cost over a million dollars, it had also ended the dominance of the Randolph-Smith House hotel and therefore was particularly well frequented by Harris and his friends, who had scant regard for the elitist "Old Money" Randolph-Smith family empire.

Walking through the main entrance, flanked either side by imposing marble columns, Andrew entered the main lobby and was instantly seized upon by the hotel owner, Mr Tweadle. "Good evening!" Tweadle called joyously while approaching with open arms and granting him the warmest of receptions. "Dining alone, are we?" he wondered while pointedly scanning around his lack of partner.

"Meeting a colleague," AJ confirmed as he cast his gaze around the large open-plan lobby to see whether he could locate his new associate.

The hotel interior was covered from floor to ceiling in dense mahogany panelling and brightly lit by several oversized chandeliers dotted across the ceiling, that were reflected spectacularly in the plentiful gilded mirrors hung on every single wall. Having thoroughly scanned for Oliver, Harris looked down at his watch to see the second hand tick over to six o'clock, their designated meeting time. And just as he looked up again a pair of shoes, blotted in oil, came into view at the top of the main staircase, beneath the Dutch painting of St Nicholas handing out gifts. Several steps later and Cunningham was revealed, still wearing his clothes from earlier on, he spotted his new colleague beside the hotel owner and walked over to greet them.

"What a splendid place!" he declared, looking around in awe at the opulence of his surroundings, a far cry from the oil fields and his humble lodgings back in Cleveland.

"This is my good friend, Oliver," Harris announced authoritatively as he turned to face the hotel owner. "I'd like you to make sure you take good care of him whenever he stays here and treat him as you would me."

"I'll make sure to honour that arrangement," Tweadle replied dutifully while making a mental note of Cunningham's face - which was currently lit up in appreciation, at AJ's considerate and most respectful gesture.

"My usual then, if you will," Harris commanded, and the hotel owner swiftly clicked his fingers in the air and instructed his team of waiters to prepare a table post-haste for their most important of guests.

Δ

The large and expansive dining room was a grand affair to say the least, with tables set out to accommodate more than four hundred of the best-dressed diners in New York. As they were led to their seats, past a pianist lightly stroking the mother-of-pearl keys on his Gilbert & Co. rosewood grand piano, Oliver could not help but feel he had really, finally, arrived. Once they were seated at their table and AJ had ordered his favourite bottle of red, he asked Oliver how he had passed his afternoon.

The answer left him gobsmacked.

Apparently, his guest had unwittingly wandered into the Five Points area of Manhattan! A notoriously dangerous area of New York where murders were a regular occurrence, and a man such as Oliver wandering around in his suit would have stood out like a sore thumb.

"Are you mad?!" Andrew exclaimed in disbelief. "You could have been killed!"

"But why would anyone want to harm me?" Oliver wondered, looking sorely confused. "I didn't do anything to them," he rationalised in his usual matter-of-fact tone, and as AJ stared at him, aghast, the man from Cleveland simply finished his starter of vermicelli soup. It was Cunningham's inimitable view of the world, to which AJ would soon became accustomed.

Then they moved on to the main course, and as AJ polished off his main of Bucks County chicken with a side of turkey wings and Oliver enjoyed his terrine of goose liver *à la* Périgueux, the host decided to turn discussions towards their new business venture together. "So your ambition to build the largest oil refinery in America..." he began, leaning back in his chair with his belly fit to burst. "How do you propose we might make that happen?"

Shuffling his chair around the table so as to be in closer proximity to his benefactor, Oliver quietly began to reveal his masterplan. "Firstly, I want to merge with my brother's refinery," he said politely, not noticing the look of shock that washed across Harris's face as he weighed up the addition of another, wholly new, partner to their business "Being larger means we'll have better economies and more purchasing power."

Realising the argument made sense but concerned that his share could be severely diluted, Andrew leaned in to ask, "And does he expect to have some holdings in our new company?"

"Your share will remain the same," Oliver insisted firmly, "while I will split my half with him accordingly."

At this, AJ's mood instantly lifted; in effect, his investment had already doubled. "Well... that's quite alright then," he said, attempting to hold back his delight, but he could not help but smile at his latest associate's approach.

"The main thing I wish to do is drive efficiency," Oliver said, before scanning the room and leaning in even closer. "I want to create my own team of plumbers, barrel makers and drivers, and bring every part of the process under one roof. Integrating is the future!"

Oliver was well aware that this was a bold proposition, and a great deal of information for AJ to process. However, sitting alongside his new partner in such opulent surroundings, he was unable to picture a scenario where he could now fail, with JR Harris & Son to back him.

Δ

Having finished their meals, the men moved out of the dining room and headed back into the hotel lobby. AJ had his mind caught up in visions of flowing oil fields, but spotted

Tweadle in the distance talking to a man, and after a couple of moments he recognised that it was none other than Alfred Roberts. *What a pleasant surprise!*

It quickened his pace to greet them, and Cunningham hurriedly followed behind.

"Al!" AJ called out. "How are you, my good friend?" he said with a big grin as Alfred turned.

"Very well, very well indeed!" Alfred replied, having already had a few tipples himself and in similarly high spirits to his comrade.

"Out for the evening, are we?" AJ enquired jovially as he jabbed Alfred in the mid-section, like two schoolkids in the playground.

"Indeed I am. And my father's just over there..." He pointed to a secluded area of the bar up ahead, and AJ saw Stephen holding counsel, surrounded by two very wide men indeed. "Shall I join you?" Alfred proposed.

"Splendid idea!" AJ agreed, and looked towards Oliver in order to gauge his reaction to the invite. However, Cunningham, as usual, lost in his own thoughts, had drifted from the conversation some time ago and was paying no attention to them at all!

As AJ nodded insistently to alert him to their waiting, Oliver suddenly snapped out of his daydream.

"Joining us for a drink, Oliver?" AJ asked genially.

In a flash, Oliver decided this was a great opportunity to make his excuses and get an early night. Having been sipping his wine out of courtesy for the past few hours and not having even finished a single glass, he did not find a night continuing in such a vein with the two big drinkers before him, the most attractive of propositions.

"While I appreciate the invitation, I've had a long day, so I think I'll retire for the evening and see you in the morning, Andrew," he said respectfully, to which AJ fully conceded, appreciative of the fact that his new business partner had endured a most tiring twenty-four hours.

As Oliver wandered off back to his room, it crossed AJ's mind that The Commander might wish to join them. "What's your father doing?" he enquired while setting off towards the main bar with Alfred.

"A bit of..." Alfred coughed overtly, before leaning in towards AJ and lowering his voice. "Late-night trading!" he revealed, raising his eyebrows.

Harris looked again in the direction of the elder Roberts and squinted his eyes in an attempt to make out through the smoky darkness, whom The Commander was speaking with. And while he could not quite see just clearly enough, AJ heard an unmistakable belly laugh, and somewhat puzzled, he exclaimed, "Is that Nelson Allen?"

"Shushhhhh..." the younger Roberts confirmed in a flap. "Father's got something going on with him and Jim Diamond at the moment," he confided.

"Not sure I'd be dealing with Allen. Isn't he a crook?" AJ mused, concerned. "Do you want me to go over and assist?"

"*No.* No," Alfred begged as they arrived at the bar to order their drinks. "He's trying to keep it discreet. That's why I'm here – I'm on lookout duty!" he confessed, while clearly demonstrating his ineptitude for the task.

"As you wish," AJ replied, acquiescing to his friend's request, before turning his attention to the barman. "Your largest and most expensive bottle of Scotch, please," he requested, while smiling contently to himself at the success of his day – so far. However with Alfred, a bottle and two glasses having just landed by his side, it appeared it may only be getting started...

Chapter 20: The Worthington Invitational

Δ

Over the month that followed, Brunson forged his new connection to Kansas, and Macdonald ably assisted him, providing the raw materials and sinking the foundations for the bridges he required. Brown continued on his travels around the southern states, and his initial scepticism over the mission soon subsided as he was warmly welcomed by the mayors and senators of every place he visited, and built strong relationships with those he met in his usual, impeccable style.

Returning to Cleveland with the full weight of AJ behind him, Oliver drafted in his brother to assist him in negotiations to buy the Ratchet brothers out. Ultimately they took the money, safe in their belief that they would be able to rebuild once again, without the assistance of Oliver. He, meanwhile, began reorganising the new business, and he retained the services of his genius chemist by offering him shares in the company and renaming the venture as Cunningham & Adams.

With the end of 1865 in sight, Christopher Worthington's "Snow Ball" did, fortuitously, correspond with a snowy evening in Manhattan. All of the members of the group attended, other than Brown and the Roberts family, the latter having decided to shun the event in order to demonstrate their contempt towards Rushbourne and Roach. The party invites were sent out months in advance to the great and good of high society. However, this social occasion was not actually a party at all, but rather a fundraiser, masquerading as a ball – unbeknownst to those excitedly making their way to the event.

The Worthington's expansive, five-storey brownstone had been the family home for the past twelve years. Situated on East 20th Street, in an upper-class suburb, the property was beautifully presented, with each of its nine windows, fronting the façade, framed by white plantation shutters which had been painstakingly pinned to the stone for decorative purposes. And while it was larger than most houses; considering the family wealth, it was far from ostentatious, old money hadn't remained old money, by simply spending all the inheritance.

First to arrive in the early evening was Levi Sykes and his wife Roza, who made their way up the substantial and steep steps, holding firmly on to the handrail for support. At the heavy double doors, Levi raised a hand, lifted the elephant-head knocker and let it drop to announce their presence. A loud thud resounded in the chilly air, and slowly, the doors crept open – but seemingly without anyone there to greet them? Sykes peered into the dark recesses of the hallway, to see whether he could discern any human life. Unable to identify anyone, he gingerly began to step inside, but just as he crossed the threshold, his knee collided painfully with something.

Ouch – that really hurt!

Stifling a cry of pain, he looked down, and saw a young girl in a rolling chair: it was certainly not what he expected. But she smiled sweetly up at him with her message for the night. "Welcome to the Snow Ball, sir. Please do go right up."

As she directed Levi and his wife towards the next floor, the girl's mother appeared from behind the door and placed a hand on her daughter's shoulder. Levi was still slightly confused at being met in such a manner but considered it not a second longer before he thanked them both and continued up the stairs aside his wife.

On the first floor – with a glass of champagne in hand, pressed there by a butler – they began a leisurely tour of the curiosities. The house was filled with artefacts from the family's globetrotting adventures, displayed in glass cabinets along with hunting trophies and works of taxidermy, the most impressive of which, being a full-sized bear in attack pose, nestled in the corner.

Over the next hour, the space filled up, as guests continued to flow into the house. Macdonald and Brunson arrived together, having travelled down from Alex's ironworks in Pittsburgh, and they chatted away merrily with Rushbourne and Roach. Enjoying the fine food and wine on offer, the men from the group mingled with the other notable attendees, including Russell Randolph-Smith and his socialite wife – the impressive guest list read like a who's who of America's upper crust.

Δ

The final arrival of the evening stood spinning the invitation that bore his name, AJ Harris, within his hands. He had debated at some length whether or not to attend the party, and had been mightily tempted to follow the Roberts family's example and decline the invitation. But ultimately Andrew was far too business-minded to stay away – and, more importantly, still not rich enough to snub those who did not fall into his way of thinking.

As he made his way up the stairs to the first floor, he was feeling slightly perplexed by the greeting at the entrance and trying to fathom why Worthington would have an immobilised child opening the doors for all his guests? Consequently, when he walked into the dining room, his head was somewhat in a spin, which was not helped by the well-spoken hullabaloo that assailed his ears. He quickly scanned his surroundings for an ally, but his attention was struck by *another* infirm child, this one wearing some sort of mechanical apparatus around his legs and assisting with pouring out a cup of tea.

What is this place?

Lost in a fit of bewilderment and with his guard severely down, he did not notice Alex Macdonald spot him from afar and hurry over, leaping at the chance to engage with his associate, with whom he had not spoken, since their last social engagement at Brunson's island.

"Good to see you, old sport!" Macdonald boomed in a manner to imitate AJ's father, but only left him feeling more sick to the stomach, than had he not approached at all.

"And you," came the tepid reply from Andrew, who refused to look the Scot in the eye, having heard about his blossoming partnership with Brunson and Sykes.

Ever the optimistic, Alex tried again.

"How's business?" he asked, though he was picking up on the undercurrent of awkwardness in the situation.

"Not bad," AJ replied, keeping his gaze fixed firmly ahead. "And you?"

"Things... are... going well," Alex said, his voice strained, underplaying his success.

Then silence filled the space between them, and Macdonald tried to think of something to keep the conversation rolling.

He could not help but be saddened by Harris's current stance, which was in such contrast to their meeting earlier in the year. But before either of them could initiate the next move, AJ suddenly staggered forward.

"Andrew!" Jack grandly announced. "Good to see you."

Brunson had discretely wormed his way around the room, having spotted the men chatting, and startled AJ with a firm slap on the back - which was how he liked to greet all his adversaries, in an effort to put them instantly on the back foot.

Andrew to his credit, had managed somehow, not to return that slap. And he stood there waiting for whatever challenge Jack was itching to deliver, knowing this conversation would be a clear test of his mettle.

"So where's our friend Mr Roberts?" Brunson wanted to know.

"Away on other business, unfortunately," was all the explanation AJ offered, having decided to keep his replies to a minimum.

"So it's not because he didn't get his little bridge plan passed by Rushbourne then?" Jack said sarcastically with a menacing smirk.

AJ remained steadfast. "That, I wouldn't know."

"Well, that's a shame," Brunson said disingenuously. He turned to Macdonald, who was looking increasingly uncomfortable standing beside them. "Although I'm not sure Alex would have had the time to help you anyway - with all we've got on together!" he suggested, staring pointedly at the Scot in a clear attempt to bring him into the fray.

"Hmmmm," Alex replied awkwardly, not actually answering the question, but doing enough to appease his business partner, who instantly followed up in his usual haughty manner.

"Exactly!" Jack patted Macdonald on the back, then turned to AJ. "Alex is far too busy building the Transcontinental with me. Over a thousand miles of railroad across our great and splendid land!" he gloated, waving his hands animatedly above his head.

At this, Harris turned his gaze to Macdonald and stared at him in disbelief. *Are you actually prepared to do business with this posturing specimen of a man?*

Alex read the sentiment in AJ's eyes and hung his head, feeling like a child being toyed over by two rival groups in the playground. But before the conversation could continue, Christopher Worthington called the attendees to attention. At the front of the room he had climbed upon a dining chair, and with his butler at his side, keeping him from teetering over, he peered down upon his guests and launched into a speech.

"Ladies and gentlemen, many thanks for such a wonderful turnout this evening," he began in the jolliest of moods. "Now, I know you will be eager to know why there are a number of children helping around my house this evening..."

"We did wonder, Christopher!" came the affable heckle from amongst the crowd, causing a stir of hoarse laughter around the room.

"Well, if I may, I would like to invite you to meet Doctor Maximus Blackman," he announced. "C'mon, Max, up you come. Get him a chair, man..."

A slightly embarrassed-looking Max made his way through the hordes and climbed onto the chair set beside Worthington.

"This man here, ladies and gentlemen, is responsible for all the apparatus you see on the children around you today," Worthington revealed.

The guests looked around at the children in the room, some of whom had come in from helping out in other parts of the house. There were ten in total, each in metal apparatus of some sort to help with a deformity or disability.

"Hear! Hear!" commended one of the wealthy guests, and support rang out for Worthington's cause.

The host smiled at their kindness, and then he became overcome with emotion and seemingly struggling to continue. But gazing over to his wife for support, she smiled and nodded to him, and he steeled himself to go on. "Max is currently working on ground-breaking treatment for our little Alice to help with her curved spine," he explained, as his wife wrapped her arms around their daughter. "And we are hopeful she will be walking by next summer," he announced proudly.

At this, his well-to-do guests broke out in deafening applause, grinning at one another as if it were their child who had just potentially been cured. Joining in with clapping, Harris let his gaze rove around the room to observe the children once again, and inadvertently locked eyes with Macdonald, who had been straining for his attention.

We should catch up again sometime soon, mouthed the Scot, but AJ quickly reverted to staring forwards before gently lifting his head; leaving Macdonald to wonder whether his suggestion had been approved or had fallen on deaf ears?

"So I suppose you'll be wondering what this has to do with you," Worthington continued as the commotion settled down. "Well, I would like to announce that, thanks to President Rushbourne, I have been commissioned to build an orthopaedic hospital, right here in New York, and I will be requiring a number of benefactors to help make that dream a reality."

The room exploded once more into clapping, this time aimed generously in the direction of the president. Only one person present was unable to applaud as she would wish: Russell Randolph-Smith's wife, Anna, who was standing next to one of the children, doing her utmost to hold back tears.

Feeling an obligation to end his poor wife's state of suffering, Russell called out loudly, in his ever-so-posh voice, "Worthington, this is indeed a worthy cause. Any child born with such a poor start in life must be restored and made into an active citizen. I, for one, shall help you in your work - just say how much and you shall have it?" He reached into his jacket pocket, pulled out his wallet and waved it high above the crowd.

That did it: within moments Christopher's guests were rushing forward, wishing to outdo their contemporaries as they announced their intention to contribute generously; leaving the host to smile broadly at the success of his fundraiser, knowing all too well that Randolph-Smith's donation alone would likely have been enough to finance the project in full.

AJ, however, realising his allies were all at home, decided sensibly to make his excuses and leave while he was still ahead. He walked over to Worthington, graciously thanked him for the invitation and promised to advance his contribution over the coming days. "You can be guaranteed of that," Harris sincerely assured his host, and received a warm and grateful handshake in response. It was only Russell Randolph-Smith, looking on, who scoffed at the lack of payment, for he did not have faith that AJ's promise would be forthcoming.

Across the room, Rushbourne and Roach were also watching the exchange with interest and feeling their eyes burning into the back of his neck, AJ turned and saw them, and then walked over, feeling he should politely acknowledge them before his departure. "Good to see you again, President Rushbourne," he said.

Benjamin returned the greeting with a light nod of the head; a gesture he had increasingly adopted since taking over the top job, feeling words should now be a privilege.

"I must dash, though," Harris added politely, before turning to make his exit.

"Be great to see Stephen and Alfred at some point!" the president called out, and AJ halted to acknowledge his comment with a respectful nod in recognition.

"I'll make sure to let them know," he said, before continuing his progression out of the room and back down towards the front doors.

Smiling generously at the little girl in the wheeled chair, he wished her and her mother well, and then stepped out onto the stone steps and peered down to the dimly lit street below. A thick fog was descending over the rooftops, sinking down to cover the super-rich folk of Manhattan, making their way home to their mansions. So pulling his coat tightly around himself to fend off the bitter cold, AJ walked down to the pavement, thinking about his evening. While on the one hand it had been frustrating, considering the hostilities with Brunson and what would have to be, a lost ally in Macdonald; on the other, it had been a real eye-opener, and seeing the children had deeply humbled him. He took a deep breath of icy-cold air into his lungs and considered that his world was a great place. His obsession with creating a business empire to eclipse his father's still burned bright inside, but for tonight he was going to relax, go see his lovely Maria, and for once just enjoy the simple little pleasures of life.

Chapter 21: Back from the Cold

Δ

1866 was ushered in as the Chinese Year of the Red Fire Dog, and with a new year came a fresh wave of optimism for each and every member of the group. Profound in their belief, that this was going to be *their* year.

During the winter and spring, Brunson and Macdonald pushed ahead with their plans to connect the rail lines of St Louis and Kansas City, with the financial backing of Sykes, whom Macdonald was pressured to utilise for all his funding needs. The splendid new railroad was connected by several spectacular bridges, and each new section was opened to wild fanfare as thousands of Americans rode the line for the first time, and whereupon the cities and towns through which it ran grew in both business and population.

Meanwhile, Harris devoted his efforts to developing the oil refining business, while at the same time offering assistance to the Roberts family where and when he could. Oliver fully amalgamated his brother's smaller oil refinery into Cunningham & Adams, and the gifted chemist continued to innovate, making them even more efficient and ever more profitable still. Yet rather than sitting back on his laurels and enjoying the spoils of his hard work, Oliver aggressively re-invested the profits, and just as planned, he integrated barrel makers and plumbers into the business, which reduced their costs by over two-thirds. With the dream of vertical and horizontal integration starting to take shape, Cunningham & Adams were able to undercut the market and drive a number of their weaker competitors out of business. Oliver also proudly made good on his promise to pay AJ back his initial investment, while at the same time not seeking a single alteration to the share distribution, which gained him even more favour with his benefactor, now a firmly established friend.

Elsewhere, Stephen and Alfred Roberts remained disassociated from the group. Pushing ahead with their own plans The Commander blindly purchased watered-down, illegitimate shares issued by Stride and marketed by Nelson Allen and Big Jim Diamond, all the while completely unaware of the illicit scam into which he was being drawn. Over the course of six months he purchased twenty thousand new shares at a cost of over two million dollars, content in his belief that he was making good progress and would soon have full control of the Erie Railroad.

Christopher Worthington spent the first half of the year building New York's orthopaedic hospital, while Dr Blackman continued to rehabilitate his daughter and alleviate most of her ailments, as well as some of his son's respiratory issues. With his boy's newfound enthusiasm for outdoor activities, Worthington took a hunting trip with him as spring approached, exploring the Black Hills at Standing Rock in North and South Dakota.

Over in Washington, meanwhile, President Rushbourne had been upsetting as many people as possible, not out of spite but simply because of his disagreeable style of decision-making that ultimately pleased no one other than himself. At Collins' behest, Walter Dixon attempted to force through Congress an extension to the Freedmen's Bureau, just as Brown had instructed, however, the president vetoed it, leaving the future of the Freedmen in jeopardy once again. Dixon had wrongly assumed he had won the heart and mind of Rushbourne, who had granted him an audience on several occasions and given all the signs that he agreed with the plan, but clearly had other ideas. Benjamin's actions alienated him from the radical factions of the party, but he deemed them unimportant compared with the moderates, whose approval he actually hoped to court with his decision.

In the months after the Bureau veto, Dixon tried again, this time submitting a Civil Rights Bill and ingeniously securing the backing of his moderate colleagues during the build-up. But the president vetoed the Bill!

Appalled, however, by his decision, Congress overruled the presidential veto for the first time in US history and passed the Bill, against the president's will.

Buoyed on by the success of defeating the president's veto, Dixon decided to push again for an extension of the Bureau, and for the second time in as many months, Congress went against Benjamin's wishes. By the end of

June, when Senators from his home State endorsed the Fourteenth Amendment against his pleas, it had become all too apparent that Rushbourne's support was not only dwindling in Washington but seemingly all across America – just in time for Brown to return from his reconnaissance mission down south.

Δ

As he walked through the presidential mansion, the war general chatted cheerfully with every member of staff he passed. Having not seen him for many months, they were overjoyed at his return, and strangely, so was the president.

"Richard!" Rushbourne gushed as Brown entered the Oval Office. He stepped up out of his seat to personally greet his colleague. "How are you, my friend?" he questioned, smiling graciously.

Walking hesitantly across the room, Brown was somewhat puzzled by the president's eagerness to welcome him, especially considering their last meeting. Yet Benjamin was genuinely pleased to see the war general return, deeming him a loyal friend in comparison to the vultures, currently circling around his head.

The two men shook hands, and then assumed the usual positions: Rushbourne seated behind the desk and Brown placed subordinately before him.

"Well, it's certainly good to be back," Brown replied heartily, placing his rucksack down by his chair with several thick reports protruding visibly out the top. "And how's the Economic Development Plan coming on?" he enquired keenly, however, the plan was the furthest thing from Benjamin's mind.

"Ah, yes, I've left all of that with Roach," he said dismissively, before getting to his own agenda. "Now, I'm glad you're back – just in time, as I need you to accompany me on a series of public speeches... you know, drum up some support for the elections."

Brown leaned back in his chair to consider the oddness of the request. He could not understand why such a lazy man as Rushbourne would wish to campaign for mid-term elections, when not a single president in history had ever trodden that path. Yet while swilling the notion around his head, the war general suddenly recalled what his good friend George Collins always advocated: *Keep your friends close, but your enemies even closer.*

So without further deliberation, Brown graciously accepted the president's request, intrigued to be at his side for this trip and find out just what Rushbourne was up to.

Smiling at Brown's confirmation, the president then sought to get back to his work.

Brown, meanwhile, stayed seated.

Staring at the crown of his colleagues head bobbing up and down before him, he wondered just how long Rushboune could continue with his ignorance. Several seconds later and Brown had found out his answer. So he rose from his chair and made his way to the door, but hesitated with the handle in his hand and stared pensively back at the president: he was still waiting for him to mention the reason he had sent Brown down south in the first place. But Rushbourne was blissfully oblivious, so content was he in having secured the services of his war general, and so Brown was forced to reach into his bag, pull out the reports and hold them aloft into the air.

"Did you want to see these at all?"

"Yes, oh God, yes, of course I do" Benjamin said swiftly, not wanting to upset his chaperone. "Just leave them there," he instructed, pointing to the edge of his desk.

Wholly unimpressed, Richard marched slowly across the hardwood floor while staring intensely at the president, before placing the hefty bundle of papers amongst a raft of other documents, scattered untidily across the desk. Unsure as to whether Rushbourne would ever read the reports or not, he forced a tactful smile before turning around to make his way out of the office.

Δ

Departing their catch-up even more confused than when he entered, as well as being irritated by the president's snub, Richard decided to check on his good friend George Collins, to get his take on the recent events. Finding his associate in the middle of business with another of their colleagues, Brown respectfully waited his turn, leaning happily against the open doorframe. As soon as George noticed his arrival however, he speedily wrapped up his meeting in order to speak with his long-absent friend.

"Richard! Great to have you back," Collins said, hurrying Brown into his office the moment their co-worker was gone. "And not a minute too soon!" he declared, before closing his door and scurrying back round to his desk.

"I believe we may have a lot to catch up on," Brown said, staring knowingly at George.

"Will you sit?" Collins gestured, towards the empty seat.

"Shall we... take a walk instead?" Brown suggested, raising an eyebrow and dropping his head forward slightly to signal his intentions.

George didn't need a second clue to deduce the war general's inference. And leaving the presidential mansion on the south side of the building, they decided it was probably wise to stretch their legs somewhat further than the main grounds this time, so made their way along 15th Street NW.

When they arrived at the Washington Monument, they stood with their backs against the half-completed memorial and took a moment to admire the beauty of the midday sun shining on the calm waters of the Tidal Basin and Potomac River before them. Surrounded by what was still a building site, with numerous timber-framed shacks that had been decommissioned alongside the project, the barely completed obelisk provided a poignant backdrop to their situation, and mirrored heart-achingly Brown's sentiment about their current state of affairs.

With their privacy secured, Richard informed his close ally of Rushbourne's plan to embark upon a speaking tour. George could not quite believe the gall of the man, and he laughed disparagingly, even at the suggestion. "Are you going to go?" he enquired, leaning forward from his relaxed position to stare directly at Brown in anticipation of his reply.

"I said I would," Richard confirmed, leaving George somewhat mystified. "But I'm still trying to work out why he's asked me to attend?"

George snorted. "I think he knows his support is waning and that your image is at an all-time high. He just wants to look good in the papers, standing next to you!" He leaned back against the monument and shook his head in disgust at the debacle.

Brown had not fully appreciated just how well the past ten months had served him. While his sole focus had been on accomplishing the mission he had been sent on, the war general had unintentionally won the respect and confidence of all the southern state leaders. Not only that, but he had also gained an insight into how the country was running, on a day-to-day basis, outside of the north-eastern enclaves, from where most of his contemporaries did not dare to stray. He had returned to Washington with a far deeper understanding of America's needs, better than anyone else in the country, and the fact that Rushbourne completely missed this was just another mistake to add to his long list of blunders.

Now, a jolt of elation flowed through Richard at the thought that Benjamin's star may well be fading. "Do you think he's feeling the pressure?" he asked.

"Most certainly," George replied emphatically, and he chuckled away thinking about some of the events his close friend had missed. "He even threatened to remove me from office! But maybe that was because he heard about my meeting with Harris?" he mused.

"What meeting?!" the war general asked at once.

"I met with Andrew Harris in Manhattan at his request," George informed him. "He seemed particularly dismayed with Rushbourne, and went so far as to say that it should be you who is running the country instead!" he revealed, to the surprise of his friend.

"I wonder if he's having issues?" Richard supposed as he stared into the distance. Then he wondered whether all the members of the group were struggling with their plans as well.

"It certainly seemed that way," Collins confirmed with a gentle nod of acknowledgment as Richard ran the information around his brain and paused to consider their next move.

"We'll have to arrange to go meet him and get to the bottom of what's going on," he said. "And we need to figure out a way to protect your position as well, George."

It was like they had never been apart.

And both men smiled warmly at each other, glad to be back in one another's company, and suitably reassured that

Brown's long overdue return would now enable them to positively influence the future direction of the country, just as they should have been doing all along. In tandem, they pushed off from their leant-back position against the stone needle behind. Then Brown turned around to lovingly pat the monument like an old friend, and reassure it that one day, just like the country he loved so dear, *it too* would be completed in accordance with Lincoln's vision.

Δ

Chapter 22: Swing Around the Circle

Δ

Setting off from Washington under clear skies on a splendid August day, Benjamin was in high spirits, feeling confident he could regain some of his popularity and salvage his presidency from the jaws of defeat. Brown, meanwhile, sat beside him in their carriage simply wondering which Rushbourne was going to turn up today and rather looking forward to observing the spectacle at close quarters. They boarded a private train that would take them up the country, through Baltimore, Philadelphia and New York, then advancing west to Columbus and Chicago, before arriving into their penultimate destination, St Louis.

The talks along the way received a lukewarm reception, however, and had to be cut short on a number of occasions due to unrest. The president persistently misjudging his audience, he managed to offend those gathered with his uncouth comments. Due to the calamitous nature of the speaking tour, the governor and City Council of Chicago actually cancelled Rushbourne's public address before he even arrived. And so battling his eroding confidence, the president felt increasingly apprehensive before taking to the podium each night.

St Louis, however, was where Rusbourne's fortunes began to change, and the atmosphere was altogether more positive, in the main due to the fact that the town was enjoying a period of prosperity under Rushbourne's presidency and further to Brunson's railroad extension. Honoured to receive the president, the mayor had arranged for a banquet to be held in Rushbourne's honour in the hours preceding his speech. The feast was to be held in Missouri's most magnificent building, the county courthouse. Each of its four wings connected in the middle under a cast-iron dome, modelled on St Peter's Basilica, which could be seen from miles around in the low-lying cityscape. The glistening white-stone building was somewhat reminiscent of the presidential mansion, and sat in all its glory just a stone's throw away from the banks of the Mississippi to the east.

Having been kindly provided with black dinner suits, pressed white shirts and dickie bows, Brown and Rushbourne were differentiated only by the military badges that the war general sewed proudly atop his shoulders. Making their way through the entrance, they were escorted up to a make-shift dining hall on the second floor of the building, and after graciously taking their seats - were instantly surrounded by people encircling the table.

Have they never seen a president before? For once, both men from Washington, were thinking exactly the same thing.

But these were not invited guests, and instead they found themselves hounded by Missourians who had put on their best attire and come to the courthouse simply hoping to orchestrate a 'moment' with the two influential White House men.

As the early evening dinner progressed and an ever-increasing number of patrons queued by their side to divulge their 'business venture', Rushbourne was placatory. "Leave your message with the Mansion House," he told them. "I promise to look into it upon my return." Though of course he had little intention of doing so.

The constant interjections and seeming success of the evening were, however, particularly starting to irritate the war general, who had become rather accustomed to seeing his adversary falter. This latest stream of respect and reverence was now becoming somewhat nauseating. And so, as the main meal came to an end and hundreds of pieces of cutlery were being dutifully cleared from the tables, Richard suddenly recollected Lincoln's teachings from Machiavelli's *The Prince,* and embarked upon a crafty little plan of his own. Pushing his chair backwards and standing tall above the seated diners around him, the war general raised his glass of wine high into the air while instructing the waiting staff to fill up any empty glasses around him. When the entire room began to quieten, and all eyes turned to him, Brown then began his ploy. "A toast!" he announced loudly, making sure he had everyone's attention. "To our seventeenth president!"

Rapturous response broke out, along with "Hurrahs!", followed by the clinking of glasses and the knocking back of alcohol – including the president.

With the natives then expecting the war general to retake his seat, they were surprised when he instead remained standing. "To St Louis!" he called out, lifting his glass once more.

This raised an even louder response from the ecstatic locals, who at once obliged and drank another toast. With the noise building up around the room, Richard gazed down at the president to make sure he too was partaking, before shouting out again: "To the Union!"

This time, it was more of a visceral roar; and the president was becoming swept up in the exuberant mood around the room and completely forgetting that he had duties to fulfil straight after the meal had finished. Pausing for a moment while Rushbourne's glass was refilled, Richard readied himself to go again, but before he could take lead, the now-boisterous crowd took over.

"To Richard Brown!"

"To restoration!"

"To Lincoln!"

So came the toasts, while the waiters frantically dashed about to keep up with the constantly emptying glasses of those present, desperately seeking another top-up. The Lincoln toast was Brown's favourite, and he carried it out with particular fervour, knocking an entire glassful of wine down his throat. He watched on with glee, as Rushbourne tried to match him gulp for gulp, and from that point on; the declarations become more banal.

"To the railroads!"

"To liberty!"

"To our sweet Mississippi"

The heavily intoxicated assembly were having far too much of a good time to care about logic, and they knocked back mouthful after mouthful, hundreds of bottles of wine disappearing in the space of five minutes.

Finally thumping back down onto his seat, and grinning merrily to himself, Richard looked across at Rushbourne, who laughed exuberantly in his direction. The two men clinked their refilled glasses once again, almost cracking the crystal in their inebriated enthusiasm, and then finished off their drinks one last time.

Δ

With the banquet coming to an end and those in attendance beginning to file out of the dining hall, it suddenly dawned on the president that he still had a speech to deliver. But buoyed on by the reception he had received here and feeling indestructible once again, Benjamin confidently swaggered out onto the second floor rotunda, before peering wobbly down at the masses below. The spectators had now crammed into every inch of the building, creating an upswell of heat, and having had such a large amount to drink,

Rushbourne suddenly felt a little queasy and had to steady himself before speaking.

Minutes into the address and the president was already feeling triumphant - mainly because he had failed to realise that the cheers he had been hearing were not in favour of his words, but coming from the folks spilling out of the dining hall and merely continuing their merrymaking around him. In contrast, the people gathered on the levels below were slightly confused by the raptures from above and were left wondering whether this was simply one big jolly for their president, as opposed to being an important political speech. Yet spurred on by the perceived enthusiasm and his eyes too blurry to pick up anything other than quiet contentment below, Rushbourne let his tongue become more and more self-congratulatory as he rambled on, and on.

"God has chosen me to unite the people," he asserted sacrilegiously. "For this country needs a vision, and I have a plan, which I promise to deliver, and I know I will succeed," he stated, just ten minutes into the hour-long speech, by which point he had already referred to himself, well over fifty times.

With those in attendance becoming increasingly insulted by Rushbourne's self-glorification, a significant number made their way out of the building - just as Jack Brunson arrived, late, and managed to swim against the tide to find a favourable spot on the ground floor, from which he could observe the remainder of his president's speech.

"And to the congressmen and senators who oppose my Union," Rushbourne continued, jabbing his finger fanatically in the air, "let them know that *Benjamin Rushbourne shall never back down*!" He was practically foaming at the mouth; unable to appreciate the slanderous nature of his comments, he instead imagined himself akin to William Wallace as he roused the Scots into battle against the English.

With a long silence and a sense of bewilderment enveloping the room, a man on the rotunda floor decided to break the deadlock. "Who are these men you speak of?" he demanded.

Rushbourne snapped back aggressively, "You know who they are." He lurched forward over the edge of the banister to try to identify the heckler. "They are the same men who want to assassinate me!"

A collective gasp echoed around the atrium, and for the first time that evening the president picked up on the charged atmosphere. Scanning more closely, the shocked faces of those gathered below, Rushbourne could only conclude that his audience must be uneducated heathens, unaware of what was actually going on in their own country. Therefore, rather than heed the warning, he pressed ahead with a foolhardy attempt to try overturn their disbelief.

"You people need to open your eyes to the atrocities caused by the meddling factions within my party. For it was they who deliberately provoked the riots in New Orleans!"

This latest outburst forced Brown to splutter out a cough, to muffle his laughter: he could not believe what he was witnessing.

For a large majority it was the final straw, and they began streaming out of the exits in disgust. However, more detrimental were those remaining, who started shouting obscenities before grabbing hold of anything not stuck down and tossing it towards the upper floors - causing the inebriated group to scuttle back swiftly into the dining room as hundreds of random objects flew across the space beneath.

Δ

As the revellers waited, stuck in the dining room, for the last of the stragglers to disappear, the mood changed from over-exuberant celebration to muttered discussions about the events that had just occurred. Tentatively walking over to Brown and Rushbourne, who had purposely placed themselves in a corner of the room so as to avoid any awkward conversation, the state governor offered his most sincere apologies. "I'm awfully sorry about that, chaps," he said kindly. "Very disappointing that one or two hecklers can ruin it for everyone."

It was a generous effort to gloss over the cataclysmic outcome of the speech and detach Rushbourne from any blame. However, the president was in no mood to reply. Bent over with his elbows on his knees and hands clasped under his chin, he sat in silent contemplation - yet with the frenzied nature of events and the level of alcohol swishing around in his blood, he was struggling to work out, just quite what had happened.

"Thank you," Brown replied thoughtfully on Benjamin's behalf, while the governor struggled for what to suggest next as he fretted over the president's evident distress.

Seizing on an idea that popped into his head, and inspired by Brown's lead earlier, he waved over a waiter, who arrived with a bottle of whisky in his hand. With Rushbourne glancing up and showing no indication of refusal, the governor instructed the waiter to pour a double measure for the president, to help drown out his sorrows.

"I'm sure it'll all blow over in the morning," the governor said in another charitable attempt to reassure Rushbourne.

However, before any further condolences could be uttered there was a loud thud on the double doors of the dining room, which began to jolt back and forth violently.

Observing the action as if in slow motion and expecting only the worst, Benjamin grabbed a hold of Brown and levered him in front of himself for protection. Bracing himself for an imminent attack, Rushbourne tightly scrunched his eyes, as the doors swung open against their hinges, and the guards dashed over to face the intruders.

"Calm down, boys - calm down!" came the call from the solitary newcomer, who strolled in with both his hands held confidently aloft.

The mayor instantly recognised the man and commanded his guards: "Stand down, men, now. Stand down - it's Jack Brunson!"

Unfettered by the approach and entirely entertained by the evening's commotion, Jack swiped a glass of wine from a passing waiter's tray without stopping to acknowledge the boy, and made a beeline for the president, with a gigantic smirk upon his face. "Well, that was entertaining!" he said jokingly as he strode right up to Rushbourne.

But so relieved was he that the entrant was not one of the unruly mob, Rushbourne completely overlooked Brunson's somewhat tactless comment – unlike Brown.

"I wouldn't call that entertainment!" he decried, shaking his head in dismay. But Brunson had little regard for the war general, now that he had the president's ear.

"Those fools don't have a clue what's going on in the real world," he surmised, disregarding the fact that he was standing next to the mayor, who counted those "fools" as his constituents, and that paid to ride Jack's railroads on a daily basis. "And don't worry if they riot," he added. "I'll pay one half of the working class to kill the other!"

Brown sat aghast, absolutely appalled with the suggestion; he had never witnessed Jack so crude. But with Brunson echoing the same sentiment the president had felt earlier, Rushbourne heard his words and suddenly felt exonerated.

"That must be it," Benjamin said, the cogs in his mind slowly whirring. "They just don't appreciate what's going on!" he concluded.

Lifted to his feet, the president exchanged a mutual grin of self-assurance with Jack, and shook his hand with good merit for his wise and timely counsel.

Looking on meanwhile, Brown could not quite believe the stupidity of Rushbourne in considering such nonsense and failing to grasp that his level of intoxication was the real reason his evening had run such a bumpy course. Not that he was going to mention such a thought, and instead let the moment pass.

Brunson, then seeking a private moment of his own, had affectionately placed his arm around the president - in the process excluding the war general - and muttered quietly in Rushbourne's ear, "Can we have a minute? I have some business to discuss."

"Of course, of course," Rushbourne all too eagerly agreed. "What can I do for you?" he said, smiling fondly at his friend.

"Maybe we should take the conversation somewhere a little more... private," Brunson said while scanning the room and gently manoeuvred the president towards a side door he'd spotted in the distance.

His plan, however, was thwarted, when on the way, Benjamin called over his shoulder, "Can you come too, Richard?"

It was all Brown could do not to laugh as he replied, "Of course, Benjamin," and he followed on, as Brunson kept his steely eyes fixed firmly on the route ahead, annoyed that

Brown would now be witness, to whatever business was to unfold this night.

They crammed themselves into a tiny office, off the main hall, which was usually reserved for local judges to store their clothing. It was all of ten feet wide, but Brunson wasn't concerned about their comfort, and so carried on regardless. Opening a roll-top desk in the corner, he pulled out his own map of America and laid it out on the desktop. The map showed his current railroad connections and was annotated with several scribblings and a number of asterisks adjacent Erie Railroad.

Running his index finger along the map, Jack outlined his next step. "I'll push west, to Salt Lake City, and then on to Sacramento," he detailed. Then he wasted no time in getting to his point. "This will be the culmination of the Transcontinental Railroad - providing a single connection across America, all the way from east to west," he stated proudly.

Both of the men from Washington stared in silence, while scanning the map. Rushbourne was practically salivating, and even Brown could not deny that while Brunson's first approach that evening was not exactly to his liking, the man's work thus far and his future plans were certainly highly impressive.

"So, can I count on your support?" Brunson quickly asked.

And without a second's thought or hesitation, Rushbourne said, "Of course! This is wonderful! Exactly what our nation needs." Then he applauded and shook Jack's hand in gratitude, like it was he, who was doing the favour.

Brown meanwhile sat surprised by the ease with which Brunson had secured endorsement for such a grand plan from the president. However, not having been present for any of the previous proposals, he could only assume this to be the standard practice for bidding: which could only be good for the group. His overarching feeling, at the end of a tumultuous evening was pleasure at the thought that Rushbourne appeared to be taking the Development Plan more seriously than he had originally thought. And he went to bed with a grin of content, knowing Lincoln's dream was moving ahead.

When the men from Washington woke up bleary-eyed the next morning, however, it soon became apparent that all was not well. And Brunson's interpretation of the turmoil that occurred at the courthouse was indeed, far and wide of the mark. Word had quickly spread of Rushbourne's "Disastrous Night in St Louis", and the press were making all they could from the evening's events.

Yet the worst was still to come.

Hecklers violently forced the president off stage during his final speech in Indianapolis, and as he and Brown hid in the backstage area, rioters began fighting one another in the streets surrounding the building. The clashes lasted several hours and culminated in the death of one of the protestors - leaving Brown to reflect that Brunson's threat the previous night, to set working-class man against working-class man, had been eerily prophetic. "The Swing", in reality, had proved a disaster for the president, and what was supposed to have drastically shored up his flailing support had only left him in an inferior position, than had he not left Washington at all.

Δ

Chapter 23: Plans Ahoy!

Δ

Over the following months, Rushbourne became increasingly paranoid about whom he could trust and retreated to an ever decreasing circle. He continued to have run-ins with Collins and threatened to get rid of him on several occasions, but Brown managed to convince the president otherwise, meaning George maintained his position, but only by the skin of his teeth.

True to his word, Collins arranged a meeting with Harris to be chaired in Manhattan, away from the glare of Washington, and more importantly, Rushbourne and Roach. Arriving at Hanover Square on a chilly February morning, both Brown and Collins were swiftly greeted by Maria, who had been standing on the pavement awaiting their arrival and she ushered them in discreetly. Then she led them into the banking hall which had been cleared of all appointments for the day, and towards the back office, as usual, where Harris was waiting, this time alongside the Roberts men.

"Stephen, Alfred - wonderful to see you again!" said Brown warmly as he manoeuvred into the cramped room.

"Good to see you too," Stephen enthused, leaping up from his seat to greet his old friend with a hearty handshake. "Thank God you're back!" he added emphatically, raising smiles all around the room.

The men quickly settled into their seats, in expectation of Brown beginning the proceedings. But The Commander had never been one for standing on ceremony, and he had been waiting for over a year to have this discussion.

Blunt as a hammer, then, he got straight to the point. "So how are we going to get rid of Rushbourne and install you as president instead?"

The other men chuckled at The Commander's belligerent nature, however Stephen sat unmoved. And it was clear from the seriousness of his tone, that he demanded some form of response.

"I don't think we can just get rid of him," Richard began to explain pragmatically, but Stephen jumped straight back down his throat.

"Well why the hell not?!" came the irritated yelp as the old man became increasingly animated in his chair, banging his hands on the armrests.

"Because the way he's going, we won't need to wait too long for him to dig his own grave," the war general advised.

While Collins agreed with his friend's supposition, he could not help but cheekily supplement his response. "Well, maybe just a gentle nudge though?!"

Brown shook his head while smiling broadly at the somewhat unhelpful remark. Then a thoughtful expression came into his eyes. “It’s strange,” he said. “I know full well why my colleague to my right” – he gestured towards Collins – “has a bone to pick with Rushbourne. But why so you chaps?”

As Brown swept a hand around to indicate the men from Manhattan, they momentarily froze in shock at the question. Not wishing to reveal the split forming within the group, they instead concentrated their attack upon Rushbourne’s lack of support. “He’s not exactly been forthcoming in agreeing any of our plans,” AJ revealed.

Brown was puzzled, at once recollecting the ease with which Jack had his plan passed by Benjamin – Richard had seen it with his own eyes? But before he could mention that fact, The Commander piped up again.

“And I just want to see you as President Richard Brown. You’re the better man for the damn job!” he declared emotively.

“Which is exactly why I can’t be seen to publicly eject him,” Brown replied shrewdly. “It wouldn’t look well on me and so would be self-defeating.”

“Humph,” said Stephen, with a grimace of annoyance.

But he knew that Brown was right. They all did.

Richard’s slow and calculated approach was clearly for the best, and there was nothing to do but slump back in their chairs and try to curb their thirst for blood.

With an impasse having been reached and a silence pervading the room, Alfred Roberts broke the deadlock, when he enquired innocently, "Why, is it that *you* dislike Rushbourne so much, George?"

The men from Washington turned their heads to scan one another. This time they were the ones under the spotlight, and with a decision to make on how much to reveal. With the men from Manhattan on the edge of their seats, a rather embarrassed Brown informed them: "Rushbourne has been threatening to remove George from his post."

The men from Manhattan looked shocked, apart from Stephen, who responded instantly. "Well, we can't have our George ousted from his position!" he said, smiling graciously at Collins. Having established that George shared his distain of Rushbourne, Stephen was keen to help. "We need to arrange some sort of protection for him."

For some time the men sat in deep contemplation, gazing around at one another, seeking a solution. Occasionally one would begin to mumble an idea, before retracting it out of hand. Then, all of a sudden, it looked like AJ might just have it. "What if we could get a law passed that stopped Rushbourne sacking *anyone* from his Cabinet - unless say, he received support from Congress? That way both George *and* Richard would be protected."

His colleagues took a moment to mull over the brainwave, and then heads began to nod vigorously, as joy washed across their faces.

"What a splendid idea!" Brown commended, almost in disbelief at the perfection of the idea.

With a sense of achievement now filling the room, as well as the stifling heat from the lively conversation, and the number of bodies squeezed into AJ's office, their host decided a break for lunch might well be in order. Manoeuvring past his associates, Harris opened the door. And as the air breezed in and instantly cooled the room, he was about to call out to Maria for confirmation that the food had arrived, when he saw that she had already organised everything in the banking hall - the table, beautifully arranged and laden with food, was ready and waiting.

Thank you, he mouthed, and her smile dazzled him from all the way across the hall.

Δ

As the men from Washington regaled Alfred with tales of their Union crusades aboard the Roberts family flotilla, Stephen took the opportunity to isolate Harris, so he could seek his private counsel.

"Would you take a look into some shares I've recently purchased?" he asked while gnawing incessantly on a turkey leg. "I expected to have assumed control of the company by now. I just don't understand what's going on," he confessed to AJ, who could feel in his gut, exactly where this was leading.

"What's the name of the stock?" Andrew enquired considerately, so as to avoid placing Alfred in the firing line for refusing his assistance in the first place.

"Erie Railroad," said The Commander, just as AJ had suspected. But by now he had invested more than five million dollars in illegitimate shares, on top of his already sizable three-million-dollar equity stake in the company.

"Of course I'll look into it, Stephen. Anything for you," AJ said obligingly, and the elder Roberts sent an appreciative smile his way.

With business seemingly taken care of for now, and having finished their last delicious mouthfuls of food, Brown and Collins thanked Maria for the lunch before saying their goodbyes, and making their way towards the exit. However, just as they were about to cross the threshold, Richard turned back for some parting words.

"And I'll take a look into that East River project for you, Alfred. See what I can do," he offered kindly – leaving The Commander to stare, aghast, at his son, who had clearly been working his audience, rather than simply listening to their tales.

Chapter 24: The Sack Race

Δ

True to their word, Brown and Collins returned to Washington and without hesitation secured the services of Walter Dixon to pass a Bill in Congress to safeguard all of Lincoln's Cabinet members. Dixon had been a lieutenant colonel during the Civil War and had led his troops into battle alongside Richard, so they had established their friendship in the entrenchment of battle. Having also studied in law, Dixon had a similar disposition to Collins, and as a militant intellectual he stood on principle as someone who was unwilling to back down from what he believed to be fair and correct. The three of them now forming a formidable team, patrolling the halls of power around Washington.

After lobbying fellow senators and submitting his Tenure of Office Act, Walter was not at all surprised when Rushbourne vetoed the Bill. However, once again the president's will was overruled, and the law was ratified on 3rd March 1867. Incensed by the actions forced against him and by being constantly overruled, Benjamin was not prepared to be shackled by his contemporaries any longer and instructed a firm of lawyers to analyse every inch of the Act. With the

Bill having been swiftly scripted and rushed through Congress to protect George, the lawyers picked up on an ambiguity within the wording, which opened the door to doubts over the Act's validity and effectiveness as a tool to use against Rushbourne.

Feeling self-assured once again and desperately seeking an opportunity to demonstrate his power, Rushbourne decided that with the Senate closing for a five-month break in August, it was time to pounce and make his move. He marched commandingly across the presidential mansion towards the office of George Collins, but found his target deep in discussion with Brown. He halted abruptly by the doorway as the men turned to look at him. "Richard, I did not expect you here," Rushbourne began. He had hoped Collins would be on his own so he could try bully him without protection. "Nevertheless," he said after a quick ponder, "it's probably quite handy that you are." And as Richard and George looked at one another in confusion, the president smiled disingenuously and announced, "George shall no longer be required as part of my Cabinet, so you can pack your things and leave."

"But Benjamin, are you sure?" Brown appealed softly, playing his role as Rushbourne's close confidant, now with such consummate ease.

"I know we've discussed this before, Richard, but you won't convince me again," Rushbourne said, before adding resolutely, "Mr Collins cannot be trusted!"

Glaring at the president from behind his desk with a look of hatred in his eyes, George considered submitting his defence. But then, remembering that Rushbourne was falling directly into their trap, he dropped his head and grinned ruthlessly, out of sight. Not wishing to ruin the opportunity, he simply reached into his drawers and began pulling out his effects and calmly placed them on the top of his desk, in preparation for his departure.

Realising that tomorrow he would be jobless ought to have worried him; however, all Collins could hear were screams of *Hara-Kiri* running around his head, bringing a broad smile across his face. He was more than prepared to fall on his own sword if it meant taking Rushbourne down with him, and so he merrily carried on with his packing while his colleagues spoke over his head.

"What evidence do you have that he cannot be trusted?" Brown asked on behalf of Collins, who turned his glare towards his friend.

What on earth are you doing, helping him?!

He had expected Richard to simply stand back and watch the fireworks ensue when the Senate reconvened in January.

"I've been reliably informed that Mr Collins" – he jabbed his index finger violently in George's direction – "has been meeting with members of the group without my authority," he announced. "So what do you think to *that,* Richard?!"

Staring at Collins with a panicked look of disbelief on his face, Brown anxiously considered whether the president was referring to Collins' original meeting at St Pauls Church or their most recent meeting with AJ and the Commander, which would mean he himself was in the firing line as well.

"I... I'm not sure what to say," he squirmed.

"What would he be doing meeting them?" Rushbourne insisted forcefully, demonstrating his knowledge of only the first meeting. "I don't like it at all, Richard, and *I smell a rat!*"

Brown tried to look sombre as he inwardly breathed a sigh of relief. Collins, meanwhile, had been happily playing along with the pretence to this point, but he was not best pleased at being labelled vermin, and he halted his fumbling to stare directly into the president's eyes.

Detecting the resentment and recognising he had overstepped the line, Benjamin braced himself for the outbreak of conflict. However, George had no intention of becoming physical, and simply slung his bag over his shoulder and began marching towards the exit. Quickly stepping aside, Rushbourne allowed George to pass and looked on as he whistled merrily to himself while waltzing down the corridor, in a deliberate display to unnerve and bewilder his adversary.

Back in George's office, Brown decided to craftily ascertain the president's next move. "But what about the Tenure of Office Act?" he asked, apparently innocuously.

"What about it?!" Rushbourne snapped vehemently, still flustered from the exchange with Collins. "I don't even think it's enforceable," he added authoritatively.

"And who'll be secretary of war now you've removed George?" was Brown's next question, and this time he had the president tongue tied.

Having stormed in on a whim to remove Collins, Benjamin hadn't actually considered his plans thereafter. He stared around the vacant office, and several faces flashed through his mind, but he rejected them all out of hand. Then the president rested his gaze upon his colleague, standing right in his eyeline, before him. "Well, why don't you do it?" he nodded.

"Me!" Richard recoiled in surprise and the cogs in his head turned lightning quick as he attempted to analyse whether that was a good outcome. "I can," he replied slowly. "If you're sure. But it could only be on a temporary basis." He figured, settling on a halfway position which would allow him more time to think about the best way to play the situation.

"So it's agreed then," Rushbourne happily concluded, and he nodded in appreciation and offered his hand to shake Brown's. "I'm sure you'll do a splendid job!" he told him, before making his way back to the Oval Office.

Scanning the ransacked room and considering the enormity of the events that had just unfolded, Brown flopped down into Collins's now vacant chair. Mulling the numerous possibilities, a map of America suddenly caught his eye, atop the piles of paper scattered across the desk. He discerned that the scribblings represented battle strategies he had so effectively devised with his recently dismissed colleague, and feeling in a similarly tactical position now, Brown held the map aloft and quietly considered his next move: to push them closer towards victory once again.

Δ

1868 arrived and Congress duly returned to their seats. Yet in a surprising turn of events, rather than hiding from the fact he had defected from the Tenure of Office Act, Rushbourne proudly notified the House of his decision to suspend George Collins. Within twenty-four hours of receiving the information, the Senate voted to reinstate Collins in a decisive demonstration of defiance against Benjamin's act. Complying with their command, Brown duly stood down, but the ease with which he followed their decision deeply angered the president, who expected him to stand firm and refuse.

Now losing his faith in all of those around him, Rushbourne decided to employ someone he could trust from outside the political arena, and on 23rd February, he ordered Collins to his Oval Office for round two of their feud. "Do come in – this won't take long," he said merrily, beckoning to George as he hovered in the open doorway.

"What is it now?" huffed Collins, feeling every inch superior to his hamstrung colleague, as he took a seat opposite his desk.

"You see this man...?" the president said forcefully while pointing behind George – who spun around to see the vaguely familiar face of Wheldon Baker sitting hidden behind the door. "He shall be taking your position," Rushbourne announced gladly.

Collins rolled his eyes. "Not this again!" he said insolently, shaking his head and chuckling to himself.

"Indeed, *this again*!" he replied, rising from his seat and slapping his palms firmly on the desk. "And this time you're gone for good!" Rushbourne promised.

Baker, watching over proceedings, was becoming increasingly twitchy. But Collins made sure not to move an inch as the president stood tall, towering over him, and allowed several seconds to pass so he could openly demonstrate his disobedience. Then he said plainly, "As you wish," before slowly pushing up from his chair to depart.

Sauntering towards the exit, George shook his head in dismay at Wheldon Baker, who sat nervously, clutching his leather satchel close to his beating chest. "Good luck with him," Collins advised with a mirthless laugh.

Rushbourne overheard the comment and began to search frantically in his top drawer. He snatched at the first thing to hand. "Get out of my office now!" he yelled, lurching over his desk and tossing the presidential Bible as hard as possible. It hit the closing door and rebounded, landing straight on Baker's head.

Having been alerted to the commotion in the Oval Office from along the corridor, Brown arrived outside just as Collins exited, and walked straight past his friend still shaking his head in utter amusement.

"What's going on?" Richard enquired, coming to a halt.

"Go see for yourself," George chuckled, before continuing on his way.

Entering the presidential office and finding Benjamin in a fit of rage, Brown motioned to speak, however, the president quickly overruled him. "You!" he snarled, turning his anger on the war general.

"Yes," Richard replied calmly, as he bent down to pick up the crumpled Bible and return it to the president's desk.

"Why did you step down?" Rushbourne demanded, gritting his teeth and breathing heavily down his nose in frustration.

"Because the Senate required it?" Brown reasoned.

But this only exacerbated the situation, and Benjamin continued to berate him.

"Those meddling muckrakers are not your boss, Richard – *I am*!" he spat across the desk. "But don't you worry. Baker, here, is going to take the position and do the job you should have done!" he contended, eyes wide and manic.

In the face of Benjamin's unhinged behaviour, the war general suddenly realised: all battle lines had been drawn and there was little chance of going back. In that moment, he gave up on trying to appease the president, and his strategy turned full circle. "As you wish," he said simply, unintentionally echoing Collins' earlier sentiment and stoking the paranoia of Rushbourne, who stood aghast at the comment as Brown walked silently out of the room.

Δ

Back in his office the following morning, Rushbourne sat behind his desk to undertake his work for the day. He was feeling in a much more relaxed mood than before, assured that Baker was his answer. Hearing a knock upon his half-open door, he peered up and noticed one of the mansion clerks stood waiting. At his nod, the man walked respectfully up to the president and handed him an envelope.

"Much obliged," Benjamin said pleasantly, taking hold of the unexpected delivery with a puzzled look on his face.

He reached for his letter opener and sliced the top of the casing, and then unfurled the recently stamped document, across his desk and thighs before beginning to read.

Dear President Rushbourne,

The House has considered your most recent actions, and in dismissing Mr George Collins, you have herein enacted a flagrant breach against the Tenure of Office Act, itself, a measure created to forbid any such occurrence. By those who ratified the Act comes this letter, to inform you that the House has voted, 126 votes to 47, in favour of a resolution to impeach you for your actions, of high crimes and misdemeanours.

Yours, The House of Representatives

Having slowly read through the Impeachment notice served upon him, more than several times over, Rushbourne leaned back in his chair and nonchalantly tossed the document onto his desk. Staring up longingly at the John Turnbull painting positioned above the mantelpiece, depicting the Battles of Saratoga, a devilish smile crept slowly across his face. This, he confidently considered, will be the turning point he had so desired; and he began to chortle lightly down his nose, before slamming the palm of his hand forcefully upon the document, and licking his lips at the prospect of finally proving everyone wrong.

Chapter 25: The Impeachment

Δ

With two weeks before the start of his trial, the president was determined to fight on all fronts, and true to form he was back out campaigning. However this time he was targeting fringe senators he believed could be swayed by his very simple plan: he would offer to bestow positions of power and concessions, in exchange for support in defeating the charges brought against him. Bribes, he knew, often went a long way.

Rushbourne travelled to Iowa to meet with Senator Butterfield, one of the leading moderates within the party and thus an influential ally to have on board. Sitting in his office in the centre of town, Rushbourne made his bid.

"I promise you, Henry, if you can convince your friends to acquit me, I shall visit your office once a month and provide full backing for any plans you wish to pursue in this fine city of yours - money is not an issue"

From there he made the two-hundred-and-forty mile journey south to Kansas, where he was granted an audience with Senator Butler.

"If you can guarantee your support and drum up that of others; upon acquittal I shall grant you any position of power you may desire," he bargained.

"How about if I were to be our representative in Britain?" was Butler's speedy response.

Rushbourne had not expected any such proposal. Nor did he stop to consider whether it was practical. The point of the exercise was to entice influential men into his web by readily guaranteeing to deliver on an assortment of promises; whether or not Rushbourne would actually be *able* to deliver on his promises was immaterial to him at this stage.

"Consider it done!" he told Butler emphatically, and then departed to his next port of call.

As a secondary, and less subtle tactic than personally lobbying senators, Benjamin decided that offering cold, hard cash would likely serve him well. Of course, being president, he could not be seen to offer such obvious encouragements of favour, and nor did he have personal access to the levels of funding needed. So he would need to bring in the assistance of someone who did? For some reason his mind cast back to Worthington's party, at which he had spent a good deal of time speaking with the great and good of New York. And suddenly he recalled a particularly affluent gentleman who had attended that evening, so decided to pay a visit to the wealthiest of them all – Russell Randolph-Smith.

Arriving under cover of night and wearing a full-length raincoat with the collar turned up to meet his cowboy hat, Rushbourne skulked outside the side entrance of the

Randolph-Smith House hotel, while he waited for the door to open. Russell himself ushered him in, providing his guest with safe passage away from the public's eyes, and whisked the president along the service corridor, up the private residents' steps and to his personal apartment, on the upper most, fifth floor.

"Make yourself comfortable," Randolph-Smith said kindly once they were in the front room. He walked across to his enormous drinks cabinet in the corner and took out two glasses aside a large bottle of whisky.

Rushbourne removed his soaking wet disguise and settled himself on one of the comfy sofas in front of the large open fire, and Randolph-Smith took a seat on the sofa adjacent. Placing the glasses and liquor on the table between them, and with the fire crackling away, casting a gentle glow around the room, Randolph-Smith opened up the conversation while leaning forward to pour the drinks. "To what do I owe the pleasure, good sir?" he said in his ever-so-polite and most upper-class of dialects.

"I've come to seek your help in defeating a couple of schemers who are trying to get me out of office," was how Rushbourne portrayed his side of events. "With the sole purpose of taking my post for themselves!" he declared to Randolph-Smith, who shook his head in disgust at such ungentlemanly behaviour.

"Who are these men, Benjamin?" Randolph-Smith demanded, as he sipped delicately on his whisky.

"George Collins and Walter Dixon have been plotting against me for months," Rushbourne revealed, purposely opting to omit Brown from the conversation, lest he scare Randolph-Smith off from the start. "And if they succeed then who knows what will happen to the continuation of projects such as the orthopaedic hospital?" he remarked pointedly, shrugging his shoulders and leaving Randolph-Smith to assume the rest.

The multi-millionaire, instantly took the bait.

"Well, that would just be awful!" he replied rapidly, with just the look of disgust that Rushbourne had hoped to glean.

"Exactly!" the president said and, seizing the momentum, he continued his enticement. "The only reason I removed Collins from office is that he was holding private meetings... Just think what information he could have passed on!"

"Meetings? With whom?"

"Andrew Harris."

Rushbourne had remembered Randolph-Smith's distain of AJ from that night at Worthington's fundraiser. And he was using it to make Randolph-Smith play directly into his hands.

"Well, that's an utter disgrace!" he declared, becoming increasingly animated. "And I can imagine that Harris chap lapped it up like a dog!" he blasted.

"Do you think Harris would do something like that?" said the president, feigning innocence while stoking the fire – knowing that an angry man is a man that will be called to arms.

"Of course he would! He's *new money*!" Randolph-Smith raged. Suddenly, he felt queasy at the notion of Harris becoming more successful than he. "Tell me, Benjamin, whatever can I do to assist?"

Rushbourne took a moment to casually sip on his whisky, biting lightly onto the rim of the glass to conceal his utter delight. Then he briefed Randolph-Smith about the support he had gained on his recent trips to visit senators; but inferred that there were others who may require "a level of incentive I'm unable to provide".

Russell grasped his insinuation in an instant. "And I know just the man," he replied cunningly. "Because as you will well appreciate, Benjamin, there is only a certain 'level' on which I can operate too!" he concluded, and they grinned in unison at their cunning plan.

Leaving Randolph-Smith to enact their mission, Rushbourne headed home to Washington, arriving at the presidential mansion just before daybreak. Determined to foil Harris, Randolph-Smith went straight to work, employing the services of Nelson Allen and supplying him with a bottomless pit of cash, to make sure he got the job done correctly. Nelson, affectionately known by his close friends as The Chief, was the head of the corrupt political machine in New York called Tammany Hall. He had connections to a wide range of senators, a number of whom he had helped place into power himself, and whose eternal support should be easily guaranteed.

Δ

The trial began on 5th March, but to the astonishment of everyone in the courtroom, Rushbourne was nowhere to be seen. His lawyers had decided it best he did not appear throughout any of the trial, both to demonstrate his condemnation of the whole affair, and, more importantly, to avoid him potentially exploding and compromising their defence.

The case was to be heard in the United States Senate Chamber within the Capitol Building. A large rectangular room, it contained a viewing gallery around the uppermost edges, with the senators' desks arranged on the ground floor in a semi-circular pattern, facing the front. The prosecution and defence sat on two long tables ahead of them, facing the elevated rostrum, where the judge sat to preside over events. And for the case in question, the judge was chosen to be, none other, than Chief Justice William Roach.

As they presented his plea, Rushbourne's lawyers maintained that the president's dismissal of Collins did not fall under the umbrella of the Act, as Collins was never formally appointed but instead, was simply transferred over from Lincoln's Cabinet. Over the following two months both sides scrutinised the wording of the document and argued in great detail, as the defence did their utmost to demonstrate that the articles were not unequivocal. Meanwhile, Chief Allen continued to fight the president's case outside the courthouse, utilising Russell Randolph-Smith's exorbitant funds to great effect: he systematically bribed as many senators as possible, meeting them in hotel bars, restaurants and even the back of stagecoaches as they made their way towards the trial.

With only twenty-four hours remaining before the final verdict was to be handed down, Brunson made the lengthy journey from his island home to Washington. Having requested a private audience with Roach, he arrived at the presidential mansion in a fluster of worry. And aiming to keep their meeting as clandestine as possible, they convened in the ground-floor library, as far away as possible from the prying eyes surrounding the main administrative blocks and living accommodation on the upper floors.

"Mr Brunson!" Roach said gleefully as he entered the room with a look of gaiety at seeing his old friend once again.

"Good day, William," Jack replied rather sullenly. He shook his head in despair – severely concerned for the president's future and, more importantly, his own. Hesitantly, in expectation of the worst, he enquired, "How's Benjamin?"

"He's pretty optimistic," replied a relaxed-looking Roach.

Jack frowned back in disbelief.

How could he possibly be optimistic?

Yet it was true that his allies from Washington remained generally unconcerned. With William having been appointed to preside over the trial, he had been leading proceedings somewhat, allowing certain evidence to be heard and ordering other discussions to desist.

"Don't worry, Jack," he reassured him, leaning a heavy hand on his shoulder. "Let's just wait for the outcome."

Jack, however, remained sceptical and was not going to rest on his laurels, or leave anything to chance. He walked over to the doorway, checked along the corridor, and then seeing it was clear, Brunson closed the door for complete privacy, before beginning to deliberate their remaining options. "But let's just say Benjamin is found guilty - what then, William?" he asked pointedly.

"Well, I suppose Vice President Altidore would replace him," Roach assumed, quite sensibly, but this only left Brunson fretting even more.

"Good God, that would be awful!" he said indignantly. "There's not a chance he would be re-elected - and he certainly wouldn't be interested in the Development Plan."

Roach concurred woefully, shaking his head in agreement with Brunson's damning prediction.

Racking his brains for a solution and wondering what his world might look like beyond tomorrow evening, Jack decided that critical action was needed to uphold his interests in the event of Rushbourne losing the presidency.

"Why don't *you* put yourself forward for president?"

"Well, I mean, I... I guess I could..." Roach stuttered while considering his suitability for the task. "It's not something I've ever considered!"

"Well, you can count on my full backing," Jack said at once. "I'm more than happy to pay whatever it takes to get you into the job."

Brunson was strategising as if Rushbourne had already been condemned, wiping him away without a second's consideration.

"Let's just see what happens tomorrow," Roach suggested calmly, having pulled himself back from daydreaming of being elected. "I have a good feeling it will all be okay," he reaffirmed.

This time Brunson willingly accepted. And having now established a backup plan, he could attend the verdict tomorrow knowing it would be a win-win situation, and that he would certainly sleep somewhat better, than he had the night before.

Chapter 26: The Verdict

Δ

The morning of 26th May arrived and Rushbourne made his way to the Senate for his first and last occasion. Amongst the packed-out House, he sat anxiously with his lawyers, as the hands on the clock moved ever closer to the moment when the future of his presidency would be revealed.

Walter Dixon and his close aide, John Peters, stood to deliver the verdict, while Benjamin remained seated beneath them. As they ran through the articles in full as part of the official process, the tension inside the Senate continued to build, and even the usually unbothered Rushbourne began to feel the heat.

Holding the Impeachment Resolution, with its fifty-four signatures, aloft in his hands, Dixon knew that a guilty verdict required a two-thirds majority - meaning the magic number of not-guilty votes Rushbourne needed in order to be acquitted was nineteen. Reading out the votes in running order from the first eleven senators, Dixon maintained a professional demeanour, and held back his delight at only two finding the president not guilty.

This is going to be a landslide.

Quickly calculating the ratio across all fifty-four senators, Rushbourne realised that at this rate he would be woefully short of his target. Perspiration sprang up on his forehead and he lowered his chin to his chest while staring glumly at the floor.

His mood, however, was almost instantly reversed as Walter announced the following three results, all not guilty, leaving the result thus far at five not guilty to nine guilty.

With the result swinging back and forth, Dixon pushed ahead in reading out the next twenty-six decisions, to reveal fifteen guilty votes and eleven not-guilty, leaving the result thereafter standing at sixteen not guilty to twenty-four guilty.

Barely able to believe his luck, Benjamin glanced across at Roach, while concealing his excitement, knowing he required only three more supporting votes from the remaining fourteen senators!

His stomach was doing cartwheels.

However, as the next six votes were read out, he suffered another drastic change of fortune: all were announced as guilty. And Rushbourne's optimism swung in the opposite direction.

With only eight senators now remaining, he held his breath while Dixon read out the next results.

"Senator Lamb, representing Indiana – not guilty."

"Senator Butler, representing Kansas – not guilty."

The latest announcement placed Rushbourne on the verge of a full acquittal, and he could not help but smirk upon hearing of Butler's support.

My trip to Kansas clearly paid off!

"Senator Booth, representing Maryland – not guilty."

That was it, the nineteenth not-guilty vote announced, and with it, a loud screech went up from the viewing galley as a wave of outrage broke out across the courtroom. Tilting his head to observe the commotion, Rushbourne looked on with a mix of shock and elation as he bit his lip to hold back from unfurling in his seat.

"Order, order, order!" Roach demanded, smacking his gavel onto the sound block several times, until those in attendance returned silently to their seated positions.

With his hands shaking, Dixon steadied himself to read aloud the remaining five votes as best he could, his voice croaky and fraught. His opposition against the president fully exposed, but now he stood there without the safety of victory to protect him. The remaining votes were all guilty, but with the one-third majority having already been met, the senators missed out on impeaching the president by a single vote.

Brown, who had been standing discreetly at the rear of the room with his back against the wall, shook his head in dismay and promptly exited via a side door to avoid drawing attention to his presence. But sitting in his elevated position at the front of the room, Roach spotted him above the crowds like a hawk. Watching Brown leave so disheartened and without offering the slightest congratulation to the president, it was eminently clear to him just exactly where the war general's loyalties lay. For the first time in years, Richard had let his guard down, and shown his true colours in full...all for the chief justice to witness.

Finally finding the energy to stand, Rushbourne defiantly scanned the room, feeling an uncontrollable urge to demonstrate his indignation to his detractors. But before he could utter a single word in anger, his lawyers approached to congratulate him on the result.

With an avalanche of praise ensuing all around him at what a "Magnificent job!" they had done and what an "Outstanding result!" it was, Benjamin peered over at Roach, who subtly nodded in his direction. Returning the gesture with a veiled smirk, the president could not help but chuckle. Yet his satisfaction was suddenly interrupted when he noticed Senator Butler, from Kansas, packing up his belongings, seemingly looking to depart.

"Excuse me, chaps," Rushbourne said to his lawyers and he quickly made his way across the room towards Butler, whose brow furrowed when he caught sight of the president heading directly his way.

"Senator Butler!" Rushbourne crowed merrily, raising both his arms high in the air as if preparing to hug him.

"What the hell are you doing, man?!" scoffed Butler in a muffled tone.

The president looked surprised and his arms slumped back down by his sides. "I just wanted to offer my thanks." He nodded suggestively.

Butler continued to pack up his belongings. "Well, you can do that by delivering on your promises," he replied somewhat abruptly. "But don't do it here, in front of all these prying eyes!" the senator ordered in a fluster, before thrusting the last of his documentation under his arms, and waddling quickly out of the courtroom.

Rushbourne considered the exchange to be somewhat peculiar; but notwithstanding, decided to thank some of the other Democrats who had voted not guilty, but whom he had not approached personally, and so must have been influenced by Randolph-Smith and Chief Allen.

"Senator Lamb," Rushbourne began, stooping his head in an attempt to make eye contact with the portly representative from Indiana. "I'd like to thank you for your support," he offered. His gesture earned him yet another curt response.

"Benjamin," said Lamb very quietly, while refusing to acknowledge his presence, "I do believe we're being watched, and I would appreciate it if you ceased this conversation at once!"

At that, Rushbourne frantically spun his head around to scan the floor and upper viewing galley and identify to whom Lamb could be referring. The president was so preoccupied with his search that he did not notice as the senator from Indiana swiftly moved aside to his colleague at the adjacent desk and struck up a conversation, leaving Benjamin staring at his back, and standing unaccompanied.

When he did discover himself - the president, the vindicated hero! - standing all alone, Rushbourne felt himself becoming increasingly angry and confused at the situation. He spotted a group of Republicans who weren't privy to any promises or bribes but still had voted in his favour. *They must be my true supporters.*

Brushing aside the previous rebukes, he walked over confidently to the men from his party to thank them, and with a view to discussing the upcoming Republican ticket for the presidential elections. Interrupting their intimate conversation, he loudly announced, "Thanks for the support, chaps."

The four men abruptly halted their chatter and turned their eyes upon him.

"A joy to know there's still some loyalty within our party!" Rushbourne declared with his very best, toothy smile.

An awkward silence ensued before he tried again.

"And I'd like to invite you all to Washington in the coming weeks so that we can discuss our plans for the election."

But this affable invitation was met with another wall of silence. The eldest senator gazed knowingly around at his colleagues with a look of cynicism etched on his face and then taking a solitary step towards the president, he leaned forward and spoke in a low voice. "The only reason we voted for you was to keep that fool Altidore out the door. And in the upcoming nominations, we shall be backing nobody other than General Richard D Brown!" he confirmed bluntly.

Rushbourne stood there immobilised by the news. He did not know how to respond. Indeed, it seemed within a flash, that there was no need to respond at all.

"Good day to you, Benjamin," said the elder senator and, as one, the group turned their backs on the president and slowly walked away.

Suddenly recognising the hollow nature of his victory, Rushbourne lowered his head and walked despondently in the other direction. He cast his gaze across at Roach, but his closest friend was wrapped up in carousing with his fellow magistrates, and he did not notice the president glumly exit the courtroom, entirely deflated, and with nobody but himself for comfort.

Chapter 27: The Campaign Trail

Δ

Later that evening, Brunson returned to his usual lodgings at the Willard Hotel, where in hopeful anticipation he had reserved the entire Round Robin Bar, in order they could celebrate without being bothered by the press. Booking the room prior to the result having being revealed, he had been somewhat fearful it could end up in disaster; however, in the hours after the trial's conclusion, Jack was most impressed with himself for having had the foresight to make the arrangement. He had requested the room be unstaffed in order to keep the merrymaking as private as possible, and had arranged for the bar to be adorned with red, white and blue garlands. Now, he was starting the party in advance of his esteemed colleagues' arrival, by pouring himself a large glass of Old Overholt in eager enthusiasm.

Yet when the double doors swung open and Brunson sprang up to greet the arrivals, he was shocked to see Roach and Rushbourne come skulking in, their feet heavy as they stomped forward with expressions of abject misery on their faces. Expecting a whole roster of other government officials to be following in line behind, Jack peered down the corridor.

But to his surprise, there was nobody to be seen.

"What's going on, chaps?" he enquired worriedly. However, his question was met with a forlorn silence as his company stared pointedly at one another.

Finally, Roach solemnly suggested, "Maybe we should get a drink."

After hurriedly closing the doors and dashing back towards the bar, Brunson speedily poured three glasses of liquor, inadvertently soaking the wooden bar in his impatience, as he desperately awaited an explanation for their mood.

"What's going on, chaps?" he asked once again, and laughed nervously. "We just beat the impeachment... surely we should be celebrating?!"

He handed them each a glass and clinked his against theirs in an attempt to rouse them out of their gloomy mood. But with the president unable to even muster a smile, let alone speak, Roach then took the lead.

"I'm sorry to disappoint you, Jack, but the support from the Senate is not what it seems," William revealed soberly, before looking despondently across at Rushbourne. "They won't be backing Ben for another term," he concluded wearily.

Brunson looked at them, perplexed.

He could only assume this must be some cruel joke they were playing on him – acting in a defeated manner, but about to spring forth and reveal the punchline, or so he desperately hoped. "I... I don't understand," he said, while scratching his head and frantically trying to rationalise their sentiment after such a wonderful result earlier in the day.

The crestfallen president felt he owed it to Jack - one of the very few, apparently, who loyally supported him - to clarify the situation. "I spoke with a number of senators after the result, and they informed me they are all looking to back Brown at the upcoming Convention," he revealed pitifully, before gulping a large mouthful of his drink and looking, stoney-faced, into the distance.

Staring at the president in astonishment, Jack could not fathom the news to be correct. However, with no time to dwell on the defeat, Brunson said firmly, "Well, we just need to form another plan then."

"I think our road may be run," Roach replied despondently.

The ease of his surrender incited Jack to the core, and he slammed his glass down onto the bar; the ferocity of the strike indenting the wood and nearly smashing the glass within his grasp. "It's never over!" he yelled. "There's always an answer! We just need to bloody well think."

Silence filled the room, broken only by the sloshing of more whisky into glasses as the men desperately scrambled for a solution. Then, with several minutes having passed and nothing being offered by Rushbourne or Roach, Brunson suddenly began grinning widely at his allies and nodding his head enthusiastically, having smartly deduced their only avenue.

"You can run for the Democrat ticket instead!" he announced. Having noted the number of Democrats who had acquitted Benjamin, this seemed a plausible suggestion. "And you should run too, William," Jack instructed to Roach.

At this, the Chief Justice fully expected a rebuttal from the president, yet Rushbourne only stood in silence, for once feeling a sense of his own limitations.

With a new plan in place, the men rested against their bar stools and gazed across the empty room, which at this moment in time was supposed to be filled with America's political elite engaged in fervent celebrations. Rushbourne and Roach turned to refill their glasses and drown their sorrows for the night, but Brunson remained in deep contemplation as he considered his other options outside the room in which they stood. Switching his mind to Brown, Jack grimaced heavily to himself, and began to construct a plan - for how he could get back in favour with the man he had disregarded for so long.

Δ

A mere seventy-two hours later and on a blisteringly warm and sun-kissed morning in Chicago, Crosby Opera House proudly opened its doors to host the 1868 Republican National Convention. Thousands of delegates from across the country were flooding into the city, and among them, arriving by carriage from the station with Collins by his side, was Brown. Expecting a long day ahead, and with the trials and tribulations of the past year weighing heavily on his mind, Brown prepared to summon up every last ounce of energy he had to get through the day – unable to even contemplate winning, this early on in proceedings.

Crosby Opera House had only recently been completed, and was already one of the crown jewels in Chicago's entertainment district. The opulent building was resplendent with white marble; set over five floors under a tiled mansard roof, with several goods stores spanning its full width at street level. As Brown and Collins made their way through the arched entranceway, they were greeted by a rather over-excited Senator Marcus Demille, who led them swiftly towards the main auditorium, whereupon he thrust open the heavy double doors.

As they entered the packed-out, yet strangely hushed theatre, a resounding ovation exploded across the hall: senators and their staff alike rose up from their seats, clapping and cheering to welcome the new arrivals. Initially dumbfounded by the reception, Brown could only assume that all of the candidates had been greeted in such a manner, and he slowly cast his eyes around the layers of upper galleries, while acknowledging the three thousand faces turned towards him. Next he peered down the central aisle in front of them, and noticed Walter Dixon. Standing on the stage some forty rows ahead, he excitedly motioned for them to come join him. So the war general and his good friend began to make their way down the sloped, central concourse, ushered forward with congratulatory handshakes and pats on the back by those able to outstretch and reach them. And as they arrived on the stage, the vigorous clapping intensified when they closed in on Dixon, who leaned in to Brown.

"All for you, my friend - all for you," he said warmly in his ear, before stepping towards the front lip of the stage.

Dixon raised his hands, palms out, and slowly brought the audience to a quiet yet vibrant hush. Then he marched back to Brown, grinning euphorically, grabbed hold of Richard's hand, and thrust it into the air to proclaim loudly:

"I proudly present our Republican nomination for the 1868 presidential election!"

And with barely a millisecond having passed, a deafening roar rang out around the theatre, as hundreds of top hats were tossed jubilantly into the air.

Brown and Collins stared at each other as realisation dawned. Without either of their knowledge, the party had, prior to the conference, unanimously decided Brown to be the sole nominee, and therefore he would go unopposed for the ballot. In that moment, the war general's concerns over the day instantly subsided, and he stood completely humbled at the front of the stage while waving his hand aloft in appreciation of this most overwhelming act of support. Then Brown moved to take his place at the podium. The audience stood, electrified in anticipation of his acceptance speech, but unable to quell their enthusiasm for even a second, so Brown kept it simple.

"Let us have peace!" he boomed, while slowly raising his fist into the air.

All over the auditorium, fists shot up to mirror him, and a cacophony of "Brown for president!" calls filled the air. Then one senator shook his neighbour's hand, and another shook his neighbour's too, and so it went on, until all were stood congratulating one another, on their most splendid decision.

Δ

As June passed and the news of Brown's nomination as the Republican candidate became common knowledge across America, both the Harris and the Roberts families publicly backed their man and privately financed him behind the scenes.

Elsewhere in New York, Rushbourne and Roach arrived in Manhattan outside Tammany Hall for the Democratic National Convention. Gazing across at Union Square, they could not help but cast their minds back to their previous visit, when their fortunes seemed so much rosier than today.

They had arrived early, and so found the vast main hall empty – for now. It was extravagantly decorated with red-and-white-striped bunting hanging down from the circular, upper viewing gallery, and hundreds of rows of benches crammed into the lower floor. Come a few hours' time, it would be a very crowded space in which to try to circulate.

Standing there rather gormlessly, while staring up in awe at the gigantic chandelier hanging from the domed ceiling above, neither Rushbourne nor Roach noticed the burly figure of Chief Allen as he stomped his way around the edge of the room to accost his visitors. Nelson was a brute of a man, not afraid to command others' fists to get what he wanted; he maintained a ruthless control by extorting the lower-class residents of Manhattan Island for his benefit and had little sympathy or interest in anyone, other than himself.

"You!" he snarled in his deep, gravelly voice while progressing towards the president, whom he had expected to be a shoo-in for the Republican nomination after his hard work to have him acquitted. "What happened?!"

"It was a stitch-up!" Rushbourne said haplessly, hoping the simplistic reply would resonate with Chief Allen.

But although he was not the brightest of men, Nelson was a decent judge of character, and he could tell when he was being lied to. His lip curled in distaste.

"Well, let's hope you get the nomination today, because you have *a lot* of promises to deliver... and there's a very big one waiting for me!" he warned, before brushing past the president and storming off to the entrance foyer, to see whether there was anyone else who he could rattle.

Rushbourne and Roach were standing there motionless, in fear of what losing today's vote might mean for them, when the host of the event, Winfred Skinner, entered the auditorium and spotted them from behind.

"Great to see you, chaps," Skinner said pleasantly. "As I understand it, you're both running?" he asked, seeking confirmation for his final numbers, as he hovered a pen above his list of candidates' names.

"Indeed we are," replied Roach proudly, and Skinner happily ticked them off the list.

"Well, good luck to you both, and may the best man win," he said in his overly subservient manner. Then, all teeth and smiles, he bounced off to the stage in order to practise his opening speech.

Δ

Over the next hour, Tammany Hall filled up to the brim with a mix of rich politicians and local New Yorkers; all of whom paid patronage to Chief Allen as they entered the building. Proceedings got going at around midday to scenes more reminiscent of a saloon than a serious political conference; Nelson's men plied those in attendance with free booze as Winfred took to the stage.

"Welcome to the 1868 Democratic National Convention!" the host yelled squeakily, in an effort to overcome the melee of noise.

It suddenly dawned upon Rushbourne and Roach that the nominations were going to be a free-for-all and seemingly decided by the rule of "He who shouts loudest - wins".

And the voting system turned out to be convoluted as well, with no less than twenty-two rounds. The president fell out of the running within the first fifteen minutes, and with the omnipresent threat of hostilities he stood torn: exit now, or stay and support his comrade? With a constant barrage of bickering being thrown back and forth across the auditorium, the noise only added to his anxiety, and he began to plot an escape route, in preparation, should Roach also fail in their mission.

As the fifth ballot was announced, Winfred Skinner, oddly, amassed nine votes from nowhere, to the total surprise of everyone in the hall, apart from Allen and his closest cronies - who sent the room into a choir of primeval bouts of cheering and forceful chest-thumps of glee. However, Skinner had no desire whatsoever to be chosen and so, after a long minute of gesturing for hush in the auditorium, he addressed the rampant crowd. "It appears my name has been put forward, which can only be a mistake," he said nervously to the increasingly intoxicated rabble. "Unfortunately, I cannot run for president. No matter how much I love this country, and our beloved party –"

"Well, take the bloody nomination then!" came a roar from the back of the upper floor: Allen, hidden within his band of men, and stoking the fire once again.

His jibe incited the masses into boisterous applause, and as Skinner started to wilt, he was forced to rush from the stage to be violently sick in the wings. Ably stepping up, his assistant took control, only to announce several further ballots that kept Skinner firmly in the running.

With the final few ballots being drawn, Nelson instructed his sidekicks to spread around the room, so they could rouse the crowd in support for Winfred at every given point. And while he busied himself organising his men, the stand-in announcer revealed that in the latest ballot, Roach had fallen short of the required votes needed to progress.

Realising their race was run and now desperate to escape, Rushbourne grabbed Roach, and they ducked and dived through the hordes of drunks, fighting their way towards the exit. At the doors, they paused for a moment, as the final ballot was drawn.

"It gives me great pleasure to announce that our Democratic representative shall be none other than... Winfred Skinner!"

And without a second more contemplation, the president and his number two stampeded out of the building and dashed away from New York, before Chief Allen and his goons had a chance to get hold of them, and exact their pound of flesh.

Chapter 28: The Result

Δ

The campaign trail was more gruelling and hard fought than anyone had expected, as both candidates did their utmost to win - even Skinner, who grew into the role as the months passed by. And as the firecrackers fizzled out on New Year's Eve, America awoke to 1869, with the final result now only two months away.

On the day of the final result, Brown remained at the Fifth Avenue Hotel, where he had stationed his campaign HQ throughout the election. In attendance at the gathering alongside Richard's campaign team were all the familiar faces, including Alex Macdonald, Jack Brunson, Levi Sykes, Christopher Worthington and Alfred and Stephen Roberts. AJ, however, was running late, as he had a most important guest to pick up from the station, prior to his arrival.

The hotel had cost over two million dollars to build and was one of Brown's favourites in Manhattan; not only because it provided some of the grandest lodgings in the city, but because its more than four hundred employees ensured the service was second to none. Set across six floors and extending a full Manhattan block, its structure was so imposing that some commenters likened it to Buckingham Palace when it opened.

Brown had commandeered the Reading Room, usually reserved for well-heeled businessmen to browse the daily newsprints, and it was from here the presidential candidate was hoping to make the headlines himself. And with his assistants still working diligently to analyse the polling updates as they arrived via telegraph, he was approached early on by Jack Brunson, who pulled him aside for a private conversation.

"What an honour to be present for your victory," Brunson said. The flattery was not necessary, however, as Richard harboured no ill feelings towards him. He viewed Jack as a somewhat overzealous member of the group, yet a hard-working one, who had successfully undertaken a number of projects – just as he and Lincoln desired.

"Well, we'd best hold off celebrating just yet!" Brown exclaimed with a chuckle. "How are things with you?"

"The Transcontinental is well underway," Jack told him, "and I hope to complete it within the next year."

"Now that really is progress!" Richard replied, looking suitably impressed, as he kept half an eye on his campaign team and the roll numbers coming in.

Their conversation was then suddenly halted, as the doors of the Reading Room abruptly swung open, and Chief Allen swaggered in, uninvited. *Who would have invited him?* Was the thought on everyone's mind, and the words on the tip of their tongue.

But with no reaction from around the room, and labouring under the assumption that he must be on someone else's guest list, Nelson continued across the black-and-white-checkerboard tiles to speak with the Roberts family. Slightly amused, but also somewhat perturbed by Allen's presence, Brunson turned his attention back to Brown. "So, can I therefore assume you'll wish me to continue?" he hastened to ask.

"Let's see how this goes, and if all's well, then I'll sign it off first thing for you," the war general confirmed, to the absolute delight of Jack, who could now relax, with his politicking complete.

As both men brought their business conversation to an end and moved on to more genial matters of the heart and home, Harris arrived with an unfamiliar guest by his side. He had decided this was the right time to formally introduce Cunningham to Brown, and with Oliver now having developed their business venture into the dominant oil refiner in Cleveland, AJ needn't hide his protégé away any longer.

Walking into the room, Harris instantly noticed Brunson standing directly ahead of him and could not believe his gall in cosying up to Richard, however, held back on displaying his discontent. He nodded politely in acknowledgment at Brown alone, and then made his way across to the Roberts family, where he was even more stumped to find them talking to Chief Allen!

What the devil is going on here?

Without any introductions, Harris pulled Stephen aside. "I need to speak with you immediately," he whispered forcefully in his ear.

The comment, uttered through gritted teeth, caused Stephen to lean back from his position and regard his friend more carefully. Upon observing the exceedingly serious look in AJ's eyes, he decided not to question him, and instead grabbed hold of his son and followed Harris and Cunningham straight out of the room, somewhat to the surprise of the others.

Δ

AJ scanned the corridor for a private location and noticed a doorway in the distance. He marched up and twisted the knob vigorously, but found the door was locked. Frustrated, he looked around again and spotted another door. He darted towards the entrance, with his three colleagues zig-zagging like sheep behind. However, The Commander was unable to contain his frustration at the ensuing spectacle any longer. "What the hell's wrong with you, man?!" he cried.

Ah-ha! Success, thought AJ, as this time the door opened and he peered inside to see an empty office.

"Quite a lot, Stephen," he replied knowingly. "So please do follow me..."

Entering the room, he tossed his coat onto the desk and stood leaning against the edge, while his associates took up the limited seating, available within the tiny office.

"My first bit of business," he said, once they were all squeezed in place, "is to introduce you to my fine friend, Mr Oliver Peter Cunningham." He grinned as he gestured to his guest from Cleveland.

"A pleasure," Stephen offered tersely, knowing that Harris would not have dragged them away if this was all he wished to detail.

"A pleasure it will be," Andrew replied readily as he looked fondly upon Cunningham. "Oliver owns the largest oil refinery in Cleveland - moving more freight throughout the land than anybody else."

The Commander, now seeing his worth, suddenly became more appreciative of the introduction. "This is my boy, Al..." Stephen motioned to his son. "He'll deal with anything you may wish to discuss, Mr Cunningham," he advised. Then he returned his gaze to Harris and enquired cynically, "Right, so what's the bad news?!"

Pursing his lips and becoming altogether more austere, Andrew looked Stephen dead in the eyes. "It may be best if we speak about this, alone..." he said. He turned to the others. "Oliver, Alfred, that gives you chaps the opportunity to discuss your mutually beneficial business in closer detail."

Sensing the change in the air, the two men readily stood, and left the room without question, leaving Andrew to deliver the news.

"Millard Stride has been selling you watered-down stock," AJ revealed quietly. "Meaning that what you've bought is worthless. It's a sham," he confirmed, while flashing a sympathetic grimace in the direction of his comrade.

"What on earth does that mean?!" Roberts said, scratching the top of his head. "And if so - surely we just report them?" he surmised, feeling assured that the authorities would come to his aid.

However, he was overlooking one rather important issue.

"And cite whom?" AJ questioned. "Where were you buying the shares from, Stephen?"

With that, the dastardly scheme began to unravel before Stephen's eyes. Yet rather than being enraged as AJ expected, he sat sunken and deeply embarrassed at having fallen foul of the deception. As Stephen struggled to find the words to reply while he contemplated being on the losing side for the first time in decades, to his alarm, Harris had more to come.

"I'm afraid it gets worse..." he added.

"I'm *five million dollars out of pocket*, AJ! How could it get any worse?!" he seethed through gritted teeth, and stared his young friend dead in the eyes.

Andrew braced himself and continued.

"Because it wasn't just Stride, Allen and Diamond," he revealed, gripped by concern over how Stephen would react to the bombshell. "Jack Brunson is involved as well!"

Stephen leapt from his chair.

"I'LL KILL HIM!" he raged and lurched towards the door, the mobility issues conferred by age seemingly vanishing, as he snatched at the handle and flung himself down the corridor.

"I think we need to decide how best to play this," AJ called out, before hurriedly turning to grab his coat and chase after The Commander.

However, he was unable to catch up with his ally, who had a decent head start, and quickly hobbled along the corridor before barnstorming back into the Reading Room.

"You retched little man! You robbed me of FIVE MILLION DOLLARS!" he yelled out at Brunson, and everyone instantly stopped what they were doing. *"If I were twenty years younger, I'd have you!"* Stephen threatened, before raising his limp, grey fist into the air and stumbling towards Jack.

Standing next to Brown in a room full of his contemporaries, Brunson was never going to be drawn into a physical conflict, and the need was swiftly removed, as the other members of the group swarmed in between them and halted The Commander's progress.

In the ensuing melee, AJ grappled his way through the hustle and jabbed his index finger towards Brunson. "This man is a *crook*," he insisted forthrightly, while Jack suddenly appeared worried. "He's been selling illegal shares to Mr Roberts and *he should be incarcerated for his actions*!" he announced. It was not exactly the plan of calculated retribution AJ had ideally hoped to deliver. However, with the future president, he hoped, looking on and expecting an explanation, it would suffice!

Shocked that Harris had exposed his corruption, and in such a pivotally public arena, Brunson was for once shaken and unsure what action to take. "I... I don't know what you mean!" he said, instinctively lying – and compounding his deceit under the spotlight of so many eyes.

"He's lying to you, Richard!" The Commander yelled. "He's bloody lying to your face!" His feet scuttled on the spot and his associates had to work against his will, to hold him back from Brunson once again.

Closely scrutinising both men in an attempt to ascertain the truth, the war general struggled with how best to handle the situation. And as a hush of anticipation fell in the room, his examination was cut short by his campaign runner, who jumped to his feet in jubilation.

"Richard! You've won the public vote!"

The news caused Brown's campaign team to erupt in rapturous applause and swarm around the new president to congratulate him on his victory. Richard's legislative advisor picked up a concertina accordion and began playing away, and with the merriment escalating in the room, the men put their inquisition to one side – for now.

Chapter 29: Making Concessions

Δ

With the initial celebrations dying down and plenty of cake and fine wine having been consumed, the tension of the argument still remained thick in the air. Realising the party would not get into full swing until the issue was resolved, Brown decided to take matters into his own hands and he departed the room for a private discussion with AJ and Stephen.

In the Reading Room, meanwhile, Chief Allen quickly stomped over to Brunson with some discreet advice, delivered within earshot of Macdonald and Sykes. "I suggest you get out of here now and go on a little voyage. Preferably somewhere out of the country!"

Jack gaped at Allen, shocked by the suggestion, having felt sure his lie, that he knew nothing of the scam, had been successful. But now the gravity of Nelson's delivery made Jack question his safety.

"I'll speak with some of my people and see what I can do," the chief said. "But don't come back until I say, or *you will* end up in prison!"

Without taking even a second further to ponder, Jack pulled his cape from the coat stand, and not offering a single "Goodbye" to anyone, scarpered from the room.

Standing in disbelief, having overheard the entire exchange, Macdonald struggled to take in the fact his associate could be seemingly involved in such underhand dealings. "Did you know anything about this?" he enquired indignantly of Sykes.

"You know Jack..." Levi said nonchalantly in an attempt to brush the issue aside. "I'm sure it won't lead to anything."

It wasn't quite the explanation, the young Scot was hoping to hear. And a somewhat disillusioned Macdonald did not return his colleague's smile, but instead scanned the room, wondering exactly whom he could trust: all of a sudden feeling, his world to be a rather callous and lonesome place.

Meanwhile, in the small private office down the corridor, AJ had just concluded his meticulous account of the events at Erie, as well as presenting a whole raft of additional information he had unearthed regarding Brunson's prior business misdemeanours, that brought into question his integrity on the whole. Deeply disturbed by the accusations, but still desperately seeking a solution that would keep the group together, Brown tried to placate the men sat demanding answers, all around him.

"Firstly, I'd like to say that I'm completely dismayed by this information, and if what you say is proven correct, Jack shall be struck off from this group forever," he began.

Stephen and AJ remained unimpressed by this, however, having expected Brown to get rid of Brunson that instant. And the newly elected president discerned their notable indifference, so pressed on ahead apprehensively. "And secondly, I promise to rubber-stamp your Brooklyn Bridge plans as my first duty in office," he said.

It certainly made for a great start.

But yet again his audience sat in splendid silence.

Carefully considering the offer before them, and to see whether anything more would be forthcoming.

Several seconds ticked by as the men weighed each other up. Then The Commander, in his inimitable style, decided to grasp the situation by the throat and push Brown for further concessions. "I have another idea..."

Richard dutifully nodded for him to continue, while inwardly squirming in preparation for the request and hoping it would not be too colossal so that he could comply, and bring to an end this moment of unrest.

"Manhattan has several railroads, but not one central hub," said Stephen, and the new president wondered where he was leading. "So what I'm proposing is to bring them all together under one roof."

Instantly intrigued by the idea, but also concerned by what it would cost him, Richard enquired tentatively, "And what will you require from me?"

"The development requires twenty-one acres of land. So you'll need to sign that land over to me," Stephen demanded straightforwardly, putting the ball firmly in the president's court. Brown sat there thinking it over.

Reading between the lines, he got the sense that if he endorsed the project, it would be enough to satisfy Harris and Roberts, however, he was stumped by the size of the request. If the land grant was way out west, where few would notice the giveaway, it would be inherently easier. But clearly, resolution of this current situation called for him to be bold, and make the first major decision of his presidential term.

"If you send me your plans, I'll have the land allocated over to you next week," he announced flatly – to the sheer delight of his associates, who knew that the two projects, the bridge at Brooklyn and now the central railway hub in Manhattan, would secure both their futures for the coming decade.

Brown wiped his brow in relief and began to stand, confident that business had finally been settled, when AJ piped up with one final request. "May I add something, Richard?" he said lightly with a contemplative look on his face.

Brown hesitantly lowered himself back into his seat, knowing that he could not grant even a single further concession.

"With you now having won the presidency, I believe there's an opportunity to speed up the Development Plan," AJ said, piquing Richard's interest, who was somewhat relieved this did not sound like the start of another demand. "If the government were to act in partnership on funding, rather than simply granting land, we could expand beyond our wildest dreams."

But Brown instantly found fault with the suggestion. "My only income is from the tax system, Andrew, and that's used to pay off the war debt, not to support public programmes."

"Indeed that has been the case, however, I have spoken with my European associates, and we've calculated that their debt will be paid within a decade."

This was news to the president, and he sat up in his seat and listened extra carefully now.

"So, if you were to smooth out those payments across, say, a century, then the tax leftover each year could be committed towards development," said AJ.

Richard ran the theory through his head, but was unable to comprehend how it would actually play out in real terms.

Sensing that his friend was struggling slightly with the notion, Andrew tried to exemplify. "You also have to consider the effect of multiplication. If we can develop the country and boost the population now, then a *million* tax payers are going to bring in a lot more income than a hundred thousand; so you'll pay the debt off more quickly anyway!" he stated unequivocally.

Leaning back in his seat, Richard was gobsmacked at what appeared to be such a simple yet brilliant idea. His eyes scanned back and forth between the men as he furiously worked through the plan.

"And remember," said AJ, to give Brown more food for thought, "less than five per cent of Americans qualify for tax payment, so only the rich will pay - yet everyone will benefit."

Stephen jumped in to cement their proposal. "And why struggle paying off all the debt during *your* presidency, Richard," he said craftily, "Just so the next guy can reap all the rewards?!"

Richard allowed another moment for the information to sink in properly, as he sat there bedazzled by the plan.

"It's... it's absolutely astounding," he muttered, shaking his head in astonishment. "Thank you, both of you. What a wonderful plan to benefit us all!" he concluded. Then the men rose up to congratulate one another, awash with a sense, they were standing on the cusp of a brave new frontier.

Δ

With their business now complete, Brown opened the door and respectfully offered his associates the lead into the corridor. However, first the men from Manhattan wished to offer one final word of warning.

"I think you're making a terrible mistake with Jack," AJ advised with a grave look. "He'll betray you in the end."

Stephen raised his shoulders and opened his palms in agreement, while shaking his head in a disappointed, yet respectful manner at Brown.

Feeling similarly dissatisfied with the whole affair, but just hoping the accusations did not prove true, the new president assured them, "I'll go speak with him right now."

But as they re-entered the Reading Room and scanned those in attendance, the men could see no sign of Brunson. Recognising their puzzled looks, Sykes quickly made his way over to privately defend his friend's desertion. "Jack was called away on business at short notice, but he told me to pass on his best regards," he said, hating that he was having to lie - especially given that he was not proficient at it, and made even worse as AJ and Stephen looked straight to Brown with unconvincing glares.

However, Richard was saved from his rather awkward moment as Christopher Worthington abruptly climbed atop the depositary desk in the middle of the room. "Gentlemen! May I have your attention? I wish to tell you about a great set of plans I have for the city!"

As Worthington continued his oration, which held the attention of those in the room, Stephen Roberts leaned over to Chief Allen and sneered under his breath, "I thought we had an understanding. How dare you work against me!"

Yet Nelson replied without a modicum of concern. "The stock's legitimate, Stephen, but if you'd like to discuss it further, I'm more than happy to take this outside," he offered with a malevolent grin at the seventy-five year old, who instantly recognised his limitations and was only able to offer a grunt in response. He knew all too well Allen's band of goons, would likely be waiting nearby.

Meanwhile, Worthington was concluding his speech to the group. "So, it's my intention to create two new museums; one for art and one for natural history, right here in New

York! But I'll require all of your help to achieve it," he appealed, and the men moved across in unison to generously offer their assistance, while Brown gazed upon them and let out a great sigh of relief – finally, able to relax, he could now enjoy his own victory!

As the drinks began to flow and the female members of Brown's campaign team, danced back and forth with the men to the accordion being played by Alex Macdonald, AJ waved Cunningham across to introduce him formally to the president. He found Brown with a drink in his hand and a rosy glow now upon his face.

"Richard!" Harris said merrily, while steadying the new president as he chuckled away to himself amongst the liveliness of the room. "Allow me to introduce my very dear friend, Mr Oliver Peter Cunningham. I think it would be most sensible and beneficial for him to join our group," he proposed.

"Very good to meet you," Brown replied, warmly shaking his new acquaintance's hand. "If you're a friend of Andrew's; then you're a friend of mine!" and easily as that, Oliver was initiated into the group.

Chapter 30: The Golden Spike

Δ

Following Chief Allen's advice, Brunson quickly informed his fellow co-conspirators of the urgent need to leave the country, before speeding out of New York and back to his house on Lake Erie. He frantically packed some bags, while his wife anxiously looked on, wondering what was happening, and then kissed her goodbye and promised to return soon, before rushing down to his dock. His allies, Millard Stride and Big Jim Diamond, were awaiting him there with overnight bags. Not that he cared either way, but it would provide some comfort, having the only other men with dirty hands, close by under his watchful eye.

Aboard his boat, they set off due north and sailed past Detroit, before bottlenecking into the St Clair River and shooting out at Lake Huron. For Brunson, these were unchartered waters, however he pressed ahead, refusing to sleep, and working in shifts with his fellow crew as they made their way through the shallows of St Mary's River. Finally reaching the promised land, they sailed onto Lake Superior, then crossed towards their final destination, of Thunder Bay in Canada.

Meanwhile, back in Washington, President Richard D Brown was sworn in, and after making his inauguration speech, he signed off on his first bit of business by authorising the bridge over the East River, as well starting the ball rolling, on the area of land for Roberts's Central Depot. Having no knowledge of the underlying rift between Harris and Macdonald, Brown passed the bridge plan as it was originally submitted, meaning the Scot was included as the main partner for the works.

With two such large projects running concurrently, The Commander heeded Harris's advice and only publicly put his name to the depot, in order to avoid being in the heavy spotlight from the public and the press. Paying his chief engineer and designer of the bridge to front the project, Stephen happily allowed him to take the credit for its creation, while he concentrated his efforts on bringing Brunson to justice.

For the two months that followed, Stephen was locked in a battle with Chief Allen, as the two men spent every waking hour lobbying members of the legislature. Roberts, wishing to level the playing field against the underhanded tactics of the chief, instructed his lawyers to offer bribes in order to ensure the share dealings at Erie were looked into properly. However, unfortunately for The Commander, Nelson not only had a similar amount of purchasing power, utilising Brunson's funds, but he held more political sway, having previously bribed many of the senators involved, and was therefore able to leverage them for their past indiscretions.

In what became typical of their exploits, several senators in Albany were approached and offered large sums by both men. In some cases, they refused to take the bribe of the one who arrived second, and in other cases they took both bribes, then voted for the one who furnished the largest offer! Such efforts culminated in another victory for Chief Allen, as the Senate legalised the newly issued Erie stock. But while it was now classed as legitimate, this still conveyed no ownership over any of the assets at the company – leaving The Commander in a state of absolute shock and severely out of pocket.

Having been informed of the outcome by Nelson, Brunson made his way back from Canada. But rather than feeling relaxed, he realised that his spat with Stephen had now brought their hostilities into all-out, open warfare, and hereafter it would be a case of "kill or be killed". With the Transcontinental soon to be finished and with no new projects in the pipeline, Jack invited Macdonald and Sykes to meet him, in order to discuss his latest set of plans.

As he guided *The Olive* to its mooring at Brunson's island, Jack was most delighted to find his friends standing on the jetty, awaiting his return.

"Alex!" he called gregariously, his confidence surging. "Good to see you!" He beamed down from the starboard side.

"Glad to be here," Macdonald replied hesitantly, feeling slightly more assured of his partner's character, now he had been cleared of all the charges.

Jack jumped down from the boat and landed thunderously on the jetty. He slapped his arm around the Scot, grinned at Levi standing quietly to one side, and declared, "Well, I'd best show you the new bowling alley then!"

After which he marched Alex and Levi off towards the house, leaving Millard to try get Big Jim down off the boat, and without falling haplessly into the lake. Once they made it to terra firma, they chased their associates up the garden and caught up with them outside Jack's castle, just in time to view its latest addition. Opening the double doors, Jack enthusiastically grabbed hold of a ball and smashed it down the middle one of two lanes, knocking over the beautifully arranged pins. "Unstoppable!" he yelled, throwing his arms wildly in the air as his guests applauded politely. Yet before they could request a turn themselves, Jack directed, "Let's go inside. I have some business which will no doubt be of interest to you all..."

Δ

In the dining room, Jack's guests took their seats, while he stood at the head of the table holding a long, thin, red box. "My Transcontinental Railroad is set to complete in the coming weeks," he announced and he slid open the container to reveal a spike made of gold. "Here is the final spike that shall be hammered in to complete the connection."

It was no bigger than his forearm, yet this small piece of ceremonial gold, represented just how far he had come.

"Bravo, Jack, bravo!" Sykes joyfully applauded the achievement, along with the other men.

To their bemusement, however, Jack appeared stony-faced and he waited for silence to ensue.

"Now, is not the time to be complacent," he told them, shaking his head and glaring around at his colleagues. "And so to guarantee success for the Transcontinental, Mr Diamond and I have devised a plan... to control the price of gold!"

He and Big Jim exchanged proud nods at their scheme. Macdonald looked surprised, and then intrigued. Sykes just looked confused. "Whatever do you mean?" he said. "How do the two relate?"

"Well..." Jack said slowly, and then sniggered along with Diamond. "If we drive up the price of gold, it will have a direct impact on the cost of grain - meaning producers in the west will start shipping more freight to the east."

Macdonald no longer looked intrigued, and Sykes no longer looked confused: the two men sat there aghast at Jack's plan to undertake yet another dubious scheme - having just avoided jail time for the last one!

However, before either could speak out against this folly, Big Jim got to his feet and began exuberantly skipping around the room, pretending to ride a hobbyhorse between his legs. "Yee-hah!" he cheered exuberantly, circling the table, and swinging a hand aloft as both Brunson and Stride cajoled him onwards. Sykes and Macdonald did not quite know where to look, and were feeling strangely out of place, amongst Jack and his new associates.

Wishing to pull the conversation back from the jaws of idiocy and bring an end to Diamond's childish display, Macdonald politely enquired, "And what of your second port of business, Jack?"

"Well, I'm rather glad you asked, Alex," Brunson replied, flashing a fiendish look towards the Scot, "Because this one mainly involves you!"

Macdonald's stomach twisted in knots, and he almost wished he hadn't asked, as Brunson began telling the story of how his new plan came to be.

"Sailing to Canada, I suddenly realised - those rivers go all the way to the Atlantic. So I took a trip to the head of Lake Superior, where it meets America, and found myself in a place called Duluth; which is not only a growing mining town, but also the furthest shipping port in America."

A somewhat puzzled Macdonald hastened to interject.

"But Duluth's not a shipping port?"

His host rubbed his hands together with glee.

"Not yet, it isn't! But if I can create a line due north from Kansas, then our great and splendid country will finally have a better solution than shipping all its goods through east America!"

For this little brainchild Brunson received a flurry of enthusiastic congratulations from around the table.

Macdonald, though, could only muster a slow clap, having instantly grasped what Brunson was attempting to do.

"We'll really need to invest heavily to make it work, Jack," Sykes said, becoming increasingly excited at the thought of the project. "The land out there is particularly tough to master," he warned. However, the host had no such concerns.

"Don't you worry about that," he said, holding the gaze of his friend with a wicked look in his eyes. "I *never* fail!"

And with that, Brunson pulled out the ceremonial golden spike, spinning it above his head. Then he thrust it back and forth towards the men like a dagger, while in his head he danced a glorious vision: of finally exterminating the Roberts family for good.

Chapter 31: The Road to Success

Δ

The next day, at the Union Depot at Erie, the men boarded Brunson's newly built, personal locomotive, to deliver the golden spike to its final destination, at Promontory Summit in Utah. The luxurious carriage had been stripped out and rebuilt to resemble a gentlemen's club, with comfy leather sofas, wingback armchairs and a pool table dominating the central space. A further carriage, to the rear, provided bedroom accommodation alongside washing facilities and a cloakroom. In all, the train afforded Brunson and his guests the most sublime way to travel by railroad, that anyone had ever dared conceive.

They departed the station in the early evening and began the first leg of their journey towards Kansas City, whereupon, they were due to welcome President Brown to their party in the morning. Settling into their surroundings and thoroughly enjoying the many luxuries aboard, Millard and Diamond started early on the alcohol, while fooling around on the pool table. Sykes, meanwhile, buried himself deep in his notebook, brainstorming plans for Duluth, and allowing Macdonald to seize the opportunity to speak to Brunson alone. The Scot had tossed and turned in his bed for most of the night before, while running over the ramifications of both Brunson's proposals. The scheme to manipulate America's gold had weighed heavily on his mind. However, Jack's plan to try and undermine New York by turning Duluth into a shipping port was the main reason for his concern. Just like Brown, Macdonald hoped the group would work together, and so he decided to see whether he could convince his associate to take a less combative stance.

"Duluth sounds like an ambitious project," he began, smiling pleasantly at Brunson and taking a seat by his side. "It'll change the entire landscape of the country," he stated, trying his best to seem indifferent.

"Therein lies my plan," came the self-assured reply from Jack. It was then the coach abruptly jolted on it rails, causing Stride and Diamond to laugh out loudly, while they attempted to keep the pool balls atop the table.

"Well, I was thinking about it last night..." Macdonald said, and Jack turned to glare at him, having suddenly realised this was not merely a passing conversation. The scot swallowed and continued. "I was thinking, and it seems the plan is to drag all of the European trade to Duluth?"

"Right," Jack said warily, placing his whisky glass down on the half-moon table by his side and wondering where Alex was going with his line of questioning.

"Well..." Macdonald nervously approached his final enquiry. "Won't that cause a lot of pain for those in New York?" he pondered, as innocently as he could manage.

But Jack did not like his tone, and frowned suspiciously at this level of interrogation. "And why would I give a damn about anyone who lives in that godforsaken swamp?!"

Alex was stunned by Brunson's hard stance. However, holding his nerve, he brought up an issue he thought Jack may have overlooked. "But what about Chief Allen? Wasn't he responsible for, making sure justice prevailed?"

Brunson leaned over and whispered menacingly into his ear, "He's a big boy, Alex. I'm sure he'll work something out!"

Thinking on his feet, with his mind now in a tailspin from Jack's latest admission, Macdonald quickly burst out laughing to avoid exposing his true feelings. "Damn them all!" he roared, while offering his glass in a toast to Jack.

After a moment's calculation, Brunson clinked his glass back to Alex, and alerted to their salutations; Big Jim, never one to miss out, walked over and generously topped up their glasses, before initiating another round of drinks. As the journey descended into inebriated disorder, Macdonald could only thank his lucky stars for the most useful interjection, leaving Brunson with no time to dwell on their conversation as they sped merrily into the night.

Δ

Arriving in Kansas, the men woke with mightily sore heads, and little memory of the outrageous events of the previous evening. A journey during which they had stopped at St Louis and stocked up on not only alcohol, but women, cigars and guns. Trailblazing under the dark night sky through mid-America, the emptiness of the plains had never heard such debauchery, and it was oozing from the cabin.

Steadying themselves for the imminent arrival of their esteemed colleagues, the men did their best to make themselves look presentable and hurriedly cleared the locomotive. Then, after welcoming Brown and Collins aboard, they set off once more towards their final destination.

The president chose a seat, and sat comfortably, enjoying the company with a sense of relief, that the charges levelled against Brunson had not come to fruition, and hoped they could all now move forward with the Development Plan as a group. Their other latest arrival, Collins, obsessed with anything mechanical, wandered around the carriage alongside Macdonald, who kindly explained to him the many innovations around the locomotive. And with Stride and Diamond having indulged the most, they made their excuses and headed to the rear coach for a spot of rest. That left Sykes and Brunson to take their places adjacent the president, and get down to the business of putting their new proposal forward.

"How have the first two months in office treated you, Richard?" Sykes enquired, by way of opening the conversation.

"Getting used to being called president?" Jack added cheekily.

Sykes looked somewhat alarmed by this jest, but Richard took it in his stride with a laugh.

"I am indeed," Brown confirmed, smiling graciously at his associates. "And how are things with you, Jack? Glad to hear you weren't involved with any wrongdoings at Erie."

That wiped the joviality right off Brunson's face, as he was desperate to look sincere. "I guess we all make mistakes," he said soberly, trying to come across diplomatic, in front of the president. "But I don't hold grudges," he said, the very epitome of reasonableness.

Overhearing this, Macdonald struggled to contain his derision. He decided to remove himself from the carriage and avoid making an outburst. "George, how about we go take a look at the engine room?" he suggested.

Collins agreed, as eager as a child offered a plateful of cookies, and off they walked to the front of the train, the Scot muttering to himself as they went.

With the floor now entirely his to command, Jack opened up on his latest plans to Brown. "I was hoping to speak to you regarding an extension to the Transcontinental," he began. "I propose building a line north to Duluth."

The president, understandably, looked puzzled.

"Duluth?" he said brusquely. "What the devil is the attraction with Duluth?"

Brunson accepted that his project may require a little more promotion in order to obtain Richard's full approval – this was not Rushbourne after all! And he needed to tread extra careful, unable to reveal the true aim behind his plan, to eradicate Manhattan as a port.

No president would agree to that.

"While visiting, on a fishing expedition, it came to my attention that there's a silver mining operation underway. A rather *large* one, that the locals suggest will be like a second Gold Rush there soon!" his story began.

Richard's ears had pricked up at those two little words, Gold Rush. "Yes?" he said. "Go on."

"Well, it seems the Canadians are coming down and taking it all for themselves!" Jack declared – a false claim, engineered, to galvanise his president's will to act.

"Is that right?!" Brown exclaimed and he started to fidget uncomfortably in his seat.

Sykes stepped in to provide some factual support. "The original Gold Rush attracted over three hundred thousand speculators to California, who then settled and sparked the evolution of the West," he reminded Brown. "If we can attract the same migration north, we'll expand the country and its appeal worldwide."

Brown nodded in approval, and couldn't help but be reminded of Harris's advice about expanding the tax take. And so finally confident of their rationale, he concluded, "Chaps, I'm more than happy to back your plans" – to the sheer delight of his associates.

Meanwhile, beyond the cosy events taking place within the carriage, Macdonald and Collins stood with the wind whistling through their hair as they built on their newfound friendship.

"How are things now that Richard's president?" Macdonald shouted over the roar of the locomotive.

"Much better than before!" yelled Collins, with a hint of irony, as he chuckled away and made light of his struggles under Rushbourne.

"I believe Richard will do us proud," Alex hollered emphatically, holding on to his flowing locks and grinning at Collins, who motioned for them to sit and avoid screaming at one another against the wind.

Relaxing with their backs against the warm engine chamber, Collins turned to Alex and said cheerily, "Well, he's done you proud already!"

The Scot looked on confused.

"What, ever do you mean?" he wondered.

"Richard passed the bridge over the East River project!" Collins exclaimed, delighted to be the one to inform Alex, who clearly had no idea.

"Well... that's... great news!" Macdonald replied, somewhat apprehensively, as he was left to consider just how long Stephen had known about the endorsement.

And as the men aboard speculated and fretted and plotted, the train chugged on across the sun-scorched land, towards a new era of development set to be unleashed across America's soil.

Chapter 32: The East River Bridge

Δ

The summer of 1869 passed with Brunson beginning the initial stages of his new development to Duluth. And applying Harris's logic, Brown offered to provide not only the land but also financial support, including the sale of government bonds in partnership with the new scheme - which Sykes more than happily had his firm take to market. Jack also commissioned Macdonald to build Hannibal Bridge, heading north out of Kansas City, and work began soon after. However, Alex, with a mounting sense of disillusionment, remained distant, and only briefly visited the site in Kansas, to avoid bumping into Brunson.

Having made contact with the Roberts family, the Scot then travelled to New York in order to discuss their bridge crossing to Brooklyn. And on a beautiful August morning, as his hired carriage conveyed him along the busy roads towards the footings of the bridge, he gazed out of the window at the city passing by, fondly reminiscing about the time he had spent with AJ at Delmonico's, and when life had seemed exponentially simpler.

Sunbeams reflected on the choppy waters of the East River as he made his final approach, and Alex was feeling quite calmed by the sight – until he peered out of his carriage to see it was not only Alfred and Stephen waiting for him at the footings, but also a grumpy-looking AJ.

Stepping from his stagecoach, the Scot was somewhat uneasy; he could already feel the simmering tension. But he did his best to ignore it as Stephen's chief engineer explained the plans and Macdonald listened intently while offering his opinion on timescales and deliverability. Throughout the discussion he could feel AJ's eyes burning into him, watching him like a hawk, and ready to denigrate him should the opportunity arise. However, having now established himself as a most competent operator and being well skilled in his profession, Alex provided a faultless account of himself, and left Harris standing in silent frustration.

Don't think you've got away with it that easy.

AJ allowed Stephen's engineer to depart before reverting to more direct tactics in the hope of pressuring the Scot into walking away. "So, is our project big enough for you then, Alex?!" he questioned with a scowl. "No doubt you'll be terribly busy assisting *other* members of the group?"

Macdonald said nothing to this childish jibe.

But the Scot's eyes could not hide his true feelings and he winced with sadness at the claim.

"Come on, Andrew," The Commander gently implored. "Let's just leave him alone," he reasoned, seeing little point in being antagonistic, if Brown had instructed that Macdonald be involved in the project.

"Leave him alone?!" AJ berated Stephen, his pride still smarting from having been cheated by Alex for all these years. "The man's in the pocket of Jack Brunson! How can you stand here and trust him?" he ranted. "I wouldn't be surprised if he was involved in the scam against you at Erie!"

That was a wild accusation, and it sorely offended the Scot, who felt compelled now to defend himself.

"I can guarantee you, I had *no part whatsoever* in such dealings," he said staunchly, in a state of barely checked anger. "And as I understand it, Jack was acquitted of any wrongdoing anyway!" Macdonald pointed out – but that only riled Harris further.

"Only because Nelson Allen bribed every senator in America!" he countered, yet neatly failing to mention Stephen's attempts to do exactly the same thing.

Shocked at hearing this news, Macdonald stood silently in splendid isolation. He was the one individual, out of them all, who'd had access to both sides, and was able to connect the dots. Looking around at the eyes bearing down upon him, he realised a decision was needed. He could no longer sit on the fence.

With the power in his hands to condemn either Brunson's mob or Harris's clique, he quickly assessed his options and decided his future pathway.

"There's something I need to tell you," he began. He took a deep breath and told them: "Jack's going to try and manipulate the gold price."

There was a moment of hush, and Alex swallowed the large lump in his throat. Then AJ burst out in a fit of derisory laughter. "And we're supposed to believe that?!" he scoffed, shaking his head in disgust. "I bet it's another one of Brunson's schemes and he's sent you here as his stooge!"

"I swear to you, it's true!" Alex said imploringly, and he went on to explain the finer details of Brunson's plan.

The group from Manhattan weighed up the information. It seemed, from his emotional state and accuracy of the account, that Macdonald was likely telling the truth; but given his past history, AJ was given to erring on the side of caution.

"We just can't trust him, Stephen."

And as The Commander transferred his gaze to Macdonald, before reverting back to Harris, he could not dispute his ally's rationale. "I'm sorry, Alex, but Andrew's right. Our business is built on loyalty and trust, and you've always stood next to my biggest enemy. It's just too much of a risk," Stephen said regretfully.

He had always been a fond of Macdonald as an individual, but he was not prepared to chance getting burnt again by Brunson, or any of his associates.

Andrew was delighted with the outcome.

And aiming a disdainful grin at the Scot, he placed his hand on the elder Roberts' shoulder and gently turned him to walk away.

However, now that he was fully exposed, Alex had no other choice but to push again, in the desperate hope of regaining their trust. "He's going to build a railroad to circumvent New York," he announced flatly to the back of their departing heads.

That stopped the men dead in their tracks, and Stephen turned around with a look of absolute fury in his eyes.

"What? What did you say?"

This better not be a lie.

"Jack has a plan to extend his Transcontinental north from Kansas to create a super-port in Duluth and divert the Atlantic traffic away from Manhattan," he detailed meticulously, in order to demonstrate the legitimacy of his confession. "And he's got President Brown to approve the plan."

Now, Stephen may not have been the most learned of men, but he knew the waters around America like the back of his hand, and he stood there with his mouth agape, picturing the route forming in his mind. He could tell exactly what Jack was trying to do, having sailed the route on a number of occasions himself. And with a dark dawn of realisation setting into his bones, the old man's legs began to wobble like jelly, leaving AJ and Alfred to help prop him up either side.

"I'll kill him!" he muttered under his breath while trying to regain his footing.

Staring across at Alex, a sudden sense of uncertainty washed through AJ's bones. He certainly had not expected this when he began goading the Scot, and still didn't know what to suppose now. The only thing he did know, he was not prepared to mellow.

"I still don't trust you, Macdonald," Harris said with a steely look in his glare. "But I shall keep an eye on the gold market, and if your prediction proves correct... Well, then we'll gladly receive you back with open arms!" he declared contemptuously, leaving all the collateral in his court.

The situation played particularly well into AJ's hands, being one of the founding members of the New York Gold Exchange, would mean he had direct access to all the trading information. If any anomalies were to arise, he would be able to witness them at first hand. But at this point, that fact did little to help the Scot.

Feeling somewhat unnerved at having greatly exposed himself, without gaining any further trust of the Manhattan group, Macdonald was seemingly left in limbo. However, knowing he could do little more to persuade them, Alex reassured himself that Brunson would carry out his plans, and he determined to allow the matter to run its course over the next few - anxious - weeks.

Chapter 33: The Gold Run

Δ

As sure as eggs is eggs, Brunson and Diamond did roll out their plan to manipulate the gold market. They began on the first day of September, when Big Jim met with two fresh-faced New York City bankers and made them an offer they could not refuse: act as dummy accounts, and they would receive a most generous bonus at the conclusion of the run. The two men in question, Turnbull and Bradley, were forbidden from knowing the real reason behind the mission; they were only told they must keep the plan confidential and purchase stock, as and when directed. A simple task for such a large reward, they more than willingly accepted being the pawns in Brunson's scheme.

Entering the Gold Room on the corner of William Street and Exchange Place, the young racketeers gazed out across the trading floor and witnessed for the first time, hundreds of men waving their hands at one another amongst a din of deafening noise. Armed with enough funding to purchase millions of ounces of gold, Turnbull and Bradley surreptitiously placed order after order throughout the day. Their efforts gently nudged the price up, from one hundred and thirty-two dollars at the start to one hundred and thirty-three dollars at close.

They then repeated the trick for the following three days, and left the exchange on 5th September having driven the price of gold to one hundred and thirty-seven dollars an ounce. With their plan seemingly working impeccably, Turnbull and Bradley became increasingly confident they were going to succeed in their instructions, and make themselves very rich young men indeed.

Unbeknownst to them, however, Harris had been keeping a watchful eye over proceedings for several weeks and patiently waiting for any abnormal price rises. Looking through the log books at the end of each day, he analysed the trades, and the names of Turnbull and Bradley stood out starkly against the usual suspects - particularly at such large denominations. Sensing that these two men may have something to do with Jack's scheme, AJ rose early the next day to personally open up the exchange.

Standing by the entrance, he welcomed everyone who passed, until he spotted the culprits, and marched straight up to greet them, "Mr Turnbull, I presume?"

Turnbull's jaw almost hit the floor.

He was aghast that Andrew John Harris, no less, was personally welcoming them to the exchange. Shaking AJ's hand, he stood there completely speechless, then Harris turned his attention to Bradley. "Which must make you Mr Bradley," he concluded, and robustly shook the man's hand.

With both men suffering a fit of paralysis, Harris politely instructed them to "Follow me this way, chaps", and he proceeded to usher them into the banking hall, and towards the counting office at the rear of the building. Like lemmings, Turnbull and Bradley followed on, past the morning Bulls and Bears standing ready, and licking their lips for the onset of the clacker.

When they reached his office, AJ gestured the men inside and pointed to two seats. The naïve young traders sat down quickly, looking at each other with the same thoughts mirrored in their eyes: *Why has Harris apprehended us?* and, *I hope this is just a friendly introduction!*

"So, you chaps are buying gold on behalf of Jim Diamond and Jack Brunson, right?" Andrew said bluntly.

How does he possibly know?

Turnbull and Bradley pushed back their seats in horror, giving their game away, without uttering a word. Desperate to explain their way out of the situation and trying to salvage what remained of their seemingly very short-lived careers on Wall Street, they anxiously looked at each other before erupting into pleas.

"We were given instructions!"

"We just followed orders!"

"We didn't mean any harm, Mr Harris."

"Please don't strike us off!"

Andrew stepped back and leaned against his desk so he could glare down upon both of his newly acquired detainees in tandem. Rubbing his chin in contemplation, he ran several options through in his mind for how best to utilise the men, before landing upon a cunning idea. "What you boys did was very silly. But... I'm willing to forgive you," he proposed, to the sheer relief of the young traders. "On one condition, however."

"What?" Bradley asked desperately.

"Anything!" said Turnbull.

"I want you to go back onto the floor and begin selling off all your positions at one hundred and thirty-two dollars an ounce," AJ told them uncompromisingly.

His apprentices nodded fervently, in appreciation of being let off the hook. And while they knew all too well that agreeing to such a deal would be a direct assault on Brunson and Diamond, it was a risk they were willing to take to avoid falling foul of the formidable AJ. Gleefully thanking him for the opportunity, they wasted no time, as they leapt up and scrambled to leave the office, but Andrew stopped them in their tracks with one final addendum.

"And, gentlemen... this meeting never happened. So when Mr Brunson comes asking why you sold off his positions, you're going to have to come up with some other explanation," he instructed, just as the clacker roared loudly behind them, to signal the start of trading.

"Yes, sir," said Turnbull.

"Thank you, sir," added Bradley

And with that, they dashed out onto the floor with their new set of instructions.

So desperate were they to please AJ that Turnbull and Bradley completed their sales with extreme efficiency, and by the end of the day's trading, the gold price had fallen back to its original position; the reversion costing Brunson more than two million dollars - *success!*

That evening, AJ returned to the offices of JR Harris & Son with a single mission: to celebrate his achievement by taking Maria out for a meal. An hour later, he was seated at the best table, in their favourite restaurant, happy in the knowledge that he had averted a gold run that could potentially have damaged the country; as well as halting Jack in his dastardly scheme, and putting a dint in his bank account for good measure!

Δ

At the Randolph-Smith House Hotel, Brunson sat in the lobby area, awaiting the arrival of his recruits, just as he had for the past few days. Yet as the time ticked by, there was no sign of his associates, and he became increasingly fretful at their unusual tardiness. Unable to leave the hotel, lest he be seen, to quell his nerves and boredom he began to delve deeply into a bottle of scotch, while burning through a full pouch of tobacco. Sitting alone and feeling increasingly intoxicated, Jack started to question how anyone would dare disobey him. And muttering to himself, he came to the conclusion that no one possibly would, so decided to wander around the ground-floor foyer to see whether he had simply missed Turnbull and Bradley entering earlier on.

Meandering into the bar, he noticed a group of men sitting on stools with a set of gold certificates piled up beside their drinks, and he staggered up to confront them.

"You!" Jack slurred, pointing at the men. "You, what happened at the Gold Exchange today?"

"The same as every day!" replied one of the group humorously, and he took a drink, and deliberately turned his back on Jack, while his circle of friends chuckled loudly around him.

"What price did it close at?" Jack demanded, as he grabbed hold of the rather portly man by his collar, causing him to spill his drink all over himself.

The man reacted at once. Spinning off his stool and shoving Jack, who lost his balance and landed on the floor in a tangle of limbs.

"One hundred and thirty-two dollars an ounce," the man said, looking down on Jack in disgust. "Now leave us in peace!"

One hundred and thirty-two dollars, how could that possibly be? Staring wildly, around the many evening revellers, Jack suddenly realised he was in a sorry state – all alone, and a long way from home. What he needed was some help to pull him out of the hole in which he found himself. So he struggled up and weaved his way straight to the telegram office by reception, where he sent a message for Big Jim to return from Erie – it had been the most unfortunate of timing, for him to have returned to take care of the depot. Yet, even Diamond's return would not reveal to him the whereabouts of Turnbull or Bradley - who, quite sensibly, had decided it would be best to abscond until the furore died down, rather than face the wrath of Jack Brunson.

Waking early the next day after a fraught night of disturbed sleep, Brunson decided to take breakfast in his room. Having been holed up in the hotel for the past week, Manhattan's lively and bombastic atmosphere suddenly seemed to be grating on him immensely.

Ever loyal to his friend, Big Jim arrived promptly, later that day, and was surprised to find Jack at such a low ebb. They sat together in a private area of the bar, and Jim provided Jack with his own explanation for what must have happened, before offering his cunning plan for going forward. "I've obtained a list of the top hundred brokers who've borrowed gold at the exchange..." he revealed excitedly, drawing Jack's attention. "Why don't we place an advert with a local newspaper calling in all the loans at one hundred and sixty dollars an ounce?!" he proposed - absurdly - but with a wide grin of satisfaction on his face.

"Surely that's only one step away from blackmail?" said Brunson, who preferred to keep his deceitful activities somewhat more covert. "And besides, no one will fall for that!" He puffed out his cheeks in disbelief, dearly hoping his ally had some better suggestions up his sleeve.

"Okay. Well then, we just take the simple route," Jim said bluntly. "You dip your hand in your pocket and we go back in again!"

In reality, it was the only option they had, but Jack instantly identified one glaring flaw with that plan. He could not be seen walking into the exchange and placing large bets on the market, especially if he wished to keep his image squeaky clean with Brown.

As such, he had another idea in mind. "So *you'll* go in there tomorrow and start buying again?" he said, placing the onus firmly on his friend.

"I guess if we can't trust anyone else then I'll have to," Jim confirmed, and for the first time that day, a smile lit Brunson's face. What a delight it was at having so many stooges, happy to undertake his dirty work.

Δ

Striding onto the trading floor on Monday 9th September, Big Jim was desperate to make amends for his good friend. So much so, he soon forgot about playing things steady, and began purchasing gold at a rate that made the trades from the week before seem like small change. Swept away on a wave of excitement, across the following three days he invested so heavily, and so frequently, that Brunson's stake in the plot rose to over twenty million dollars.

AJ watched in astonishment as the events unfolded, but this time he was powerless to intervene, or use his influence over the man responsible. His only option was to put down his own money in an attempt to combat Brunson and Diamond; though it would be a brave man who would take them on, in what would effectively be: a race to the bottom. Watching the market rise consistently back to its peak and knowing he could not financially outmuscle them, Harris decided he had no other choice but to speak with Brown and inform him of the activities going on in New York. So he took the night train to Washington, and arrived at the presidential mansion early the next morning.

With his logbooks tucked underneath his arm, he was all prepared to take his knowledge to a higher source, but when he arrived at the Oval Office, he was disappointed to find that the president was nowhere to be seen. He decided to go seek out his trusted ally, George Collins, who he was sure, would know of Brown's whereabouts.

He found his old ally standing reflectively on the South Portico, taking a moment of fresh air. "George, my good man - do you know where Richard is?" he enquired, expecting the president must be held up, in meetings somewhere nearby.

"He's not here, Andrew," Collins divulged, and then coughed roughly and wheezed before grasping his chest. "He's gone to Pennsylvania - visiting his aunt."

"Thanks, George," AJ said warmly. He gently placed a hand on Collins' shoulder. "Are you okay, old sport?" he asked considerately.

"I'm fine, Andrew, I'm fine," George replied, but then he spluttered once again, this time covering his mouth, to shield away his germs. "Thanks for your concern, though."

AJ was of a mind to stay and ensure that his good friend was indeed all right, but the matter at hand that had brought him to Washington, was pressing to say the least. With George doing his best to muster a reassuring smile, AJ accepted that his friend would be fine, as he professed, and he bid him farewell to head off in pursuit of Brown.

Little did he know, but that would be AJ's final farewell to good old George Collins, whose health would continue to deteriorate for the remainder of the year, until, come Christmas Day, he succumbed to his final rest.

Δ

Next, Harris undertook the cross-country journey to rural Pennsylvania, arriving at Washington train station on 14th September. *Rural - there are more people working in my office building than live here!*

He was unable to find a suitable stagecoach for hire in this quaint, single-track town, so he consulted with some locals over the direction of his destination, before setting out on his journey on foot.

The two-mile trek with the mid-morning sun beating down upon his brow was arduous, and he was soon soaked with perspiration, beneath his heavy suit. Unwilling to slow his pace, however, until he'd resolved the issue, AJ pressed on along the sandy and desolate track. Finally, he arrived at the foot of the long driveway, and spying the president enjoying a spot of croquet on the front lawn, Harris pushed ahead with a building sense of relief.

Brown spotted his friend labouring up the path, and rushed straight over to greet him. Somewhat perplexed, but delighted to receive him, the president promptly led AJ into the whitewashed wooden house and provided him with a cold glass of lemonade. Then they sat together at the kitchen table, while outside hoots of laughter and the thwack of the croquet mallet indicated that Brown's family were playing on in his absence.

"So what can I do for you, Andrew?" the president enquired, looking genuinely relaxed away from the tribulations of the capital.

AJ took a moment to quench his thirst with the refreshment provided, drinking it deep into his gut. Then he set down his glass and said, "I need to warn you about a gold run that's occurring in New York."

"And you came all the way here to tell me that?!" Richard jested, not fully understanding the implications of the drastic revelation.

Andrew was resolute. "Jack Brunson and Jim Diamond are going to cause a run on the gold supply, and it could severely damage the country," he warned.

Brown sipped slowly on his lemonade while contemplating the information brought to him. And as the drink slipped down his throat, cooling and refreshing him on this humid day, he suddenly recalled the last time AJ had *warned* him of wrongdoings by Brunson, and he wondered whether Andrew's judgment may have become clouded when it came to issues concerning Jack. However, he did not wish to pour scorn on Harris's advice, especially given how far he had travelled.

"Okay, Andrew, let me speak with John Peters when I return to Washington," he said. He hoped it would placate AJ to have the Secretary of the Treasury investigate the matter in closer detail, later in the week.

Harris, however, understanding the true gravity of events, was unable to hold back. "In a couple of days' time, Richard – and I say this with the utmost respect," he said politely through gritted teeth, "... it might be too late!"

Leaning back in his chair and placing his glass upon on the table, the president stared out of the window with a reserved look upon his face. He felt this to be something of an imposition – he really did not want to leave his family during their holiday time together. "I'll be back to Washington in three days' time and shall look into it then. I can't say fairer than that," he concluded, and he rose to signal that the discussion was at an end.

Respectfully, Harris rose alongside him.

He was annoyed by the president's lack of urgency, of course, but realised there was little point in pushing him again, safe for losing his ear completely. He could only hope that the delay did not cost them too severely, and that they could still be able to rescue the situation, once Brown had returned to Washington.

As the men moved out of the house and back towards the gardens, Richard could sense Andrew's obvious disappointment. Out of courtesy, he asked, "And if your information is correct, what do you suggest I do?"

"You'll need to sell plenty of government gold and buy back bonds," he advised, looking pointedly at Richard in the hope he would remember.

"Thanks, Andrew," Brown quickly concluded. "Now, come say hello to the kids!" he commanded cheerily; and biting his tongue, AJ smilingly acquiesced.

Δ

Chapter 34: Black Friday

Δ

As soon as he returned from his vacation, Brown sought out his Secretary of the Treasury as promised, and ordered an investigation. And he soon found out that John Peters corroborated Harris's information, about the ensuing bull market for gold across America. But while Peters agreed that it was a strange occurrence for the price to have increased so rapidly, at its current level, he deemed the rise sustainable!

Their hands were soon forced, however, as between the 18th and 22nd September, Big Jim - buoyed on by the success of his earlier splurges - became progressively greedier, and increased their position to forty million dollars, which subsequently drove up the price of gold to one hundred and sixty-two dollars per ounce. With the price now hitting unsustainable levels, and deciding they needed to consult with all parties involved before taking any affirmative action, Brown and Peters packed their bags, and made the trip north to New York immediately.

When Brown received information that Brunson had been residing in Manhattan for the past two weeks, the evidence appeared increasingly damning for their main culprit. Brown however, wished to reserve judgement until he had spoken with his fellow comrade - but this did not mask his irritation of the fact, that he found himself placed in this position once again.

Marching through the entrance doors of the Randolph-Smith House hotel, Brown found Brunson reading the *New York Tribune* whilst lounging on a sofa. Richard quietly strode across the foyer and stopped beside his associate.

"Mr Brunson!" he said sternly.

Jack started violently. Slowly lowering his newspaper, he peered over the top to see the one man he hadn't expected.

"Hello, Richard!" he said sheepishly and a smile edged across his face.

By now Brown's presence was attracting attention, and the ground-floor lobby had transformed into a hub of noise as the hotel guests marvelled at seeing their new president in the flesh. Jack quickly grabbed the opportunity to avoid any potential interrogation in front of the masses, and he leapt to his feet. Scrunching up the newspaper and tossing it on the couch, he suggested they move to one of the more discreet rooms off the lounge?

When Brown gave him a disgruntled nod, then Jack led him the way, yet peering up ahead it became clear that nowhere in the hotel was quiet at that time. "Everyone up! The president requires the room," he yelled authoritatively as they entered the room, leaving those in the space to quickly finish their drinks, before dashing out with the bartender following on their heels.

"So what can I do you for, Richard?" Brunson enquired spiritedly, seeking to mask his guilt. "Drink?" he offered, motioning across to the bar, thinking perhaps he could delay the onset of the conversation, and charm his way out of any potential unwanted questioning.

"Not just yet," Brown replied in his most serious tone. "Do sit down please," he instructed, with authority.

Jack relinquished the whisky bottle in his hand and started to comprehend fully, that this was not a mere social call. He walked over with an uncommonly grave look about his person, and took a seat opposite the president.

"What do you know about the gold run we are witnessing at present?" Brown asked, getting straight to the point and still, despite the man's evident unease, he desperately hoped Jack was not involved.

"I don't –" Jack began, but Brown cut him off in mid-stream.

"And I need you to tell me the truth, Jack!"

"Well, I..." he began tentatively, racking his brain for a believable answer. An idea sparked, and he jumped in feet first. "I heard about it too, Richard! And so I came down here to speculate a bit, just like everyone else is doing." Brunson sat back and breathed a sigh of relief, confident he had covered himself with his crafty little explanation.

Slowly scanning his associate up and down with a blank stare, and offering no inkling as to his internal conflict, Brown could not decide whether to believe Jack. His gut told him, *he should not.*

Yet with no hard evidence at hand with which to challenge Brunson's excuse – which was, after all, plausible – the president decided he would hold the matter in abeyance.

"Okay, Jack," he said soberly, slowly rising from his seat and maintaining eye contact throughout. "But you need to cease this activity right now!" he advised.

It was a most generous advisement indeed.

And both men knew what Brown was silently saying: *I will overlook this possible indiscretion, if you leave this instant.*

Springing to his feet, Brunson extended his hand. "I'll go home right now," he promised, smiling gratefully at the pardon.

Richard could only stare back, feeling a huge sense of doubt, before simply wishing him, "Good day," and sweeping out of the room, leaving Jack standing alone, still waiting for the handshake.

For a while he remained there, in the private bar, cut off from the distant hum of the hotel in the background, and trying to analyse the turn of events. Angry with Diamond for over-speculating, he blamed his colleague for bringing the spotlight upon them. Either way, it didn't matter, and Brunson knew the game was up. So with only the whisky bottle for company, he began to plot his way out of this mess.

Δ

Meanwhile, outside the Randolph-Smith House hotel, John Peters was waiting for Brown, in a stagecoach.

Together, they travelled the short distance across Lower Manhattan to Hanover Square. As they walked into the offices of JR Harris & Son, Brown was instantly recognised by the staff, who leapt to their feet like corporals on early-morning inspection. Only Maria had been half-expecting the president's arrival, and she quickly guided them to AJ's office.

"Richard! Great to see you again," Harris greeted Brown warmly, before turning to his companion. "And Mr John Peters, I assume?"

John Peters, a man of few words, merely nodded politely. He had started his career as a Democrat, but having found little support within the party, he became a stalwart Republican. He had demonstrated his loyalty during Rushbourne's impeachment, which was why Brown had subsequently appointed him to his Cabinet after his inauguration.

"How was your vacation?" Harris enquired politely as the men settled into their seats.

Brown let out a rueful sigh.

He was completely humbled by AJ's cordial approach and knew he didn't deserve it. Andrew could just as easily have chosen to be sanctimonious and lambast the president for his dithering, especially with the gold price at its current, eye-watering level.

"I want to apologise to you, Andrew," an embarrassed-looking Brown began, shifting uncomfortably in his seat. "I should have acted sooner," he admitted.

"Don't worry about it," AJ said sincerely, smiling graciously at his guests from Washington: they were here now, that was all that mattered.

"Well, that's very modest of you, AJ," Richard said. "I see now that you've only ever wanted to help me, and the country, and I won't forget that again," he declared with a fond smile.

With a warmth pervading the room, it suddenly dawned on Harris just what a pivotal moment this could turn out to be; here was a golden opportunity to evolve into Brown's go-to advisor. "I'm only here to help, Richard, you know that," he said firmly. "You know my father, you know me - we're forthright, but we're loyal. And in this day and age, that's all that counts."

Brown nodded in complete accord, before swallowing his pride and saying, "That is why, Andrew, I need you to speak with John and devise a plan to shut this gold run down for good."

AJ's chest puffed up with pride.

"It would be my absolute pleasure, Richard," he said. He turned his piercing gaze towards the Secretary of the Treasury. "Let's get to work, John."

Harris devoted his entire afternoon to going through the books with Peters, and calculated exactly how much Treasury gold they would need to release in order to bring the price of gold back down. Together, they formulated a meticulous plan that, they hoped, would avoid any adverse shocks to the system, and allow the market to return slowly back to normality.

After profusely thanking AJ once again for his assistance, the men from Washington exited the building, with his plans tucked firmly inside a leather wallet, and all three of them went to bed that night feeling armed and ready, to implement their strategy the following day.

Δ

The morning of September 24th arrived, and while Peters was preparing to release millions of dollars of gold in tranches, as AJ had instructed, Brunson had woken even earlier and was already standing opposite the Gold Exchange, awaiting its doors to open. With his position now fully exposed, he had little need to conceal his identity, but he still wanted to remain somewhat undercover, and so was looking to sneak in amongst the raft of daily traders as the floor opened for business. Harris, meanwhile, considering the whole affair taken care of, was on his way to Cleveland to attend to some urgent business with Cunningham.

When he entered the Gold Room, the regulars noticed Jack and his presence there struck them as somewhat odd. However, caught up in their hunger to continue benefitting from the current "Bull Run", they paid him little heed as they waited for trading to begin.

Brunson's task was a simple one: sell all his gold at overinflated prices to those who believed the increases would never cease. And there were plenty of those around. Releasing as much of his gold as possible without causing suspicion, he knew he would take some hits on the way down as the price began to tumble. But from his buy-in price at one hundred and thirty-two dollars, he did, however, still have a comfortable margin, from which to profit rather handsomely.

Having sold off all his positions by midday, Brunson rushed back to the hotel to collect his things, and then sped to the station and boarded a train for Erie, the matter, for him, consigned to history.

Peters, meanwhile, also sold in large tranches across the morning, but the steady fall he and AJ had planned for in their intricate scheme was scuppered by Brunson's sell-off. Thanks to Jack's actions, the price of gold dropped far too quickly for Peters to combat it, from one hundred and sixty-two dollars in the morning to one hundred and thirty-eight dollars as the afternoon session commenced. Soon, everyone was looking to sell, and the price was only heading one way.

Big Jim Diamond, who had spent the morning frolicking with his mistress, arrived at the Gold Room to witness blind panic ensuing all around. His initial reaction was amusement; he was convinced that whatever was causing such a stir would be of no issue to him. Still, curious, he decided to investigate what all the commotion was about.

Approaching a fraught trader, sitting slumped with his head in his hands at the edge of the floor, Jim asked,

"What's going on here then?" He gestured to the melee with a large grin upon his face.

"Gold price... gone... all gone," the man muttered back, unable to raise his head, so desolate was he.

Diamond, however, did not even flinch at the news. "Well, I'm sure you'll get it back tomorrow," he said pleasantly, while reassuring himself that he was unlikely to suffer a similar fate given that *his* were the hands pulling the strings of the market.

"Nope... not this time," replied the chap as he peered up at Jim with a look of horror on his face. "One hundred and sixty-two dollars an ounce at opening... one hundred and thirty-six dollars right now. We're all finished!" he cried.

"WHAT DID YOU SAY?" Jim demanded, hauling the young trader up by his underarms.

"The gold price," the man gasped. "One hundred and sixty-two dollars this morning. Trading now at –" He was cut off by furore in the room as there was another tick down on the price. "Trading now at... one hundred and thirty-five dollars an ounce!" he groaned.

Big Jim abruptly dropped the trader to the floor in shock. Raising his hands to cover his mouth, he scanned the crowd before him once again, and finally he appreciated the panic etched onto their faces as his mind automatically turned to Jack...

Where is he?

Did he sell?

Does he know?

But there was no time for his thoughts to linger. And instead Big Jim rushed across the floor, and squeezed through the mob to place himself directly in the centre of the ruckus. Raising his hand in the air, he desperately shouted out his price, and at once he was engulfed in a sea of aggressive deal-making.

In the minutes that followed, the frenzy descended into fist-fighting. And as the police came to help, and the scuffles spilled out onto the street, a most unsightly scene stunned all those who were there to witness, such desolation in the heart of Manhattan's financial business district.

Chapter 35: The Grand Opening

Δ

The events at the Gold Exchange went down in the history books as "Black Friday", a name aptly coined by the *New York Times*. The collapse caused shockwaves throughout the US, with stocks falling by more than twenty per cent and numerous firms forced into bankruptcy: nowhere was left unaffected. Farmers across the country were ruined as crop prices dropped, in some cases to half their value, resulting in large-scale layoffs in workforces. The agricultural market in America was blighted so heavily it would never regain its pre-eminence from before the intervention of Brunson – whose Transcontinental Railroad, ironically, also suffered as a result.

Initially, the reaction from the press was one of gratitude towards Brown and Peters, for their efforts to abate the gold run. However, as the public became more aware of the dealings that occurred, and they increasingly struggled to make ends meet, anger and resentment began to stir, and fingers were pointed at the president. To quell the accusations, Brown was forced to submit to a congressional investigation.

The chairman of the House Banking Committee, Arthur Franklin, was appointed to chair proceedings. An up-and-coming thirty-six year old, he had been a brigadier general during the Civil War. While propelled into his political career somewhat late compared to others, he was doing a fine job of establishing a name for himself, and trying desperately to continue his inexorable rise. One by one, Franklin interviewed all of the parties involved.

First he met with Brunson, who immediately laid the blame at Diamond's door. "I wasn't even in the Gold Room at the time all of this was going on - how could I possibly be involved?" he contended vehemently.

For his part, Big Jim – having lost millions of dollars as well as all contact with Brunson – deflected the accusations right back in Jack's direction.

And due to the ongoing investigation as well as the heavy scrutiny which he himself was under, Brown was forced to cease all association with Jack, until his name was cleared of all wrongdoing. This stalled the Duluth works for over half a year, to the absolute delight of the Roberts family.

In order to obtain all the evidence required, Franklin travelled to New York and examined the Gold Exchange accounts, which Harris kindly provided. AJ also offered to run through the trades with Franklin – a most willing and helpful aide. But not wanting to expose his own involvement, he cautiously attempted to lead the investigation towards Jack's guilt, while at the same time exonerating the president. Working together, day after day, Harris and Franklin struck up a solid friendship, and when the evidence gathering concluded, AJ had himself another useful ally in the capital.

With Franklin returning to Washington, he presented his findings to the investigative committee. The verdict of the members: there was no substantial evidence against any individual, and so they closed the case without finding anyone guilty of wrongdoing. The only clear outcome from the escapade was that Brown was no longer prepared to blindly trust Brunson, and as a result he was hesitant to approve any more of his plans, unless he had run them past Harris beforehand.

Elsewhere, The Commander was having a mixed year. On the one hand, business had proved most successful, with the bridge to Brooklyn coming on handsomely and his Central Depot taking shape. However, on a personal note he was having a harrowing year, as first his daughter and then his beloved wife passed away; and after fifty splendid years of marriage, Stephen was left lonely and depressed. The losses weighed so heavily on him, that some feared he would become a reclusive.

Feeling, at seventy-seven, that time was catching up with him, he slowly handed over the day-to-day running of the business to Alfred - who in turn brought his three sons, Stephen Roberts II, Elliot Roberts and Milton Frederick Roberts, on board to assist him. As a further relinquishing of the reigns and in recognition of their unbreakable bond of friendship, The Commander also bestowed a ten percent share of the business to Harris, knowing that the gesture would help ensure the future success of his family empire.

Δ

On a sunny day in the spring of 1871, the final tracks were laid, and invitations sent out for the grand unveiling of Manhattan's first Central Depot. Informed by everyone around him that it would be remiss of him to miss the occasion, Stephen dragged himself out of bed and skulked up the street to Hanover Square, where AJ was standing by. They took his private stagecoach for their journey towards East & 42nd Street, but rather than take the direct route through the centre of town, Harris considerately instructed his man to circle around the eastern edge of Manhattan. The six-mile journey not only allowed them to pass by the Brooklyn Bridge site, but also kept The Commander away from the hustle and bustle of the city; which, after all these years, now seemed like such incessant noise to his ears.

As the carriage trundled along the streets, Stephen sat silently, and peered out of the window at the world passing him by. Deeply concerned by his friend's emotional state, Andrew offered him a sympathetic smile.

"How are you keeping today?" he asked kindly.

"Well. You know," came the short reply from Stephen. Shoulders hunched, blackened eyes, he suddenly looked every inch his age.

AJ was desperate to revive his friend's outlook, but was struggling to know how. He decided an attempt to stir the old man's hunger, was exactly what he needed. "Such splendid developments on the bridge!"

But the success of the project offered little solace to Stephen; he only wanted something money could no longer buy. Yet seeing that AJ felt the need to talk, and with some distance left until they arrived, he decided to turn the conversation around.

"I've heard Macdonald's doing a great job," he said, turning his tired eyes towards his comrade. "He means you no harm, Andrew. You should make good with him," Stephen advised; his previously hostile take on life, somewhat diminished by recent events.

"Let me speak with him and see what I can do," AJ offered, if he thought it would please his great friend.

The old man mustered a smile as he looked upon Andrew, full of admiration and pride at what a fine young man he had become - just as Stephen had predicted all those years ago, when speaking to Harris Senior at the Union League meeting in Philadelphia.

"And what of Brunson's extension to Duluth?" The Commander asked wistfully; in a tone which lacked his usual gusto, when enquiring about his enemy.

"As I understand it, Brown has let him continue what he started," AJ replied with a look of frustration on his face. "We'll just have to hope Jack makes another mistake?"

"Well, I'm sure you'll figure something out – you always do, AJ!" Stephen accepted with a smile, as their coach came to a halt.

Quickly, Harris stepped out first, and offered his hand to help his friend from the carriage. Peering out, Stephen stared up at his Central Depot; a mammoth four-storey building, and then he looked glumly up and down the busy street, appearing almost afraid of the oncoming pedestrians.

"I'm going away after today," The Commander announced suddenly. "I need to get out of this city. The noise, the people – I just need some damn peace and quiet!"

"Well, don't you worry," AJ assured him. "I'll keep an eye on things while you're away."

The two allies smiled at each other in mutual respect, and couldn't help but feel reflective. Thinking of the tumultuous events they had endured to reach this point, they had to try and enjoy these special moments, and the future that could now lay ahead.

Δ

Entering the main hub and staring around at the monolithic structure, AJ – who had visited many, if not all, the grandest buildings in America – was blown away by the final creation. A design masterpiece containing hundreds of majestic archways, twelve rows of elevated platforms and a thirty-metre-high, curved-glass roof; it awed everyone who entered with its magnificence.

Having arrived before the grand unveiling, they were greeted by Alfred, who warmly embraced his father, thrilled to see him out of his seclusion. Both men had suffered terrible losses this past year, Al's youthfulness, the only thing that had allowed him to carry on with a little more ease than his father.

"Andrew, thank you for bringing Father," the younger Roberts said as he shook AJ's hand heartily.

"Not a problem. We're all family here," he said, while acknowledging Alfred's three boys, who stood nearby, mesmerised by Harris. "I understand you're sitting down with Oliver later on?" AJ said to ensure Alfred did not forget about the meeting, and Alfred nodded to confirm the appointment.

Soon thereafter, the president arrived with Dixon, Peters and Franklin, and when Macdonald and Cunningham joined them on the concourse; the group was then complete. AJ called over the head of catering to request a round of single-shot whiskies, before gathering the group together.

"This past year we've witnessed America's unparalleled growth under the patronage of our good friend and esteemed president," he said, and those circled around him cheered lightly. "Yet... it's also been a year of great loss, both here in New York as well as in the capital." He cast his gaze towards Brown, who nodded in sombre appreciation.

A toast was in order, and AJ knew just whom they should honour. "To the Roberts family!" he called out, lifting his glass into the air. "And to our dear friend George Collins," he added mournfully, as the group knocked back their drinks.

With Harris busy conducting the waiters as they hurriedly collected the empty glasses, Brown took aside his aides he had brought from Washington. "There may come a time when I'm not around," he said quietly, thoughts of Collins ruminating in his brain. "So if you're ever in need of anything, *these* are the men to seek out," he directed, gesturing them towards the members of the group, and his colleagues nodded their understanding.

Δ

As the time for the official opening ceremony approached, the Central Depot concourse filled with expectant New Yorkers, and a hubbub of noise inside. Alfred and Stephen Roberts took their places on a stage temporarily erected at the front of the crowd, and Alfred called the cavernous space to order. Once a relative hush descended, he delivered a brief but informative speech, enlightening the attendees about the facility, and the efforts expended to complete it. Then, finally, he proclaimed loudly:

"I now declare the Grand Central Depot... open for business!"

This was met with thunderous applause, and as the brass band started up, the most important guests were ushered to their own private area, to relax and chat - and most importantly, to network.

Over the past several years, AJ had morphed from being a somewhat introverted individual, living in his father's shadow, to an all-out leader of men. His success with Cunningham and his standing within the group had empowered him to feel confident in his own abilities, and where he once saw threats, he now saw opportunities. Spotting Worthington standing alone with his twelve-year-old son, he walked over to speak with him. "I hear plans for the history museum are progressing well?" Harris said after pleasantries had been exchanged.

"We're hoping it can add to our knowledge of the world and provide us with a foundation for further scientific research and education," Worthington explained, his eyes alight with passion.

His son interjected excitedly, "And I'm going to exhibit my findings in the museum, Mr Harris!"

Warmed by Junior's enthusiasm, AJ smiled down on him. "Well, I shall certainly look forward to seeing that, young man," he said kindly, before returning his gaze to the elder Worthington. "Seems like you've a headstrong lad here, Christopher!" he commended him, and the men chuckled away at the young boy's strength of conviction.

Meanwhile, Oliver and Alfred had finally managed to locate one another in amongst the cluster of guests.

"Shall we take this to your office?" the oil man said, looking around surreptitiously.

Heeding Oliver's recommendation, Alfred led his ally up the iron staircase to his private office overlooking the concourse, with AJ, watching them go, and pleased to see the two men finally working together. Then his roving eyes caught sight of The Commander sitting amongst a group of men in conversation, of which he was clearly taking no active part. AJ marched over immediately.

"Thought I'd come and save you!" he beamed.

Stephen wobbled up from his chair. "Thanks Andrew," he said, finally freed from the incessant gossip. "Think I'm going to go home now."

With AJ sensing he was unlikely to change The Commander's mind, he happily accompanied his great friend to the exit. When they stepped outside, into the open air, Harris's driver was waiting there patiently.

"Take my stagecoach," said Andrew. "I'll arrange something for myself later on."

Stephen looked up at him with a dignified smile and stepped aboard the carriage for his journey home. "I'll see you soon" replied The Commander, then he rested his aching back into the comfy, monogrammed upholstery.

Leaning up against the wall, Andrew took a moment to watch as his stagecoach departed into the hectic mid-afternoon traffic. Pausing for a moment to take in Manhattan's locals rushing about their business, he felt an overwhelming sense of achievement - knowing that he, and his comrades, were helping to create a bigger and better world around them. The moment, as he stood there, filled him with pride.

But his peaceful solitude was to be short-lived.

And unbeknownst to AJ, Macdonald had been monitoring him; and seeing that Harris was alone for the first time today, he seized the opportunity to speak with him in private.

"Andrew!" he said enthusiastically as he approached. "How are you?"

Harris slowly turned around, already knowing who was standing behind him; the thick Scottish accent was an instant giveaway. "I'm good, thank you," he replied politely, yet offered nothing more in return, leaving Macdonald to fumble around, having hoped for more than simply well-mannered conversation.

"Sad news about Stephen," Alex offered, which caused Harris to recall his grief-stricken comrade's advice from earlier: *maybe it was time to bury the hatchet.*

"A terrible shame indeed. That great man has taken his losses particularly hard," he confirmed, and Macdonald lit up at AJ seemingly lowering his guard. "I just wish I could do something more?"

Desperate to re-establish their friendship, Alex grabbed the opportunity to prove himself yet again. "What if we could help with one of the losses? I mean, what if we got his money back from Brunson?" he suggested excitedly.

He received a muddled look in reply from AJ, who nevertheless motioned for him to continue.

"My cousin was recently swindled out of some money I had given him to set up his jewellery business," Alex explained.

Andrew gazed at him incredulously, wondering how this would cheer up their associate. "And?"

"And the conman is currently sitting in Dunfermline jail. But if my brother were to drop the charges in exchange for his services, we could utilise him to play the same trick on Jack!" Macdonald revealed.

Suddenly, the penny dropped for Harris, and a smirk spread across his face. Staring at Macdonald, feeling a reignited rush of affiliation with the Scot, he knew he could no longer hold his grudge.

"Okay, Alex, let's put this plan into motion and see what we can achieve," he said.

The "we" said it all: for this was the first time, in a long time, that he and Alex would work together, and the Scot beamed back, elated, to have finally earned back the trust he had broken.

Δ

Meanwhile, high above the celebrations, another plan was being hatched in a first-floor office. At this stage it mainly involved Alfred, listening to a man eighteen years his junior, sit and dictate their future union.

"You see, I don't care much for competition because it only creates disorder and inefficiency," Cunningham lectured his host, who looked on like a nodding dog. "And I ferociously oppose waste!" he added, appearing sick to the stomach at even the thought of it.

"I agree," Alfred replied automatically. Truthfully, he was not entirely sure to what Oliver was referring, but he allowed him to continue his tirade.

"The railroads fight for traffic, the refiners fight for contracts – in what, I must say, is a rather undignified state of affairs," he said with a genuine look of sadness in his eyes. "However, if this were transformed into an orderly flow of business, then the whole country would surely benefit – don't you agree?" His insistence was infectious to say the least.

"So what can we do?" the younger Roberts questioned politely.

Why I thought you'd never ask...

And thus Oliver emphatically laid out his proposal in full. "My plan is to set up a rebate system between you and me, while at the same time increasing the price for shipping. Everyone will pay the higher price, but you will rebate me into a separate company that we shall set up together. I will then cover that cost to you by paying into another company, the same amount as the rebate."

Alfred's head was spinning; he was unable to comprehend the intricacy of the scheme, but he did not want to reveal his ineptitude. So analysing his decision based solely upon the fact that Cunningham was a loyal friend of Harris's, he simply replied, "Okay."

With business seemingly concluded, Alfred rose from his seat. However, Oliver had one final addition to his devious scheme. "Oh, and by the way, Alfred," Cunningham said, halting his associate on his way towards the door, "as part of the plan, I'll need daily access to your shipping reports." This would allow Oliver to review all his competitors' activities against his own - dates, destinations, barrelages and costs.

"Sure thing," Alfred agreed subserviently, and he received a nod of appreciation from Cunningham.

Now they were ready to depart the room - but just as Alfred put his hand on the doorknob, he yelped in shock as a face popped up behind the glass window in the door. Smiling wildly, AJ entered the room, followed by Macdonald, forcing Alfred and Oliver backwards on their heels. The men retook their seats, wondering why their friend looked so pleased.

"Alex has a plan that's going to put a smile back on your father's face!" AJ revealed eagerly, and Alfred looked on in anticipation while the Scot unveiled his plot, to reignite The Commander.

Chapter 36: Lord Campbell-Campbell

Δ

After happily subscribing to the plan, as proposed, Macdonald instructed his cousin, Alastair Bowman, to have the charges dropped against the charlatan in exchange for him taking on an even bigger swindle over in America. Days later, Bowman arrived by boat at the port of Manhattan with Fraser Finlay, the imposter who had conned him, and they were promptly whisked away by stagecoach to a secret location. The last thing AJ and Alex wanted was for their scam to fall short and land back upon their doorstep, so, having fully debriefed their visitors, they left the men to their own devices.

Bowman, originally hailing from Gloucestershire in England, was a polite and agreeable type of chap, simply looking for a quiet and easy life. Finlay, however, was quite the opposite - a gregarious individual with a mop of ginger hair, he had a particular penchant for all things Scottish and did not suffer fools gladly.

The unlikely pair checked into the largest suite at the most luxurious hotel that Erie had to offer, situated only a stone's throw away from the depot, and practised getting into character while they waited for their subterfuge to begin.

Having hired out one of the bar areas as part of their plan, Bowman positioned himself there in anticipation of one of their marks frequenting the bar. But as a lengthy and monotonous two days passed without a single sighting, it slowly dawned on him that this could be a long and arduous process.

He pressed on, however, into the third day, and as luck would have it, with midnight approaching, Millard Stride came breezing in for a well-earned beverage after finishing work. Seating himself at the empty and unmanned bar, Uncle Millard looked about for a member of serving staff and did not notice as Alastair approached from the corner of the room.

"Excuse me!" Bowman said politely in the best upper-class English accent he could muster. "I have this bar reserved for my Royal guest."

Instantly, Stride was drawn into the trap; the prospect of meeting a member of royalty had him practically salivating.

"Would it be okay if I stayed just a little longer?" Millard enquired meekly of the well-to-do stranger. "Maybe... meet your guest?" he propositioned, in the hope that he could impress his friends, with tales of the encounter.

Lingering for a moment and twitching as he considered the idea, as if it were an imposition, Bowman eyed Stride up and down pensively. "Well... you do seem a jolly fellow.

Maybe it will be alright," he allowed. Then, somewhat eccentrically, he yelled out, "Barman!"

Within a flash, the bartender duly appeared. And he quietly poured two glasses of whisky before leaving them alone again so that Bowman could continue his elaborate performance. Grabbing hold of a small wooden box resting neatly at the side of the bar, he slid open the front to reveal a bottle of 1825, Chateau Lafite, Bordeaux red; a rather fine and expensive vintage, it had been selected from Harris's very own collection, earlier that week! Crouching down, he picked up a hefty looking case by his feet and delicately placed it on the bar, before slowly clicking open the locks at each end to reveal two crystal-cut glasses inside. Then, with Stride, like a moth to the flame; Bowman held the first flute up to the light cast by an oil lantern, and began to painstakingly examine every millimetre of the surface.

Suddenly, he appeared annoyed.

"Hmm... this one will be for cleaning!" he muttered to himself, in clear earshot of his visitor.

Millard sat silently in shock, unable to identify even a single speck of dirt! And he continued to look on as Alastair picked up the second glass, repeating the process, and this time accepting it as suitable, before uncorking the costly bottle. "I'll just let it sit for a moment and warm up," he revealed to Stride, while looking mightily pleased with his own suggestion. "He hates anything other!"

Stride had never seen anything like it before. This process for preparing a simple glass of wine was so impressively elaborate, it did not cross his mind to consider that the man before him was anything other than the associate of a true royal. And so with the con well and truly in play, Alastair excused himself for a bathroom break.

The moment he was out of the room, however, he only had eyes for reception, and rushed over to request that the porter alert his associate that he was now required.

Δ

Finlay walked into the bar, chest puffed out, large feet at ten to two, dressed in full Scottish garb, complete with knee-high socks, tartan waistcoat and bright-orange kilt. Without saying a word, he directed his gaze presumptuously towards the wineglass. Bowman picked up on his colleague's cue and rushed to hand him the flute he was pretending to demand.

"Sorry Sir, here you are" he offered.

But as he sipped the wine, a look of disdain flashed across Finlay's face – leaving Stride, perched on a bar stool, feeling most uncomfortable as the Lord acknowledged his presence for the first time.

"Who is this standing in my bar?!"

"Sorry, sir, sorry!" Bowman fumbled again, with a look of worry in his eyes. "The gentleman was merely seeking a drink, and I said he could remain. I do apologise, it's my fault entirely" he grovelled in complete subordination.

"Hmm..." Finlay exhaled. "And who, in fact, are you?" he enquired, looking down his nose at Stride.

"Millard Stride, sir," he replied quickly, before holding his hand out to shake. "An honour to meet you, sir."

Staring into Millard's eyes, Finlay recognised the look of adulation – which was, he knew, essential for any con to work. And realising their mark had now fully dropped his guard, he began to change tact.

"Mr Stride, was it?" he said, snatching his lingering, outstretched hand. "Lord Campbell... Campbell," Finlay announced, as Stride gazed down in wonder at his fingers; covered in gold rings, adorned with opulent red stones (brought over from Bowman's shop in Scotland, they were in fact the exact same ones Finlay had swindled Alastair out of earlier in the year)!

As the three men burned the midnight oil and the drinks continued to flow, Stride felt accepted enough by his new associates to seek more details about their visit.

"So what brings you here to Erie?" he enquired. The "lord" appeared somewhat reluctant to answer, however.

He glanced around the room and then abruptly stood and crossed to the doorway to check for the presence of any eavesdroppers. "Can you keep a secret?" he asked cautiously.

"God, yes!" replied Millard readily, leaning in towards Finlay as he took his seat back at the bar.

"Myself and some friends from Europe are seeking to purchase a wee bit of land over here," he advised, luring Stride further into his web. "We want to build an entire new town with houses, churches, taverns - and we'll need a railway line connection too."

"I *own* a railway line!" Stride blurted out at once, beaming with excitement that he may be able to further their association beyond this evening. "Lord Campbell-Campbell, you should come and meet my partners. We might be able to assist you?" he offered generously.

Finlay held back a huge smirk while thinking, *Part One: Complete.*

"Aye - sounds like a fine idea," Lord Campbell-Campbell agreed, and Millard insisted on another round of drinks to toast that fine idea, before the men decided to call it a night - or morning, as it turned out.

Returning to their sleeping quarters as the early-morning sun broke through the curtains, and the birds began to twitter, Bowman sat on his bed and looked over at Fraser with a puzzled look upon his face. "What was that about?" he asked his colleague, and nodded in his direction. "Campbell-Campbell?"

"Don't know - I didn't mean for it to come out twice," he laughingly revealed. "Just glad he bought it as my full name!" The comment sending both of them into hysterics, and inadvertently waking the guests in the rooms all around.

Chapter 37: The Prestige

Δ

The men from across the Atlantic slept until after midday, and rose with heavily pounding heads. Still, they could be content that their plan was now fully in motion, and after settling their stomachs, they were ready to press ahead again. Bowman practised his best King's English in the mirror, while Finlay undertook the arduous task of changing into Lord Campbell-Campbell's full regalia, and then they made their way across to the Union Depot.

Arriving inside the concourse, they quickly scanned the station and became acquainted with the space, just in case a speedy exit was required of them later on. Their reconnaissance, however, was interrupted, when Millard Stride came running out to escort them to the offices above, all the while enthusing about Jack - who, he assured them, was "looking forward to meeting them."

In truth, Brunson had listened to Stride's story that day with more than a hint of scepticism, and he was sitting waiting to grill them, as soon as they walked through the door.

"So, what's your game, chaps?!" Jack demanded, leaning back in his chair and eyeing the men up and down with a clear look of mistrust.

Struck by Jack's hostile demeanour, Finlay froze dead, right on the spot. And uncharacteristically for him, he failed to answer the question. Fortunately, he was rescued from his hesitation, by Bowman. "Mr Brunson, we're here seeking five hundred acres on which to create our new settlement and build a railroad."

"Well, isn't it convenient that you landed in my office then?!" Brunson mocked, staring intensely at the men, and trying to unmask them.

Camouflaging his nerves in the face of Jack's aggression, Finlay finally unfroze, and decided swiftly that in order for this to work; he would have to put on the most outlandish performance of his life. "I'd say it's indeed *you* who's the lucky one," he declared firmly, glaring down at Brunson, as Stride and Bowman nervously took their seats.

Then, an eerie silence pervaded the small room.

"Lord Campbell-Campbell," Millard blurted out in an attempt to abate the tension, "why don't you tell Jack some more about your plans?" He hoped his business partner would become more sanguine once he heard the finer details.

Fraser stared directly at Brunson and matched his aggressive stance. Then he glanced over at Stride and puffed out his cheeks in a show of defiance, before stating begrudgingly, "My family owns large tracts of land with thousands of labourers. I want to bring them over here to mine for oil and gold – something they will hardly find in the Highlands of wee bonny Scotland!"

His words made Jack pause momentarily.

Then his thoughts filled, thinking of Manhattan, and how it had grown inexorably due to the influx of Irish immigrants.

Hmmm...maybe he is telling the truth?

But with New York at the forefront of his mind, it also struck Jack that there may be something amiss regarding his visitor's story.

"Well, that all sounds just splendid, Mr Campbell," Jack began, purposely dropping his title to gauge the reaction – which sufficed "However, I'm still a little flabbergasted at one small detail..."

Finlay and Bowman had to work very hard not to glance at each other nervously, as they wondered whether they had missed something, and inadvertently given their game away.

"... Why are you here in Erie?" Jack finished. "It's not the first place I would have expected your search to begin," he said shrewdly.

Without hesitation, Finlay replied with conviction: "Oh, to the contrary, Jack, naturally we went to New York first. But I must say, I'm nay too fond of that lot. Don't feel like I could trust a single one of them!"

It was Campbell-Campbell's finest moment, the perfect hook, and one with which AJ and Alex had armed him. Brunson's eyes lit up at this perceived hatred of Manhattan, of which he could so well identify. And with that common ground established, Brunson dispensed with doubt and hesitation, and started to see that this could provide his biggest opportunity to create a super-port in Duluth.

"What if I were to make you a member of the board and we built the line together?" he suggested, to ensure the lord did not seek a deal anywhere else. "I also have a piece of land in mind that would be perfect for your settlement," he said, while envisaging thousands of Scots digging in the silver mines and making him even more extraordinarily wealthy.

Peering down at Bowman, sitting on the crumpled sofa and trying not to scream in excitement, Finlay gave a little nod and then marched the few steps over to Jack before confidently offering his hand across the desk. "That, Mr Brunson, is a deal," he concluded emphatically.

They shook on it, and Brunson requested that they allow him "a day to arrange things". Then, parting as new associates, they said their goodbyes and Stride led Bowman and Finlay out of the depot.

Returning to their hotel, the imposters walked alongside one another absolutely speechless, not quite able to believe that their plan had unfolded so perfectly. Still having not uttered a single word, they entered their room and patiently allowed the door to close - and then all hell broke loose: Bowman opened a bottle of champagne and shook it up and down, splashing fizzy bubbles all across the expensive carpet, while Finlay jumped on the bed and danced a merry jig.

Back in the station office, the atmosphere was somewhat less celebratory, however, as a deadly serious Brunson disclosed the finer points of his plan to Millard.

"I want you to advance all of Jim Diamond's shareholdings to our new friends," he requested straightforwardly.

"Can we do that?!" Millard responded, looking visibly shocked at Jack's instruction.

"I can do whatever I like!" Jack snapped. "Besides, no one's going to believe him after the gold run anyway," he added, rubbing his hands in glee at the prospect of gaining a wealthy new investor, at the expense of one of his enemies.

Pondering the instruction, Millard still felt a little uneasy about the whole situation, but he recognised that he was probably better off sticking with Jack. And besides, he had just helped bring Lord Campbell-Campbell, the Scottish aristocrat, on board: there was no chance Brunson would ever seek to get rid of Stride in the same fashion now...

Δ

Within twenty-four hours of the meeting, Uncle Millard had collected Diamond's share certificates from the vault and provided them to Campbell-Campbell as evidence of their commitment. Jack, meanwhile, delightedly informed Big Jim that if he wanted to discuss the matter further, he would have to contend with "not only the railroad, but a lord, who has protection from the realm".

Finlay and Brown, meanwhile, rushed straight back to Manhattan, and on the guidance of Harris, peddled the shares on the open market in one frantic morning of trading. They sold the lot for just over six million dollars – and with a twenty per cent cut going their way, it proved a hefty payday for only one week's work across the Atlantic.

Desperate to inform The Commander, AJ and Alfred appropriated one of the company's fleet of ships and sailed up the coast to Canada. They took Finlay and Brown along, in order that they could retell the tale in full, knowing that Stephen would appreciate every last, intricate detail, and have more questions than they could answer.

Back in Erie and as the afternoon rolled on, Brunson began to hear rumblings about the shares being sold, and he was gripped by a wretched feeling, deep in the pit of his stomach. Furiously rushing from the office, he peered down at the platforms below to spot Millard happily going about his business. He screamed at him from afar, but his profanities were nullified by the overbearing noise of the trains setting off from the station.

When he had finally come to his senses, an idea struck, and Brunson left the depot straight away to seek the advice of the only other Scottish person he knew. Aboard his private train, he sped the short journey south to Pittsburgh.

Trying not to give too much background information away, in an effort to save his own blushes, Jack enquired nonchalantly. "Have you ever heard of a Lord Campbell-Campbell back in your homeland?"

Alex, of course, thought, *Yes I have; but never back in Scotland!*

"Not that I can recall, Jack," Macdonald replied, while feigning a look of serious concern. "Why - is there something I can assist you with?"

The offer, pleasantly delivered as it was, sent a shiver down Brunson's back, as a reality began to dawn on him.

Desperate to find the men and have them brought to justice, in the coming days Jack spent thousands of dollars on private investigators, who received information that Bowman and Finlay had absconded across the border. Brunson decided to pay a visit to Washington in order to seek the president's counsel, and he provided Brown with a full account of the crime that had been perpetrated against him, and pleaded with Richard to use his presidential powers to extradite the men.

Unsure that the matter required such a forceful measure, Brown did however offer to speak with the Canadian prime minister and request that he ensure the suspects did not leave his borders, in order that Jack could go and collect them himself. Yet in a shock twist, Canada refused to get involved with the issue, citing it a mere business affair, and so, not wishing to incite a row with his cross-border neighbours, Brown returned to Brunson with his conclusion.

"I'm sorry Jack, but there's nothing more I can do."

Frustrated by the lack of action, and realising he would have to go it alone, Brunson begrudgingly accepted Brown's position. And with no other options available, he ploughed even more cash into apprehending the men, instructing a crack squad of bounty hunters, whom he led into Canada aboard his ship.

However, having been forewarned by Macdonald that Brunson was on their tails, AJ and Alfred jumped back aboard their steamer, and returned to New York with their two stowaways on board. Arriving in the dead of night, Bowman and Finlay transferred directly to one of the Roberts family's ocean-going liners, and as the sun lifted over Manhattan's harbour, they set sail across the Atlantic, for a safe passage back to their homeland.

Chapter 38: Metropolitan Museum of Art

Δ

As 1871 concluded and the New Year was ushered in, details of Alfred Roberts and Oliver's rebate plan began to gain public attention. Having set up their private subsidiary, and increased shipping rates across the lines, they fully expected their plan to succeed. However, the inflated prices led the independent refiners to become suspicious of Roberts' actions and they called a summit to discuss their grievances, their anger clear to see on the painted banners held aloft the bated crowd:

'Down with the conspirators'
''No compromise'
'Don't give up the ship!'

All of which was perfectly arranged by John Madison, as he bellowed across the packed hall. "We cannot allow these monstrous price increases to persist!" Pounding his fist on the table in front of him, hundreds of men reiterated his stance, yelling obscenities around the room.

"This great anaconda wishes to strangle us all – but they don't know who they are dealing with!" Madison continued, further inciting the audience into a mad frenzy.

At the rear of the hall, Robert Adams, of Cunningham & Adams, stood with his back fixed firmly to the wall, veiling his face with a cap. Observing the mob-like furore ensuing around him, he was fast realising that Oliver had made a wise decision in not attending, having been concerned for his personal safety. Yet Oliver's absence only added fuel to the theory, that he was chiefly involved with Roberts' inflated freight prices.

In the aftermath of the summit, several violent protests were held outside the Grand Depot, which was subject to a stream of vandalism and boycotting of the lines; in what the Cleveland press dubbed "The Oil Wars". Like a man possessed, Madison obsessively investigated the origins of the price rises. Undeterred by the prospect of taking on Cunningham & Adams, and unrelenting in his desire to break the scheme, John unearthed payments to the subsidiary company, and he took his findings to the High Court in Pennsylvania. As a result, the company was revoked and Roberts, fearing any further implications, subsequently agreed to reduce his inflated fares. More damningly, for the first time in American history, the general public were alerted to the name of Oliver Peter Cunningham, as it was plastered across the front pages of the newsstands, where he was pilloried for his actions.

Elsewhere, and in New York, Stephen Roberts was settling back into Manhattan life once again. And having returned from Canada a few weeks later, unexpectedly for those around him, The Commander's thirty-three-year-old cousin, Ella-May, joined him at the family boarding house. The two had become well acquainted during his visit across the border, and Ella-May arrived with a strong head, full of ideas for spending his vast fortune!

First she convinced him to purchase a church for her congregation, and then she had him donate more than one million dollars to create the Roberts University in Nashville, Tennessee. While costing him a not insubstantial amount of money, his philanthropy did have a positive effect on The Commander, who slowly climbed out of his slump. That, and of course, coming home to the affections of someone forty-five years his junior, may also have contributed to his rude upturn in health!

Δ

In February, the day arrived for the grand opening of Worthington's Metropolitan Museum of Art, and the usual entourage of upper-class New Yorkers arrived in all their splendour outside the five-storey, brownstone townhouse that had been granted for the museum. The location was perfect for his assembly, situated in Upper Manhattan amongst the mansions of the elite, the RSVP replies had come flying back in their droves, with all the socialites of

New York wishing to demonstrate their support for Christopher, as well as their impeccably good health to their fellow millionaires.

The building had formerly been a dancing school, and the reception was held on the uppermost level, in a room that still retained a shiny wooden floor and the dancers' handrails. The real feature, though, was the magnificent glass ceiling overhead, which allowed the stars in the night sky to shine resplendently into the space, and illuminate the paintings crammed somewhat chaotically onto every the inch of the walls.

Standing atop the museum docents' desk in his usual and unmistakable style, Christopher warmly welcomed his guests to the opening. "Dear one and all," he called out as his VIP's huddled around in the compact and busy space, "tonight we celebrate the opening of the Metropolitan Museum of Art! I want to thank you all for your generous support..." He smiled graciously around the room. "However, I don't wish to detain you, with so much on display to see. So enjoy the museum, donate where you can, and I hope to speak with you all at some point this evening." A riotous round of applause broke out, and then the string quartet began playing Vivaldi's sweeping masterpiece, *The Four Seasons.*

With his guests acting on his instructions and freely meandering around the floors of the museum while enjoying the complimentary canapes and champagne on offer, Worthington was desperate to speak with AJ and Stephen. He was hoping to capitalise on the latter's recent philanthropy, and pique both men's interest in donating to more of his charitable ventures. Finding them chatting with Oliver and Alfred, he began his seduction by kindly offering to enlighten them about some of the pieces on display, and he was more than happy when all four men agreed to join his little tour. *The more millionaires, the better!*

"You've done a grand job here," Harris commended him, while silently longing to invite Macdonald along. However, he remained tight-lipped, having agreed to keep their rekindled friendship under wraps – especially with Brunson in town.

"Thank you, Andrew – but we still have so much more to achieve." Christopher sighed in resignation, and then began his petitioning as they exited the room.

After they had viewed a number of the sculptures and paintings on display, Worthington could sense his guests were being merely courteous, with their minds far from investing, and so he shrewdly shifted the conversation to entice his business-minded friends.

"Have you ever considered buying art?" he enquired, and the men shook their heads in unison. "But surely it would be a great way to store and even build your wealth...?"

"Go on," AJ directed while glancing knowingly at The Commander, expecting this to be another ruse to pump them for donations, rather than an actual business proposition.

"Well, you see, it could be mutually beneficial. If you were to build up a collection from a certain artist, I could display the works, here on your behalf. That in turn would make them better known, which would increase the value of the works," Worthington explained. "Your artefacts would be regularly maintained and under tight security – so in many ways, it would be like having your own bank of art!"

His cash-rich associates stood there awestruck at the brilliance of the plan. And with their interest clearly stimulated, the men chattering away beside him, Worthington led them into the American sculptures exhibition while continuing his sales pitch. "I have access to all the up-and-coming artists around the world – Manet, Renoir, Rousseau, Cezanne – all at the forefront of a new artistic movement, yet still currently very affordable to purchase. Indeed, I have a number of examples on the fifth floor, should you wish to see?" he teased.

"I'd certainly be interested in anything you feel may be of interest," The Commander replied, attempting to play it cool but unable to hide the excitement written all over his face.

With the group entirely sold on the idea, Worthington was preparing to take them back to the top floor, where Mozart's *Symphony No. 25* was building to a crescendo, when suddenly Russell Randolph-Smith arrived in the doorway and blocked their exit.

"There you are!" he sniped, uncharacteristically.

A committed board member, Russell had being wandering around the museum with his wife and their twenty-year-old son, looking for Christopher, with whom he had expected a private audience. And he was further aggrieved to find that, instead, Worthington had apparently been courting his "New Money" associates.

Visibly flustered as he glared at the group, Randolph-Smith brusquely snatched the leather briefcase in his wife's grasp and jolted it towards his host. "And there you go!" he offered coarsely.

Christopher peered down, looking baffled at the delivery, now in his possession. "What's this, Russell?" he politely enquired.

"Well, I did want to give you this at the start," Randolph-Smith grumbled, feeling annoyed that his gift was to be passed over with so few eyes in the room to witness his generosity. "It's my wife's collection of Chantilly lace from Louis XV's court. I thought you may wish to exhibit it," he revealed, before helping Worthington to open the briefcase.

AJ rolled his eyes and instantly reflected, *But who on earth would wish to see your wife's smalls on display?!*

It didn't go unnoticed.

Out the corner of his eye, Russell spotted the derisory look, and he confronted his foe head on. "So do inform us, what *you* have brought then, Mr Harris?"

AJ simply stared back with a look of contempt, as Worthington looked to deflect the confrontation.

"Well, I was just explaining to Stephen, Alfred and Mr Cunningham about the –" he began, but was rudely interrupted by Randolph-Smith.

"Cunningham? Not *Oliver Peter Cunningham,* of Cunningham & Adams?!"

"That's the one," Oliver confirmed plainly, having been drawn into the conflict, of which he had been taking not a single jot of notice beforehand.

"The... the one from the papers?" Russell panicked while frantically waving an extended finger up and down, and looking around in abject disbelief. "How could you let him in the building, Christopher?! Do you not know who he is?"

"I do know, yes. Oliver was invited along with Andrew, as part of the group," Worthington replied calmly in an attempt to diffuse the situation - but the attempt failed miserably.

"Group?! What group?!" Russell scoffed. "You should not be involving yourself with men like these. They're just common thieves - *true robber barons*!" he spat out unequivocally, twisting his finger to the ceiling and staring upon them with a cracked look, deep within his eyes.

That did it: AJ was no longer prepared to simply stand there and say nothing. He quickly stomped towards Randolph-Smith, causing his wife to shriek in fear.

"How dare you!" Harris barked, just as the quick-witted Worthington jumped in between the two in an effort to hold them at bay.

"Gentlemen, gentlemen - please!" he cried. "This is neither the time nor the place. And you should be ashamed of yourselves - there are ladies present!" he added, hoping to pour water onto the raging fire.

For a moment longer, they glared at each other, hands fisted and with gritted teeth. Then, with their host's plea ringing in their ears, the both of them backed down.

Shaking his head in disapproval of Worthington's choice of company, and in condemnation of them all, Randolph-Smith huffed down his nose before exiting down the stairs without saying a word, his family following hurriedly behind.

"Sorry about that, chaps," said an embarrassed Christopher. "He must have woken up on the wrong side of the bed!" he joked, before rushing off to catch up with his friend and smooth things over; not wanting any of his sponsors to leave disgruntled.

"Who is that man, Andrew?" Cunningham enquired from across the room, in his usual monotone style.

It caused AJ to burst into a fit of hilarity.

"Exactly!" he said. "Who is he indeed?"

But Oliver did not care for frivolities and remained deadly serious. "No, really. Who. Is. He?" he stressed.

"Russell Randolph-Smith. He owns half of Manhattan," Harris confirmed, before casually departing the room with the Roberts men, and leaving Oliver standing by the window.

"Is that so?" mused Oliver as he watched the Randolph-Smith family down in the street below, dashing across to their stagecoach outside St Thomas' Church. "Is that so..." he slowly repeated with a wicked scowl on his face; fixating on their carriage, he followed every wheel that turned, as it took off into the cold night air.

Chapter 39: The European Partners

Δ

Up in the main hall, another man was standing alone and contemplating escaping into that cold night air. Feeling like he had been in the lion's den all evening, Jack had not been his usual exuberant self, and had shied away from spending too long in conversation - specifically to avoid any awkward questions regarding the gold run or Lord Campbell-Campbell. Now that he had shown his face, he was desperate to return home. But just as he decided to depart, Brunson noticed Sykes through the throngs, admiring a painting, and couldn't leave without saying 'hello'. So as the string quartet began playing Hungarian Dance No. 5 by Brahms, Jack weaved his way across the room. Yet when he arrived at Levi's side, he struggled to catch his friend's attention, so engrossed was he in a painting of a water scene.

The gentleman banker leaned in close to read the plaque, at the bottom of the golden frame. "La Grenouillère," Levi whispered in a dazed fashion, before gazing across to the picture hanging adjacent, of a small boy riding a rocking horse atop tricycle wheels, labelled Jean Monet on his

Hobby Horse. "Fascinating, Jack... absolutely magnificent, they are," he enthused, completely enthralled by the mastery.

"Indeed," Brunson agreed tersely, to placate his associate. But Jack had no care for what he saw as merely doodles, and would much rather be discussing more important matters: like his business.

"Did you hear about Jim Diamond?" Sykes enquired heavily, seemingly unable to take his eyes from staring at the wall.

While Sykes knew little of what had occurred during the Lord Campbell-Campbell fiasco, he was well aware of the death of Big Jim – who had been shot dead by his lover's husband on the steps of the Grand Central Hotel, in broad daylight, only two weeks prior.

"Sad news..." Jack offered, as he shook his head to display a sense of dismay. "A big loss to us all," he lied, doing his best to conceal his absolute delight.

Finally, Sykes shifted his focus from the paintings to scan around the room, and more importantly, check for the presence of Harris and his gang. Then he moved in closer to Brunson and asked in a hushed tone, "What's happening with the extension?"

"The ground's proving somewhat difficult to break – and even more so, are the locals!" replied a clearly frustrated Jack. Yet his friend offered no words of sympathy, having warned him that would be the case.

"Brown's agreed our loan repayment though, so we just need to keep selling the government bonds and it should all work out okay," he said in an attempt to reassure Sykes.

"But Brown's re-election is barely a year away. What if he doesn't make it?" Levi suggested to his ally - who looked puzzled. "Don't you recall what happened with Rushbourne? You need to focus all your energies on completing this now!"

Realising that he had been caught up in escapades elsewhere, and had severely taken his eye off the ball, Jack considered the full ramifications of the upcoming elections - it hadn't even been a consideration before, he had simply expected Brown would secure a second term. So appreciating Levi's sage advice, he nodded respectfully, and promised to put all his effort into completing the line to Duluth, before rushing out the door with a new sense of urgency.

As the evening drew to a close and *Air* by Bach swept gently through the building, Worthington returned to the upper main hall - and was instantly apprehended by Stephen, who was clutching a frame under his arm. The painting depicted a pair of lovers, standing on a patio surrounded by flowers, with several large ships on the horizon. It was soon clear why The Commander was so desperate to purchase the picture. "How much for this?" Stephen demanded, turning the painting around to show his host. "Ella-May wants it."

Alfred, meanwhile, was looking on with some concern at his father's sudden flippant attitude to spending; especially when it appeared to be going in the sole direction of his new love interest.

"Ah, a fine choice, Miss!" commended the host, beaming with delight. *"Garden at Sainte-Adresse,"* he read from the label on the frame. "A Monet. You'll not be disappointed!" he enthused.

At this, Stephen's young fiancée clapped her hands together in glee, before jumping into an embrace with The Commander, and nearly knocking him off his feet.

After stabilising his friend before he could fall over, Worthington took the picture from his grasp and placed it very carefully back on the wall. Then he leaned in to speak to Harris as he passed. "See, Andrew," he whispered, "They're already selling out!"

Δ

AJ was the last to leave the party, but he did not get far: he stood frozen on the doorstep, outside the entrance to the museum, peering down at his stagecoach, awaiting him on the street. Bizarrely, the carriage curtains were twitching and a large piece of luggage was visible bulging in the rear boot: *how odd?*

Harris glared down at his driver, who placed a finger to his lips and nodded towards the rear, just as the curtains were pulled back ever so slightly to reveal... AJ's father: James Robert Harris had returned to Manhattan!

In a flash, AJ was eagerly rushing down the stairs and jumping into the carriage. "What are you doing here?!" he exclaimed excitedly, his mind running at a thousand miles per hour, as the wheels set into motion.

"Well, firstly, I want to congratulate you on everything you've been doing," James said proudly, while offering his son the warmest of smiles. Then he turned serious. "However, I'm also here because there is something of vital importance of which I must inform you."

"What, Father?" AJ replied anxiously, perching on the edge of his seat in anticipation.

"The party's over, son," James announced soberly. "Our European partners are pulling back funds across the world!" he revealed.

The younger Harris gasped at the news, and his eyes bulged wildly out of his head. "But why - what for?" he said frantically as he scratched his head in dismay, considering all his hard work undone.

"They're concerned about several issues," the elder Harris began. "The run on gold over here didn't help, but really it is the imminent announcement that the German Empire is to move on to the gold standard that has them very worried. They just want to hold back for now and see how it all plays out," he concluded. Andrew was absolutely floored. And he could barely hide the dissatisfaction, written all across his face.

Appreciating it was rather big news to absorb, JR allowed his son to sit in silent contemplation for a moment, as the stagecoach bumped along the road, before offering his advice. "All will be fine, AJ. You just need to batten down the hatches for a while. A storm causes no damage, my boy, if you're well enough prepared for it!"

Andrew slowly nodded, but he still could not help but feel shell-shocked by the news, and unsure how to make sense of it all and what it meant for his future. "So what should I do, Father?" he asked.

"Ensure that you and your closest are prepared," JR advised. "But don't spread the word too far - otherwise it could potentially destabilise the whole country." The words made sense, but AJ was still processing it, when his father then asked curiously, "Talking of your allies, whatever happened to Alex Macdonald?"

Andrew was still caught up in his thoughts, so replied simply, "He's really proven himself of late," to the absolute delight of his father.

"Well, he has the same potential Cunningham did," JR said, awash with excitement. "Look at all the men of great empires throughout history – Archimedes in Rome, Newton in Britain, Aristotle in Greece. Progress is fostered through new innovations, and if you can get a hold of men such as these, you'll own the future of this great country," he declared authoritatively.

But before he could respond, the driver shouted, "Here, sirs!", and their coach came to a stop outside AJ's abode.

"That'll be us then!" JR said, looking on merrily.

Then AJ helped his father down from the carriage.

Out on the street in the dead of night, feeling calmed by his father's guidance, Andrew had some news of his own that he wished to share. "Do you recall our head secretary, Maria?" he asked while leading his father up the flight of external steps to his front door. "I'm thinking of asking her to marry me!" AJ announced proudly.

"Oh, well, that's wonderful news, Andrew," James said. "Although... do you not wish to marry someone..." He paused while he sought the most diplomatic approach. "... a little more, well... wealthy?" he suggested tentatively.

The younger Harris halted, as they reached the final step. "Maria is my rock and has backed me in every venture from the beginning," he said passionately. "I'd rather marry someone I know to be completely true and loyal, than someone who wants me only for my money!"

For the first time in his life, AJ had argued his father down. *What a fantastic moment to behold.*

The elder Harris regarded his son for a moment, and then nodded his head and broke into a wide and affectionate smile; so proud of the man his boy had become.

As they walked across the threshold together, James concluded sincerely, "Well, I shall look forward to the wedding with great anticipation." Then the door closed slowly behind them, and they continued their discussions, strategising late into the night.

Δ

Chapter 40: The Cleveland Massacres

Δ

With his father safely back in England, AJ arranged a meeting at his office with the Roberts men, Cunningham and Macdonald. In the middle of the night, whilst the rest of America slept, the five men sat in his banking hall under candlelight, and Andrew informed them of the tsunami set to engulf the world in the coming twelve months. His ultimate advice: they should consolidate their operations in preparation.

Both the elder and younger Roberts were happy to heed the advice, as was Macdonald. Their only concern of note was the Brooklyn Bridge development, however the project looked likely to require almost a decade to complete, so the delay of a year or two would be only a minor irritant.

Cunningham, however, sat fidgeting uncontrollably in his seat, becoming more agitated by the minute. Having ignored his shuffling for as long as possible, AJ could no longer bear the constant distraction. "What is it, Oliver?" he asked in a considerate yet stern tone.

Cunningham did not want to defy his mentor, especially in such company, yet at the same time he was desperate to say his piece. “But I had plans to take over all the oil refiners in Cleveland this year,” he said with frustration.

“Well, just hang on a bit and we’ll mop them up when they are struggling,” AJ said affably, smiling merrily at his good friend and considering the matter closed.

“But it won’t work like that,” Oliver objected instantaneously, catching Harris with his mouth half-open about to speak.

AJ swallowed his announcement, and reverted back to his oil-friend. “What won’t?” asked Andrew, trying his best to remain emotionless and uphold his level of respect for Cunningham.

“Waiting until after the crash won’t work, because none of the refiners are overstretched. They’ll simply cut back during the downturn and ride it out until things pick up,” Oliver revealed, demonstrating his intimate knowledge of their competitors’ inner workings.

AJ sat silently for a little while in contemplation.

And not wanting to stifle his ally, or question his impeccable judgement, he came up with a plan he believed would satisfy them both. “I’ll give you six months to round up as many as you can, and after that we pull back until I say. Deal?” he offered.

These were the fairest terms AJ could come up with, and his partner gratefully acknowledged that.

“I won’t fail you, Andrew,” Oliver promised confidently.

Matter: solved, or so the other men thought.

But before he moved the meeting on, AJ identified one potential stumbling block with regard to the plan. "What will you do about John Madison?" he asked, which raised a friendly titter around the room. "That chap downright hates you!" he chuckled, in anticipation of hearing his ally's no doubt inimitable idea.

"Oh, don't you worry about that, AJ," Cunningham said, grinning mercilessly. "I have a plan all ready for him!"

The group laughed at his reply, and Harris thought, *I don't doubt you do Oliver, I don't doubt you do...*

Δ

Cunningham returned to Cleveland after the meeting and went straight to work arranging meetings with the owners of all twenty-six refineries, in which he would employ a strategy that was simple but fair – or so he thought. Each meeting was to follow the exact same pattern. First Oliver detailed the current state of the refining market; wholly appreciating that the owners would be aware of the challenges within the industry, he wanted to reiterate these at the outset, to gently unsettle their nerves. Then he followed up by informing them of how well Cunningham & Adams had fared over the past three years, before producing his financial accounts to demonstrate, explicitly, the clout they held over their rivals. Finally – in what Oliver viewed as his most gracious of considerations – he offered the going rate for the business plus twenty per cent, so that no one could possibly feel aggrieved, and therefore be incited to seek revenge on him.

How can I say fairer than that?

Given his ever-so-clinical nature, Cunningham wanted the takeovers completed quickly and efficiently, with as little time wasted on negotiations as possible. So when he encountered someone who wished to quarrel, the strategy went out of the window and he simply said: "Take my offer and your family will never want for anything again. However... decline my offer, and I can only assume that to be a slur upon my person. Then you will do well to survive in business barely a single year longer, for I shall make it my mission to see that you don't."

The majority of owners took upon the offer gleefully and retired to a life of wealth, while concentrating on reinvesting their monies elsewhere. The big question, however, as posed by Harris, was what to do with John Madison – the man who had scuppered Cunningham's rebate system with Roberts, and unmasked him to the press.

Oliver and his brother Michael arrived at Madison's refinery feeling confident of success, having devised an altogether different strategy to employ, against their learned and smartly turned-out adversary. Somewhat perversely, Oliver had grown rather fond of John further to his exploits against him, and he viewed the twenty-eight year old as a slightly younger version of himself, albeit, a little less quirky!

Having observed the men from Cunningham & Adams walk across the yard before entering his office, John was wholly expecting a dog fight and he sat behind his desk ready for battle. However, Oliver's approach caught him off-guard.

"So, how much would you like for the business, John?" he put forward politely.

Oliver had decided his plan for Madison would be unique: he would offer him the opportunity to name his price, and whatever the figure, he would happily pay it out of respect, no matter how extortionate the sum.

For a moment, Madison looked with confusion at his adversaries. *They can't be serious, can they?*

Then he steeled himself to remain steadfast to his original conviction. "Respectfully, may I say, Mr Cunningham, the business is not for sale."

Michael Cunningham began lowering his hand into the leather satchel by his feet, to pull out the company accounts. But before he could remove them, Oliver reached across his brother's thigh, and signalled for him to cease.

"John, I like you. In many ways you remind me of myself," Oliver disclosed, to Madison's utter shock. "And whilst I've successfully purchased twenty-one of the other refiners, I'd prefer not to purchase yours," he stated.

John was now awash with confusion, wondering whether this was some form of reverse psychology, and feeling like a ball of wool, being toyed with by these two big cats.

"Well, why did you come here then?" he asked hesitantly, eyeing Oliver and thinking what an intense aura surrounded the man – he barely even needed to speak these days, to make you feel fear and a kind of begrudging respect.

"I don't want to purchase your business, John. I want to incorporate you!" Oliver announced unexpectedly. Now that really was an offer, he had never expected to hear.

Madison sat speechless at the opportunity laid out before him, and took a moment to deliberate the moral conundrum. Should he refuse, he faced an uphill struggle and potential annihilation. However, if he accepted, Madison would be joining the man he had previously attempted to bring down, and someone he had at times, publicly denounced as *the Devil!*

With the clock ticking on and pressure mounting for a reply, he quickly ran through all avenues in his mind, before gazing across at the brothers.

"I'd be honoured to join you," John confirmed, thrusting his hand across the table and sealing the deal with a handshake that would make him an instant millionaire.

Leaving Madison's premises with the agreement in their hands, left four refineries remaining, and now Oliver hit stumbling blocks, even after guaranteeing to "spoil them". Oliver and Michael's hostile tactics were met with equal aggression, and in one unfortunate incident the brothers were turfed out of Benjamin Turnbull's family home by threat of shotgun - while his seven-year-old daughter threw the household spit bucket at Oliver, hitting him on the back and ruining his suit jacket.

At the end of their run of meetings, Cunningham & Adams had absorbed twenty-two of the twenty-six refiners in

Cleveland and achieved the feat in less than four months, beating AJ's allotted timescale.

Amalgamating the refiners provided the company with greater efficiencies and reduced levels of competition, as Oliver organised their operations into a newly built central refinery - the likes of which had never been seen before. The men had taken a huge leap forward with their successful venture, and AJ's advice of late, to all his allies, was to be make sure they were more conspicuous. So, in an effort to promote their unbeatable standards, under one brand name, Oliver unveiled his new corporation to the world, simply naming it: Criterion.

Chapter 41: Brown's Inauguration

Δ

In the capital, the president was running for his second term in office. This time, both AJ and Brunson had met him separately to assure him of their full support, and they forwarded large sums of cash to fund his campaign. Once again Brown was successfully nominated for the Republican ticket; however, he was not universally backed, as in the previous nominations. A number of the party favoured newspaper editor Harvey Martin, one of Brown's fierce enemies, who took a particularly tough stance against the president over the gold run. While Richard ultimately prevailed in the nominations, Martin's campaign was not concluded there: and the Democrats poached him to lead their campaign, and utilised his newspaper to depict the incumbent president as a crook and a drunk, while republishing details of the gold run, and questioning again his involvement in the scandal.

Yet despite their best efforts, Richard remained popular with the public, and in a strange twist of events, on 29th November, only a day before the Electoral College cast their votes, Harvey Martin suddenly died. This left the Democrats in utter disarray. In the panic they rushed forward four replacement candidates, but as the results came in, it became quite clear early on that Brown was going to roar into a landslide victory, and he triumphed over his nearest rival by more than two hundred votes.

On 4th March 1873, Richard was sworn in for his second term as president, and masses of people congregated before the steps of the Capitol Building to hear his inaugural speech. With the crowd huddling together in the frightful chill of the autumnal day, Brown warmed his hands with his breath, as he took to the rostrum to speak.

"Our country remains in its infancy, and whilst the states shall grow through adversity, we still require careful dedication to bring fairness and freedom across the land. It is my aim to complete the restoration of good feeling between the different sections in our common community and create an America that offers opportunity, for one, and for all," he called out, and the crowd erupted into applause that warmed their hearts as much as it did their icy hands.

Δ

Later that evening, and as was customary, Brown hosted his Inauguration Ball. He had chosen for its location a gigantic hall on Judiciary Square. Capable of holding over six thousand guests, it was laid out with circular tables around the edges of the room, a space for dancing at the front, and a buffet-style arrangement by the entrance. However, with the new building still requiring heating to be installed and the coldness of the day worsening into the night, the hall appeared somewhat bleak and barren, with the couple of thousand guests strewn around, forced to remain in their coats as they watched the brass band struggle to hold their freezing instruments.

And while those in attendance lined up to congratulate the recently re-elected president, AJ gathered his closest allies on the far side of the room to reveal the second phase of his masterplan. "Everyone is now prepared for the storm, yes?" he asked around the table, and the men nodded and smiled in appreciation that they had been graced with the warning. "And so... the final part of the plan is to put an end to Jack Brunson!" AJ divulged.

Stephen Roberts impulsively, began rising from his seat.

"How, Andrew?!" he blurted out, most excited.

But Harris offered him a stern gaze in response and the old man, recognising he could have drawn unwanted attention, apologetically slid back down into his seat.

"From what I understand, our friend Mr Brunson has been overstretching himself massively in an attempt to complete his extension to Duluth," AJ said, scanning from one man to the next as they leaned in closer. "So what we need to do now is encourage him to invest even more."

A smile of admiration crossed Oliver's face; he had already grasped the outcome of his business partner's devilishly cunning plan. "We'll bankrupt him forever!"

The Commander's eyes lit up at the prospect.

"Exactly! So what I need you to do this evening is shout from the rooftops about how well business is going," Andrew instructed. "I want him frothing at the mouth with jealousy, because if I know Jack like I think I do, he'll react by trying to fight fire with fire!"

Content that the plan was understood, AJ led his friends away from the table - all but Alex, whom he left alone as a tactical move, to maintain the illusion that Macdonald was merely a business associate. Then the entourage moved towards the crowds surrounding Brown, who was currently holding court with Brunson.

"So can I assume our agreed loans will now continue with regard to the Duluth extension?" Jack enquired quietly.

"That should be fine," replied Brown, in a most carefree mood having successfully secured a second term. "All will be taken care of, Jack."

Brunson then spotted the Manhattan group approaching and instantly ceased the line of conversation.

As they took their final few steps, navigating through the masses, pure adrenaline ran through Harris's body. He glanced back at Macdonald and saw him making his way towards the refreshments. There was no underestimating the vital role the Scot had to play here; he was the only one who could get relatively close to Jack without causing real suspicion. AJ just hoped he had not succumbed to the greatest double-cross of all time!

As the men congregated around Brown, the Roberts family knew this would be their only opportunity to get near to Jack, and so they quickly pressed ahead in attempting to subliminally influence their enemy.

"Another four years, Richard," Alfred greeted the president vociferously while shaking his hand animatedly. "Congratulations, my friend!"

"Thanks for your support, chaps!" Brown replied merrily, looking just as thrilled as his colleagues.

The younger Roberts quickly stepped in to continue the ruse. "And thank you for our Central Depot," he gushed.

To which his father quickly added, "And don't forget the Brooklyn Bridge," with a look of smugness aimed directly at Brunson, so he could not fail to pick up on the boasting.

"And every other plan you're assisting us with!" Alfred offered graciously. A lie, just to land another blow.

Stephen piled on the coercion. "One hundred and seventy trains we see pass through the depot, Richard – every single day! We're looking at *fifteen million passengers* in the first year alone!" he exclaimed excitedly, feigning a look of utter astonishment.

Jack quickly ran the sums through his head and a nerve was sorely hit. *That's a hell of a lot of train fares.*

Exacerbated by the Roberts family's self-glorification, and not wanting to be drawn into revealing his own plans in retaliation, Brunson decided sensibly, to leave the conversation. Spotting Macdonald in the distance, standing alone and eating a plateful of food, Jack made his excuses and left the group in a huff.

"Alex!" he called, alerting the Scot to his approach. "Long time no speak!" he jested.

Macdonald chuckled pleasantly at Jack's introduction. "Far too long, my friend," he replied genially, before quickly putting down his plate and wiping his hands in order to shake Brunson's hand. "But you always seem so busy these days!" he said, as if it were just like old times.

"Yes... I've been... very busy," Jack deflected, not wishing to delve into his embarrassing losses of late. "And how are things with you? Did I see you talking to that repulsive bunch from New York earlier?" he asked, not necessarily thinking anything untoward was afoot, but still requiring some justification from Alex.

"Brown's involved me with their Brooklyn Bridge project, so I'm having to deal with them," Alex explained, and he added a heavy sigh for effect.

Across the cavernous room, Harris was observing the exchange with interest and attempting to decipher just what Jack and Alex were discussing. Unable to grasp the gist of the conversation from such a distance, and desperate to ensure nothing faltered at this critical stage, he decided to make the boldest of moves, and wandered up to interrupt the two old allies, dragging Oliver along at his side.

"Jack!" he said with the most gregarious of smiles. Undeterred by Brunson staring blankly back at him, he enquired politely, "How are we?"

Jack was suspicious of the approach, but he decided to engage with his foe, especially considering how well he had outwitted Harris, last time they duelled at Worthington's house. Brunson was looking forward to giving him another tongue-lashing.

"All's well with me, Andrew. Brown's back in power and it's full steam ahead," he said, masking a sneer as he pictured their faces when he opened the super-port at Duluth.

"Indeed it is, Jack. Now Brown's back in, we can't possibly fail," AJ concurred hastily. "In fact, my good friend Mr Cunningham here has just bought out all the independent refineries in Cleveland and now supplies ninety per cent of America's oil. What do you think to that?!" AJ said exuberantly, wiggling his eyebrows up and down and smiling wildly at Brunson, who didn't wish to provide him with an answer.

And while he had enjoyed every minute of goading his opponent, AJ decided he had pushed it as far as possible without arousing suspicion. "Anyway, good luck with the Development Plan" he closed, and left Jack to chew on the thought, as he merrily swept off to join Brown once more.

Back in conversation with the president, he continued to watch over Brunson and Alex's interaction for the remainder of the evening; only praying that the Scot remained true to his word.

Δ

With the evening winding down and Macdonald having departed the party, Jack stood all alone. His anger continued to build as he watched the leader of his sworn enemies across the other side of the room, holding court and entertaining the president, alongside his numerous Cabinet members.

Arriving so late to the party that the room was almost deserted, Levi Sykes noticed his friend standing somewhat desolate and aggressively smoking a hand-rolled cigarette. "Evening, Jack. Everything okay?" Sykes asked pleasantly. "How's the extension going?"

Brunson kept his vision locked firmly on Harris.

"We need to press ahead twice as fast," he replied, through gritted teeth. "Look at them, thinking they're winning. But they're not, Levi... they're not! And those *fools* need teaching that lesson!" he declared menacingly with a crazed look upon his face, breathing heavily through his nose.

Sykes gazed at his ally with some concern. He had never seen his close friend display such animosity in public; he seemed completely consumed by his hatred. Unfortunately, Levi had some further news to stoke Jack's simmering discontent. "Well, regrettably, we may have to put our plans on hold a little..." Levi began tentatively, and then quaked somewhat as Brunson's look of irritation was suddenly turned in his direction. "I can't be sure, but I'm hearing mutterings from Europe that world markets may be cooling. We might need to hold off for a year or two."

It was the last thing Brunson wanted to hear.

"What?!" Jack snapped, looking again at his adversaries, who were frolicking about without a care in the world. "A year or two?" he scoffed dismissively. "I don't think so, Levi. Not now Brown's back in: we can't possibly fail!" Jack argued confidently, not realising that he had just reiterated, exactly what Harris had told him earlier.

Sykes stood there uneasily, trying to think of some way he could convince his ally to change his mind. But then Brunson latched on to a plan to counter any potential downturn, an ingenious plan, in his mind - stolen from none other than Cunningham. "Well, you don't have to worry anyway, because I've come across an idea that will allow me to complete the line much quicker. I'm going to visit every independent railroad and *buy them out*!" Jack revealed. "But to connect them all together I'll require *a lot* more finance."

At this, Sykes looked somewhat concerned.

And while he could see the merits of the plan, he was hesitant to submit any firm promises at this stage. "I'll see what I can do. But as I said, funding appears to be drying up, Jack, and I may struggle," he concluded, yet his fanatical friend barely heard him, so engaged was he in glaring at Harris and his merry band of men.

Chapter 42: The Money Supply

Δ

Across the summer of 1873, Jack Brunson arranged to meet the minor railroad operators between Kansas City and Duluth in an attempt to purchase their operations. He adopted a similar uncompromising stance to Cunningham, but it soon became apparent that he was not going to be able to simply pressure these men financially. Unlike the refineries, the railroad companies were run by small-time locals who simply wished to make a small living for themselves as well as those in their tight-knit communities, and they did not dare risk the livelihoods of their fellow men by handing control over to an outsider. The message finally hit home for Brunson when he spoke to Peter Stephenson, one of the railroad owners.

"But what would I do with all that money in a small town like this?" Peter asked him innocently.

"Move!" said Jack. "Move to a bigger city. Move to a better city!"

"But I quite like it here," came the quaint reply from Stephenson, and Jack dropped his head into his hands, feeling utterly dismayed. He had not envisaged it would be quite this difficult, when he set out on his mission.

With a sense of increasing desperation, and with what felt like an impending deadline to beat Roberts, Brunson decided that his only option was to offer way over the odds for control of the lines. But he wanted the advice and assistance of his main supporter beforehand, and so Jack jumped aboard his private train to make the long journey south, to visit Sykes at his summer home in New Orleans.

Arriving in good spirits with the finish line to his project almost in sight - all he needed was to secure some more funding - Jack took a hired stagecoach from the station to Levi's quiet country ranch in a secluded area northwest of the city. He found his ally riding on horseback around Louisiana's Jockey Club's Creole Racetrack, situated on grounds that Sykes had donated from his thirty-acre estate. Riding alongside him was his son, Michael Faraday Sykes, who was there to celebrate his twenty-eighth birthday with his fiancée, Rosie (daughter of the Adler banking family in New York). Their marriage had been arranged between the two Jewish dynasties to help maintain their heritage.

Spotting his friend resting happily on the boundary fence, Sykes dismounted his horse, removed his riding helmet and wiped his furrowed brow, before walking over to greet his guest and lead him back towards the house. As they passed under the wooden garden archway with its "Sykes Mansion" sign swinging delicately in the breeze, Jack gazed around at the stately homestead and could not help but be impressed.

The luxury house was the largest and grandest in all New Orleans, extending to a mighty twenty-two rooms, with landscaped gardens and a private boating lake overlooking the Bayou St John –Sykes's tranquil little bit of paradise that he had lovingly built, as a getaway from the stresses of everyday life.

They took a seat on the first-floor veranda and quenched their thirst with a cool glass of water. In this peaceful setting, Sykes's mind was a million miles from work. "Do you ride much?" he enquired genially.

Jack looked at him in bewilderment. "I can't say that I do, Levi!" he replied, somewhat abruptly.

But his host was far too relaxed to pick up on the contemptuous tone, and he merely smiled while gazing across to the sun-kissed racing grounds. "My boy's ever so good at riding, you know," he said, a look of contentment on his face. Then he turned to Jack. "However, I'm sure you're not here to discuss my son's riding ability. So let me have it: what's going on?"

"The independents won't sell to me. The only way I can persuade them is to offer way over the odds," Brunson confided.

Sykes leaned forward and placed his glass on the hand-crafted mosaic table in front of them before resting back in his seat. Sitting with his legs and arms folded while gazing regretfully upon his friend, he took a deep breath before breaking his silence. "I'm sorry, Jack," he said, exhaling heavily, "but the situation hasn't changed. Funds are scarce. I can only suggest holding back for a period and hoping it gets better," he advised pleasantly.

But Brunson hadn't travelled all this way to accept 'no' for an answer. "What do you mean, funds are scarce? *How can they be?!*" Jack raised his voice in anger, inadvertently attracting the attention of Levi's staff around the house. *"Everyone else seems to be obtaining loans freely!"* he raged.

Jack was questioning Sykes's ability to do his own job, and that fact was not overlooked by the host. However, not willing to be drawn into a shouting match, Sykes opted instead to clarify his position calmly.

"I've spent the past three days contacting everyone I know. We're all facing the same problem, Jack," he stated categorically. Then he added sternly, "And if the 'everyone' to whom you're referring to is Andrew Harris, then maybe you need speak with him instead!"

The distain in his friend's response was evident, and Jack realised he had overstepped the mark: Levi never spoke words in anger.

At once Brunson knew he must back down, in order to maintain their relationship. He decided to direct the conversation elsewhere, so that the moment did not linger. "What about other avenues of finance? How about the bond sales?"

"It's the same story there, Jack," Sykes said, calmed once again. "I'm struggling to offload them," he admitted.

What an absolute waste of my time! Brunson took a long gulp of his drink to cool his frustrations, and stared off into the distance.

With his associate now refusing to look his way, and sensing that Brunson was not best pleased with the conversation thus far, Sykes tried to smooth his ruffled feathers. "Honestly, Jack - and I say this to you as a friend - the markets seem very strange right now. If you want my advice, just sit tight for a while."

Expectedly, it fell on deaf ears.

"Don't worry, Levi," Jack said dismissively, still refusing to acknowledge his friend. "I'll arrange something myself," he concluded somewhat coldly, having already started to formulate another plan in his mind.

Leaving that instant, Brunson sped to his Lake Erie home determined in his quest. But having only ever dealt with either Sykes or Diamond in the past, he was left to speak with a number of minor banking acquaintances, with little to no success. Consumed by his hatred of Harris and the Roberts family, as well as his spiralling fear of missing out on his opportunity to ruin them both, he decided it unfeasible to simply sit back and wait, and was compelled into taking decisive action.

Stuck for alternatives, Jack approached the independents once again, but this time he offered unsold government bond certificates that were promissory of payment in expectation of their future sale, on top of his initial offer of cash. In some cases this meant the owners were receiving double what their holdings were worth. At the same time, he invested every last penny of his own money into iron and ore from Macdonald, to build the final set of interconnecting tracks. Making strong progress and connecting a number of key lines, by the end of August Brunson reached Minneapolis, and with only a hundred and fifty miles left to connect the northern line to Duluth, he estimated that it would finally be completed by no later than the end of the year.

Δ

While Jack's men broke ground at Duluth, in a sun-glazed New York, AJ received a telegram from across the Atlantic. Hot off the telegraph, it had been passed to him from the bank's operator, and Andrew held the message aloft in front of him, while standing alone in his office at JR Harris & Son. With his door ajar, he squinted through the gap, across the banking hall at his staff going merrily about their business, before shredding the paper into little pieces and flittering them from his fingers, into the bin beside his desk. Standing there motionless, in silent contemplation of the communication from his father, Harris was startled when Maria appeared suddenly at the door.

"Anything I can do?" she asked worriedly.

Harris paused for a moment longer, to consider his exact reply.

"Organise a meeting with Brown for the morning," he requested robotically, while gazing off into the distance. "And, tell him I'll come to him."

No further questions, she grasped the importance, and quickly arranged the appointment.

Arriving at the presidential mansion, Andrew received the warmest of receptions from a particularly cheery Brown. And joined by John Peters, they settled down in the Oval Office; just any other day for the men from the capital.

"Many thanks for accommodating me at such short notice," AJ said humbly.

"Not at all, Andrew," Brown replied jovially, offering his broadest smile. "I know when you come calling, it must be worth hearing!" he quipped. But this was no laughing matter.

AJ smiled modestly at the kind remark, then a seriousness swept over his whole being, as he leaned forward and stared his colleague directly in the eyes. "Unfortunately, not so good news this time, Richard."

At once, Brown dropped his playful nature and looked with concern at his advisor.

"The world economy is soon to be thrown into turmoil," said Harris gloomily, "and I wanted to inform you as soon as possible, so we can prepare for the ensuing storm."

Brown raised his hands to clasp his face.

"What...? How...? But why?" he muttered as he began to turn a shade whiter, so dumbfounded was he by the news.

"There are a number of factors," AJ said, "but the gold run has damaged the country more than we could have imagined. And like other countries, we've overextended ourselves, laying railroads to nowhere that will never repay their collateral." AJ spoke carefully, hoping that if the coming crash did not put an end to Jack, then his condemnation of him would at least finally eliminate the man from any future association with the group.

The president was confused, and deeply concerned about the state of the nation, as well as his own leadership. "So... so what are we going to do, Andrew?" he appealed frantically.

Time for Harris to come to the rescue.

"We need to pull back on spending, and the Development Plan needs to be placed on hold," AJ directed. His face scrunched up in a discernible display of agitation. "Which is *most* infuriating, because Stephen was coming on a pace with the East River Bridge. *But we must cancel them all!*" he finished, demonstrating the clear severity of his orders.

Unable to process the numerous potential outcomes of this disastrous information, Brown sat immobilised. Peters, meanwhile, at least managed to grab a piece of paper to hastily scribble down Harris's directives, and urged him to continue with his advice.

"Then we need to reduce the money supply and raise interest rates," AJ instructed. He knew that would hurt Jack, by restricting his wider options for funding and increasing the payments on any debt he held, but he also knew that this was the best way forward for the country as a whole.

Staring at the men sitting startled in front of him, AJ offered them a warm smile and tried to ease their tension. "I don't want you to worry, Richard. My backers and I will support you through this," he reassured him. "And when things have settled down, we'll be back to full speed with the Development Plan."

What ever would we do without you...?

The president felt overwhelmingly relieved to know that he had the unyielding support of Harris. "Thank you, Andrew – thank you so very much!" Richard said, feeling completely indebted to his friend and saviour. Little had he expected, when Harris wandered into his office only ten minutes before, that his entire world would be so significantly tipped upside down.

Chapter 43: The Panic of '73

Δ

The following day and without hesitation, Brown sent out several private telegrams informing all members of the group that he was suspending expenditure on their development projects indefinitely. The news came as no surprise to the Roberts family and Macdonald, and was only a mild annoyance to Worthington, who would no doubt continue to obtain funding from wealthy benefactors, and had already secured the sites for his museums. However, when the news reached Sykes, he leaned back in his plush Manhattan office and his thoughts turned instantly to his ally; he wondered just what Jack had been doing since they last spoke.

Upon receiving the news Brunson rushed to Washington in a state of panic, to engage with the president and urge him to reconsider his position. Storming into the Oval Office unannounced and without an appointment, he marched across the floor and directly towards Richard, who was taking an afternoon coffee at his desk.

"What's going on?" Jack demanded as Brown calmly placed his drink upon the table. "Why now?!" he boomed.

"I'm sorry, Jack, but there's nothing I can do," Richard advised softly as he stood to walk around the desk and console his guest. "It's not just you - everyone's been affected," he revealed.

"But please! I beg of you..." Jack stumbled, and in desperation, gripped hold of Richard's lapels. "I'm almost there - can't you just help me complete this final bit?"

Peering down with some embarrassment at his friend, and certainly with a hint of confusion over his impatience, Brown said, "When things have settled down, we'll be back to full speed, Jack. However, as things stand, that's the best I can do for now."

Brunson released his grip and fell onto his knees, neurotically massaging his forehead with his fingertips, he felt a sharp pain in his chest and suddenly breathing became a struggle. The president offered to help, but refusing, Jack picked himself up, and stumbled uncontrollably out of the presidential mansion.

Wandering out onto the streets, he looked dishevelled, and the locals stared down their noses at him, pointing in revulsion, coming to the only assumption; he must be a drunken beggar. Peering about through bleary eyes and with his mouth agape, a sudden realisation befell Brunson: *A day ago I stood on the brink of being the richest man in America...now I stand to be the poorest of them all.*

Somehow, he managed to get himself back to the station, in what was a blurry expedition across the city, and he fell into a carriage on his train and sped the short journey north to seek the counsel of his only friend.

Δ

When he arrived in Lower Manhattan, Jack stormed into Sykes's office, only to be informed by Levi's secretary that her boss was "currently unavailable". Ignoring her, however, Brunson pushed her aside and strode across the floor, before forcing his way into Sykes's office.

"Jack!" Levi exclaimed gravely at the sight of his friend, whom he had been expecting to see at some point.

"I need to speak with you," Brunson demanded manically, as Sykes's current client turned his head in disgruntlement at the disruption going on around him.

"Can you give me a minute?" Levi requested politely of the man, who generously acquiesced; more out of fear than benevolence, having noted the unhinged state of the intruder behind him.

Inviting Jack to sit, while anxiously closing the door behind his client, Sykes turned to his friend. "You've no doubt heard the news from Washington?" he said, praying it would not affect them too harshly - because Jack had heeded his warnings in New Orleans.

"Yes... yes, I have," Jack replied restlessly, while sweating profusely, having stormed up three flights of stairs to arrive at the office.

"But you're going to be okay...?" Sykes ventured tentatively. "I mean... you did hold back, like I suggested... didn't you?"

But as Jack took a deep gulp of air and averted his eyes to the floor while rocking back and forth, Sykes could already tell that was not the case.

"Jack! What have you done?!" he cried anxiously.

"I built the line to Minneapolis," Brunson slurred, seemingly unable to stop shaking. "A hundred and fifty miles to go, and we were... this close... this close!"

Tears started to form in his eyes with the realisation that his race could now be over; when he was so frustratingly close to the finish line.

Stepping out from behind his desk to kneel beside his associate and caught in a whirlwind of despair at his good friend's miscalculation, Levi had no concern for reminding Jack about his warning and was only regretful that he could not go back in time, and enforce his advice even more vehemently.

"With the development funding on hold, we'll just need to work something out to cover your loans," he announced, trying to put a plan into action and salvage what remained. "So tell me, how much was Brown going to give you?" Sykes enquired, hoping for a relatively small figure, which he could try to mitigate.

"One hundred and fifty million dollars," Brunson replied flatly. And with those six words, Levi knew the end was nigh.

No coming back from that.

"Well... then, I think you just need to concentrate on protecting yourself from here on out," Sykes said, looking at his crestfallen friend beside him; shoulders sunken and broken in two, a mere pittance of the colossus he had always known Jack to be. "And so I see no other option than bankruptcy. Unless... we can convince someone to purchase your railroads with all the liabilities. But I can't imagine a single person who would?"

The two men sat silently, in the office together, deep in contemplation, until Jack's attention was abruptly caught by a loud steamer hooting its horn on the East River. He cast his eyes to see the first footings of the Brooklyn Bridge, standing tall in the distance - and winced with a dawn of realisation.

"Roberts..." he declared gravely under his breath. "Roberts will buy it."

Levi recoiled in utter shock. "Are you sure you would want to hand him all your hard work!"

"No. No!" Jack cried. "Roberts will want to buy it to further his lines. So we need to sell it *elsewhere* and keep his dirty little hands off it!"

Sykes suddenly grasped his friend's proposal.

"Well, you'll have to be prepared to sell at rock bottom," he advised regretfully. "The market will know you're facing insolvency."

"You can give it away for a dollar, for all I care," Jack said, though each word made him seethe with fury and disgust. "Just make sure you keep it out of *his* hands!" he demanded.

Δ

With his plans being put in place, Jack loitered around in the waiting room, smoking incessantly. He peered down over the busy streets of the financial district below and shook his head at their existence, while Sykes worked diligently on a deal late into the evening. After systematically contacting every major rail operator, he managed to negotiate a stock sale of the Transcontinental, transferring all debts to the purchaser, the Penny-Penny Railroad Company, which purchased Brunson's operations for the un-princely sum of one dollar. Although a hard pill to swallow, the sale cleared Jack of all his obligations, meaning he no longer had to file for bankruptcy, and so saved his personal assets including the family home in Erie.

Stooping over Levi's desk as the clock ticked towards midnight, Brunson hovered his hand over the dotted signatory line. Thinking of all the events that had occurred flashing before his eyes, he took a deep breath before stroking the pen across the paper, and passing it over to Levi to co-sign. And as his ally dipped his pen into the inkwell for one last time, Jack halted him for a moment, having had a flash of inspiration.

"When I visited Duluth, I met a man and gave him fifty thousand dollars to invest in a silver mining operation," he disclosed, his eyes lighting up. "Do I have to declare that too?" he wondered.

"Is your name on the company deeds?" Sykes replied inquisitively, while refraining from signing the document.

"No," Jack confirmed. "I just gave him the money and off he went!" How unsubstantial that sum had once seemed, he realised, now that he couldn't just simply hand it out.

"Well then..." Levi grinned reassuringly. "You'd best go find him and see what he's getting up to!" he advised keenly, and the atmosphere in the room transformed, as they gazed pensively upon one another.

With the news of Brunson's fire sale spreading out into the market, a panic ensued as investors scrambled to protect their own positions. Added to the restricted money supply initiated by the president, this led to a series of bank runs and subsequent failures across America. As the situation continued to worsen by the day, on Saturday 20th September John Peters shut down the Stock Exchange to avoid any further bankruptcies, and travelled to Manhattan to consult with JR Harris & Son as to the best way forward. But with the domino effect already beginning to take a firm grip around the throat of the economy, any advice could not halt the thousands of businesses that failed. And as factories began to lay off workers, and the effects rippled around the country, a further sixty railroads failed in quick succession, over the three months that followed.

Chapter 44: The Harris Wedding

Δ

With the nation on its knees and development across the land grinding to a halt as well as asset values falling steeply, it was perhaps not the best timing for the future Mr and Mrs Andrew Harris to be hosting their lavish wedding. However, the date had been set many months ago and AJ was riding the crest of a wave, having finally got rid of Brunson. So, with little thought of cancelling, on 25th December 1973 the invitees packed St Paul's Chapel to the rafters, desperate to obtain the best seat from which to view the happy couple, on this most joyous of occasions.

Andrew and Maria were married in front of an exultant crowd of friends and family from all across America, and with the ceremony complete, the congregation began to spill from the church and spread out around the grounds. Tucked up warmly in their heavy winter coats, they momentarily enjoyed a glimmer of mid-afternoon sunshine as it broke through the clouds, and radiated across their faces. Such a serene moment, it caused a silence to fall amongst the guests.

All that was, apart from one.

With business forever on his mind, Oliver noticed a new building across the street, standing high above those beside it, and he approached the groom with a look of excitement on his face. "What's that, AJ?" He pointed it out.

Andrew burst into laughter, having expected his comrade to be offering his congratulations and not enquiring about work. "It's the Equitable Life Assurance building. They even built her with a passenger elevator," Harris confirmed. He grinned suggestively at his friend. "We should go take a look sometime?"

"Indeed we should," Oliver agreed calculatingly, "indeed we should," and already AJ could sense the plan forming in his best man's head.

With everyone having vacated the church, the elder Harris ushered his son and his stunning bride through the crowds, in order that they could make their getaway first and save poor Maria any further discomfort (rather commendably, she had been standing without complaint in solely her wedding dress and white-fur stole for the past ten minutes).

"Over to the Union League. We'll see you there!" JR announced loudly, prompting the gathered masses to make a quick dash towards the warmth of their stagecoaches, lining the full length of Broadway, for as far as the eye could see.

Watching over proceedings with great interest, meanwhile, while leaning against his fifth-floor windowsill and rolling a large glass of strong whisky in his hand, was

Russell Randolph-Smith. He stared down at the commotion below him and scoffed loudly at their brazenness.

"What a deplorable bunch of peasants," Randolph-Smith proclaimed as Chief Allen came lurking out from the dark recesses of the room to stand and scowl beside him.

"Don't worry," Nelson asserted confidently, "their day of reckoning will come!" Randolph-Smith flashed a menacing grin in agreement, before inhaling the remainder of his drink.

Δ

With the cake cut and the Soyer ham in champagne sauce having been well appreciated, Andrew and his father undertook their speaking duties, entertaining the hundreds of guests with their most erudite recollections. Then the party moved into full swing, with a crescendo of alcohol and dancing, as their guests enjoyed the music provided most exceptionally, by the New York Philharmonic.

Taking a moment to stand and watch over proceedings while ordering a drink at the bar, Harris smiled broadly to himself as he considered the success of the day. Most particularly, he was touched by the sight of his beautiful wife at the centre of the dancefloor, very gently dancing with none other than his aged father, who was positively fizzing with humour and life tonight.

AJ was not alone for long, however, as a cheery-looking Macdonald spotted him from across the dancefloor and approached.

"What an eventful year it's been!" the Scot said knowingly, grinning in delighted recognition that the two of them had made it to be standing here in such fine circumstances.

"Indeed it has, my friend," AJ confirmed jovially, laying a hand on his ally's shoulder. "But there's so much more to come – especially for you!" he nodded.

"What do you mean?" an intrigued Alex replied, and he moved in nearer so as to not miss a word over the noise of the band.

"I think your iron business has much more room to grow," AJ suggested, while leaning in close to his friend. "We should arrange a meeting to discuss where best to take it," he proposed generously.

The Scot's eyes lit up as he considered how far Cunningham had risen since Harris had offered his assistance. "That would be wonderful, Andrew!" he said ecstatically.

AJ flashed him a sincere smile. "Good. Now then, I see my lovely wife has taken a rest from dancing. I really mustn't neglect her..."

"Of course," said Macdonald. "But if I may, just quickly, there was just one other thing..." Harris halted in his tracks, and Alex continued quickly: "A banking friend of mine in Pittsburgh is struggling due to the panic and I wondered if we could help him? I didn't reveal anything to him before the crash of course, in case the news spread too wide," he added, in order to demonstrate his undying abidance to Harris's instructions.

The inference not wasted on AJ, he read clearly between the lines. Gazing upon Macdonald, Harris felt deeply gratified that they had managed to turn their friendship around. He could only wonder where they would have been, had they merely teamed up earlier. "I'm more than happy to assist Alex," AJ replied cordially. "Any friend of yours is a friend of mine," he stated with a glint in his eye.

Both men stood quietly, in mutual delight at their alliance and their growing trust in one another. The moment, however, was broken, as Maria skipped over with her head bridesmaid, Audrey. "You're not going to stand by the bar all night, are you?!" Maria quipped spiritedly, causing AJ and Alex to snigger like schoolboys.

"No, dear!" AJ apologised gladly, and he smiled lovingly at his bride, who turned her mock derision towards the Scot.

"And how long are you going to wait before asking Audrey for a dance, Alex?" she asked forthrightly.

Poor Alex nearly spat his drink across the room.

"Oh, yes... yes... of course," he exclaimed, before quickly taking hold of Audrey's hand and leading her merrily to the dancefloor.

With the newlyweds finally left to enjoy a moment on their own, Maria leaned against her husband and he encircled her with his big arms. Content with the world and their embrace, they watched quietly, while their friends danced amongst the masses of wedding guests. Then peering down at his wife, AJ gently placed his palm atop her stomach and rubbed it softly, as the couple smiled lovingly at one another.

"Forevermore, the twenty-fifth shall be celebrated with great gifts and the most lavish of parties," Andrew declared, and his wife rose up on tiptoes, to kiss him on the cheek.

Δ

As the early morning hours arrived, and only those with the strongest constitutions remained strewn around the ballroom, AJ gathered the members of his inner circle and led them towards the front entrance of the building. Exuberantly driving open the large double doors, he dragged Macdonald, Cunningham and the Roberts men out into the freezing night air and demanded that they join him, in the middle of Union Square.

At this time of night, it was devoid of life, save for pigeons seeking shelter amongst the trees, and the men looked out dubiously, reluctant to leave the club. But never wishing to question or deny their leader, they followed Harris across the slippery ground and congregated under the recently erected Lincoln Memorial.

With condensation forming all around from their deep exhales of breath, AJ huddled his men into a circle and smiled avidly at his compatriots.

The Commander, however, did not return the smile; he was struggling with the conditions, gasping for air as the cold filled against his throat. "You'd best have a good reason for dragging us out here, AJ!" he grumbled, albeit with an edge of joviality.

Harris let out a boisterous laugh that echoed into the night. "Indeed I do, my friend, indeed I do," he said, while scanning around the square. "Just look where we stand!" he said proudly. The men peered up from their hunched positions and waited for him to continue.

"Eight long years ago we attended a meeting in there," Andrew stated, pointing at the Club. "And who could have envisaged we would end up here today?" He stared nostalgically at the statue of Lincoln, looking down upon them. "Between the five of us, we have helped build this great country, but there's still so much more to come. First America... then the world!" he proclaimed - outlandishly, and yet with all his heart.

"Hear! Hear!" applauded Stephen, in the hope his commendation would call an end to the meeting and allow him to return to the warmth of inside. However, it only spurred Harris on.

"This group, Stephen, that you so called the New World Order, is now in our hands," AJ declared profoundly, while staring at them all with great intent. "The politicians will come and go, other members may come and go, but our four families shall forever be the top-tier members..." He paused to allow his words to resonate, and once again cast his keen gaze around the square, and then high into the night sky.

Detecting the first onset of snowflakes, falling from high above, he returned his attention to the group and placed his fist into the middle of the circle. His allies laid their hands on top of his, and Harris authoritatively concluded:

"Dependable to The End. Loyal to The End. Steadfast to The End."

Dear Reader

Thank you for your support and for embarking upon this journey into the light. I do apologise if your world now seems upside down, but knowledge is a powerful thing. So keep on reading and keep on researching – the truth, you will ultimately find, is even stranger than the fiction.

The Author